CAMERON

"Her narrative is rich, her style is distinct, and her characters are wonderfully wicked."
—*Publishers Weekly*

"No one does suspense and sensuality like Stella Cameron."
—*New York Times* bestselling author Linda Lael Miller

Praise for

JANICE KAY JOHNSON

"The characters are complex and alive. [Janice Kay] Johnson takes a familiar story and makes it authentic and intriguing by forcing the characters to be real people who have to face the consequences of their actions."
—*Old Book Barn Gazette* on *Maternal Instinct*

"Remarkable in scope, beautifully realized with plot and characterizations, *The Word of a Child* comes very highly recommended."
—Cindy Penn, *WordWeaving*

STELLA CAMERON is the bestselling author of more than fifty books, and possesses the unique talent of being able to switch effortlessly from historical to contemporary fiction. In a one-year period, her titles appeared more than eight times on the *USA TODAY* bestseller list. This British-born author was working as an editor in London when she met her husband, an officer in the U.S. Air Force, at a party. He asked her to dance, and they've been together ever since. They now make their home in Seattle.

The author of more than forty books, **JANICE KAY JOHNSON** has written for adults, children and young adults. When not writing or researching her books, Janice quilts, grows antique roses, spends time with her two daughters, takes care of her cats and dogs (too many to itemize!) and volunteers at a no-kill cat shelter. Janice has been a finalist for the Romance Writers of America prestigious RITA® Award four times. In July 2003, Janice will begin a new trilogy called *Under One Roof* for Harlequin Superromance with the book *Taking a Chance.*

STELLA CAMERON

JANICE KAY JOHNSON

WRONG TURN

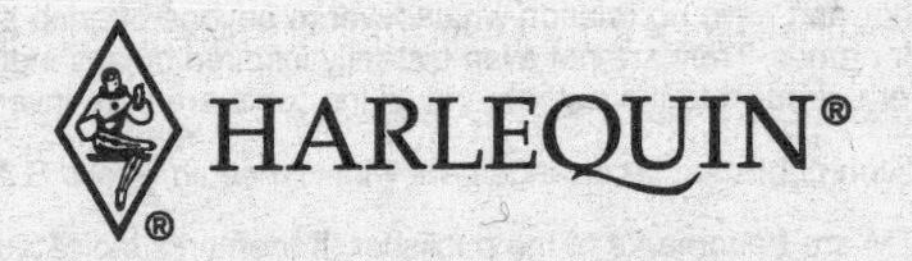

TORONTO • NEW YORK • LONDON
AMSTERDAM • PARIS • SYDNEY • HAMBURG
STOCKHOLM • ATHENS • TOKYO • MILAN • MADRID
PRAGUE • WARSAW • BUDAPEST • AUCKLAND

ISBN 0-373-83556-6

WRONG TURN

This edition published by arrangement with Harlequin Books S.A.

Visit us at www.eHarlequin.com

Printed in U.S.A.

CONTENTS

THE MESSAGE

Stella Cameron

CHAPTER ONE

"HEY, HARD BODY! How's business?"

"Busy, Peeler, busy," Page said. She dodged the off-duty guy from another bike courier service and rode on.

Getting mad wasted valuable energy and time, but the next smart aleck with a wisecrack was likely to get the full benefit of her inventive tongue.

To give her tailbone a rest, she stood up on the pedals of her bike and coasted, gathering speed, down Kearny. San Francisco could be a bike jockey's nightmare. It could also be a dream. Despite too many hours on duty, tonight Page thought the city was terrific. An autumn fog was rolling off the bay, and the cold, pungent air bore scents of exotic food to mix with the wreathing damp that turned the lights ahead of her into converging neon wires of red, blue and green.

The radio, hooked to the neck of her purple satin racing shirt, crackled. She pressed a button and lowered her head. "Yeah, Waldo?" At this time of night, Waldo Sands was her only customer. She made the 10 p.m. to 2 a.m. deliveries for his twenty-four hour delicatessen, Touch Tone Gourmet.

"You on your way, kid?" Waldo always called her

that. Page smiled. At twenty-seven, a woman had to be grateful to be called kid by anyone.

"On my way." A cable car clanked alongside and a cab cut in front of her. "Laguna and Green, right?"

"Right. They just called back. Been waiting twenty minutes for their truffle pâté and champagne, they said. Need it pronto."

Need it. Who *needed* truffle anything at midnight? Maybe the customer was pregnant. "They'll get it when they get it. Soon. Talk to you, Waldo." She cut him off, jumped the curb and shot far enough forward to overtake the cab and bump back to the street.

She mouthed, "So long," over her shoulder at the cabbie and made it through a light just tickling red.

This job for Waldo was a blessing and a curse. A blessing because starting your own bicycle courier service in San Francisco was a hit-and-miss undertaking and any extra money she could make took her that much closer to success. The curse in working for Waldo lay in spending a good portion of every night, when she should be sleeping to get ready for the next grueling day, delivering goodies to people who didn't have a thing to do in the morning.

Still, she'd always be grateful to her roommate, Tanya, for finding Pedal Pushers the extra work. One day maybe she'd parlay the unusual aspect of a night-time delivery service into a real money-maker. At the moment she didn't want to ask any of the four riders she employed to take on more than the relentless ten-hour shifts they already shouldered. In time there would be more riders. Page pedaled harder. In time there would be mopeds—and real quarters for the dispatcher and repair shop, rather than the garage behind the house where she and Tanya rented an apartment.

The cab caught up, passed, and the driver called to Page through the open window. "Hiyah, toots. Don't you ever take a night off?"

She aimed a foot toward a dented rear fender, grinned at the man's raised fist and made a sliding left turn onto Green. Uphill again. This was where the legs took it. Unlike any of the people she employed, Page preferred her single-geared, balloon-tired Schwinn to a racing bike, but the machine didn't make it on the steep grades of San Francisco without a lot of muscle help.

At Laguna, Page took a right and started looking for house numbers. The Pacific Heights area had always appealed to her, with its big Victorians, each one unique—and each one worth more than her fledgling delivery service was likely to net in more years than she wanted to consider right now.

This was it. White, big columns, fretwork around the windows and too big to miss.

Page considered going to a side entrance just visible through a trellis archway, but opted instead for the front door. She hauled her bike up wide redbrick steps and across the portico.

No bell. The hollow thunk of the brass knocker made her flinch and step back. An insistent beat of music played too loudly came from inside. Page lifted the distinctive black-and-gold Touch Tone Gourmet box from the basket attached to her handlebars.

The radio blipped again. "Yeah, Waldo? Making delivery now."

Waldo had his own radio at the store and enjoyed

using it more than Page would have liked. "Do it fast and get back. We've got another rush job." He chuckled. "You sure are quicker than me taking the van out half a dozen times a night."

"I'll be there." She switched off and knocked again. Waldo looked like a sleek, well-fed cat when he laughed like that—a big, handsome, sandy cat. Page wondered, not for the first time, just how close Tanya and Waldo were. Tanya had evaded the question when Page asked, and just said they were friends. But Waldo Sands wasn't a man who spent time with a beautiful woman like Tanya just for friendship.

Despite the music, no light showed through the leaded-glass panels in the door. Maybe she had the wrong address.

Page leaned her bike against the wall and jogged back down the steps to look up. Ah, a steady glow shone against pale draperies at three of the upstairs windows.

She knocked once more, waited a couple more precious, money-making minutes, then turned the handle cautiously. The door wasn't locked. Either the owner was overly trusting or careless. From the delivery slip in her hand, the truffle pâté and champagne lover-in-residence was an Ian Faber. From the volume of the music, she decided he probably couldn't hear her knock, any more than he'd hear any other intruder.

As she opened the door, a pale wedge cut across the darkened hall, crept over walls covered in watered silk, glistening curved banisters, and up wide stairs.

Music blared down.

"Delivery!" Page called.

Nothing but unintelligible melodic yells from the

entertainment, and high-pitched laughter. Damn. She couldn't afford this kind of time waste. Muttering, she hauled her bike inside onto Italian marble and shut the door. If the choice was between leaving a little dirt on the floor and losing her wheels...there wasn't one.

By the size and weight of the box she carried upstairs, she'd been turning a magnum of champagne into a bubbly shake all the way from Sutter Street on the other side of Chinatown. Page made a wry face. Better warn the customer. Then, if he cared as little as she had a hunch he would, she'd get clear of the blast area before the cork went into orbit.

At the top of the stairs Page shouted, "Delivery, Mr. Faber." The noise came from the left where a wall sconce at the entrance to a corridor spread blush glow on thick red carpet.

She advanced, the box held in both hands, until she came to closed double doors.

For an instant she considered knocking, setting down the box and sneaking away. But she needed payment and a signature on the delivery bill. She knocked, waited, knocked again. Waldo wasn't going to be pleased with her efforts this evening.

There was nothing else to do but open another door she'd rather not touch.

An eardrum-puncturing blast met her, and the gyrating vision of a stocky man with curly brown hair, his pleated evening shirt open almost to his black satin cummerbund, dancing with two stocking-footed women. Another man lay, one hand over his eyes, along the length of a beige leather couch.

"Excuse me." Page cleared her throat.

One of the women, a generously endowed blonde, wiggled past, her upper torso moving independently of a strapless white dress. Her eyes were tightly closed.

Page took in a litter of highball glasses and scrumpled napkins on a coffee table in front of the couch and decided this crew didn't need any champagne. Not that what they needed was her business. What she needed was a signature, immediately.

''Ma'am.'' She walked all the way into the room. ''Hey, excuse me.''

Finally she was sighted. The second woman, a diminutive siren with waist-length black hair that slipped around white shoulders to form a cape over a green chiffon creation, opened her eyes and stopped undulating.

''I don't believe it!'' Her voice came to Page as a scream with words. A long red fingernail stabbed in her direction. ''Kiddies, will you *look* at this?''

Amid choking guffaws, three pairs of eyes studied Page. She noted dimly that the man on the couch, his head propped on one arm, his feet on the other, seemed to be asleep.

The woman in green turned the music down a fraction. ''Who *are* you?''

''Delivery for—'' Page glanced at the sheet beneath her fingers ''—Mr. Ian Faber.'' Her face felt as luminous as her skintight purple shirt and matching cycling shorts. Her daytime customers were used to the way she looked, and until tonight she'd never had to go farther than the front door on any of her deliveries for Waldo. In this setting she must seem clownish.

''Mr. Faber appears to be no longer with us. I'm Mr. Martin Grantham the third. Will I do?'' he offered, while indicating the supine, dark-haired figure.

''Is that Mr. Faber?'' Page asked, trying not to picture the way her long brown hair puffed up between the reinforced bands of her white racing helmet. ''I need his signature and payment. All after-hours deliveries are paid for on receipt.''

The woman in green inspected Page more closely. ''Is it Halloween do you think, darlings? Let me see—'' she consulted her watch ''—no-o-o, another two weeks to go yet. So no treats for you, my pet. A pity. Such a good costume. What are you supposed to be, anyway?''

''Would you like to pay for this so I can get to my next delivery?'' Page spoke to Martin III who rocked from heel to toe and back again with a fatuous smile on his flushed face. He didn't appear to hear her.

''I'm Deirdre,'' the black-haired woman said and giggled. ''Who are you?''

''Page Linstrom for Touch Tone Gourmet.'' Irritation and weariness tightened the muscles in Page's jaw. ''We Always Deliver'' was Waldo's unoriginal slogan, and keeping this job with him depended on an ability to find any location fast and not leave until the transaction was completed.

''You really are quite pretty,'' Deirdre told her. ''Isn't she, Liz? Not everyone could carry off that outfit, but she does. Do the elbow and knee pads come in other colors? I can't wear black.''

The laughter that followed, the tears that squeezed from Grantham's eyes while the women leaned on him, held hysteria. Contempt dissolved Page's embarrassment. People like these, empty with empty lives, were to be pitied. Busy and focused every waking minute of her life, she didn't understand them and didn't want to try.

"I think that's about enough," the man on the couch spoke and his voice was the antithesis of hysteria. Cool, deep, tinged with disgust, it startled Page and stopped every other sound and movement in the room. "What the hell do you think you're doing?"

Ian Faber—at least she presumed that's who he was—stood up, fists on hips beneath his rumpled dinner jacket.

Page wasn't interested in the reactions of the three comics. "Are you Mr. Faber?"

"Mm, what?" He shifted dark, dark eyes from a furious stare at his companions to Page. "Yes, yes I am."

"If you'll just take delivery of your order I'll be on my way."

He glanced at the box. "Of course, my *friends'* midnight snack. Martin's very good at ordering things in my name." The comment elicited no response from Martin, and Faber added, "I apologize for my guests' behavior. Let me take that from you."

The package was heavy. She handed it over gratefully and waited while he went to a teak desk between two of the windows and took out a checkbook. "My boss insists on cash," Page told him while the others, snickering explosively from time to time, drifted to sit in various chairs.

Page concentrated on Faber. His curly hair was as dark as his eyes and he was tall, slender, elegant even in the suit he'd slept in. He was reaching inside his jacket for a wallet. Page didn't like or understand Waldo's cash only rule. It embarrassed her when she had to tell customers about it, and carrying sums of money around at night couldn't be totally safe.

A muted noise from her radio made Page shift anxiously from foot to foot. Waldo wasn't going to like being kept waiting, not at all. She'd once seen him lose his temper with an inept store clerk. He'd fired the man on the spot. This episode could bring her the same fate if she didn't make up a lot of time on the way back for pickup.

"Here you are." Ian Faber tucked some bills into the envelope provided and signed where she'd marked an X on the outside. "Let me show you out."

Without a backward glance, Page left the room, Faber close behind. She trotted downstairs, shoving the envelope into the pouch belted to her waist.

"I don't think I caught everything that was said to you." Faber reached the hall neck and neck with Page.

"You didn't miss anything worth hearing," she told him.

"Forgive me, please," he insisted. "I don't put up with people being insulted in my house."

"*You* didn't insult me." She adjusted the Velcro bands at the wrists of her gloves and pulled the bike to rest against her waist. "And in this business you get used to smart comments."

"I don't suppose that means you have to like them."

"No. But you develop a thick skin. You have to. Don't give it another thought."

"That may be easier said than done." He opened

the door while she tightened her chin strap. "Isn't this unusual?"

She paused to look at him. An angular, handsome face and a nice smile, pleasant mouth. He was very tall, tall enough to make her five feet ten inches seem less than usual, and he was solid in a graceful way. "What do you mean by unusual? San Francisco's full of female messengers."

"Not at night. It seems dangerous."

"Not if you know what you're doing," Page told him. He was attractive, almost too attractive. She felt him beside her, big, commanding. "Well, enjoy your pâté."

There wasn't room to push her bike past him in the doorway.

"Do you just do this at night?"

His interest puzzled her. Her work wasn't something that she talked about to anyone but her employees and other people in the business. This obviously privileged man came from another world, and she hardly knew what to say to him.

"Do you?" he repeated.

"No. We're a new service. Started eighteen months ago. I've got four riders, a dispatcher and a part-time mechanic, and most of our trips are during the day—all of them except these deliveries I make for the deli."

"And do you work every night?" He stepped outside and turned to face her. There still wasn't room for Page to pass.

"Most nights. When you're building clientele you can't turn down an account."

His features sharpened in the muted light from the

hall. Long, arched brows showed clearly above slightly up-slanted eyes, and shadows heightened his cheekbones and settled at the tilted corners of his mouth.

A prolonged silence became awkward. "If you'll excuse me," Page said. As if surprised when she spoke, he drew in a breath and moved aside.

When she jerked her bike over the step he stretched out a hand to help, met her eyes and smiled. "You know my name. What's yours?"

She shrugged. "Page Linstrom." Why he wanted to know escaped her but she didn't mind telling him. With a last glance at his eyes, she bumped the bike down to the sidewalk and mounted.

His goodnight came to her distinctly as she rode away...so did the memory of his face.

"Goodnight, Mr. Faber."

IAN LEANED AGAINST a column and crossed his arms while he watched the woman speed off. In a few minutes, when he'd decided what to say before he kicked Martin and his two buddies out, he'd go back.

Tires squeaked and he straightened to see more clearly. Mist verging on fine rain drifted in swathes before a streetlight. Crashing on a bike would be easy in these conditions. She moved fast. Even at a distance he saw the glitter of whirling wheel spokes. Then she turned a corner and was gone.

Page Linstrom might be interesting to know. He hadn't met a really interesting woman in a long time, and he'd sensed something deeper than the lovely exterior she presented. Slowly he sank to sit on the steps, lifting his face to the mist and liking its soft touch. She was certainly lovely; tall, statuesque but graceful. And the effect of blue eyes and brown hair had always intrigued him.

A roaring, grinding sound came from the sidewalk and a gang of teenagers on skateboards shot by. Shiftless kids hungry for kicks. San Francisco seethed with potential danger at night, people on the hunt for petty, malicious diversion...or a chance for hard-boiled crime.

It took a gutsy woman to tackle these streets alone in the dark. The danger of accident on slick streets aside, any female would run the risk of attack.

Ian stood, an unfamiliar mixed-up feeling in his stomach. He had no reason to feel concern for a woman he didn't even know. But it might be worth trying to see her again. How could he pull that off, he wondered, if for no other reason than to find out if she was as intriguing as she seemed?

He glanced back at the street, silent again now. Throughout the advertising industry he was considered innovative, inventive—Faber the whiz. His family's lucrative business didn't flourish under his leadership because he was short on ideas. The idea pressing in on him now was fuzzy around the edges but sharp at its center. Meeting Page Linstrom again definitely appealed, so did learning more about her. Exactly how was the hazy element.

CHAPTER TWO

FOUR HOURS' sleep didn't cut it. Six o'clock came around just as Page was really getting comfortable, but there was no choice but to get to work. Her hair still damp from the shower, she wandered into the kitchen easing blue Spandex shorts into place.

"Good morning, sunshine."

Tanya. She sat at the scrubbed white wood table in the middle of the room. Page halted just inside the doorway, squinting. She had the start of a headache, something very rare for her. "What are you doing here?"

"I live here, remember?" Tanya tossed curly, shoulder-length red hair and hooked an elbow over the back of her chair. "You look awful. What time did you get to bed?"

Good old Tanya. Always on cue with the comment that made you feel worse than you already did. "I made my last delivery at two. Your friend Waldo makes sure I keep at it till the bitter end of the shift."

"You can always quit." Tanya slid to sit on the edge of her ladder-backed chair and stretched elegant, black silk-clad legs. Her black leather miniskirt rode high on her thighs.

Page considered reminding Tanya that without a steady infusion of money Pedal Pushers would all too quickly be a memory, but decided the effort would be wasted. The child of wealthy, indulgent parents, even at twenty-three Tanya had no concept of what it was like to be responsible for one's own fate.

"I need the job with Waldo. I'm grateful for it—and to you for giving me the lead. It's hard work but it pays well, and I get to keep the whole tag price instead of splitting it with another rider. That's a real plus."

Tanya yawned. "I don't understand all that tag price stuff. There has to be an easier way for a girl to make a living. But right now I'm more interested in your social life."

Getting annoyed with Tanya was a futile exercise. Page tossed her gloves and pads on the table and pushed aside a newspaper strewn with bicycle brake parts. The air was chilly. Winter was here, and expensive or not, they'd have to turn the furnace on.

"Did you hear what I said?" Tanya persisted. "It's time you did something besides work. And I wish you'd keep this bike stuff out of the kitchen—and the hall, and the bathroom..."

"I don't put it in the bathroom. Usually the parts are in my bedroom, but I needed the table."

Tanya rolled her eyes. "I'd love to hear how you'd explain all those oily lumps piled up in your room to a man. It isn't *sexy*, Page. In fact it's downright eccentric."

"Leave my bedroom out of this," Page said, but she laughed. "No one but me is likely to see it—except you when you decide to invade my space. Stay out, and your delicate sensibilities won't be offended."

"More's the pity that no one else sees it," Tanya said, frowning at a fingernail.

Page picked up a brake block and inspected it. "You know how I feel about that. I'm not suggesting men don't interest me." Men were Tanya's favorite topic and she refused to believe Page didn't share the fascination. "One day I may decide I have time for a relationship with someone—if I can find a man who's prepared to understand that what I've started here is too important for me to give up."

Taking a chair, Page sat down next to Tanya. "It's been a long haul. At the beginning I thought getting enough money together to leave Anchorage and just exist somewhere else would make me feel fulfilled. But that was barely the beginning. Making this operation fly is going to take years, and I have to do it alone. Men have a way of doing two things. First they can make a woman forget she has a right to be her own person with her own dreams. Second, if the romance fades she can be left with nothing but the habit of living as an appendage to someone else. Neither appeals to me."

Tanya clasped her hands behind her neck and looked at the ceiling. Like the walls, it was painted a shiny yellow. "Just because your mother and sisters are doormats to the men in their lives, you don't have to expect all relationships to be that way." She sounded almost truculent and Page glanced at her sharply.

"*You* can love 'em or leave 'em, right?" Page said. "No man will ever own you." She thought of Waldo Sands.

"You've got it. But that doesn't mean I think men

aren't important. And the romance doesn't have to go out the window once the vows are said, the way you seem to think. Anyway, regardless of your theories I think you spend too much time working or thinking about work. That's all you do. It's not that I don't admire what you've done. Starting a business on a shoestring has to take guts. But you know what they say all work and no play does to a girl.''

''In other words I'm dull. I guess I can handle that.'' The brake block left oil on Page's hands. ''James W. will have to take a look at this.'' James W. Amwell, jr. was a sixteen-year-old who lived with his grandmother in the apartment above Tanya and Page, and on weekends and after school he worked as the Pedal Pushers' mechanic. The boy was a studious recluse who loved repairing the bikes, although when asked he insisted his job was ''mindless therapy for one of superior intelligence.''

Tanya moved her coffee mug listlessly back and forth on the table and gazed into space as if she'd forgotten Page. Bluish shadows underscored her downcast eyes. Her full mouth was drawn into a tight line.

''What time did *you* get home?'' Page asked.

''Oh—'' one beautifully manicured hand fluttered ''—a while ago.''

''Figures. In other words you haven't been to bed yet.''

''How do you know I didn't decide to get up and go for an early run?''

''In a miniskirt and spikes? Tanya, when's the last time you and I were in the kitchen together before I went to work?''

"You're being judgmental."

"When?" Page smiled and Tanya's wonderful green eyes slowly took on the lazy sparkle that was part of her beauty.

"Okay, okay. Never. Some of us have more sense than to brave the streets in the dullest hours of the day. I'm a night animal, friend."

Page noticed the red light on the coffee maker. "Oh, Tanya, you're wonderful. You made the coffee."

"Yes. I could have gone to bed, but I knew you'd be crawling out here in one of your elegant getups, too exhausted from putting on your makeup and doing your hair to take time for the simpler things of life. So I decided to take care of you."

"Sure, mother. And I bet you made oatmeal and put out my vitamins." Another of Tanya's pet complaints was Page's lack of concern about leisure clothes and her preference for little makeup and a simple hairstyle. She decided this morning was a good time not to take the bait on that subject. She poured coffee and returned to her chair beside her roommate. Up close she didn't look so radiant. "Is everything okay with you? You don't feel ill or anything?" Usually Tanya fell into bed the minute she got home and left for classes at a local art college a few hours later while Page was at work.

"I feel terrific. I always feel terrific. Don't I look it?"

"Sure. I guess you do—if you can look terrific and exhausted at the same time."

"I'm not exhausted," Tanya said too quickly. "Why should I be?"

"No reason, I guess." Page caught sight of an open Touch Tone Gourmet box on the counter. Remnants of a sweet roll littered a paper towel beside the box. A parting gift from Waldo this morning? Previous subtle comments by Tanya had revealed that she waited in Waldo's apartment over the shop until one of his employees took over orders and dispatches at two in the morning. Then they spent hours together there. That worried Page. They seemed so different. Tanya always put on a worldly front, but Page had a hunch she wasn't as tough as she'd like everyone to believe. Waldo, on the other hand, *was* tough. He was the kind of man some women found magnetic simply because he was the take-charge type. Page prayed Tanya would be strong enough not to let Waldo hurt her.

Tanya met Page's eyes and smiled, but not before Page saw a shadow of anxiety. "Maybe I am a bit tired. Having a good time gets exhausting sometimes, that's all. I'm probably worn out from enjoying myself."

"You going to school today?" Page asked.

"Later maybe. I've got some errands to run after I sleep for a few hours."

Page closed her mouth firmly. Her friend's attendance at classes had become more and more erratic. Something else that worried Page. When they'd first met after Tanya had answered Page's advertisement for a roommate, Tanya had been determined to show her influential Texas family that she could go to school, become a dress designer and pursue a career successfully. At that time, almost two years ago, Tanya had worked as a waitress, insisting that she didn't want financial help from her parents. That resolve hadn't lasted, but Page understood Tanya's accepting money from her parents to go to school—as long as she went to school. What she didn't understand or approve of was what she knew her friend did most of the time: stay out all night, sleep most of the day, skip all but very few classes and use her family's generosity to support an addiction to expensive clothes. She looked at Tanya now and sighed. Not liking her was impossible. A funny, spirited charmer who was the best friend Page had ever had, she was all too easy to love. And at the back of her mind, Page didn't believe Tanya was happy.

A furious hammering on the front door almost made Page spill her coffee. "What now? If Lilian's upset the Zipper again I'll croak. I'm not in the mood for one of their spats." She pushed back her chair and went into the hall. Lilian Sweeny, a divorcée with a three-year-old daughter, was Pedal Pushers' intrepid slick-tongued dispatcher. Willy Kowalski, an ex-jockey who was better known as the Zipper, had been the first messenger Page hired. The two warred constantly, when they weren't trying to look after each other. The rest of the staff, Page included, shared a secret hope that the two would get together permanently.

The instant Page unlocked the door it swung sharply inward. If she hadn't jumped back her nose would have joined the never-ending list of injuries, minor and not so minor, that were an accepted blight in the life of a bicycle courier.

Rather than the Zipper or Lilian, Buzz Collins, nineteen and Page's youngest rider, stalked into the apartment, her bleached white hair gelled into four-inch spikes. "I gotta see you, Page."

"Sure." Resigned, Page led her into the kitchen. Tanya had left the room. "Sit down and tell me what's on your mind," Page said. "Want some coffee?" Buzz, officially Beatrice Collins, wasn't a complainer. The closed expression on her pale face spelled trouble, and that concerned Page.

"No coffee," Buzz said. She hooked her thumbs into the waistband of leopard-skin tights. "We gonna do something about what's going on?"

Page cleared her throat. "Aren't you people getting along?"

Buzz stared. Her mouth was an iridescent mauve slash, and indigo bands outlined her eyes. Page often longed to tell the girl how pretty she'd be without all the paint, the rows of earrings dangling from each ear, the bizarre clothes and studded leather wrist straps. But Buzz's mission in life was to be different.

"I asked what's wrong, Buzz."

"Zipper didn't say anything to you yesterday? Or Perkins or Ken?"

"No. What are you talking about?"

"Lilian didn't clue you in?"

Page's stomach made a slow revolution. "I just told you I don't have any idea what you're talking about. So spill it. I need to get to the garage."

"They said they were going to have a meeting with you."

Impatience jerked the nerves in Page's face. She took a slow breath. "Okay, let's take this a step at a time. There's something wrong between you people, right?"

"Wrong."

Page frowned. "There *isn't* anything wrong between you?"

"Right."

"Damn it, Buzz. Enough of the guessing games. If you've got something to say, say it. Otherwise get to work so I can, too."

Buzz crossed one foot over the other and bells jingled on the laces of her high-topped sneakers. "I knew you'd get mad. That's why I couldn't figure why you didn't say anything yet. Those chickens promised they'd talk to you so I wouldn't have to. They know I hate arguments."

"I'm trying to be patient...."

"Yeah, yeah. Well, we've got problems."

"So I gathered."

"It's this messenger outfit we don't recognize. We've all tried to track them down, but they take the kind of risks you'd kill us for taking, and we've given up trailing them every time. But so help me, the next time one of those turkeys trashes me I'm gonna ride like there's no tomorrow."

"That's it. Enough double talk." Page pulled out a chair and pointed to it. "Sit. And tell me what's going on. All of it."

Buzz perched her small shapely body on the edge of the chair and hugged her knees. "Some guys from another bike courier service are on our case."

"You mean you're getting hassled on the road? What's new about that? Banter between riders from competing companies goes with the territory and usually it's harmless."

A tinge of pink showed through the powdered

white on Buzz's cheeks. "This isn't the usual. They know each other, we can tell that, but we've never seen any of them before. Or we don't remember if we have. And they're mean. Look—" she worked one tight pantleg above her knee to show a series of deep scratches "—and I wasn't going anywhere when it happened."

Page shook her head. "I don't understand."

"I was headed for a drop at about five yesterday. Traffic was max. This guy was beside me while we waited for a cable car to cross Pacific at the bottom of Grant. He kept looking at me."

"It isn't a crime to look, Buzz."

"It oughta be a crime to *accidentally* ram a foot into someone's spokes just when they're taking off."

The little hairs on Page's spine rose. "It had to be an accident."

"Like hell. He used his shoe right between a spoke and the forkblade. I fell on my face, and that's when I got the gravel rash. The Zipper's had a couple of run-ins and so's Perkins and Ken, and I've had it. I just want you to know I'm fighting back from now on."

"Whoa," Page said. "Hold it right there, lady. You know my policy. We're a clean outfit. Spills are part of the game, but safety, particularly for other riders and pedestrians, comes first. No exceptions. Got it?"

"You mean we're supposed to lie down for these turkeys? They're after us, I tell you, Page. There's a war on and we don't even know who the enemy is."

Page tried to think clearly. Stories about this kind of thing abounded in San Francisco, but she'd never put much stock in them until today. "Okay. Down to the shop. We'd better have that summit meeting before one of you does something we'll all regret."

She swept up her gloves and pads, gathered the brake parts and led the way out of the apartment and into another gray October day.

From the garage, Lilian Sweeny's voice rose above the standard morning hum of chatter and the familiar clanging of tools and equipment. "If you ate properly, maybe you'd grow. How's a man supposed to live on hot dogs and fries and pop?"

Page grinned at Buzz, whose face relaxed into a smile. "Some things never change, huh?" she said.

"You said it. Another day, another round of baiting between our resident lovebirds. Poor Lilian, she thinks if she could feed the Zipper up he might get to be taller than five two."

Inside the garage Page was confronted by typical workday chaos—with the addition of Jemima, Lilian's little girl. The three-year-old sat on a tattered car seat amid piles of spare bike wheels, tires and heaps of nuts and bolts.

Lilian spied Page immediately. Standing, the woman was close to six feet. She was standing now, leaning over the radio to glower down at the Zipper.

"Morning, Page," Lilian bellowed. Her dark eyes, as dark as her wildly curly hair, narrowed on the Zipper. "Will you help me with this guy? Cold hot dogs for breakfast, and he wonders why he's a runt."

Most days Page would have entered into the debate. She enjoyed her colorful employees. They were loyal to her and to one another, the closest thing to a family she had here. But she wasn't in the mood to be flip.

She ducked a hanging bike frame that had just undergone the ugly painting and taping necessary to protect it from theft. All over the city, Peugots, Raleighs, Bridgestones and dozens of other expensive machines masqueraded as wrecks to save them from sticky fingers. Locking before making a drop took more time than most riders could afford.

"What's Jemima doing here?" Page asked, smiling to take any sting out of the question.

"She's got a cold." Lilian shrugged. "What else could I do? The day-care center wouldn't take her."

Jemima sniffled on cue, stuck a thumb in her mouth and clutched an old pink blanket to her face. Page went to ruffle the child's black curls. This happened regularly. Page had decided that whenever the dispatcher was short of money she brought Jemima to work to save day-care fees. Lilian had a hard time making ends meet, and although a smelly garage wasn't an ideal place for a tot, Page didn't have the heart to complain.

"You can put her upstairs in my bed when it's time for her nap. I'll leave you a key," she said. Sometimes the responsibility she felt for all these people weighed her down. "Okay you lot, let's talk about these incidents you've been keeping from me."

A chorus of dissent went up. Then Ken Moore, a muscular, sandy-haired man with green eyes who had dropped out of law school when he decided the only boss he ever wanted to work for was himself, took the center of the floor and shushed the others. He was a confident, natural orator whom Page considered wasted in his present occupation. She could only hope he'd make more of his talents one day, although at twenty-eight he seemed happy in his present life-style and intent only on perpetuating his reputation as a lady-killer.

For the next half hour Page listened to stories of unprovoked mischief by an unknown group of riders. Inquiries among messengers from other services had suggested Pedal Pushers was the only group being singled out for the unwanted attention. Even the Zipper, naturally stoic, seemed concerned. He repeatedly passed a callused hand over his head, which he shaved "to cut down wind resistance," and fiddled with the many pockets on his leather vest. Perkins, the fourth and quietest member of the troupe, added his list of incidents, and Page was forced to believe they had a serious problem.

"All right. I get the picture. All I can think is that it's a completely new outfit and they've decided to try cutting down the opposition one firm at a time."

"So what do we do?" the Zipper asked.

"Nothing, except watch out for ourselves. You know the police are never on the cyclist's side. Not that I blame them in many instances. But we don't have any official place to go. Ride defensively. If you see one of these clowns, get clear. Don't get drawn into any arguments. Don't react. Just get out of their way. Sooner or later they'll move their attention elsewhere. Meanwhile, we've got drops to make, so let's get on with it."

To Page the day seemed endless. Business had picked up steadily in the past few months. Two more law firms, a prestigious architect and a busy printing outfit had been added to her list of customers. She should be ecstatic. She was ecstatic. She was also deeply upset at the possibility of being under siege from whomever was picking on her riders. Why hadn't she encountered personal attack? Maybe the answer was obvious. She'd been marked as the owner of Pedal Pushers, and the word was that she'd be best undermined through her employees.

In between worrying about her business she thought of Tanya. Buzz's morning interruption had been ill timed. Page became convinced that Tanya had stayed up to talk because she'd been upset and was trying to find the courage to confide. Page hoped the opportunity hadn't been lost for good.

AT ONE-THIRTY the next morning, Page wheeled her bike into the white-tiled entrance of the Touch Tone Gourmet deli for the fourth time that night. She pushed open a second set of swinging double doors and entered the store. Ropes of onions, dozens of huge sausages and string-cradled wine bottles hung in swags from the ceiling. Glass-fronted cases displayed an overwhelming array of delicacies. The aroma was of cheeses and grains and dried bunches of herbs. "If you want it, we've got it," was yet another of Waldo's rash boasts for his customers' benefit. Page wondered, not for the first time, just how cost-effective the ten or so deliveries she made a night were. Waldo insisted they paid very well, but that the main function of round-the-clock service was to promote goodwill. He believed so strongly in the concept that he'd invested in his beloved radio especially for the purpose. She guessed he knew his business.

Several minutes after she'd rung the bell on the counter, Waldo came down the stairs from his apartment. To Page's sharp eye he looked slightly mussed, and involuntarily she glanced upward. He probably had a woman in his bedroom. When she met Waldo's pale blue eyes an instant later, a flicker of understanding seemed to pass between them. Page immediately busied herself removing delivery envelopes from her waist pouch. Tanya was likely to be the woman with him. Why was the thought so upsetting?

"Big order," Waldo said in his heartiest voice. "And there's a little one you can drop on the way, too. Then you're through for the night." He pushed a large box along the top of a display case and put a small one on top. "I think this part of the service is getting more popular. I might ask you for a second rider before too long."

"Wonderful." Why couldn't she feel triumphant? One of the others would probably be delighted to make some extra money. If not, she could hire a new part-time person.

"How're things going?" Waldo asked pleasantly. His straight, sandy hair fell over his forehead. He was a big, good-looking man, and he was always charming to Page. So why didn't she like him?

"Pretty good," she told him. "I figure I'll need more staff before long. Space in the garage is becoming a problem too, but it'll be a while before I can do anything about a new place."

"I suppose you'll want to go to computerized dispatching one of these days."

He was an informed man who seemed to know a

lot about any subject that came up. "I wish," Page responded. "But I'll have to get a lot bigger first."

"Let me know if there's anything I can ever do to help," Waldo said, his tone earnest. "You're a go-getter and I like that. I want to see you succeed."

Page couldn't think of a response. She smiled and nodded. His interest in her business puzzled her. Sure, he was committed to his night deliveries and needed her services, but she didn't do anything a dozen other outfits couldn't be persuaded to do if approached with a good offer.

She took the boxes and left the store with the sensation that Waldo was watching her. Not looking back took control.

Once on the road she checked the first delivery docket, then the second, planning her route. Easy shot.

Easy... Good grief, she knew the second address. How could she forget? After a long hard day, a two-hour nap and another foray into a drizzly evening, she was to be rewarded with a repeat trip to Laguna and Green.

The small delivery was to an elegant house near Lafayette Park. Afterward, with the payment envelope safely in her pouch, Page pedaled toward Ian Faber's house. Did the man throw a party every night? She prayed someone would answer the front door this time. If they didn't, she wasn't sure she could handle another scene like the one she'd experienced the night before.

When she arrived at her destination her spirits lifted a little. Lights shone through the colored windows in the door, and lamps flanking the entrance had been turned on.

She hauled her bike up the front steps and knocked on the door firmly. A breath caught in her throat and she pursed her lips. So Ian Faber was an attractive, interesting man. He was also out of her league. He'd probably laugh if he knew that, at this instant, the woman who delivered his late-night snacks and who must look to him like a refugee from a modern vaudeville show was standing outside his house trembling at the prospect of seeing him again. She *was* trembling—and breathless. This had to be the result of what Tanya had talked about. Too much work and not enough play. Why else would a realistic, intelligent woman go hot all over at the thought of a man she knew nothing about?

Footsteps sounded inside the house, hurrying footsteps. Page prayed, *Don't let it be Martin Grantham III.* She couldn't take any teasing at this hour. Almost frantically she tore her chin strap undone and pulled off her helmet.

The door opened. "Hi, Page," Ian Faber said. His smile crinkled the corners of his eyes. "Come in, please."

Speechless, Page lifted the box from her bike basket and gave it to him.

"Thanks. If you'll come up I'll write a check."

She hesitated, took a step inside the door and thrust out the envelope. "I'll just wait here." An uncomfortable jumpiness filled her chest. "And it's cash, remember?"

"Right, cash." He closed the door behind her and

hunched one shoulder. ''Might as well keep the cold out. Had a busy night?''

Page swallowed. Was she imagining things, or was he nervous? ''Pretty hectic,'' she told him.

He shifted the box from one arm to the other. ''How late do you work?''

She shouldn't feel uncomfortable because a man tried to be polite. ''Until two,'' she said and attempted a smile. ''Time to go home now.''

''That's what I thought. Please come up.''

Without waiting for her response he walked upstairs.

Page watched until he reached the top and looked down at her. If she stayed where she was he'd take her for an insecure ninny. She set her helmet on the floor inside the door and followed him.

Ian led the way into the room she'd seen the previous night. Once she was inside he set the box on the coffee table and began to unpack and examine the contents.

A bottle of wine, a wheel of Brie, several boxes of crackers and an assortment of other containers were arranged on the table. Page sighed loudly and snapped the elastic on an elbow pad. He gave no sign of noticing.

''Is everything there, Mr. Faber?''

''Ian.'' He didn't look at her.

Page opened her mouth but couldn't think of a thing to say. Tonight he wore black pants and a black crewneck. His dark, curly hair looked even darker than she remembered; so did his brows, and his eyes when he finally looked at her. She also hadn't noticed the deep cleft in his chin before, or the olive tone to his skin that suggested a tan, or the frown line between his brows that seemed at odds with a constant hint of a smile. Was stunning a suitable description for a man? Ian Faber was stunning, compelling...an overwhelming presence that made the air around Page very still.

"Are you tired?" he asked abruptly, returning her stare.

She took a breath. "No... Well, yes, I guess I am."

He went to a bar in one corner and returned with two glasses. "Would you like some wine?"

"No thank you." He was a stranger and his behavior ought to frighten her. "If everything's all right I'll leave you to your... Ah, I'll leave you." She was more excited than frightened, which probably made her a fool. For all she knew, the man could be dangerous, and he was too big to escape from if he decided he didn't want her to go.

"They told me at the deli that delivery shifts changed at two." He'd opened the bottle, poured the wine and now he offered her a glass. "I tried to work it so I'd be your last customer, and I pulled it off."

Page's heart made a slow revolution. "Why would you want to do that?" The question sounded like a fishing expedition. "I mean why...?"

His laugh was anything but confident, and Page glanced behind to locate the door. Maybe if she ran without warning she'd catch him off guard.

"You're wondering why I pulled a stunt like this, right?"

She looked at her feet.

"Right. Well, last night you hit a chord I'd forgotten all about. You interested me. You still do. Is that okay?''

If this was a come-on it was definitely a new one to Page.

When she didn't answer he set down the glasses and started to pace. ''Anyway, I just wanted a chance to talk to you again and tell you I don't think it's such a hot idea for a beautiful woman to be riding around San Francisco at night all alone and on a bicycle.'' He paused and Page met his eyes. He was serious, truly serious—at least, he looked it. ''Ever since I watched you ride away I've been thinking about it.''

She heard what he said, absorbed the words and felt a brief rush of warmth...before common sense returned. This was the best line she'd ever heard. Ian Faber wasn't the type of man who worried about grunts hired to tend his whims. She scanned the room, half expecting to see his friend Martin contouring his stocky frame behind the trunk of a ficus tree near the bar, or pressed beneath the keyboard of a baby grand piano at the far end of the room. She could almost imagine him betting Ian that he couldn't pull off this practical joke.

''I've caught you off guard,'' Ian said. ''I'm sorry. I just didn't know any other way to get in touch with you. Asking the guy at the deli where I could reach you didn't seem like such a good idea.''

''Why?'' Page found her voice, but it sounded strange.

Ian looked as if he was surprised that she'd spoken at all. He stopped pacing and passed a hand over his thick, well-cut hair. ''Isn't it obvious?''

"Not to me." Nothing about this encounter was obvious to Page.

"I was afraid he'd think you were, uh, well, you know."

She was beginning to be dimly afraid she did know. "Perhaps we should stop this conversation right now. I may be getting the wrong impression, and neither of us would want that."

"Oh, no, no, Page. Listen, I only meant I didn't want to risk giving your customer the impression you were using your deliveries as a chance to make friends..." He threw up his hands. "Oh, hell, I don't know what I mean. None of this is coming out right. It's straightforward, really. I wanted to see you again. You intrigue me..." His color heightened. "This sounds dumb. Put simply, I'd like to get to know you better. Last night I didn't think to ask you the name of your company, so I had to resort to this, okay?"

Not okay, Page thought, stepping backward. He might be the first man she'd looked at—really looked at in a long time—and he hadn't actually made a physical move on her yet, but she didn't intend to wait around and find out if he would. Being lured to a house where no one would think to look for her, by a stranger who was unlikely ever to be connected with her disappearance if it occurred, was reason to panic. At any second she was about to do just that.

He came toward her.

"Don't come any closer." Page took another step backward and stumbled on the edge of the rug. Her arms flailed and she recovered her balance. Crouched, she held out both hands. "Let me leave or I'll scream."

Ian stopped, his hands at his sides. Page saw his eyes widen and the color leave his face. "I frightened you. Good Lord, I've never frightened a woman in my life."

Her thighs and calves cramped. He looked... shocked.

"Please listen to me," he said. "I thought this would be an amusing way to get to know you. It even seemed clever at the outset. I really am sorry if I've scared you. Good Lord." He picked up a glass and swallowed some wine, watching her as if he expected her to start screaming.

Slowly Page straightened. Dull heat throbbed in her face and neck. "You really are trying to be nice, aren't you?"

He nodded, frowning deeply.

"Oh boy. I feel like a fool. I guess I'm tired and out of practice."

"Out of practice?"

The heat in her cheeks throbbed more. "With men," she said, feeling miserable.

"I see."

She doubted if he did see at all, and she still didn't fully believe he could be interested in her. There was never any doubt in her mind that she was attractive—enough men had told her so—but Ian Faber obviously moved in circles where beautiful women were plentiful.

Nothing like this had ever happened to Ian. He watched her warily, half expecting her to leap from the room and dash away. If she did he'd have no alternative but to let her go. Her reaction had made him feel like an ass, an adolescent playing silly games. And he had genuinely scared her. He hated that.

"Could we call a truce, do you think?"

She lifted the long, windblown mass of dark hair off her shoulders. Her eyes were bluer than any he remembered seeing. Damn, why didn't she speak? He looked at her mouth, wide, soft, parted a little over very white teeth.

"Here. Have some of the wine. You look as if you need it."

She laughed, and relief rushed into his tense body. Still laughing, she took the other glass and sipped, smiling tentatively at him over the rim. Ian took another swallow and quelled what could only be a self-destructive urge to hug her. She'd probably slap him.

"You must think I'm a nut," she said at last.

"Because you thought I was related to Jack the Ripper?" He wrinkled his nose. "Nah. All the women I lure here think that. I'm used to it."

She laughed again and his stomach tightened. Relaxed, she was even more appealing. Her skin shone slightly. She appeared to wear no makeup and didn't need any. Every feature was clearly defined and the light in her eyes held honest warmth.

He realized his mouth was open. "Um, sit down, sit down, please. If you've got time?" he added hastily.

"I really should go...."

"Please?"

With a faint shrug she did as he asked, choosing one end of the couch. "You have a beautiful home," she said. Her voice broke slightly. He liked the effect.

"Thank you. It's too big for me. That's why I live

on the second floor—unless I have a lot of people to entertain. I'm always thinking I'll fill the whole place up with a family one day.'' Brilliant. She could certainly make something of that comment if she thought about it for a while.

Page only nodded and rotated the stem of her glass. She was tall, with long, shapely, muscular legs. Her body, inside a pale blue leotard and knee-length shorts, made Ian think things he probably shouldn't think, at least for now. Page Linstrom had the kind of body any man would react to.

She met his eyes and glanced away quickly. He made her uncomfortable. ''Where do you live?'' he asked. Getting personal could be hazardous, but if he didn't say or do something fast he'd probably never see her again.

''Russian Hill.''

''Is that where your business is?''

She held her bottom lip in her teeth for an instant. ''Yes. I rent the garage behind the house where my apartment is.''

''And you call yourself...?''

''Pedal Pushers.''

''Cute. How long have you been there?''

The teeth dug into the lip again. ''Two years.''

''You come from San Francisco?''

''Anchorage.''

''Alaska. You're a long way from home.'' How many more questions before she told him to mind his own business? ''I was born here. My family's in advertising. Faber and Faber. Maybe you've heard of us.''

She shook her head.

Ian took a long, slow breath to calm his leaping nerves. He didn't know why for sure, but the tougher this got the more determined he was to break·down her defenses.

"Do you live alone?"

Her eyes darkened slightly. She didn't reply.

He grimaced. "Dumb question, right? Jack the Ripper question. I only meant, I wondered if you... Scratch the question."

"I share an apartment with another woman." She looked into her glass, but he saw her amusement. "And I like my job. I've got big ambitions for expansion. San Francisco's the most exciting city I've ever seen, and I intend to spend the rest of my life here. What else do you want to know? Oh, I'm twenty-seven, single, never been married—and don't intend to be. Parents living, one brother, two sisters, no pets, except for my dispatcher's three-year-old daughter, and I'd steal her if I didn't know her mother would put up a fuss." She paused, grinning broadly now. "There, total disclosure, though I don't have a clue why you care about me one way or the other."

Ian scratched his head. She was gorgeous, bright, appealing, and she didn't know it. He was going to have to step right up and see if he couldn't do something about that. It might take a lot of effort but of the most pleasurable kind.

"My turn. Then I'll ask you another question."

She gave a mock groan and leaned back. He watched the play of muscle and soft flesh and stiffened his jaw. "I'm a marital holdout, too. Thirty-six and an only child. My folks are still in the area, and

Dad sits on the board while I do the dog work around the firm.''

Page watched him from beneath lowered lashes and after a short pause said, ''And?''

''And nothing. That's all of it that's worth reporting. How about some of this Brie? I bought all this stuff to share with you.''

''No thanks, Ian.'' She checked her watch. ''Oh, no, three o'clock.''

He frowned. ''What happens at three? Do you turn into a pumpkin or something?''

''It's not what happens at three that counts. But at six I have to get up and start another day's work, so if you'll excuse me—''

''I won't.'' He put a hand on her arm. ''Not until I say what I set out to say tonight.''

She stood up, moving away from his grasp. ''Haven't you said it?''

''Not quite.'' Quickly. He had to think of something this instant or he'd miss what could be his only chance to ask to see her again. ''I wondered if you take necessary precautions on the streets at night.'' Boy, that sounded weak.

''Thanks for the concern,'' she said, ''but I do know what I'm doing.''

She probably did. Now he had to go for it and get to the point. ''Yes, well, actually there was another thing I wanted to ask you.''

She was edging toward the door. A few more seconds and he'd blown it.

''Goodnight then, Ian.''

He closed his eyes and swallowed. Not one of his

friends would believe this. ‘‘Page—’’ he rubbed his hands together ‘‘—how would you like to spend Saturday night in Sausalito with me?’’

CHAPTER THREE

FROM THE CORNER window of Faber and Faber's boardroom in the Embarcadero Center, Ian could glimpse San Francisco Bay. A shifting web of fog separated an ominous late-morning sky from the flat gunmetal water. It wasn't the picture-postcard image thousands of tourists sent home, but he liked it well enough. Dismal fitted his mood.

"Did you hear what I said, Ian?"

Samson LeBeck was holding forth on something or other. "Why don't you recap for me, Samson," Ian said, focusing his eyes if not his whole attention on the corpulent little man. Samson was a pedantic pain, and if he didn't own a big block of Faber stock Ian would consider telling him as much.

"I was addressing the question of expansion," Samson said, puffing up his chest inside his navy pinstripe suit.

Ian concentrated on a straining jacket button. The man should address the matter of his own expansion, he thought, his mind slipping away again, away from the vast rosewood table and away from the men who surrounded it.

He could hardly bear to remember last night, what he'd said, the way Page had recoiled and bolted. She'd thought he was asking her to go to Sausalito with him for the night—literally for the night. By the time he'd recovered she'd been vaulting downstairs like a hurdler and there hadn't been time to explain that he meant he'd like to take her to see his parents' home. Damn it.

The drone of voices persisted. Faber had long ago become a major force in the advertising industry, his father was pointing out. Their west coast headquarters hadn't proved a handicap, but they should think of leaning more heavily toward the New York scene. Grant Maxwell, their vice president of operations for the east coast, was doing a fantastic job, but the time had come to show him a vote of confidence and cut him loose a bit more. Grant needed a freer hand. Ian smiled at Robert Faber. His old man still had it. He never stopped thinking, moving.

Ian pushed the blank notebook in front of him back and forth, grabbed a pencil and wrote furiously: "I was a fool last night." He scratched out the words and tried again. "Forgive me for last night. I know how it sounded, but I honestly wasn't asking you to sleep with me."

"Are you with us at all, Ian?" His father sounded uncharacteristically irritated. "We need your vote on this."

"Yeah, right—you've got it."

He raised a hand, and as he did so, Clemmie, his secretary, gathered his notebook onto the pile she'd collected.

"Just a minute..."

The notebooks were handed to his father who cleared his throat and adjusted his glasses on his thin, high-bridged nose. "Okay, we've got one, two, three, four, five...yes votes. And..." His smooth, still taut skin turned an interesting shade of puce. He looked up at Ian. At seventy, Bob Faber remained a very handsome man who, with a look from eyes as dark as his son's, could wither even the most intrepid. His son was the recipient of one of those looks now. "This isn't very clear, Ian. This is your pad, the one with the, ah, explanation?"

Ian crossed his arms and nodded.

"And I take it your vote is to give Grant more leeway?"

So much for secret ballots. "Yup." He'd better get hold of himself and prepare for an onslaught from his mother. She was the only person his father would mention the note to, and then the subtle interrogation would begin. Any hint of an eligible female on the horizon sent Rose Faber's grandmotherly antennae skyward. She and his father made no bones about their impatience for Ian to marry and have children. Usually he made sure they knew nothing about his love life.

"Next on the agenda is the question of fees for television campaigns...."

Several sentences later Ian stopped listening again. What would Page look like in a soft dress, a swimsuit...in nothing at all? He swallowed and spread his hands on his thighs. He'd be lying to himself if he didn't admit the lure of a different kind of woman from the type who buzzed through his life with nothing in mind but a brilliant match.

By her own admission, Page Linstrom wanted nothing more than to make a success of a business she'd created herself, and Ian admired that. She was independent, motivated... He turned warm and shifted slightly in his seat. She had a wonderful mouth, very soft...

"Now, Ian. Is there something you'd like to—"

"Not a thing." He pushed his chair back so hard he had to stop it from falling. Addressing his father he said, "Forgive me, Dad. I seem to be having difficulty concentrating."

Bob Faber grunted, but the beginning of a smile was obvious.

"Anyway," Ian rushed on, "I've got a lot on my mind and I think the sooner I take care of it the better. So if you'll all excuse me, and if you can all clear your calendars for an hour at, say, two—we'll reschedule the meeting for then."

Murmurs of surprise followed him to the door where his father's voice stopped him. "Good luck, Ian. I'll look forward to hearing how things come out."

Ian returned to his office. For three years he'd held the presidency of Faber and Faber, which meant that his father stayed in the wings as chairman of the board and pretended to be semiretired while he continued to watch every move his son made. And Ian took pleasure in knowing he hadn't disappointed him.

"Mr. Faber!" Clemmie followed Ian breathlessly into the big, striking room he'd decorated himself. "Mr. Faber, your father asked me to give you this. He also said for you to let him know when you're free for golf."

"I'll call him later." Ian took the folded sheet of paper Clemmie proffered, knowing roughly what it was. He waited until she retreated, closing the door smoothly and softly over dove-gray carpet.

He unfolded the lined yellow paper and read what his father had written underneath his own scribbled efforts: "When you want something and it's worth the effort—go after it." Smart man, his father. He and Ian shared a special closeness, and Bob Faber was bound to have recognized that his son's behavior this morning had been out of character.

Yeah. If a man wanted something badly enough he should go after it. With purposeful strides he crossed to the simple mahogany desk that sat between two floor-to-ceiling windows.

From his pocket he took a card on which he'd written a telephone number. There was one instant when he hesitated, but only an instant. Then he picked up the phone and dialed.

"PEDAL PUSHERS. You got something to peddle? We got the push. Name your game."

Aghast, Page listened to Lilian answer the phone. Something must change around here in the telephone answering department. Success and a professional approach went hand in hand.

"Oh yes, sir," Lilian said, standing up and saluting. "Yes, *sir*."

Page whispered, "Cool it." Surely Lilian didn't ham it up every time a customer called. Usually Page was on the road and didn't hear much of this end of the business. Half an hour earlier she'd jumped the curb to avoid an opening cab door, wrapped a wheel around a fire hydrant and been forced to come back for a repair, otherwise she wouldn't have witnessed this exchange.

She'd deal with Lilian later. Deftly, she slid on a fork tip and reached for a wrench.

"Perfectly possible, sir," Lilian was saying. "Ms. Linstrom is in her office. She may be in conference, but I'll buzz her and see if she can talk to you."

At that Page stood up, hands on hips, grinning and shaking her head.

Lilian tilted up her nose. She covered the receiver. "Sounds like *big* business. He won't speak to anyone but the owner." Lilian leaned heavily on the word owner.

Wiping her hands on an oily rag, Page stepped over the bike and went to the cluttered radio table where a pile of dockets partially buried the telephone.

"Sir," Lilian said into the phone, "Ms. Linstrom for you."

Page took the phone, frowning at Lilian who chortled silently into a fist.

"Page Linstrom here."

"Don't hang up."

Ian Faber. She opened her mouth, but the air went out of her lungs instead of in. All her blood drained downward. Glancing at Lilian, she said, "I believe we spoke before, Mr. Faber, and as I told you then, we are definitely unsuited to what you have in mind."

Lilian had sat on the tattered car seat and picked up a magazine.

"Page, listen to me. You may not believe this, but I could find a hell of a lot of people who would vouch for my reputation."

"I'll bet."

He expelled a gusty sigh. "Geez, lady. I feel like I'm jinxed with you. All I have to do is open my mouth and my foot automatically finds it."

Page rubbed her eyes and smiled a little. He sounded desperate.

"Are you still there?" he asked.

"Yes, I'm still here. You ordered me not to hang up, remember?"

"Will you please forgive me for saying such an asinine thing last night?"

"Ian, I—"

"No, don't say it. Don't cut me off."

"You do have a way of wanting to tell me what to do, don't you?"

She heard him tap the phone at his end. "I want to start this conversation again. Last night was a mess. What I was trying to do was to find a way to ask you out without you thinking I was...was...you know."

He had such spectacular eyes when he was being serious. In her mind she saw those eyes now. Penetrating, sexy. And she was nuts. She had no time for this. "Thanks for the call, Ian. Don't give last night another thought."

"Please," he moaned, "don't do this to me. Say you'll go out with me. Just once if that's all you'll give it. Or just once to see if you can stand me. I'll go anywhere, a museum, grocery shopping, you name it. I just want to find out if what I feel about you is worth pursuing."

He immediately groaned and Page laughed. "Oh yes, you do have a way with words. But I understand and I thank you. If I had time I'd say yes, but—"

"But you'll make time. And by the way, all I

meant last night was that I thought it might be nice to take you over to Sausalito for the evening. My parents live there. I thought if I invited you to their home you wouldn't feel threatened."

Page sat heavily on the edge of the table. She loved the sound of his voice. He was special. If she cut him off completely would she regret it later? And would it hurt just to go out for once?

"Page, are you thinking?"

"Yes."

"What are you thinking?"

"I'm thinking that it couldn't be such a sin to take a few hours off—"

"Wonderful! Terrific! When?"

"Just a few hours and just once. I'm not the right kind of woman for you, Ian, but I'd enjoy going out anyway." She liked the sensible ring of her voice.

"Can you go tonight?"

"Impossible. The only night I don't work, or have to get ready for work, is Saturday."

"Today's Thursday." He sounded disappointed.

"Right."

He sighed again. "Okay, Saturday it'll have to be then. Name the place."

"Wherever you want to take me."

"Okay. Dress very casually. I'll pick you up at… three? I've got the address."

He would have the address by now, Page thought wryly. "Three's fine." If they went early, she could get back early. "Goodbye."

"'I'm getting married in the morning. Ding dong the bells are going to chime…'"

Page had forgotten Lilian, who reclined in the seat,

her hands clasped behind her head, smiling beatifically as she sang.

"That's enough," Page said and climbed back to her spot beside the bike she'd been repairing. "Don't make something out of nothing and don't mention what you heard to any of the others."

"'You do have a way with words,'" Lilian said in a high voice. "And what did happen last night, boss?" She jumped up and stood beside Page. "Tell Auntie Lilian all."

Page looked up and realized, not for the first time, that Lilian was a beautiful woman in a strong, unconventional way. She sat on the dirty floor and clasped her knees. "Last night, Lilian, I met a magnetic, rich, handsome, incredibly sexy guy who asked me to spend the night with him next Saturday. And I just told him I would."

With that, she got up, tested the wheel and left the garage.

CHAPTER FOUR

SPRAY WHIPPED over the bow of the ferry. Page licked her lips and tasted salt. Even in her fur-lined, army-surplus parka and jeans and with thick socks inside her tennis shoes she was cold. She suppressed a shiver but pulled up her hood and tucked her hair inside. The wind was cool but not so bad that she should be shivering. Tension must be closing down her circulation.

She shouldn't have come. She didn't belong here with Ian Faber of the charming smile and easy manner. At least, his manner had been easy when he picked her up. An hour in her uncommunicative company had made him as silent as she was.

After he'd ushered her into a glistening black Mercedes coupe and seated himself behind the wheel, he'd announced that he'd decided to follow his first instinct and take her to Sausalito. His parents might or might not be at home, he'd said. Page instantly decided they wouldn't be there. A man didn't take a woman home to meet Mom and Dad on a first date, particularly when he was simply "deciding if she was worth pursuing." Why had she agreed to come?

They'd parked at Fisherman's Wharf, boarded the ferry and were now among a handful of passengers brave enough to venture from cover onto the foredeck. Ian sat beside her on a slatted wooden bench, his arms spread along the back, one ankle propped on the opposite knee. Page peered at him from inside her hood...and he looked back and smiled. He was dressed much as she was, but his parka was navy instead of the drab olive Page knew didn't suit her, and his jeans fashionably faded rather than just old. His polo-necked sweater, also navy, of heavy oiled wool was obviously expensive, and Page hoped she could get through the outing without having to take off her coat. Her own high-necked sweater was dark gray and did suit her, but the elbows were baggy and many washings had stretched the bottom edge. For once she wished she'd heeded at least one of Tanya's attempts to make her buy some new clothes.

She turned her head away and scanned the scenery. They sat facing the boat's starboard side. Over her right shoulder San Francisco's skyline was a hilly gray jumble against dense white cloud. Abreast of the vessel lay the barren rock pile that was Alcatraz Island.

Page got up and went to lean on the rail. Sausalito grew steadily clearer through a film of mist, its colorful buildings stacked from the waterfront to the top of steep, lush slopes.

Ian joined her, resting his chin on crossed arms. "Not much of a day, huh?" he asked. The wind flattened his hair, then tossed it forward.

Page sensed tension under his nonchalance. "I like it," she said and pressed her lips together. If she thought before she spoke she might at least manage to say something less argumentative.

He stood up and faced her, hooking his elbows over the railing. "What *don't* you like? Apart from me."

Heat rushed to her face. "I don't even know you."

"And you don't want to?"

She wasn't equipped for this.

"Why did you agree to come, Page? You're obviously hating every second you're with me."

"I..." She pressed her hands to her cheeks. "I'm sorry. Really I am. But you're wrong...and right in a way." She'd never felt more foolish or more trapped.

Ian tilted his head. "Could you expand on that?"

He had a right to be terse. "The other evening I told you a bit about myself," Page said. "I explained that I was out of practice with men. I should have said I was out of practice with anything but work. Not that I'm apologizing for that. But I am sorry I accepted your invitation."

"Thanks." He walked around her and stared at the faint outline of the Golden Gate Bridge.

Page took a deep breath. This was awful, absolutely the pits.

She wasn't a kid. Life in an Anchorage suburb hadn't exposed her to a lot of smooth repartee, but surely she was mature enough to spend a few hours with a perfectly nice man without insulting him.

Page rubbed her temple, praying for a graceful exit line. Then she noticed two women watching them from a bench. Watching Ian would have been more accurate. A "perfectly nice man" was a lousy description of him. He was one of those rare males who would capture attention wherever he went, probably until he was at least a hundred, yet he appeared unaware of the effect he had on women.

"Ian." She touched his back, half expecting him to shrug away.

He didn't. Nor did he say anything.

"Could I try again, do you think?" she asked.

"I pushed you for this date." He faced her. "If it's a flop it sure isn't your fault. You gave enough signals you didn't want to go out with me. We can stay aboard when the boat docks and go right back to the city. And I'm sorry, okay?"

"Not okay. Please, Ian. Let me say something."

Before he could respond the boat caught the wake from a passing tanker and nosed into a trough. Page stumbled and Ian steadied her as he was thrown against the side. He held her while the bow came up again. His body was solid, his braced legs hard where they touched hers.

He held her only until the deck leveled. When he dropped his arms they stood almost toe to toe for several seconds. His eyes, so serious and questioning, mesmerized Page. She stared into them. When she'd said she didn't know him it had been the truth. But she'd like to know him—well.

She breathed in and became aware of her fingers clutching his parka. Flustered, she let go. "Thanks," she said.

"For what?"

"Stopping me from falling flat on my face," she said and laughed. "Now let me see if I can crawl out of the hole I dug myself into."

He smiled and the effect electrified Page. She had to smile back. The somber set of his face was transformed into captivating expectancy.

"You know how it is sometimes," she told him.

"Each time you open your mouth you just keep putting your foot in it."

He laughed aloud. "I think you just stole my line. Must be a catching condition. You'd better watch it."

"I'll try. But I do want to go to Sausalito with you. I need the break and I need to learn to let go a bit. What I was trying to say when I made such a mess of it was that, although I don't know you very well, I do like you. The reason I said I wished I hadn't come was because I feel so awkward." She paused, watching for his reaction. He nodded and she gained courage. "I'm comfortable in my own arena, Ian, but I guess I feel out of my depth with you."

"You're very honest." He put an arm around her shoulders and pulled her beside him at the rail. "Can I let you in on a secret?"

"I—"

"Good. I knew I could. I'm a bit nervous around you, too. Whoever perpetuated the myth that men are always sure of themselves did his fellow males a disservice."

His arm was warm. Page leaned a little closer. He felt nice, very nice. "Maybe it was a woman who did it to all of you. Some women want men to be in control."

He turned toward her and she met his gaze. "You wouldn't want that at all, would you?" he asked.

"It's not something I need to think about one way or the other."

"If you say so." He pointed at the nearing headland. "When was the last time you were in Sausalito?" he asked. He took his arm from her shoulders. Page wished he hadn't, then wished she didn't care.

"I've never been there," she told him.

"Never?" He leaned to see her face. The ferry was nudging into the dock. "It's just a hop, skip and a jump from Fisherman's Wharf. If you stood on the roof of your house you could probably see it. Everyone goes to Sausalito. Some of the best art galleries in the area are there."

The gap between them was yawning again. Page had a quick vision of her bedroom with its bent-bicycle-parts motif. She tried not to compare it to Ian's sumptuous home, but failed. "I doubt if *everyone* goes to Sausalito," she said. "Some of us spend more money on bicycle equipment and tools than we do on art."

He pursed his lips as if deep in thought. "Bicycle equipment. Are you really hooked on this courier stuff? Or do you think you'll grow out of it?"

Page poked his chest with a long finger. "You know how seriously I take my business, and if I didn't know better I'd think you were trying to pick another fight with me."

He raised his right hand. "No. Honest. But can I just say that someone as elegant as you would look a damn sight better in a gallery than shuttling around San Francisco on a filthy old bike?"

"Aha." Page grinned. "You are trying to bait me. Listen, my friend. My filthy old bike isn't a filthy old bike. It's a very expensive bike deliberately made to look like a heap of junk to discourage anyone who happens along with sticky fingers and no wheels of their own. Every machine used by my riders looks that way."

"Fascinating," Ian said. "You'll have to tell me

more, but if we don't get off this ferry we'll be going back to San Francisco whether we want to or not."

They joined the line of disembarking passengers. Page noted how many cyclists were aboard and checked to see if any appeared to be messengers. "This might be an interesting place to expand to," she said, thinking aloud. "I don't think I know of an outfit that comes over here. It wouldn't be cheap for the customer. You'd have to allow for the ferry fare and the lost time, but if you consolidated—"

"Page."

She glanced up, reluctantly shifting her mind from her new idea to the slightly exasperated expression on Ian's face. "Yes?"

"We're on a date. For a while we aren't going to talk about bicycles. Okay?"

"What are we going to talk about?"

He threw up his hands. "I give up. Let's grab a cab."

"Mr. Faber, sir!"

A man's voice. Page swung around, searching for its owner. She heard Ian mutter something that sounded hostile before he gripped her elbow and guided her from the ferry landing to the sidewalk.

"Good afternoon, Mr. Faber and Ms.…ah?" A portly man in a chauffeur's uniform, his cap under his arm, held open the door of an immaculate black limousine.

"This is Ms. Linstrom," Ian supplied in a tone Page interpreted as surly. "How did you know I was coming, Banks?"

The chauffeur's surprise looked genuine. "Why, your folks told me, sir. They always send me when you're coming." He squinted at Ian as if considering his mental state.

"My folks?" His hand tightened on her arm. "My folks said they'd be..." Page thought she heard his teeth snap together before he arranged his face into a bland mask and stood aside to let her get into the car.

She slid across the softest leather seats she'd ever sat on, buried herself in a far corner and hid a smile by shading her face to look through the tinted window. *My parents may or may not be at home.* He'd been pretty certain they wouldn't be, but his little plan for an exclusive get-together had been scuttled. She did wonder how the Fabers had known Ian intended to come here.

He joined her. His smile went no farther than his mouth. Page saw the way he wiped his palms on his jeans, and her amusement at the failure of his little deception fled. She felt her own small welling of apprehension. These parents of his must be formidable if they intimidated their own son. Then another thought hit. She didn't want to meet his parents. She hadn't thought about the possibility becoming reality. And she also wasn't dressed for an audience with people who must be used to the best. That was Ian's fault. He'd been the one to tell her she should dress casually. She'd been grateful, since she had a limited wardrobe, but she wasn't grateful now. Who was she kidding? She wouldn't have come at all if there'd been any question of meeting his family.

Banks started the engine and turned into traffic along the busy, tourist-clogged waterfront. Ian chewed on the inside of his cheek. Clemmie would hear about this. She'd found out the ferry schedule for him. The pieces were already dropping neatly into place in his brain. He might have known his father—or more likely his mother, after his father reported on the note—would grill Clemmie for any information on a new woman in his life. Rose Faber could wheedle information out of anyone. Ten minutes of logical reasons that Clemmie, for Ian's own good of course, should spill anything she knew would be all Rose needed. Not that Clemmie knew more than that he'd intended to go to Sausalito while his parents were in San Francisco. But his mother could easily make a nice little package of possibilities out of his reasons for going without telling her of his intention. At this moment he felt less than a loving and respectful son.

He hadn't meant to lie to Page, but he did think his parents' home would be a good place to take her. He'd considered and quickly discarded inviting her to his own place. Too threatening after their last encounter. And his father had said he and Ian's mother planned to spend the weekend at their city apartment, damn it.

Ian felt an unfamiliar fury welling. He glanced at Page, but she stared out the window. Her throat moved sharply. He must be giving off tangible waves of annoyance, he thought. "You'll like my parents," he said, deliberately pulling his shoulders down and settling into the seat. "They'll want you to call them Rose and Bob. They're informal, easy to get along with. Everyone gets along with them." He was talking too much.

"Yes," Page said. Her voice, a pitch higher than usual, caught him off guard. She was nervous. Holy hell, just when she was starting to overcome her distrust of him, they were back to square one.

"I didn't expect them to be here," he said, resigned to revealing all. He'd never been good at deceit.

"I know."

Ian turned to her sharply. "You did?"

"Mmm. Taking a woman you just met home to Mom and Dad doesn't sound too likely, does it?"

His face burned for the first time in as long as he could remember. "I guess it doesn't." Trying to protest that he was more than casually interested in her wouldn't help at all. Maybe he should analyze his reasons for wanting to be with Page. She wasn't like any other woman he'd ever known or dated. His parents wouldn't miss that fact.

He pictured how she would look to them. To him she was lovely, fresh, with a sparkle that came as much from the inside as the outside. And he liked her dedication to independence, her unconscious femininity that wasn't diminished by her less-than-glamorous job. He found her incredibly sexy. How would his parents see her? As odd, too quiet, lacking sophistication? Would they be horrified if they found out what she did for a living…or even that she did anything at all for a living? His mother had never worked and made no secret of her hope that one day he'd end up with a woman who would mold her life around him and their children.

Ian closed his eyes. He didn't intend to marry the woman, for God's sake, only to cultivate what might become a relationship that would ease the boring routine he'd fallen into outside the office. He did find his job exhilarating, but he wasn't fool enough not to know that living for Faber and Faber alone wasn't enough.

Banks had cruised along Front Street as far as Napa and turned up into the hills. Ian crossed his arms and tapped his feet. His parents lived about as high up as you could go in Sausalito, which was pretty high. He loved the house, Spanish outside, all glass and dark wood inside and with a view over the water that didn't quit.

"How far is it?"

Page's voice had the effect of making him want to sink inside himself. With effort he said, "Not far. About ten minutes more at the most."

"You look uptight," she said softly.

He turned toward her. "I'm not uptight." *Liar.* "Just thinking. I feel guilty that I wasn't honest with you from the outset. I wanted us to go somewhere quiet so we'd have a chance to get to know each other. But you don't believe that, do you? You think I planned to take you to an empty house and seduce you."

She colored, and he rammed a hand into his hair. Ian Faber, silver-tongued devil, had struck again.

Page's hand closed on his wrist, and she pulled his hand down. "I didn't think that. Not consciously." She gave a short laugh. "Although it may have crossed my subconscious. Truly, I know I've blown way out of proportion what should have been very straightforward and simple. And I feel like a fool about it. You're great to be with and I'm a pain."

"No—"

"Yes, yes I am. At least let me wallow in my humility for a while."

Now Ian laughed. She was wonderful when she showed herself as she really was. "Okay," he said. "Wallow if you like."

"Thanks. I've finished now. Everything's fine. I can tell you aren't thrilled that we're getting a reception committee. Frankly neither am I, particularly when I'm not dressed for one, but we'll make it through."

Damn it all, he was pouting and she was coaxing him along, trying to convince him they were having a great time. "You bet we will," he said. She still held his wrist and he covered her hand, holding it between both of his. "I'm beginning to think I'm a good judge of character. I could tell there was something more interesting about you than the fetching purple outfit and those delectable knee pads you were wearing the night we met."

She wrinkled her nose, but before she could respond the limousine made a sharp right turn and started down a steep driveway.

Below her, behind a vine-covered, white stone wall, she saw a red-tiled roof. Huge skylights dotted its surface. Banks parked on a gravel swathe by the wall and leaped out to open Page's door. She took the hand he offered and emerged into air scented by orange trees.

"Thank you, Banks," Ian said. He had followed her out. He put a hand on the back of her neck and walked her down some steps into a shady courtyard, where jade plants grew higher than their heads. The house was of white stucco. No windows faced the area. They passed through black, wrought-iron gates into an atrium, where a small fountain bubbled amid random clusters of flowering shrubs in containers.

Page's heart sped. She was definitely out of her element.

The hand on her neck began a massaging motion. "Loosen up, will you?" Ian said in a low voice. "I could play these muscles in your back like a guitar."

She breathed through her nose, pulling her mouth tight. "I'll be fine," she told him, not at all sure she would be. "I'm always nervous when I meet someone for the first time."

With his hand still firmly on Page, Ian opened a brass-studded oak door and walked into the house. She was relieved to notice that he, at least, seemed more relaxed. He even smiled when he called, "Hello. Anyone home?" The smile turned to a narrow-eyed grin when a small, dark-haired woman rushed across terra-cotta tiles to throw her arms around him.

"Ian, darling. What a lovely surprise!"

He held her off. "Hi, Mother. Surprise, huh? Do you send Banks down to meet every ferry just in case I decide to surprise you?"

She made a little, slightly coquettish moue and lowered thick lashes over a pair of bright blue eyes. "You know I don't. I meant it was a lovely surprise to find out you were coming."

"Mmm." Ian bent to kiss her cheek. "We'll talk more about that later. Mother, this is my friend Page Linstrom. Page, this is my mother, Rose."

Page cleared her throat, extended a hand and finally found her voice. "How do you do, Mrs. Faber." Ian's petite mother made her feel like an Amazon, and the sensation didn't help her composure.

"Hello, Page. Please call me Rose. Everybody does."

Reluctantly Page relinquished her parka to Ian who made an apologetic face as his mother dismissed him, insisting that he search out his father while she showed Page the house.

"So," Rose began, her high heels clacking as she led the way down a corridor lined with illuminated curio cabinets. "Your name is Page. Very nice. Simple. I've always liked simple names."

Page murmured what she hoped was a polite response and followed Rose into a vast, airy kitchen, tiled floor to ceiling in dramatic, umber Indian patterns.

"Sit down." Rose pulled out a stool from a butcher-block counter flanking three sides of a central cooking island. "Ian and Bob will be talking business for a while. They won't miss us, and we need to get to know each other."

Not asking why they needed to get to know each other took restraint. Page slid onto the stool and watched Rose pour coffee into two mugs.

"Cream and sugar?"

"Black, thank you." Any minute now this woman would find a way to tell her how unsuited she was as a companion for Ian. And Page would gladly agree and go home.

Rose sat on a stool where she could face her guest. "When did you and Ian meet?"

It was coming. "Um, quite recently…about a week ago, I guess." The next question would be how they met and then even the composed Rose Faber was likely to have difficulty thinking of an appropriate response.

"Have you always lived in San Francisco?"

For an instant Page's mind blanked. "I'm sorry?"

"I wondered if you were a native San Franciscan."

"I'm from Anchorage, Alaska," Page said, relaxing slightly.

"How long have you been in California?"

"Two years." A few more minutes, and Rose would probably know how much Page had in her bank account. She sipped her coffee to hide a smile.

Rose drank, too, her small, perfect hands laced around the mug while she fell into a moment of thoughtful silence. Planning attack, Page thought, without rancor. Ian's mother gave off vibes that felt friendly.

"How about your family?" Rose asked at last. "Are they still in Alaska?"

"Yes."

"They must miss you."

"We aren't particularly close. We talk on the phone regularly and I went up for a visit a year ago. I like to know they're fine, but I don't get homesick."

Rose frowned. "That's sad. Don't you get lonely?"

This was an area Page avoided. "I'm usually too busy to be lonely." She made sure of that. "But there are times when I envy close families. My folks were always too engrossed in working hard enough to pay the bills. They barely kept ahead most of the time. There wasn't much time for getting to know one another the way most families do. But that kind of childhood teaches you independence, and I'll always thank them for it.''

She cleared her throat and closed her mouth firmly. There was something about Ian's mother that invited confidence. Page couldn't remember the last time she'd given conscious thought to her not-too-cozy childhood.

''You know how to make the best of things,'' Rose said, dropping her voice as a woman in a white overall bustled in with a basket of vegetables. ''We'll get out of your way in a minute, Cass,'' Rose said, and turned back to Page. ''It doesn't do any good to mope about things gone by, does it? You can't change them, so you might as well learn from them. When you have your own family you'll be able to give them the attention you didn't get. I expect you want a family?''

''I...'' Page couldn't think of a reply.

Rose smiled and her eyes held genuine warmth. ''Oh dear. I always dive in with the personal questions. Bob—my husband—says I'm intimidating, but I don't think I am, do you?''

''No,'' Page responded promptly and realized, with surprise, that she meant it.

''Thank you, dear.'' Rose checked her watch. ''I'd better give you the grand tour and take you back to Ian.''

For the next half hour Page trailed through spectacular rooms, each one eligible for its own page in *Architectural Digest*. And finally, feeling slightly disoriented, she followed her hostess to a library overlooking all of Sausalito and the bay beyond.

Ian sat in a dark leather chair that matched one occupied by a man who could only be his father.

"Page." Ian sprang to his feet. "We thought Mother had kidnapped you permanently."

"This is a beautiful house," Page murmured, resisting an urge to press the bottom of her sweater closer or cross her arms to cover her elbows.

"Page is from Anchorage, Bob." At full pitch, Rose's voice was big and resonant for so small a woman—like that of a diminutive contralto.

"I know." Robert Faber rose, smiling, and shook Page's hand. In comparison to his wife, he seemed reserved. "Ian's been telling me all about you, Page."

Wonderful, Page thought.

For the next hour she did more listening than talking. Although polite and interesting, Bob, as he insisted she call him, concentrated on discussing business with his son while Page became a spectator, mentally retreating to a place where she observed the two men as if from outside a thick glass window. Rose had left to "do something about dinner."

Page's gaze followed the path of heavy beams to the apex of the vaulted ceiling. Then she rested her chin on a fist, lowered her eyes and let the soft blues and greens of the huge rug lull her.

From time to time Ian or Bob spoke to her, but the father immediately steered the conversation back to business, and she couldn't go there with them.

The sweeping green arches on the rug cradled endless blue circles, one after another. Page was getting drowsy. On Saturdays she usually tried to get some extra sleep. Sighing, she glanced up directly into Ian's eyes.

While his father thumbed through a sheaf of papers, Ian looked at her. She thought he had probably been looking at her for some time. The corners of his mouth twitched up, but not in a real smile, only in a signal that came more from his eyes. He was telling her silently that, despite what she might have thought, his mind was more on her than whatever he was discussing with his father.

Then Rose called them to dinner and the moment passed.

At the vast shimmering table in the dining room, Ian tried and failed to concentrate on what was said around him. Page was a trouper. He'd seen her occasional tugs at the old sweater she wore and longed to tell her she was a woman who could wear a flour sack and still command the rapt attention of any man in the vicinity. But she held up under his mother's not very subtle interrogation and his father's pleasant but irritatingly disinterested comments.

At last a maid removed the dessert dishes and began to pour coffee.

Ian looked at his watch. "Good Lord. Eight-thirty. I had no idea it was that late. We'd better get going." He pushed back his chair and Page did the same.

"Nonsense," Rose said. "You men have done all the talking and now you want to go home, Ian? We want our liqueur, our coffee and your undivided attention for a while, don't we, Page?"

With a sensation close to horror, Ian avoided looking at Page.

"We certainly do," he heard her say in a firm voice, and he blessed her courage. This had to have been one tough experience for her. He'd have hated it if he'd been in her position.

"Right," Rose said, clearly satisfied. "Bob, tell Madeleine we'll take our coffee into the library."

With that Ian's mother led the way and fussed over seating them all in the leather furniture he'd always found uncomfortable.

"Now," Rose said when she was settled with her coffee and a generous measure of Cointreau. "Back to you, Page. I'm sure Ian told Bob all about you, but he hasn't told me. How did you come to settle in San Francisco? You have decided to settle here permanently, haven't you?"

Now would come the questions Page had hoped Rose wouldn't ask. "I intend to stay in San Francisco," she said. "It excites me. That's why I chose it."

Rose was silent for several seconds as if digesting the idea that someone might choose where to live on the basis of excitement. "There must be more to your decision than that. I've always thought it was a wonderful city to raise a family in. Don't you?"

"Mmm. I suppose it would be," Page said. This was definitely a woman obsessed with one subject. Since her own life probably revolved around her husband and son, she must expect everyone else's interests to be similar.

"Mother, I do think Page and I should—"

Rose interrupted. "You don't have to rush off. The ferries leave all the time and Page and I are only just getting to know each other."

This would probably be their first and only meeting, Page thought. She could cope with anything once. The sooner she told Rose Faber everything she wanted to know, the sooner she could get out of there.

"I don't know if Ian told Bob *all* about me. Not that I'm very interesting. I run a bicycle courier service out of a garage behind my apartment." She caught Ian's eye, and the amusement she saw there warmed her. He really was attracted to her, and she had the feeling he admired her just as she was. She gathered confidence and turned back to Rose. "I have six employees. Four of them are riders. I ride myself. I guess you'd call Pedal Pushers a seat-of-the-pants operation." She realized she was digging her nails into the arms of her chair and carefully relaxed her fingers.

There was a short silence, then Rose clapped her hands. The effect was like hearing a child holler in a library reference room. Page took in a breath and held it.

"Do you hear that, Bob?" Rose said, her eyes round. "Page has her own business. My, I do admire your courage, dear. And you ride those bicycles around the city yourself? In and out of all that traffic and up and down the hills?"

"Yes." An almost childish defiance fueled Page. "I enjoy it. Particularly at night."

"At night?" Rose whispered now. "Oh, Page. You *don't* go around the city at night, dear. Not on your own."

Page glanced at Ian. He shook his head slowly, a rueful grimace on his face.

"I'm very careful," Page said, tempering what she would have preferred to say. "And I'm always in radio contact with my client. Ian will tell you how careful I am." Let him try to help her out if he felt she wasn't doing so well in this exchange.

"Page is very sensible," he said, but he didn't return her smile. "She always weighs what she does."

And that, Page thought, *can be taken any way you want it.*

"Well," Rose continued after a sip of Cointreau, "I think it's very good for a young woman to have some experience in the world before she gets married and settles down."

Ian felt himself shrink in his chair. He'd assumed his parents would disapprove of Page. The kind of remark his mother had just made suggested the opposite. He checked Page's expression. It showed nothing.

"Have some more Drambuie, dear," Rose offered. Page shook her head, smiling. "As I was saying," Rose went on. "I've always thought it's easier for a woman to be satisfied to spend her life backing up her husband and children if she's already had a good look at the world."

News to me, Ian thought, looking at his father this time. His eyes were lowered, and his face betrayed nothing of what he was thinking.

Rose gathered momentum as she talked. "So many of my friends have married children with families of their own. And they tell me over and over how these young wives feel they've missed out if they were never on their own for a while. I think I understand why. Once you've been on your own, you not only gain maturity but you get ready to really appreciate a good husband who can take you away from all that nastiness out there."

Ian cringed. His mother sounded like someone in a matrimonial agency. He couldn't believe it. For some reason, occupation and background aside, she'd decided Page was a prime candidate to become Mrs. Ian Faber. And even if he'd ever considered such a thing, which he hadn't and didn't intend to, she was doing an embarrassingly thorough job of making sure Page would never want to see him again, much less consider any kind of deeper relationship.

When Page suddenly stood up, Ian started. "Ian," she said, "I'm having a wonderful time, but six o'clock in the morning comes around early and I'd better go home."

Ian stood also, as did his father and mother. "Six?" Rose squealed the word. "You get up at six?"

"I have to be at work shortly after that on weekdays and on Sundays I still get up at the same time because I have to catch up on my chores and paperwork." Page smiled with a genuine warmth, which Ian appreciated, and submitted to his mother's hug. Oh, but she was lovely, and graceful, and so sexy....

"Well, if you have to go you have to go," Rose said and Ian could tell she wasn't feigning disappointment. "But promise me you'll make Ian bring you back."

Page cast him a pleading look. "Thank you for the invitation," she said. "I'll remember it."

"Thank you for coming." Ian's father spoke with less enthusiasm, and he and his son exchanged sympathetic glances. They were both used to Rose's attempts to push Ian into marriage, but this had been one of her more flamboyant efforts.

Throughout the ride back to the ferry and the crossing itself, Page said little, and Ian allowed her the peace he knew she must need. Again and again he looked at her, watched the play of emotion over her elegant features. The wind had turned her hair into a riotous mass that caught shining slivers from the boat's spotlights.

Minutes from Fisherman's Wharf, the ache of expected disappointment hit him. If things went as he expected, he'd drive her home, she'd thank him politely and he wouldn't have the gall to press for another date. Then he'd go back to fantasizing about her when he should be doing other things, and probably make a fool of himself by calling and being turned down.

"May I kiss you?"

They were alone on the deck in the gathering darkness. Had he really said that? He couldn't have asked her to let him kiss her, out of the blue, not when they'd had a rotten few hours together in the company of his parents and no chance to even approach closeness.

"Yes."

Page's voice came to him as a muffled whisper. She stood in front of him at the railing where they could see San Francisco emerging from the gloom.

He didn't move immediately. He'd asked and she'd said yes.

Page faced him, her arms at her sides. Her eyes shimmered, and he was afraid she was close to tears. This was all beyond him—the emotion he felt, the answering emotion he felt in her.

The pressure of her hands on his chest was light. She pressed her palms flat on his sweater beneath the parka. Then she wound her arms around his neck and pushed her fingers into his hair. Her face replaced her hands on his chest.

"Pretty awful afternoon," he said. "I'm sorry."

"Don't be. Your folks are nice." She rubbed his neck, and Ian's stomach tightened.

He touched her hair, stroked it, kissed it. He had to see her again. He had to.

In the gloom she raised her face, and he brought his lips slowly to hers. Soft. She felt so very soft and warm. Her mouth moved beneath his, brushed with exquisite care, then opened a little. She wasn't leading or following, simply doing what seemed so right to him and, he knew, also to her. He let the seconds slowly unreel while they touched fingertips to one another's face and brought their mouths together again and again. Then he stilled her head and made the contact harder. With his tongue, he parted her lips, tested the soft places just inside and reached. And Page held him close again, forced her body against his until he was certain she felt his arousal and equally certain that the wanting wasn't all on his side.

She pulled away a little, rested her forehead on his jaw and he felt her tremble. Why didn't he feel euphoric? Why did he feel so incredibly sad? Was it too late for his shot at enjoying someone like Page Linstrom, for as long as they wanted to enjoy each other?

"We'd better get off this thing."

Her voice startled him and he turned his head. The boat had docked and the last few passengers were moving down to the landing.

With his arm around her shoulders, Ian walked Page back to the Mercedes, settled her inside, then got in himself. The sinking sensation wouldn't go away, the conviction that even though she'd kissed him with passion she might not want to see him again.

The drive to her apartment took too little time, and when they got there she opened the car door and was on the sidewalk before he could turn off the engine.

He joined her and tried to take her in his arms.

Page bent her head and held his wrists. "Thank you for taking me. I hope I haven't embarrassed you with your parents."

The desperation he felt was like nothing he'd ever experienced before. "They liked you. Couldn't you tell?" It had surprised him how much they had liked her.

"They're too polite not to try to make someone feel at home. I'm sure they're wondering where on earth you found me." Her laugh was unconvincing. "I'd better go in. I'd invite you for coffee, but I really do need to sleep."

"Yes," he said. There was nothing else to say. "May I see you again?" He was sure he didn't have a pulse at all.

Her indrawn breath was soft but still audible. "I wish I could say no. I ought to say no. But I can't. Not right away though, Ian. Let's both do some thinking and decide if we should even try to go on with this. I'm not sure we should."

"I am." He could barely stop himself from grabbing and kissing her.

"You may not be tomorrow when your parents start pointing out how unsuitable I am for you even as a casual acquaintance."

"I'm the one who wants to be with you, not my

parents. Can I pick you up tomorrow when you finish work?''

She chuckled. ''At two in the morning?''

''If you like. Call me from wherever you make your last delivery and I'll come and get you.''

''You didn't hear what I said.'' She stepped back. ''We have to think our way through this. I don't have any idea how soon we'll see each other again, only that I'd like us to. Think about my work schedule, okay? And think about how hard it will be for us to do more than grab a cup of coffee and a sandwich while I'm on my lunch break or before I start my evening shift. It could be something you don't want to bother with.''

He opened his mouth to protest, to say that he didn't give a damn about anything *but* bothering with her right now, then managed to stop himself. ''Go on in,'' he said with what he hoped was restraint.

She leaned close, kissed his mouth so quickly he barely had time to feel her lips, and turned to run up the steps.

''I'll call you tomorrow,'' he said as she opened the door.

''What?'' She was silhouetted against light from the hall.

''I said lock the door.''

''Right,'' she said and disappeared inside.

Ian did a soft shoe jig on the sidewalk. ''I'll call you tomorrow, Page,'' he said aloud. ''And the next day. I'll eat sandwiches for lunch, and dinner every day if necessary—until I can persuade you that there's more to life than work.''

He drove home, noting with satisfaction how short a distance he lived from Russian Hill.

CHAPTER FIVE

THE PHONE RANG as Page replaced a last handful of books on the cinder block and plywood shelves in her bedroom.

"Hello." She expected to hear Tanya, who hadn't come home again last night.

Ian said, "Hello yourself. You aren't still sleeping, are you?"

Page's hold on the phone tightened. So did every muscle in her body. "Yes. I'm still sleeping. I'm snoring. Can't you hear?" She made several snorting noises.

He laughed. "Okay. Dumb question. I meant I hope I'm not waking you."

If he only knew how little sleep she had managed since they'd parted the night before.

"Did I wake you, Page?"

"No, of course not. How are you?"

"Lonely."

She closed her eyes. "I'm sorry."

"Are you lonely?"

Yes, yes, but I can't get in too deep with you. "I'm too busy to be lonely. Today's cleaning day. This afternoon I'll get a nap if I'm lucky, then tonight I'm back on duty for the deli."

"Can't you make enough money by working normal hours?"

He wasn't getting the message. "No, I can't, Ian. I've already explained that."

"Why?"

"Because my business can still go either way, and I need all the money I can get my hands on. The daytime stuff isn't enough yet. If that sounds crass I'm sorry. But it's also life—my life. Now please, have a nice day and let me get on with mine. Sunday's catch-up time, and there really are a million things to do around here."

"Don't hang up."

She sighed. "You like saying that, don't you?"

"No, I don't. But I don't like feeling you're going to smack the phone down in my ear, either. How about going for a drive this afternoon? We could—"

"I can't, Ian. I already said I'm knee-high in work."

"You couldn't leave it just for an hour or so?"

She wanted to. How she wanted to. "No, I can't. But thanks anyway."

Silence followed. Page could almost hear Ian formulating his next offensive. "What time are you off for lunch tomorrow?" he asked.

She didn't believe this. She must have become some sort of challenge to him. He was determined to beat her down. "I'm not sure what time I'll get a break."

"I'll call your dispatcher and she'll let me know. Is that all right?"

Page remembered Lilian's last poetic telephone effort with Ian and rolled her eyes. "Don't do that. I'll call you when I'm free."

"Sure." Sarcasm didn't suit his voice. "Then you'll give me a location I can't get to before you have to go back to work again. I don't think you want to see me."

"That's not true." Damn, she shouldn't have said that. "I mean I would like to have lunch with you, but you could be right, it could be very tough to pull off."

He was silent for a moment. "Got it. Pick a location where we can meet. How about Golden Gate Park?"

"Well—"

"Yeah, Golden Gate Park. Right by the Baker Street entrance to the Panhandle, First bench you come to. I can take a long lunch tomorrow. I'll get there at eleven-thirty. You wouldn't be there before then, would you?"

Page tugged at a piece of hair. "No, but—"

"Great." He spoke rapidly. "I'll be there at eleven-thirty then, with lunch. And I'll just wait until you arrive."

He was cutting off any escape route. "What if I can't get away before one? That happens sometimes."

"You may not get much lunch." His laugh made her laugh, too. "Get back to work and be careful tonight. See you tomorrow."

He hung up without giving her a chance to say anything else. She considered looking him up in the phone book and backing out, but didn't. If she didn't want to go, she wouldn't. It would be his fault if he sat in Golden Gate Park for two hours. Not that she believed he would. After all, she hadn't agreed to go.

Page pushed at her hair with the back of her hand. She'd already flipped a duster through the apartment and cleaned the kitchen. Her own bathroom, tiled in shocking pink, was immaculate. Ugly, but clean, right down to the cracked pumpkin-colored linoleum. Finishing her bedroom was all that remained of her weekly domestic chores.

As she pulled the magenta down comforter over her futon, another jolting ring of the phone startled her.

Maybe it was Tanya. "Yes," Page said into the receiver, more shortly than she intended. She was worried about her roommate's increasing moodiness and repeated absences.

The telephone line crackled before a woman's voice shouted, "Page? Is that you?" Page's mother had never accepted that she didn't need to shout on the phone just because she was thousands of miles away.

Page sank to the floor and crossed her legs. "Yes, Mom. How are you?" The old guilt came. She should remember to call home more often.

"Fine, fine," Molly Linstrom yelled. "Got to keep this short. Costs, these long-distance calls, I can tell you."

"I know, Mom." Page rested her forehead on the heel of one hand. "Why don't you hang up and I'll call you right back?"

"Just wanted to let you know your brother has a new baby boy," her mother went on as if Page hadn't spoken. "Nine pounds and doing great. He looks just like Tony."

Her brother had a boy. Not her brother and sister-in-law had a boy. Not that Sally was or wasn't doing well. Linstrom women were supposed to be no more than conveniences for men. "That's good news," Page said. "How's Sally?"

"Good," her mother said. "Anyway, that's all I wanted to tell you, so—"

"Mom," Page interrupted. "How are you and Dad and everyone?"

"Oh, we're the same as usual. I've got to go."

"Yeah." *And how are you, Page? We think about you sometimes.* She was a dreamer and should know better by now than to care about being a nonperson to her parents. "I'll send something for the baby. Tell Tony and Sally... Tell them I love them."

Her mother had already hung up.

She sat still for a moment, her head in her hands, before the chime of the old clock in the sitting room reminded her she couldn't afford moping time.

One of her Sunday tasks that she hadn't mentioned to Ian was her consultation with James W. Amwell, jr., upstairs neighbor and part-time mechanic for Pedal Pushers.

When she'd done everything possible for her bedroom, Page made a giant tuna-fish sandwich and put it in a brown sack with a large bag of potato chips, an apple, a banana, a pint carton of milk, and two cans of cola. James was one of Page's favorite people. When she allowed herself to analyze the reason, the answer made her sad. James reminded her of the Page she used to know—optimistic, single-minded, invincible. He hadn't yet learned, nor admitted that anything could make his goals more difficult to reach than his lack of money and family support already did.

Whistling breathily, she made her way out of the house and down the alley leading to the garage. Classical music, played at James's favorite high volume, met her. Wagner's Valkyries were doing their thing, as James would put it.

With a finger jammed in each ear, Page entered the garage through the small side door. "James!" She couldn't see him. "James, where are you?" Scrambling, she climbed onto a pile of boxes to snap off the button on his cassette deck.

"Where...? What on earth are you doing?"

James sat on the floor in the lotus position, his eyes closed, hands turned up atop his knees. Each forefinger and thumb touched in a circle. He didn't answer.

Immobile, his thinness was more pronounced. Usually he was in perpetual jerky motion, and although the sticklike wrists that protruded from too short sleeves were something no one would miss, his animation overcame what might have been an impression of frailty. Sitting still, he looked pale and poor, and Page's heart contracted.

She approached on tiptoe and whispered, "James, it's me. I made too much lunch, so I brought you some." She said the same thing every Sunday, and every Sunday he accepted her offering solemnly but never ate until she'd left.

Page worried about him. He wanted one thing in life—to become a structural engineer. For that he needed a college education, and the only way he'd get it was by his own efforts. From the day she'd met him, a scraggly fourteen-year-old who needed braces he still didn't have, he'd talked of his savings for college. Page had long ago figured out that one of the ways he saved was by not eating very often or spending money on clothes. He lived with his youthful grandmother, a self-centered woman who tolerated James as long as he kept out of her way.

He opened his eyes slowly and blinked several times. "Yoga," he said. "It helps you focus your inner self and avoid distraction."

"So I've heard," Page said. "How does everything look?" He would have been working since early morning, oiling, greasing, checking the machinery and the radio.

James pushed long, tow-colored hair away from his face, leaving oily stripes on his forehead. "Not so good."

"Good...what?" She paused in the act of setting the paper sack on the radio table. As far as James was concerned, "terrific" was the prime word around here. Everything was always terrific.

"Ken was in yesterday while I was working," he said. "He wanted to talk to you, but you were out."

"He came in on Saturday? Why? He never puts in an extra minute if he can help it."

James unbent and got to his feet. "He said he wanted to talk to you and only you. When he got in Friday night you'd already left to do deliveries for Waldo Sands, so he came back yesterday."

"Did he tell you what his problem is?" Page asked. Ken was often surly, but he did his job and he did it fast without undue complaining.

"Look at this." James ambled to a bike leaning against one wall. Page recognized the machine as Ken's Peugeot. "He didn't say anything about it. Or I guess he did. He said to leave the damn thing alone." The boy colored slightly. "Sorry. Just quoting. Anyway, I didn't touch it, but I did look."

Page dropped to her knees and examined the bike. "What about it, James? Looks the same as usual to me."

"Drive chain," he said shortly.

She put her finger on top of the chain and moved it. "Oh, hell. I see it. Geez, I don't believe it. Someone took a hacksaw to the thing. It's almost cut through. Ken should have contacted me somehow." Not that she had any idea of what she was going to do about it.

"He was so mad he punched me out of his way," James said. "Went on about someone trying to kill him and how you didn't pay him enough to take the kind of risks he was taking."

Page got up and went to sit in the old car seat. She was still such a simpleminded idiot. She'd assumed that, in this business, hard work and determination would get her where she wanted to be. That she'd have to deal with threatening competition had never occurred to her. "Did Ken say anything else?"

"Not much. Just that he wasn't wasting any more of his weekend, but he'd see you on Monday."

"I guess I'll have to wait till tomorrow morning, then," Page said, more to herself than James.

"Afternoon," he said. "He was also going on about all the extra hours he'd wasted coming in here looking for you. He's taking the morning off. Look for him around two, he said."

"Two!" Page buried her face in her hands. "Just what I need. One less worker for a whole morning. Then I suppose he'll get everyone else riled up."

"It'll be okay."

She lifted her head. James stood beside her, his big hands knotted together. Anxiety pinched his face.

"Sure it will." Smiling, she held out a hand and he hauled her up. He was a tall boy, taller than she was. One day, when he put some meat on his bones, he'd be a big man. "I'm not used to this kind of thing, James, that's all. Will you do something for me?"

"Anything."

"Replace the chain on Ken's bike and give the broken one to me. I don't want him giving some sort of performance and getting the others uptight. I'll talk to Lilian in the morning and have her make arrangements for a meeting after lunch."

James shifted uncomfortably. "I heard about the guy who kicked Buzz."

"Her bike. He kicked her bike, not her."

"Yeah." His grimy fingers made their way through his hair again. "But some outfit is picking on our guys."

She wanted to snap at him that she didn't know what she could do about it and that all she wanted was to be left alone. "Don't worry," she said, and patted his shoulder. "Like I told Buzz, this kind of thing happens. The best way to defend ourselves is to stay calm and not get dragged into a petty war."

"Is cutting a drive chain petty?" He turned the power of sincere blue eyes on her. "If that thing had broken while Ken was flying, it could have been all over for him.''

Everything he said was true, but she didn't have the answers he hoped for. ''Just fix the chain, okay?'' she said. ''I'll figure it all out and calm everyone down. Now I've got to check out my own wheels. Sunday night's busy for Waldo.'' She had a hunch she was going to get more and more grateful for Waldo's business. It might be good strategy to look for more night clients and another rider or two willing to take on the work. Then there was her Sausalito idea. The realization that being down one courier could throw her completely off schedule made her all too aware of the need to grow and grow fast.

''WHAT MADE YOU CHANGE your mind about playing today?''

Ian watched his father's ball soar off the tee and track a straight course down the fairway. ''Guilt probably, Dad,'' he said with only a twinge of remorse at the deception. When Page had refused to spend the afternoon with him he'd immediately called his father, then headed for Sausalito and the golf course.

Bob Faber stood back. ''Guilt, son?''

''I haven't been spending enough time with you lately.'' He met the older man's eyes and smiled. ''I've missed our times together.'' And that was completely true.

''Me, too, Ian. Let's take time to catch up again.''

Ian's own shot angled high and veered to the left, disappearing behind a stand of trees. ''Hell, I'm rusty.'' He crammed his club back into the bag and they trundled off. They'd long ago decided to spurn jitneys in favor of getting some exercise.

"You seem different lately," Ian's father remarked, squinting at the gray sky. "Quieter somehow. Do you still see Martin and the others?"

"Martin occasionally." Though he no longer enjoyed his company as he once had. "We play the odd game of racquetball. The others have kind of slipped away. Guess I'm getting old, slowing down too much for them."

"Or growing up too much for them?" Bob Faber arched a brow. "I liked that young woman you brought over yesterday." Now he stared straight ahead.

Ian suppressed a chuckle. Neither of his parents could contain curiosity about their only child's love life for long. "I like her, too," he said evenly.

"Pretty spunky, doing a job like that. Can't say I'd fancy it."

"Page has guts." Maybe more than were good for her.

They'd reached Bob's ball, and Bob fussed, drawing and replacing several clubs, then leaning on the one he finally chose. "You like her a lot, don't you, son?" He didn't wait for a response. "I can see you do, and your mother said the same thing."

"You didn't think she was a little offbeat for the Fabers?"

"Not at all." Bob took a practice swing and lined up on the ball. "Can't tell an orange by its skin, I always say. Not that she doesn't have great skin...." He paused, shook his head and bent over the club once more. "Could be elegant in the right clothes.

And she speaks well. Sounds bright. Sturdy girl, too. Make a good wife and mother, I'd think. At least, that's what your mother was saying. Some man's going to be very lucky.''

Ian blew into a fist and remained silent. His parents were unbelievable. Wonderful but unbelievable. He really couldn't accept yet that they wouldn't prefer to see him attached to some socially prominent woman; yet, faced with the possibility that he might be an indefinite marital holdout, they would push him into the arms of the first candidate for whom he showed more than a casual interest.

''What do you think our chances are on the Daniel Max account?'' he asked, determined to change the subject. ''Samson's talking as if we've got it in the bag, but I think it's too soon to relax a muscle.''

His father's ball sailed in another straight line but landed in a sand trap. ''Damn.'' He stuffed the club back in his bag and shoved his hands into his pockets. ''I'm with you on Max. We're the best and we've got the best concept, but like they say, it isn't over till the fat lady sings. Somebody else could still get the account.''

''Yup. But we're up front, I know it. Max wants to change its image from middle-priced merchandise for middle-income customers to upscale products at prices the average folks can afford. By forming a link with a British manufacturer who's prepared to keep costs down for the size of the account, and leaning heavily on the prestige of wearing British-made stuff without spending a fortune, it can work beautifully. With the right advertising, that is. And we're the right advertising.''

His father laughed and slapped Ian's back. "Right, son, right. And with you spearheading we could probably refuse the account and then have Daniel Max crawling to our door begging us to change our minds."

Ian had to smile. "I do get carried away, I guess. But only around you. The rest of the world thinks I'm made of ice."

"The rest of the world, son?"

"All of it."

"Including Page Linstrom?"

Ian stared at his father, who pursed his lips in a soundless whistle. "Dad," Ian said, "sometimes you aren't too subtle."

IF HE WASN'T THERE—right now—she wouldn't wait. She shouldn't be taking time out to stop for lunch at all.

Page rode through the entrance to the park. All morning she'd rushed from job to job with a sense of barely contained panic at the prospect of the interview with Ken and the rest of the riders that lay ahead. At eleven she'd made up her mind she wouldn't attempt to meet Ian. By eleven-twenty she wasn't sure she'd get through the day at all if she didn't see him, talk to him...ask his advice maybe.

Benches lined the walkway in the center of the narrow strip of Golden Gate Park dubbed the Panhandle. They all seemed occupied, but there was no sign of Ian. People strolling alone and in twos, joggers, children, dogs—the place was crowded for eleven forty-five on a Monday morning. He must have come with the same thought as she had, that he wouldn't be kept waiting, and left almost immediately when she didn't show on time.

Page dismounted and slowly took off her helmet. She felt close to tears. He'd said he would be there, until one if necessary, and he hadn't even lasted fifteen minutes. If he'd come at all. She knew she was being unreasonable, that she'd considered not coming herself, but that didn't matter. She needed someone. She needed Ian.

A jogger passed and whistled. Page dropped her helmet into the bike basket and braced herself against the seat. The silver satin racing outfit she wore had been a frivolous waste of money bought because for once she'd given in to temptation. She knew she looked good in it, good enough to make sure she got the kind of attention the runner had just given her. And she'd worn it for Ian. Even while she'd pulled it on early this morning, denying all the time that she intended to meet him today, she'd been visualizing his reaction.

So much for that. She guessed he wasn't lonely anymore.

She reached for the helmet.

Pressure on her back brought the start of a shriek to her lips. "Don't put that on." A broad hand climbed to rest beneath her hair. Ian kissed her before she could speak, drew her against him with both arms wrapped tightly around her body. "Wait here," he whispered. "I'm going to catch up with that jogger and kill him. But I'll be right back."

Page gasped and kept her hands tightly locked behind his neck. "You'll do no such thing."

"For what he was thinking he deserves to be punished."

She laughed. "How do you know what he was thinking?"

"Mmm." He rubbed his cheek on her hair. "I know because I've been watching you for five minutes and thinking the same things."

Warmth suffused her and she laughed. "Where were you?"

"On the first bench, like I said I would be."

Turning her head, Page saw that she'd ridden into the park without noticing a bench immediately inside the gates. "I thought you hadn't come."

Satisfaction loaded his smile. "You were afraid I wouldn't, huh? You've been missing me since yesterday?"

For an instant she felt off balance. Then she returned his smile as coolly as possible. "I came, Ian, because I'm too polite to leave a busy man sitting in a park on his own for two hours."

"Afraid someone else might get me?"

"You're impossible."

"I'll take this." Pushing the bike, he returned to the bench with Page beside him. A willow spread its almost naked branches over the area and he leaned her Schwinn against its trunk.

"Don't do that around anyone but me," Ian remarked, taking her hand and guiding her to sit down.

"Do what?" Page asked. She glanced at her watch. Much as she wanted to be here she mustn't take long.

"Wiggle when you walk. And while we're on the subject, I don't think you should wear that outfit at all."

She bowed her head and looked up at him. "You've got a lot of instructions to pass out today."

"Yup. Got to take a little control around you. Show you how strong I am—and possessive. Lady, in that suit I can see just about all of you and my imagination fills in the rest. I don't think I like the idea that other men are doing the same thing."

She'd wanted this, so why did she feel irritated? "The suit's no different than any other piece of functional equipment. It serves the same purpose for me that your clothes serve for you. Fits the image and feels good. And by the way—" it was her turn to do some careful eye work "—no man should look the way you look in a business suit. You, Ian Faber, are a first-class knockout. Navy blue is your color, and the way that shirt fits has to have every woman in your office wanting to take it off. And your legs—did I tell you I'm a leg woman? Ian, the way those pants fit your fantastic legs makes me want to see you in shorts."

First he turned pink. Then he laughed, tipped back his head and howled until his lashes were wet.

Page crossed her arms and, with a struggle, kept her face perfectly serious. "Didn't Rose teach you how to accept compliments?"

He sobered a little but continued to chuckle and wipe his eyes. "You are something. No woman ever said those things to me."

"You didn't like it?"

"Well." He coughed and straightened his tie. "I didn't say I didn't like it. In fact, when would you like to see me in shorts? How about after work tonight?"

She wasn't getting dragged into another when and where battle. "How about the lunch you said you'd bring? I'm starving."

"Chickening out on the sexy come-on?" He grinned, and the effect was definitely wicked.

"Lunch, Ian?"

"Right, right. Lunch. I was afraid I'd be late, so I ran into a deli and bought sandwiches, coffee and fruit. Is that okay?" He looked suddenly anxious. "If it's not we can hop in the car and go to a restaurant."

"What kind of sandwiches?" He made her feel good, lighthearted in a way she'd almost forgotten.

She hadn't noticed a big box under the seat. Ian pulled it out and opened the top. "Pastrami on rye, or ham and swiss, or roast beef or vegetarian. There's egg salad and tuna salad and liverwurst and shrimp croissants. I got some bagels and cream cheese and—"

"Stop. You bought out the whole store. I don't know about you, but I only eat one sandwich at a time." Amazed, she peered into the crammed box.

Ian shrugged. "I didn't know what you liked so I brought one of everything."

"That's a waste."

"We'll give the rest away."

"Sure." Page looked around, wondering if he intended them to go from person to person offering food. "I'd like the shrimp, please."

They ate without speaking and drank coffee from Styrofoam cups. Being silent with Ian beside her felt all right, comfortable. Page began to wish they could stay here indefinitely and that she didn't have to face the afternoon.

"Something's wrong, isn't it?" Ian said suddenly.

Page almost spilled her coffee. "No. Everything's fine."

"There's something else you should know about me," he said, taking the cup from her and setting it on the ground so he could hold her hand. "I'm psychic. I can see inside your head."

"Of course you can. Just the way you can see inside my clothes." She winced. That was the kind of thing she never said. "I didn't mean to say that."

"It's perfectly okay. I bring out the worst in you. I understand. But I still want to know what's on your mind."

It would feel so good to let it out. She had no one to talk to about the decisions she had to make, and earlier she'd considered telling him. But she was supposed to go this alone. That was what she'd set out to do from the day she'd left Anchorage.

"Page," Ian said, keeping his voice low, "tell me, please."

She sighed. "A long time ago I promised myself I was never going to need anyone's help to make my way."

"Everyone needs help sometimes," Ian said and raised her hand so that he could kiss her knuckles. "I sure need help from time to time."

"You're something, Ian. Do you know that?"

He hitched an ankle onto the opposite knee and shifted to look at her. "What's up?" One slightly rough fingertip traced the tendon from beneath her ear to her neckline and back.

Concentration was tough when he touched her like that, but she began, haltingly, to explain what had been happening to her riders. When she'd finished he didn't say anything, and she began to feel foolish. Maybe she was overreacting, making a lot out of very little.

"I'd better get back," she said when several minutes had passed. "I have my little summit meeting to attend and a lot more deliveries before tonight rolls around."

Ian opened his mouth. What he was feeling was totally foreign. Fear. Possessiveness. Anger. "You're not going anywhere," he heard himself say and immediately cursed the patterning that made him forget he couldn't order this woman around. He clamped a hand on her arm to stop her from getting up. "I mean, I don't want you to go, Page. Not yet, please."

"I've got to. I'm going to be late if I don't."

"Too bad," he said between clenched teeth. Then he took a deep breath and tried to relax. "I don't have one damn right in the world to tell you what to do, but I can say what I think."

She was trying to look calm. He could see and feel her effort to shrug off the importance of what she'd just told him. If he had to guess, he'd say she was already wishing she'd refused to confide in him.

"What's the name of this outfit that's causing the trouble?" He still sounded like a schoolteacher, or a father. The breath he took through his nose did nothing to take the knots out of his jaw. "A name, Page. Give me a name so I have something to go on."

What he saw in her eyes next was a mixture of annoyance and panic. "I didn't tell you this because I expect you to take care of me. And I don't know who they are. My people haven't seen any of them before."

She'd be next. Ian swallowed acid. One day soon he'd call Pedal Pushers and find out Page had been injured...or worse. "We're going to the police." He started shoving sandwich wrappers into the box.

"We are not going to the police." Page grabbed his sleeve and waited until he looked at her. "I shouldn't have told you. I didn't have any idea you'd react like this. All I wanted was...was..."

Tears welled in her eyes, and horror. She attempted to turn away, but he held her shoulders. "All you wanted was what?"

"I don't know. Someone I trust to talk to, I guess."

As if she'd turned on a heater somewhere, some of the fear dissipated, and he warmed, glowed. She trusted him. "And I blew up like a faulty grenade. Sorry, sweetheart." He saw her lashes flicker at the term he'd used, and he smiled. "Tell me what you intend to do and how I can help you."

Her breasts rose as she took a deep breath. "I'm going to line up all the incidents that have happened. Then I'm going to make an all-out effort to find out who these people are. We've talked to other courier services and none of them say they're being hassled. That may or may not be true. This is a closemouthed, competitive business. I am going to file a police complaint. Not that it'll do any good."

"How come?"

"The police don't like us. Or they don't like bicycle couriers, I should say. There are a lot of accidents every year caused by careless riders. My riders aren't careless, but the cops have no way of sorting out who's who most of the time."

He felt sick and out of his depth. "I wish you didn't have to go through this." And he wished he knew how to help.

"So do I, but I don't have a choice." She stroked his cheek, and the blood in his veins felt like water. "I need the money. Period."

There had to be a way. An idea came to him, and so did her likely reaction. "Why not get a business loan to carry you until things really take off? That way you could stop riding and concentrate on the administrative angle." He didn't like to think of her out there, and so vulnerable.

"I'm already paying off two loans." She crossed her arms and stared at two small children chasing a ball. "I don't intend to owe any more money."

Careful. "I could help you—"

"No!" She was on her feet, marching around to get her bike. "Thank you. I appreciate your concern, but I don't borrow from friends."

He met her as she wheeled from behind the bench. Standing astride the front wheel, he placed his hands on hers. "I respect your feelings. And I admire you one hell of a lot." At least he was a friend now, and he was trusted. Whatever happened he had that to get started with.

"Thanks. The feeling's mutual."

The effect she had on him was a heady thing. "Will you at least help me out by saying you'll be very careful?"

"Yes. I'll be very careful. And I will get to the

bottom of this. I've got a hunch it'll all blow over if we keep cool."

"You really think so?" She could be right. He hoped to God she was.

"I do. I've got an idea where I can go to get some information on new people coming into the business."

"Where?"

"Just a bar at the Hotel Utah where bikers hang out after work." She looked at his hands, but he didn't move them.

"Let me come with you."

Her burst of laughter stung him. "No. Thanks for the offer anyway."

"What's so funny about my wanting to come to a bar with you? You shouldn't go alone."

Page nodded, still smiling. "I won't go alone. I probably won't go at all. I'll get the Zipper to go for me, and maybe Perkins."

Something close to jealousy turned him clammy. "Who are the Zipper and Perkins? Friends?"

"They work for me." Pressure against his locked arms conveyed her anxiety to be gone.

"How did last night go? Lots of deliveries?"

"Ian, I've got to get back to the garage."

He sucked in his lower lip. She wouldn't agree to meet him again like this if he made it tough. "Go then." He stood aside and gave her a mock salute. "May I call you when you get off duty tonight?"

"I don't—"

"I won't talk for long."

"I may not be back before two-thirty or so." She was already moving away.

This was hopeless, exactly the kind of thing that had never happened to him. He was handling her all wrong. She said she trusted and liked him. The next move should be hers. "Two-thirty is kind of late. I forgot for a minute. Listen, give me a call some time if you feel like it and maybe we'll go out again. Okay?"

The spokes stopped turning. His stomach didn't.

"Good idea," she said. "What are you going to do with all those sandwiches?"

He glanced from her to the box. He'd forgotten the silly sandwiches. "Uh..."

"If you don't want them I'll take them. I've got a hungry young friend who doesn't have much money. I can give him a couple for dinner each night."

"Fine." He handed her the box and she put it in her carrier. "I hope your friend enjoys them."

"He will. Thanks."

She rode away, turning back to give a nonchalant wave before she left the park.

Jingling keys in his pocket, Ian started toward the exit and his car. Maybe his little table-turning effort hadn't been such a hot idea.

Damn. Was it his hormones or his ego that kept him chasing one woman in a city full of delectable females?

CHAPTER SIX

BRACED FOR COMBAT, Page pushed her bike into the garage. She was met by total silence.

The radio blipped, and Lilian, who sat beside the Zipper on the table, reached back to answer. "Yeah, yeah," she said in a subdued voice. Then, while she wrote on a dispatch pad she said, "Yeah," again and then, "Out."

"Hi, everybody." Page scooted her Schwinn against a wall and faced her staff. Buzz was sprawled in the car seat with Jemima on her lap. Ken Moore, his back to the room, was looking out of a grimy window. Perkins was the only one who answered Page with a soft, "Hi," from a spot in a gloomy corner.

This was worse than she'd expected. Page took off her helmet and gloves and dropped them on a pile of old sacks. "All right, folks. Let's talk and talk fast. Time's money around here."

The Zipper's fist, coming down on the table like a sledgehammer, made her flinch. "We aren't giving up, Page. We aren't creeping away like a bunch of rabbits. I don't give a... I don't care what he says." He glared at Ken Moore's back.

"Ken?" She walked over and stood beside him. "Ken, what was said when I wasn't here?"

He gave her a sidelong glance, his dark green eyes spoiled by hardness. "I told that kid to leave my machine alone. Where's the chain that was on it Friday?"

She'd been right. Grandstanding was in Ken's nature. And rabble-rousing. He'd come in ready to whip the others into a rage, and she'd stolen some of his thunder. Page looked around. Only Lilian and the Zipper met her eyes. Ken had done a pretty good job without Exhibit A.

"Forget the chain. Fill me in. You've obviously had a head start on our discussion period. Who wants to tell me what's been said?"

"Plenty," Ken said, flexing broad shoulders displayed to full advantage in a skintight, black tank top.

Page flipped her fingers. "Gimme, Ken. Can the hints and give it to me straight." Two years with these people had taught her to put on their lingo like an extra coat.

"He says we gotta get tough," Buzz said, in a bored voice that didn't ring true. "He says we gotta fight back."

"Stupid sonov—"

"Not in front of Jemima." Page cut the Zipper off. "I called this meeting and I'll run it. In case any of you've forgotten, this is my business and I make the decisions."

Ken toed a brake block across the floor like a hockey puck. "From where I stand, boss lady, you aren't looking so good. Every one of us here has had more than one run-in with these jerks—except Lilian and you. Maybe if some sucker had taken a hacksaw to your drive chain you wouldn't be so cool.''

''I'm not cool now,'' Page retorted. ''I'm...I'm mad. But going down to their level won't solve anything.''

''It'll make us feel a hell of a lot better,'' Buzz said, the attempt at disinterest gone. ''I already know what I'm gonna do.''

''Yeah,'' Ken said. ''Me, too.''

''Fools—''

''Stop it!'' Again Page interrupted the Zipper, but she gave him a tight little smile of gratitude. He had always been the best and most likable of the bunch. She turned to Buzz. ''What do you intend to do?''

Buzz shrugged and smoothed Jemima's curls. ''Nothing much, do I, baby?'' She brought her eyes to the level of the toddler's and they giggled.

''Cut it out,'' Page said, breathing harder. ''Just answer the question.''

''And for this I left law school.'' Ken dropped into a rickety wooden chair and looked at the ceiling. ''You've missed your calling, Page, baby. You should have been a prosecuting attorney.''

''Don't you ever call me baby again,'' Page said. ''If you don't want to talk about this calmly, you know what to do.''

He locked his hands behind his neck and crossed his ankles, but his face became wary. ''What would that be?''

''Take a walk. And don't come back.'' She almost wished he would. He might be a good worker, fast and with a hound dog's nose for direction, but his attitude was bad news and she already had enough trouble.

"I say we do whatever Page says we should do."

Everyone stared at Perkins. His voice was rarely heard for more than a word at a time.

"Yeah, Perk," Lilian said. "I'll go for that."

Ken shifted and recrossed his feet. "So would I if I was safe behind a radio all day."

From the corner of her eye Page saw the Zipper move. "Speak to her like that and I'll see you don't do much talking for the rest of your life." He'd grabbed Ken's hair and jerked his head down before Page could react.

"Stop it!" She wasn't ready for this. She never would be.

"Enough, you two," Lilian echoed. She crossed the small space from the radio table and pulled the Zipper back. Page noticed she looked at the wiry little man with something close to adoration. "Zip, honey," Lilian continued, "Ken just likes to get you all riled up. We've got to do like Page says and be calm. The whole lot of you be calm." She glowered around.

"Give me some paper and a pen," Page said before anyone else could speak again. "I want a list of every incident."

"I'm carrying a coat hanger from here on," Buzz muttered.

When Page looked at the girl she kept her eyes down. "You're going to do what, Buzz?"

"You heard."

"A coat hanger?" Page nodded slowly. "Brilliant.

I don't suppose you want to explain what you intend to do with it?''

''You already know.''

''I hope I don't, but if it's what I think, you won't ride for me anymore.''

Ken snorted. ''Riders are going to get pretty thin on the ground around here if you fire us all. No riders, no business, boss lady.''

''You can cut the 'boss lady' bit, too, Ken,'' Page told him. ''Buzz, a coat hanger or anything else rigid enough to ram between spokes could kill someone. I want your word you won't pull a stunt like that.''

''A foot in the spokes didn't feel so good,'' Buzz said under her breath.

''Your word, Buzz,'' Page persisted.

Buzz passed stubby fingers through her white crew cut and sighed long and low. ''Are we just gonna wait till they kill one of us?''

''No, we are not,'' Page said. ''Every one of you has had some sort of trouble, right?''

There was a chorus of agreement.

''So you must be getting some sort of descriptions you can compare. The riders, their bikes and so on.''

''I've never seen the same one twice,'' the Zipper said.

''They can't be ghosts.'' Page tossed the pad Lilian had given her back on the table. ''It's too bad some of the competition hasn't reported any incidents. A united front would help. But we can track this down alone, and we will.''

''If I've got to do it with a smile on my lips I'll need more money to keep me sweet,'' Ken said, not looking at her.

Page's heart gave a big thud. She'd been expecting this, but she wasn't ready with an answer.

"Knock it off, Ken," the Zipper said while she was still thinking. "Page is working round the clock herself. We all know things are tight."

"That's not my problem."

Too bad Ken Moore was such a good rider, Page thought. She longed to tell him to leave. "Ken," she said, "jobs aren't that easy to come by, but if you want to go look for one, be my guest. I'll be sorry to see you go, because you're good at what you do. But I flat can't afford to pay you more than I do. Half the tag price is standard. You won't get more anywhere else."

"That's what you say."

"That's the way it is," Perkins said. "And I'm getting behind on my drops, so let's move."

Again Page was surprised at the quiet man's vehemence. "There is something I'd like a couple of you to do for me," she said.

"Name it," the Zipper said immediately.

"How many of you get together at the Hotel Utah with people from other outfits? You know what I mean, the after-work, horror-story session?"

Within two minutes she had four volunteers—Buzz, Lilian, the Zipper and Perkins—to go to the city's bicycle messenger hangout and ask questions. Ken made no comment one way or the other, but he did pick up his job numbers and get on the road as soon as Page said the meeting was over.

When all the riders had left, she turned to Lilian who continued fielding radio messages. "How do you think it went?" Page asked.

Moving the mouthpiece of her headset aside, Lilian gave Page her whole attention. "I think you're one gutsy lady. But I don't get any of this. It doesn't make sense for someone to pick on an outfit as small as ours. Page, for the first time in my life I'm scared to death."

"ANYBODY THERE? Tanya?"

Page opened the door to the apartment slowly. Light shone from the kitchen. She never left lights on. Too many years of patterning by a parsimonious father had made her careful about waste.

"Tanya?" Her voice cracked, and she swallowed a flash of nausea.

She was tired from the night's work, mentally as well as physically. There was nobody waiting to jump on her. She must have forgotten the lights this time. The sooner she got to bed and slept, the sooner she'd be her old calm self.

To reach the bedroom she had to pass through the kitchen. She leaned on the table to unlace her shoes and slip them off, then rose to her toes to stretch cramped insteps. A rancid odor made her wrinkle her nose and glance around. A glass stood on the counter by the sink. Page walked over and picked it up. She smelled the gin even before she raised it to her nose. Tanya occasionally drank gin—when she was depressed.

Instinctively, Page looked over her shoulder, mentally ticking off the days since she and her friend had crossed paths. Close to a week.

Page entered the narrow corridor that divided the two bedrooms from the kitchen and sitting room.

Tanya's was the room opposite the kitchen. Light showed under the door.

Was this a good time to try to talk, or would Tanya resent the intrusion? Like Page, she was trying to carve a life for herself away from her family. The big difference between the two of them was that Tanya received financial help from her parents, enough to keep her in college and a spectacular wardrobe. It had always puzzled Page that Tanya had chosen to live in a less-than-luxurious apartment, but she'd never questioned her friend on the subject.

Pursing her lips in a soundless whistle, Page tapped on Tanya's door. She heard the rustle of bedclothes and wished she hadn't knocked.

The strip of light under the door disappeared and Page's reticence was replaced by irritation. Damn it. They shared this apartment and had tacitly agreed to look out for each other. Page didn't need a watchdog, and Tanya probably didn't, either, but Tanya's long absences were odd, and as a friend Page felt she was owed an explanation.

She stood, hands on hips, jiggling a socked foot for several seconds, then knocked again—loudly.

No response.

Page opened the door and walked firmly inside. "Tanya. Sorry to barge in, but—"

"I'm sleeping."

Page took a step backward and half turned away. No. Something was wrong here. The voice was blurred but not by sleepiness. Tanya had been drinking—plenty.

"Um, Tanya, can we talk for a few minutes?"

"Sleepy," Tanya responded.

And I'm sleepy, too, Page wanted to retort. Instead she approached the bed and switched on a bedside lamp. Only a fan of red curls showed above hauled-up covers. This was ridiculous.

"Do you have an early class?" she asked.

Tanya didn't reply.

"Darn you, Tanya. Speak to me, will you? Let me in to whatever's going on in your life. I've got troubles of my own. Sharing them with you wouldn't be so bad, either. Will you give me a break and talk to me?"

Long fingernails curled over the covers and Tanya's face emerged, fully made-up, flaming red lipstick smudged, mascara caked into the paths of dried tears. "What d'you want, Page? I don't want to talk right now." A gold ribbon, bow askew, sagged over her forehead.

In a swift motion, before Tanya could react, Page pulled the covers farther down. "You're still dressed," she said, nonplussed. "What is it with you?"

"Leave me alone." Tanya rolled away, hiding her face. She wore a rumpled, red satin dress with a peplum and short shirt. A high-heeled red sandal with rhinestone-encrusted straps still clung to the toes of one exposed foot.

"Are you sick?" Page asked, real fear coiling in her. "Where have you been all week?" *And when did you manage to get in and out of here to change clothes, and have you been to school?* She mustn't pile on all the questions that screamed for answers.

"With a friend," Tanya said, a fuzzy, sullen coating on her voice. "So what?"

"So nothing, as long as you're all right."

"Don't worry about me."

"I do. I can't help it. We're friends, remember?"

Tanya rolled onto her back, one hand over her eyes. "If we're friends, don't push, okay? I'm not having such a hot time right now. Happens to everyone."

The arm Tanya had raised was thin, thinner than it should be. And the dress, which Page had never seen before, fitted so tightly that it showed prominent hip bones and ribs. Something near panic rose in her throat. "How is school going, anyway?" She tried to sound casual, cheerful. "I'm living for the day when I see fashions by Tanya at the end of some TV show, or in a magazine layout."

"Don't hold your breath."

Page sat on the edge of the bed and took a thin hand in hers. The skin was unnaturally warm. "Is it a man?" She didn't want to say Waldo specifically. If she did, Tanya would have immediately protested that he wasn't the only male on her horizon.

"I think I kind of love someone." The statement amazed Page. She couldn't think of an answer. "He loves me, too, only he's fighting it. That's a tough scene, Page. If it ever happens to you, you'll know how it feels."

Page Linstrom, the workaholic without a heart. She looked at their joined hands. "I guess you're right." Some of the feelings she was having about Ian came close to pain. There were a lot of potential stumbling blocks to a relationship, and while they might vary from couple to couple, they didn't hurt or confuse any less because a woman seemed directed in other areas of her life. In many ways, having a goal you couldn't give up made caring for someone even harder.

Tanya had closed her eyes. Page looked at the ceiling. She'd turned to Ian when she was desperate for support. Did that mean she wasn't as comfortable with her lone existence as she liked to think?

"Do you want to tell me who he is?" she asked, keeping her voice soft. "It might help to talk about what's happening." Even as she asked she tried to remember the last time someone had come to the apartment to pick Tanya up. Months ago. Tanya always left alone in a cab.

"I can't tell you. He doesn't want anyone to know."

"How could it hurt for you to tell me?" She gently pushed the ribbon to the top of Tanya's head.

"That's the way he wants it."

Page sighed. "Okay. You love him and he loves you. Why is it tearing you apart?"

"It's not." But Tanya's voice rose a pitch and she pulled her hand free.

"Of course not." Pushing wasn't Page's style, but she sensed Tanya's need and her vulnerability. "You've got it all together. That's why you've been drinking, and that's why you're in bed with your clothes on and makeup smeared all over your face. Why—"

"Leave me alone!"

Tanya swung her feet to the floor. When she stood an ankle gave out, and she caught herself clumsily against the wall.

Page knew roughly what the answer would be but

had to ask. "Please let me help you. This man, whoever he is, isn't doing you any good."

"Don't say that." Tanya sat down again and buried her head in her hands. "We'll work things out."

"Maybe you need a break. You could go home to your family for a while and—"

"No! No. You don't understand." She straightened, smoothing the wisp of red satin over her thighs. "Anyway, Mommy and Daddy are in Europe at the moment. And I'm fine," she added, casting Page a defiant stare.

"Sure you are." She was weary now, too weary to go on fighting, and a fight was what this felt like. "I'd better get to bed and let you do the same."

Tanya didn't answer, and Page left the room to go to her own. On the way home she'd planned to take a relaxing bath, but it no longer sounded like a panacea for her overcrowded brain. The growing problems with Pedal Pushers and her constant dread that she wouldn't get ahead fast enough to make the business a success were now crammed together with her concern for Tanya. At least where the business was concerned she could keep doing something. About Tanya she was helpless, unless Tanya allowed her into whatever the trouble was.

Preoccupied with the stream of questions that passed through her head, Page stripped off the silver racing suit and stretched out nude on the futon. Even in winter, San Francisco seemed warm to her, and she enjoyed the freedom of not wearing clothes to bed, a luxury Anchorage had never afforded.

She'd scrap the bath altogether and make do with

a quick shower, although even that seemed too much trouble.

Ian had told her to give him a call when she felt like it. She felt like it.

But he'd also let her know that he didn't want to be disturbed very late. She looked at the clock on the bedside table. Only two. Tonight the deliveries had been light and Waldo sent her home early. Ian had thought she wouldn't be back before two-thirty.

Page curled on her side. She was splitting hairs. Two was almost as late as two-thirty. He hadn't been as persistent about seeing or talking to her again as she'd expected. Not that it mattered. Better that way. If they did have a chance to be friends, even very casual friends, that would be nice. But it could never be more.

The phone was on the same table as the clock. But maybe he wasn't listed in the phone book. No, probably not. She ought to take that shower.

She kept the phone book under the phone. There wasn't another convenient place for it. Propping herself on an elbow, she eased out the book and scuffed aside pages. A listing for Ian Faber stood out as if in darker print, which it wasn't.

Calling was out of the question. What if this wasn't the same Ian Faber? She rested her head down again. A little nap before the shower sounded good.

There weren't two Ian Fabers, not living on Laguna.

Damn. She wanted, more than she remembered wanting anything before, to talk to Ian. Without sitting up, she pulled the phone onto the floor beside the futon and punched in the numbers.

"Hello."

He'd answered immediately and he didn't sound sleepy. For a moment Page listened, half expecting to hear music and laughter. All she heard was Ian breathing on the other end of the line.

"Page, is that you?"

Annoyance flickered. Was he so sure of himself that he'd assumed she'd call him after work? "Yes." She was being childish. Who else was likely to call him at this hour?

"I thought you were going to be too tired to talk to me."

She was a fool. Dozens of women might call him in the early hours of the morning. "Does that mean you're too tired, Ian?" On the other hand, hers had been the name to come automatically to his lips.

"I've been sitting here trying not to call you. It's not two-thirty yet. I'm not sure I was going to hold out once it was."

She smiled, then smiled more broadly at her own transparent pleasure. "I just wanted to thank you for the picnic. It was fun."

Seconds ticked by before he replied. "That's all you wanted to say? Now you want to say goodbye?"

He wasn't attempting to hide how much he wanted to talk to her. She ignored his questions. "How was your afternoon?"

"Busy. Things are hopping at the office. Ask me how my evening was."

"How was your evening?"

"Dull. I played racquetball with Martin—you remember Martin Grantham? He was drunk the one time you met him, but he's really not such a bad guy.

Only he beat me tonight, which doesn't usually happen. I guess I wasn't concentrating."

"That's too bad." Talking to Ian was taking away the tiredness.

"It was all your fault. You and that silver suit you had on today. I kept seeing it when I should have been seeing the ball."

She turned hot. She rested a hand on her breast and then remembered she was naked. Her fingers groped for something to cover her body, before she registered that no one could see her.

"Page?"

"I'm here. My afternoon was awful." She hadn't intended to, but she went on to tell him about her problems when she got back to the garage.

"Sounds as if you coped well."

His response surprised her. Some remark about how unsuitable her job was would have been more in character. "Thank you." More seconds passed. "I guess I'd better let you get some sleep."

"Don't hang up."

They laughed.

"I know, I know," Ian said. "I'm always saying that. Page, can I tell you something—honestly tell you something without your getting offended?"

She sat up and pulled the comforter over her knees. "That'll depend on what you tell me."

"I'd better not say it."

He was manipulating her, making her insist that he say his piece. "Don't keep me in suspense." She'd play his game.

"I'm in bed. Where are you?"

She swallowed. "Sitting on my bed."

"I wish we were in the same bed."

Page breathed in but felt suffocated. She had no slick answer for him.

"Does that offend you?"

If she wasn't careful she'd be admitting she wished the same thing. "No. I'm not a kid."

"You sure aren't, thank God."

She pressed a palm to her flaming cheek.

"Are you still there, Page?"

"I'm here. And for some reason I'm suddenly overheated."

"Maybe you wear too much to bed." She heard him pull in a breath. "Sorry. I'm not saying the right things tonight."

She *must* be suffocating. She imagined his big, well-formed body stretched out on a bed. She made a mind picture of him lying on his back, a sheet around slender hips, one hand behind his head while he talked to her. His broad chest would be covered with dark hair, his biceps flexed. The ridges of muscle on his stomach would be hard and lean....

Ian listened to their shared silence. He lay a few miles, only minutes from her. One day that distance would be put aside. The conviction hit him with exhilarating force.

Tonight, after Martin had left, he'd sat sorting through emotions that were virgin for him. For the first time in his life he wondered if he could be moving toward feeling something more than physical attraction for a woman. Oh, Page wouldn't be the only woman he'd ever liked, as well as wanted for a lover, but there had never really been anything deeper than that.

He sat up and hugged his knees with one arm. ''Page, forget anything I've said that you found offensive, okay?'' Staying rational was the answer. The different element here was that she wasn't falling into his arms and his bed. That made her more desirable.

She sighed into the phone. ''You didn't say anything offensive. And Ian, the heat had nothing to do with what I've got on. I don't wear anything to bed.''

CHAPTER SEVEN

WHEN HAD Faber and Faber become big enough to employ five people in the mail room? Ian clasped his hands behind his back and walked slowly between long, Formica-topped counters lined with wire baskets.

Two women who appeared little more than teenagers continued to work, feeding envelopes through a postage meter. Each had flashed him an acknowledging smile before returning to their tasks. Probably didn't know who he was, which was just as well.

The other woman in the room, and the two men, gave him their full attention.

"Is there a problem, Mr. Faber?"

He looked at his shoes, then returned his attention to the woman's face with a brief detour to her name tag. Mrs. Pellett.

Smiling, he pulled a high stool from beneath a counter and sat down. "Not a thing, Mrs. Pellett. I decided it's been far too long since I checked in with some of Faber and Faber's most important departments." Too much. Too effusive. He coughed. "I wanted to make sure you people know that although you don't see some of us very often we don't forget you, or the essential work you do down here." That sounded okay.

"Thank you, sir," Mrs. Pellett said. But she looked uncertain and Ian noticed from the corner of his eye that the other two women had paused to listen.

"It's good to see you, sir." One of the men—Ian noted his name was J. Grimes—held out a hand. "Feel free to look around. Not very exciting, I'm afraid." While Ian shook his hand, Grimes blushed and added, "Not that excitement is what we expect... I mean, efficiency's the thing, isn't it, sir?"

Ian squared his shoulders, broadening his smile. "Absolutely. How long have you been with us, Mr. Grimes?" Most other departments were on a first-name basis. The formality felt strange.

"Fourteen years, sir." A faint suggestion of pride entered the dry voice.

"Fourteen years?" Ian nodded and wondered how he himself would survive for fourteen years in this narrow room filled with transient things. "A long time, Mr. Grimes, and we're grateful for your loyalty."

"Thank you, sir."

It occurred to Ian that he might sound as if he were working up to a gentle firing. If there was such a thing. "We thank you, Grimes." His sincere smile took in the entire mail-room staff. "We thank all of you."

He got up quickly and started reading cards on the fronts of baskets. Eventually he found one marked local, then another beside the first.

"Was there something in particular...?" Mrs. Pellett's voice trailed away, as Ian pretended to be deeply engrossed in the contents of the two baskets.

Twenty-six packages and envelopes addressed to

businesses in San Francisco. Ian riffled through them again, checking his count. Twenty-six extra deliveries in one day, or even half that number, should bring in as much money as any one bicycle messenger could make on several nights.

"I have been wondering about our local deliveries," he said, not raising his eyes. "How do we deal with these?"

"Courier," Mr. Grimes said promptly.

Ian picked up a cardboard tube addressed to a seafood firm with offices on Bay Street. "Any particular service?"

"We use several. A lot of these outfits come and go, so we keep our options open and spread the business around. Keeps them all on their toes that way."

Ian admired Grimes's directness. "True," he told the man. "But with all these outfits do you find the reliability factor constant?"

"They do vary, sir." Mrs. Pellett crossed her arms. "In fact they can be a bit of a nuisance. Here one day and out of business the next."

"I see," Ian said. "In that case I think I'll look into this and see if I can come up with one or two firms that'll really give us the service we demand."

His last impression of the room as he left was one of stillness. There would be lively discussion over coffee this morning.

Rather than use the elevator, he charged up flight after flight of stairs, his shoes clanging on concrete. He needed exercise—and a chance to get over the awkwardness he'd felt in the mail room. But it had been worth it. Now he could proceed with the plan he'd devised while he'd lain awake in the night after talking to Page.

He reached his floor and paused for breath before opening the door to the plushly carpeted hall. While he walked swiftly toward his suite, he smoothed his hair and settled his jacket more comfortably on his shoulders. He felt hot. But he felt hot every time he thought of Page.

"There you are, Mr. Faber." Clemmie rose from her desk the instant he entered the anteroom. "Your father wants to know if you'll have lunch with him."

Ian waved her back into her seat. "Clemmie, be a dear and call Dad back for me. Tell him I'm caught up in something and can't make lunch. Ask him if we could get together around three. We'll have coffee in his office if he likes and catch up a bit." All this was said while he walked into his office. Before Clemmie could answer he closed his door.

He checked his appointments for the day then called Pedal Pushers.

"You got something to peddle—"

"Yes." He smiled, wondering if Page knew about her dispatcher's answering technique.

Minutes later he hung up and settled smugly into his chair. He'd never thought of himself as devious, but he was learning. "*Big business. Guaranteed volume. Chance to increase that volume*. He'd baited his hook carefully, grateful Page was "unavailable." And he'd made sure the dispatcher told him when Ms. Linstrom *would* be available before suggesting she come to the offices of Faber and Faber at eleven-thirty for an interview.

He buzzed Clemmie. "I'm expecting an eleven-thirty appointment,'' he told her. ''Until then I'm out. To anyone.''

There. Page wouldn't be able to reach him to question or cancel the date. If she chose not to turn up, there was nothing he could do about it. But he didn't believe she wouldn't show. If there was one thing certain about the lady, it was that she would be unlikely to turn down business.

For an hour he tried to work up a treatment for a toothpaste television commercial. He'd long ago passed the point where he had much time for hands-on work in the creative end of the business, but he still enjoyed involving himself as a copy writer on the ground floor of occasional projects.

By eleven-fifteen he gave up. Photos of smiling mouths, puckered mouths, mouths kissing mouths, littered his desk—the pad where he'd scribbled theme line and jingle ideas was a crosshatched disaster.

He felt disheveled. In the compact bathroom off the office he splashed cold water on his face, scrubbed it vigorously with a towel and made an ineffectual attempt at taming his hair.

Eleven twenty-five.

Damn, he'd splashed water on his pink silk tie. It would dry in puckered circles. Usually he kept a spare in a drawer but he'd used it and forgotten to bring another.

Eleven thirty-five.

She was a hardheaded, cantankerous tease. So what if she didn't show? There were plenty of other women waiting in the wings. All he had to do was pick up the phone and he'd have dates every night for as long as he wanted them.

A sharp pain at the end of his right index finger startled him. He'd chewed a fingernail to the quick. That was it. The end. No woman would reduce him to this. He stopped pacing and sat behind his desk once more. A buzz from the intercom jolted him like a blow. He flipped the switch.

"Your, ah, eleven-thirty appointment is here, Mr. Faber."

A beatific calm slipped over Ian. He wasn't sure why he felt that way, and he wasn't going to analyze the reason. "Show her in, please." How could he have doubted, even for a second, that she'd come?

Page came through the door Clemmie opened for her. Ian avoided looking at his secretary before she left. He didn't have to see her face to know what her expression would be.

"Come in, come in." He stood and waved Page to a chair on the other side of the desk then sat down again. "I'm glad you could make it. Coffee?"

She shook her head. "What's this about, Ian?" Her blue eyes glittered with skepticism.

Ian rocked back, lacing his fingers behind his neck. "Business," he said. She'd obviously been working. Her hair was windblown and she wore the purple outfit she'd worn the night of their first meeting.

"Business, Ian? What kind of business?"

Her waist was so small. Did she wear leotards and shorts all winter? he wondered. He'd feel better if she wore oilskins, or even jeans and a baggy sweatshirt. There were so many kooks out there—watching.

"You make me uncomfortable when you stare," she said.

He started. "I wasn't staring. I was thinking."

"And staring."

"Yeah, I guess I was." He puffed up his cheeks and slowly expelled the air. "I was wondering…" All he needed to do to ensure failure with her was deliver a lecture on how she should dress. "Did your people find out anything at the Hotel Utah?" he asked, suddenly inspired.

"You didn't ask me here to talk about that."

This was one woman he'd never be able to snow. "Not entirely." Swinging forward, he rested his elbows on the desk. "But I think of you as a friend, Page. You don't need me to say that I'd like to think of you as more than a friend." His concentration slipped quickly from her eyes, her mouth, to the toes of purple, high-topped sneakers.

Page shifted and he glanced back at her face. She was blushing and it suited her. "I don't think this is the time or the place to get into personal stuff," she said, and lifted her hair from her neck.

Her turn to feel hot, Ian thought with satisfaction. "Possibly not. But can we at least agree on the fact that we are friends? I'll settle for that for a while." As if he had a choice until she changed the rules.

"I think of you as a friend, Ian."

"Good. What about the Hotel Utah?"

In an unconscious gesture, Page gathered her hair together and piled it at the back of her head. The action, the way it lifted her breasts, arched her ribs, mesmerized him.

"I don't know what to think about it all," she said. "Not only didn't they get a good look at any of the guys who've been giving us trouble, but no one else seemed to see them, either. Not a single description.

It doesn't figure. How can a whole group of riders be invisible to everyone?''

''Pedal pushers—I mean the pants—are fashionable again now, aren't they?'' As soon as he asked he felt ridiculous.

Page looked blank. ''I don't follow trends. Why?''

He made an airy gesture. ''Oh, I don't know. It just popped into my head that it would be kind of cute if you wore pedal pushers and sweatshirts for work. Kind of a trademark, you know?'' *Hell.*

When she laughed he wasn't sure how to react. ''You haven't met my people,'' she said. ''There's only one other woman apart from me, and if it doesn't have spots or glitter, or if it isn't made of leather with studs, she won't wear it. And the guys might not think pedal pushers were too cute.''

He didn't feel like smiling, but he managed to turn up the corners of his mouth. ''I bet they wouldn't. Forget it. Just the old advertising instinct rearing its head. So, no leads on these people, huh?''

''No leads. But so far today we haven't had trouble, so I'm keeping my fingers and toes crossed and praying they've lost interest.''

Ian's prayer was the same, but dread still lay in the pit of his stomach. ''Let's hope so.''

''I don't want to hurry you—'' she looked at her watch ''—but we'd better keep this really short. In fact I have to get on the road just about now.''

''Sure, sure.'' Even as he searched for more ways to detain her he knew it was a mistake. ''It meant so much to me to hear your voice last night. When we were in the park yesterday it took everything I had not to push you for another date.'' He'd always been honest, but this was making him feel too vulnerable for comfort.

Page leaned across the desk and put a hand on top of his. "Maybe we're more alike than we think. Part of me was glad you didn't push. But I think a bigger part was disappointed."

He lifted her fingers toward his mouth, studied her palm, then kissed it. "True-confession time, huh?" He was too old to be a cockeyed optimist, but he was enjoying these few minutes of forgetting the rest of the world.

Page couldn't help closing her eyes. Ian's mouth on her palm was soft yet firm, as erotic as if he'd kissed her lips. "I'd..." She swallowed. Her mouth was so dry. "I'd better get going. But I'm glad we got to talk for a few minutes. Maybe we'll get a chance to see each other again soon." She wasn't used to making the moves, but if he could lay himself open, so could she.

He held her hand a while longer, then took in a gusty breath and released it. "Yes, yes. But I almost forgot what made me get you here in the first place."

She slid to the edge of her chair. Lilian had talked about Ian saying he had work for them. She hadn't really believed that.

Ian had difficulty concentrating on what he would say next. "Um, I've been doing a study on our mailing department. Reliability, cost-effectiveness, you know the routine." This had better not sound as thin to her as it did to him.

Page crossed her arms under her breasts, and Ian quickly averted his gaze. At least for now he was going to have to separate his mind from his libido.

"Anyway, we've decided at Faber that we'd like to deal with one or two really reliable courier services rather than go through the hit-and-miss routine of calling half a dozen in the space of every week."

He saw interest in the serious set of her features. "You mean you don't already deal with just one firm? That's fairly unusual."

Ian suppressed a satisfied grunt. More ammunition when he informed the mail room that he'd decided to eliminate most of the outfits doing local work for Faber. "I agree," he said. "Now, I realize you aren't fooled by my offer. Obviously I would never have thought of you...it's because we know each other and..." He was never this bumbling. "You know why I'm doing this."

Her smile was uncertain. "Are you sure that's such a good idea? I mean, I want the business of course, but—"

"But could conflict of interest become a problem? Why should it? You and your people will come and go from the dispatching area and you probably won't ever see me. Whether or not you and I continue to...ah... Whatever happens between us need never affect the other."

She stood up, beautiful, lithe, unselfconsciously graceful. "Then I'd be happy to take on the work. Thank you. Do I talk to your dispatch people?"

"I'll do that," he said in a rush.

"We won't expect any preferential treatment, Ian. If there's a problem, I want to hear about it."

"Oh, you will." And he meant it.

Page inclined her head. "Then we have a deal. I'll tell my dispatcher to expect calls."

"You got something to peddle?" Ian grinned and was rewarded by a grimace from Page. "I've spoken to her about that," she said. "I guess I'll have to speak some more. What kind of volume are we talking about, by the way?"

She was more in control than he was at the moment. "Ah, minimum of twelve to fifteen packages a day, I'd say. Could be much more on occasions."

He noted triumphantly that she was surprised. "That much? Great. Thank you very, very much. We'll perform well for you, I promise."

Much as he longed to address the question of her giving up riding and spending all her time on management, he gauged that the timing was wrong. "I'm sure you'll do just fine. By the way, this isn't very professional, but since getting in touch with you isn't the easiest thing, what are you doing on Saturday?"

That old uncertainty entered her eyes. "I've got a lot of catching up to do around the apartment," she said. "And shopping. Tanya says it's time I stopped—"

The abrupt snapping shut of her mouth intrigued him. So did her heightened color. "Tanya's the woman you live with?"

"Yes, anyway, I really do have loads to do on Saturday."

"I wasn't thinking of the daytime." Actually he'd been thinking, or fantasizing, of all day and all night. "How about dinner?"

"Well..."

"Come on." Cajoling was foreign to him but he could learn. "Be a sport and keep a lonely man company for an evening. We'll go somewhere spectacular. Do you like to dance?''

''Yes, but I don't have anything—''

''Wonderful. It's a date, then. I'll be by around seven. We'll go somewhere for a drink first and eat late. How does that sound?'' A mistake, he realized instantly. Never go for the close on a question.

''It sounds very nice.'' Her smile was fixed and he felt her rallying for a turndown.

''Good. Saturday at seven, then. And now, you'd better get back to work and so had I.''

Swiftly he went to put an arm around her shoulders and usher her to the door. It opened the instant before he reached for the handle and his father put his head inside. ''Busy, Ian?''

He thought fast. ''Come in, Dad. You're exactly the man I wanted to see. Page was just leaving. You remember Page?''

''I remember Page very well.'' Robert Faber came all the way into the room and shook her hand. The flicker of his eyes was subtle, but not so subtle that Ian didn't know it had taken Page in all the way to the purple sneakers. He pushed his shoulders back and hoped he didn't look as off balance as he felt.

''Good to see you again, Mr. Faber.'' Page was polite but not effusive. ''I intend to write Mrs. Faber and thank her for a wonderful dinner. Please tell her she'll hear from me when I have a few minutes. I'm sure having too much to do and not enough time to do it is something she understands.''

Ian couldn't hold back a pleased smile. To hell with the way she dressed and her oddball occupation. Any savvy man or woman would admire her. His father's appreciative expression suggested he certainly did.

When Page had left, Bob Faber faced his son with raised brows and a quizzical smile on his face. "She's quite a woman, Ian. But I guess you've noticed that."

"ARE YOU SURE, operator?"

Static crackled in Page's ear before a nasal voice repeated, "There is no listing in Dallas for a Jasper Woodside, jr."

"Wait!" She had to be absolutely sure that her hunch about Tanya's family was right. "Is there a Jasper who isn't a junior?"

"No, ma'am. But I have two J. Woodsides. Would you like those numbers?"

Page listened and scribbled, hung up and immediately tried the two J. Woodsides of Dallas, Texas. Neither John nor Jerry had ever heard of someone named Tanya.

This time Tanya had been gone three days and Page's concern approached panic. That the wealthy family that supposedly supported her friend's every whim didn't exist wasn't a surprise. The pieces were falling into place. Tanya's choice of an inexpensive place to live. Her saying she didn't receive mail from home at the apartment because she had a post-office box.

On Tuesday and Wednesday nights, after she returned home from working for Waldo, Page had considered calling the deli to see if Tanya was there. Each time she'd decided against the idea, afraid she'd run the risk of having Tanya shut her out completely. Maybe it shouldn't matter so much, but it did. In a city where Page had arrived as a stranger, Tanya had been her first friend, and she didn't make friends easily. She didn't want to lose her.

Tonight, Thursday, Page felt an unaccustomed emptiness. The work she'd started getting from Faber and Faber was a wonderful shot in the arm to her cash flow. Page had made several pickups there herself, and each time she entered the building she couldn't help hoping for a glimpse of Ian. She never saw him, and her disappointment had grown.

When she thought of Saturday, her stomach turned queasy. Somewhere spectacular, Ian had said. And dancing. Before seven o'clock on Saturday evening she'd have to break down and buy a dress. She didn't even know what was in fashion anymore. If Tanya were around she could help.

Tanya took over her thoughts again—the way she'd looked on Monday night, thin, drawn. With more difficulty than she would have liked, Page turned aside her preoccupation with Ian and went to stand in the doorway of Tanya's room. She switched on the light. Everything looked as it had on Tuesday morning.

Her mind a blank, Page wandered about the room. Tanya was so tidy. No wonder her own disorderly space was an irritation sometimes. Tanya must have a family. If only there was a clue somewhere.

Page opened the drawer of a warped writing table on one side of the bed. A jumble of papers confronted her. Odd. So tidy on the outside, so disorganized on the inside. She left the drawer open and checked the closet for a suitcase. But then the idea that if one was missing she could assume this was a planned absence immediately made no sense. Surely Tanya would have said if she was going away for a while—if she knew she was going anywhere. The problem remained the same. These disappearing acts had no pattern, and Tanya was definitely in worse shape each time she returned.

The closet was also messy. Page closed it, feeling like a snoop. She also felt helpless. Where could she go for help? And she was more and more convinced that whatever was happening to Tanya was serious enough to necessitate help from someone.

Back at the writing table, she lifted one scrap of paper after another, hoping to find a telephone number, or an address to lead her to Tanya's parents. Bills, mostly unpaid, messages and notes that made no sense, checkbook stubs; the mishmash was endless and also useless for Page's purpose.

She sat on the bed and continued searching. There had to be a lead here somewhere. Idly flipping through sheets of paper, she came to another checkbook stub and picked it up. The first page showed a large deposit. A huge deposit even for Tanya, who always seemed to have plenty of money. Page squinted. Her eyes were tired. A rim of shiny black caught the light. Awkwardly easing her hand under the tabletop to free the object, she pulled the drawer all the way out. Crushed at the back was a familiar, shiny black box. Touch Tone Gourmet. The gold lettering was creased, but plain. Hesitantly Page opened the flaps and looked inside. Bills, wads of new bills in big denominations. There had to be thousands of dollars.

Page's skin prickled. Waldo had a preoccupation with cash. He wanted things paid for in cash, and it made sense that he would pay for what he got in cash, too. She closed the box and shoved it forcefully back, hating to touch it, to think of what it might mean... that Tanya was tied to Waldo by her own dependence.

"Find anything interesting?"

At the sound of Tanya's voice, Page jumped so hard her neck hurt. She slammed the drawer shut. "Thank God. Where have you been? Where do you keep going? I've been so worried about you."

"You don't have to be. I've already told you that. And I don't need a keeper, Page. I don't like the feeling you're watching me. I left home to get away from that."

Goosebumps shot up Page's back. She stiffened, totally at a loss for something to say.

"What are you going through my things for?" Tanya continued. "Would you like it if I waited until you were out and searched your room?"

This was a side of Tanya that Page hadn't seen before. Her roommate was sober, but there was a meanness about her. "I'm not interested in your things," Page said. "And I'm sorry if I'm trespassing on your turf. I was worried, okay? You haven't looked well for a long time." And with this she took in the rumpled man's shirt Tanya wore and loose jeans and tennis shoes. She looked as if she were dressed in a larger woman's clothes, and haggard didn't describe the condition of her face. "The only reason I opened this drawer was to see if there was a phone number or address for your parents. If I'd found either I'd have used it." This wasn't the right moment to bring up the issue of why Tanya had lied about her family. "I also checked your closet to see if you might have packed for a trip. Then I realized I wouldn't know anything more about what's going on with you if I found out you had taken a trip. That's it. All. If you want to call it quits as friends, fine. Otherwise tell me what's eating you so I can help you."

If Page didn't feel so dried-up by the effort she'd just put out, she'd cry.

"I'm sorry." Tanya did cry. "Look, I'll try to give you a call or something if I'm not coming home. Would that be all right?"

Page nodded, unable to speak.

"And I shouldn't have said all that stuff. You're very important to me, Page. You're kind of...well, kind of my anchor, I guess."

"I want you to see a doctor." Page hadn't planned to say that, but as soon as she had she was glad. "You've lost too much weight."

Tanya fidgeted before she answered. "You're having your own troubles, Page. Maybe that's making you blow mine out of proportion."

The avoidance of her suggestion didn't escape Page, but she was more interested in what Tanya said. "How do you know I'm having problems? We haven't discussed that."

Tanya's back was to her. "I...I just heard some things, that's all."

"What things?" Page needed to know if there was some general talk about Pedal Pushers. Not that it made sense for Tanya to have heard any gossip.

Tanya shrugged. "Not a lot. Just about some accidents and things."

Page took a deep breath and let it out slowly. "Ken told you, didn't he? He's made comments about you from time to time. Did he find a way to talk to you, to talk about Pedal Pushers?"

"That's right, Ken told me." Tanya turned around, smiling. "He's quite a hunk, that guy."

"I might have known it," Page muttered. "He may be a hunk, but he's no prize. I wonder how many other people he's told."

Tanya turned around. "I wouldn't worry about that. I just happened to bump into him the other day when I was leaving, and he started a conversation. The bike accidents were probably the first thing that came into his head to say."

"Yeah," Page agreed, "you're probably right. I wish I didn't need him, though."

"Listen. Nothing's changed with me. Remember the man I told you about?" Tanya didn't sound as if she needed an answer. "Well, we're still working things through and it's hard on both of us. Go to bed and stop fussing over me. I promise I won't drop out of sight without a word again."

Tiredness was making Page's head fuzzy. There was a great deal more she and Tanya should talk about, but at least they'd made a start at openness. "Thanks," Page said. "I feel a bit better hearing you say that. I guess I will hit the hay."

She closed Tanya's door as she left. Maybe they should keep a pad on the kitchen table for messages in case there wasn't time to bother with a phone call.

She opened the door again to tell Tanya the idea.

Tanya stood bracing her weight on the foot of her bed, her back arched over. She'd taken off the shirt and the black lace straps of her bra were stark against her white skin.

So were clusters of purple and red bruises.

CHAPTER EIGHT

"DON'T COME IN HERE!" Tanya straightened and whirled around, clutching the shirt to her chest. More bruises marred her thin arms.

"Oh, Tanya. What's happened to you?" Page put a trembling hand over her mouth.

"I fell." Tanya pulled the shirt back on and crossed it tightly about her. "Stupid accident. You know the way these things happen?"

Page was wide awake again. "I never saw that many bruises from one fall."

Tanya's eyes flashed and she spoke through gritted teeth. "Are you calling me a liar?"

Page flinched but stood her ground. "I'm not calling you a liar. I'm just asking questions."

"You ask too many questions. We already went over that."

"And you said our friendship meant something to you, and in future we were going to be open with each other." She began to feel angry.

"I know," Tanya said quietly, "and I meant it. I'm extra touchy at the moment, Page. I wish I weren't." She sat on the end of her bed. "I fell down some steps and I rolled over and over. It hurt a lot."

Page went to sit beside her, started to put an arm around her shoulders, then changed her mind. She gave an awkward laugh. "I'm afraid to touch you. You must still hurt a lot. Where were the steps?"

Tanya's mussed red hair obscured her face. "At a friend's house. The man—you know who I mean. I ran out of there after an argument and slipped. There are metal railings down each side of the steps and I think I hit some of those, too." Her voice cracked.

The little room felt stuffy and dismal to Page, and Tanya's perfume smelled cloying. "When did it happen?" she asked.

Tanya shrugged. "Yesterday, I think."

She thought? Wouldn't a person know when they'd fallen hard enough to do the damage Page had seen? "Did you hit your head as well?"

"No." Tanya turned her face, and up close she appeared even worse than Page had feared. A smile did nothing to improve her appearance. "And I'm so hardheaded it probably wouldn't have hurt me anyway," she added.

Page smiled back. "Thank goodness for that. Boy, I don't know about you, but I'm just about too tired to sleep. Would you like a hot drink? I'll make it."

"I don't think—"

"Please. I need your advice on something."

One delicate eyebrow raised, and Tanya's green eyes regained some light. "What kind of advice?"

Page feigned shyness. "Something to do with a man. You don't have the corner on that market, you know."

"Really?" Tanya got up, buttoning the shirt. "You've got my full attention. Lead the way to the kitchen."

An hour later Page crawled onto her futon and, as

she always did, pulled the comforter over her head. Her plan had been to get Tanya talking and then draw her out about what was really happening in her life. It hadn't worked. Tanya had wormed out the whole story of Ian and shown genuine delight that Page was at last interested in someone and something other than work. No matter how hard Page tried to turn the conversation back to Tanya, it remained on herself, until finally she gave up and asked for some hints on what kind of dress to buy for Saturday.

The magazines Tanya had rushed to collect were now beside the futon. Pages were marked to give guidance to shops Tanya preferred and styles she thought would suit both Page and the occasion.

Page wasn't sure she could afford Tanya's taste, but she'd do her best. And it wasn't the dress that kept her awake now.

She stared unseeingly into the darkness and remembered bruises on pale skin...and money stacked in a black box. Were Waldo and Tanya just in an unhealthy relationship, or something more?

THE HALIBUT WAS probably wonderful. Page couldn't taste a thing, concentrate on a thing. *Eyes for no one but you.* She didn't remember where the line came from, but it fitted Ian's present state. Without looking at him, she knew he watched every move she made. Her hands seemed to have grown larger and clumsier, and she was sure the heat in her face must show as ugly red.

"Good?" Ian asked.

She glanced at him and then at the elaborate hairstyle of a woman seated behind him. "Very good. How's yours?"

"Good."

Page toyed with her wineglass, took a sip and picked up her fork again. Their conversation had been this way from the moment Ian came to the apartment for her. Desultory. She really wasn't comfortable with him in his natural settings. That confirmed her theory that, as much as they were attracted to each other, and they were, they didn't belong together. Wasn't that what it proved?

"That dress looks wonderful on you."

Was he eating at all? "Thank you. Actually it's two pieces." She set down the fork and placed her hands in her lap. He didn't want to know silly details about her clothes.

"Something wrong, Page?"

She looked up at him. "No...yes. Ian, I'm lousy company. Admit it. You bring me to this wonderful place—" she indicated the mirrored walls of the restaurant, the crisp linen cloths, the flickering candles and fresh flowers on each table "—and I clam up. Frankly, after our last official date I'm surprised you asked me out again."

Coming perilously close to settling a shirt cuff in a candle flame, he reached for and caught one of her waving hands. He laughed and trapped her wrist on the table. "Why must you always analyze? Why don't you just *feel*? You know perfectly well why I asked you out again. You also knew I would and that you wanted to come."

She relaxed slightly. "Pretty sure of yourself, huh? What was your major? Humility?"

"Smiling suits you." The pressure on her wrist lightened, and he turned it to stroke the base of her thumb with his own. "So does blue. I've never seen you in a skirt before."

"Thanks. I bought this today..." She rolled her eyes heavenward. "Don't you admire a sophisticated woman, Ian? I bet all your dates let you know they buy a new dress when you're taking them out."

"Please don't get sophisticated." He trailed his fingers to the tips of hers and waited until she returned his gaze. "Keep on being yourself for as long as you can."

"You sound as if being yourself isn't easy around here. Who are you, Ian? Have I met you yet?"

"You've got me there. I don't think I put on an act most of the time. But I guess most of us have a few masks we aren't aware of."

He was showing himself now, Page thought, letting her see the way his mind worked on at least one level. "Sometimes we have to cover up," she said, "when we know we'll be taken advantage of if we don't. You should see me at work. My father should see me at work. You wouldn't believe what comes out of my mouth, or how. But Dad never did understand why a woman wouldn't want to stay home and be 'provided for.' Of course, being provided for also means—as far as he's concerned—that you're on duty and answerable for your actions twenty-four hours a day. Still, he'd see that as what I should want. He'd never work out that I find it a challenge to run a business where I deal with people, day in and day out, who can be pretty rough and tough." She withdrew her hand from his and drank more wine. She'd said too much. Too much, or too little. Why couldn't she develop better social skills?

"Your father did you a favor."

"What?" She looked at him sharply.

"He did you a favor. And me." Ian laughed. Even when he confused her, she loved the way he laughed. "He made you determined to find freedom. You chose San Francisco to do that in. Good for you and me."

She shook her head slowly. "You have a lovely way of making things sound so simple. But you're right—at least about it being good for me. Your dinner must be cold."

Ian speared a carrot and put it into his mouth, chewing thoughtfully. "My mother does that."

"Does what?" She was beginning to feel very relaxed now.

"Changes subject in mid-conversation. The dress is sexy."

Page choked and blushed at the same time. "Now who's changing subjects in mid-conversation?" She coughed and felt tears form in her eyes. "And you deliberately go for shock value, Ian Faber. Dirty pool."

"No way. I was thinking that if you wore the dress, or top or whatever it is, back to front no man in this room would eat his dinner."

"Ian! That qualifies as a lewd suggestion." The outfit, of soft, midnight-blue cashmere, was a draped, crossover-cowl style at the back, leaving her skin bare to the waist. Shopping alone, she'd been unsure it suited her, but an enthusiastic salesperson had assured her it was perfect, and Page decided it was at least flattering.

"Lewd?" Ian said when he stopped laughing. "Garbage. Wishful thinking, that's all. Not that you don't have a delectable back. In fact, you have a delectable every—"

"Thank you," she said hurriedly. "You're pretty delectable yourself."

He chuckled. "I'm crazy about the way you do that. It's sort of naughty and totally out of character."

Page gave him an arch stare. "How do you know what's out of character for me?"

"Hmm." With his elbows planted on the table, he rested his chin and started one of his disconcerting but provocative inspections of as much of her as he could see. "You'd be surprised how much I've figured out about you. And you've told me more than you think. Where did you buy the, um, dress? The skirt does nice things, too, by the way. I'm glad it's not too short. Not that I don't like looking at short skirts."

"You mean who's wearing them. But not on older women, right?" Page was enjoying herself. The banter teased something inside her, warmed her, created an intimacy that was subtly arousing.

Ian snorted. "Lady, I've seen your legs, remember? And what *wonderful* legs. The truth is I don't think a tall woman with phenomenal gams needs miniskirts. I believe long legs inside a clinging skirt are one of the biggest turn-ons there is."

A faint blush started again. "I'm glad I can give you a thrill."

"You make that sound obscene." The humor in

his eyes took any sting out of his words. "But it's true. Where did you buy the outfit?"

Why would he care? Only women were supposed to care about things like that. He must be humoring her, trying to react on her level as he saw it. "Well." How did she deal with this gracefully? "I did go into Neiman-Marcus."

"Good choice." He drank some of his own wine, nodding approval. "You can always rely on Neiman-Marcus. I do a lot of shopping there...or, to be more precise, I shop there when I can't put it off any longer."

"You don't like shopping, either?" Page leaned forward conspiratorially. "I absolutely hate it. I know women who can't wait to spend all day making their feet swell. Not me."

"But your trip to Neiman-Marcus paid off."

"No. It was too rich for my blood. I got this at Macy's."

For an instant Ian stared, his glass halfway to his mouth. Then he set it down and laughed. "You are wonderful. Any other woman would have let it go. You just have to be honest, don't you?"

"Yes," she said tersely, and thought: too honest. He might find her simplicity intriguing, and even find her intriguing because of that simplicity. She didn't like the idea very much, or the probability that he wouldn't take long to get bored with such a simple diversion.

A waiter removed their plates. He made no comment about how little had been eaten—he didn't have to. The disapproving downturn of his mouth said it all. They ordered coffee and brandy.

She leaned back in her chair and let her eyes wander over the other diners. The ambience of the place was one of understated elegance. She was glad she'd bought the outfit. It felt good and appropriate.

"The music's nice," Ian said. He also sat back. With his hands spread on the arms of his chair, his navy suit jacket gaped to show a white shirt, probably hand tailored, that fitted him without a wrinkle. He did have a broad chest and a slim waist. Page decided some men were born to wear beautiful suits and silk ties and handmade shirts, and Ian was one of them.

"Hey, dreamer. Do you like the music?"

A pianist played a grand piano. The pieces were gentle, nonintrusive, mostly old and familiar. "I love it. This place is so peaceful, it wouldn't be hard to fall asleep."

Ian, jolting forward, startled Page. "Ruby's is supposed to be romantic. It's not supposed to put you to sleep. Or is it the company that's doing that?"

She narrowed her eyes at him while the coffee and brandy arrived. When they were alone again, she brought her face nearer to his across the table. "If you think I'm going to fall into any of your traps and tell you how irresistible you are, forget it." Up close his dark eyes appeared opaque, pupil and iris all one. She withdrew several inches. "You are pretty irresistible."

"Page—"

"Ian, darling! It *is* you. I told Martin I was sure it was, and he said I'd had one too many, didn't you Martin, darling? You're so mean sometimes."

Page looked up into the avid face of Deirdre of the long black hair and vicious tongue, and wished for divine intervention, like the fire alarm going off. Clearing out the restaurant seemed incredibly appealing at the moment.

Martin Grantham III stood at Deirdre's shoulder. He wasn't swaying this evening, and Page acknowledged, unwillingly, that in a foppish way he was quite attractive.

"Hello, Deirdre, Martin." Ian sounded as enthusiastic as Page felt, and at least one or two of her knotted muscles softened.

"Darling, we haven't seen you for simply ages. Poor Liz is pining away for you. Says you won't even talk to her on the phone." With this Deirdre pulled out a chair and sat down, motioning Martin to the other side of the table. He appeared uncomfortable. "Maybe Ian and, er... Maybe Ian doesn't want company," he said.

"Nonsense," Deirdre said. So far she'd managed to behave as if Ian were alone. She hailed the waiter. "Be a good boy and order me some more champagne, Ian. You know how I love champagne."

Ian glowered from Deirdre to Martin, who slid awkwardly to sit where Deirdre had indicated.

"We were about to leave," Ian said in a flat voice Page hadn't heard before. "Do you both remember Page?"

"You can't leave yet." Deirdre ordered the champagne herself, a bottle of Dom Perignon, then took a sip from Ian's brandy snifter. "You've got to finish this, and we just arrived."

"How are you, Page?" Martin asked. His discomfort was strong enough to make her feel sorry for him.

"You are the lady we met at Ian's that night, aren't you?"

"Of course she is, silly." Deirdre made a cross moue. "I expect Ian is... Well, Ian always was one for little experiments."

Page put her napkin on the table. Cold climbed her spine and tightened her scalp. If this was so-called sophistication, she hoped she never got it. The woman was a boor. But she was also someone Ian had entertained in his home, together with a clone who must have been his date. Little experiments. Like taking out a member of the working class?

She'd bowed her head and didn't realize Ian was standing until he said her name.

"Page," he repeated. "It's time we got to that dancing I promised you." He motioned for his check.

"Aren't you going to have some of your champagne?" Deirdre asked, ignoring Martin's whispered, "Shut up, Deirdre."

"No thanks," Ian said. "And it's *your* champagne." He was making it clear that he wasn't paying for Deirdre's self-indulgence.

Martin stood and shook Page's hand. "Nice to see you again," he said. "Sorry about that other time. You know what they say: when the wine's in the wit's out? It's true."

She couldn't help liking him. "Forget it," she said. "I had until tonight, and I will again now. Enjoy your evening. You too, Deirdre." No need to take lessons from lesser beings.

As they left, Martin was reminding Ian that he owed him a rematch on the racquetball court. Ian's only response was a thin smile.

Outside the night was cool, the sky clear and silver black in the light of the moon and the city's illumination.

Sitting beside Ian in the car, Page fell silent. He'd switched on the engine but made no attempt to pull away from the curb. They both stared straight ahead.

"I'm sorry about that," Ian said.

"Why should you be?"

"Because they are friends of mine, or Martin is, anyway." He ran his hands around the steering wheel.

"Martin's quite nice, and I'm sure if Deirdre were sober she'd be okay, too." The inside of the car felt warm and Page opened her window. Night scents, dark and soothing, crept in.

"I doubt it," Ian said. "But then, I don't remember seeing her sober."

Page laughed. "Then feel sorry for her."

"You're too forgiving."

"Don't bet on it. I'm putting on a good front."

"Thank God," Ian said on a sigh. "Saints make me feel guilty. Are you up for dancing?"

She wasn't. "Um...well..."

"Neither am I. Would it make you nervous if I invited you back to my place? I'm not ready to let you go yet."

Whatever that meant. "It might make me nervous, but I'd probably say yes."

He put the car in gear.

Traffic was light and the drive from Brannan Street to Ian's place took what seemed to Page only minutes. When they eased into the narrow alley beside his house, she was still wondering if she'd appear a fool if she told him she'd changed her mind and wanted to go home.

"I hope the cupboard isn't bare," Ian said as he ushered her through the front door. "If it is, I suppose I can always call Touch Tone Gourmet." Was his laugh hollow?

Page said nothing. She was probably projecting her own tension on him.

"It's chilly in here," Ian said after showing her into the salon. "These big old houses are the dickens to heat. I'll get a fire going, then we'll raid the kitchen."

"We just had dinner," Page reminded him.

"Correction. We just paid for dinner. I seem to remember that neither of us ate too much."

She wrapped her short sheepskin coat more tightly around her. It didn't complement the blue cashmere, but was as close as she'd been able to come to something dressy.

Ian knelt on the hearth of a large, gray, marble fireplace and set light to paper beneath a pile of logs.

Page glanced around the beautiful room. "How do you keep everything so tidy?" It would take hours to clean the place.

"I have a housekeeper who comes in every other day," Ian said, still engrossed in poking the fire to life.

"Of course." How could she be so naive? It wasn't likely that the wealthy president of an advertising agency did windows.

At last, satisfied with his efforts, Ian stood. "The kitchen's downstairs. That's the one inconvenience to living upstairs. Do you want to stay by the fire while I see what I can find to eat?''

Being alone in the big room didn't appeal to her. ''I'll come with you. I'd like to see the kitchen.'' Not strictly true. Page didn't enjoy cooking, and kitchens had never interested her.

This kitchen was huge. Square, white tiles covered the lower halves of the walls. An incongruous paper depicting blue cupids cavorting among impossibly large pieces of blue fruit filled the space to a carved ceiling. Everything was spotless: rows of copper pans and utensils hanging from racks over a central cooking island; dishes visible through glass-fronted cabinets on two walls; a double, white enamel sink; a blue, linoleum-covered floor strewn with a hodgepodge of rag mats.

Ian watched her reaction. ''Strange, isn't it? I keep saying I'm going to do something about it. I like to cook, so I had new appliances put in, but I haven't gotten around to the decor. God knows who chose this.''

Page made a sympathetic noise. ''I hate cooking.'' She applied fingertips to temples. He didn't need to know she had difficulty boiling spaghetti.

''So we balance each other,'' Ian said, oozing cheer. ''That's exactly as it should be.''

She resisted the temptation to ask if that meant he'd like to stay home and have someone like her ''provide'' for him.

He took off his raincoat and tossed it on a chair. ''Ready to take yours off?''

She let him ease the sheepskin from her shoulders, conscious that the pattern of his breathing changed slightly and that his knuckles lingered too long on her bare back.

As soon as her hands were free, she moved. The change in atmosphere was subtle, but even without looking at Ian she knew it had happened. "May I check out the refrigerator?" she asked.

"Be my guest."

His voice was no longer falsely cheerful.

As if she spent every evening coming up with nice little snacks for company, Page took out cheese and sliced roast beef and mustard and mayonnaise and set them on a round oak table by a bay window. Then she found lettuce and a tomato, a loaf of bread and added them to the array.

While she busied herself, Ian stayed beside the chair where he'd put their coats.

"I thought you said you didn't like cooking," he said when she started setting out plates and flatware.

"I don't. Sandwiches aren't cooking, and I'm not going to make them. I just thought I'd do my bit first."

"Maybe I don't want sandwiches."

She paused in the act of opening the mayonnaise jar. He must see that she was keyed-up and not thinking straight. "What *do* you want?"

"To kiss you."

Her breathing quickened. "Are you always so blunt?"

"That wasn't blunt."

Her warmed skin turned fiery. "Can I make you a sandwich?"

"You can, but I probably won't eat it."

She made herself meet his stare. "What is it with

us, Ian? Why does it feel like this whenever we're together?''

His laugh was short and jarring. ''You're not that innocent.''

''No. Maybe I should go home.''

''Do you want to?''

Page crossed her arms and turned away. ''I don't know.''

She heard him move, but she still jumped when he slipped his hands under the draped back of her sweater. ''If I'd been blunt just now I'd have said I wanted to make love to you.''

''I know.'' Her voice sounded loud inside her head.

''Shall I explain exactly why we fence the way we do? Why there are all these long silences?''

He didn't need to. As he'd said, she wasn't that innocent.

''I'll tell you anyway. It's because we've got something special starting. Or already started. I felt it from the first time I saw you, and if you're honest you'll admit you did, too.''

He traced bare skin at the edges of the sweater all the way to her waist. Page shuddered.

''Sexual tension can make conversation tough. That's why the silences.''

His hands were inside the sweater now, circling her waist, and she felt soft wool sliding from her shoulders. She didn't try to stop it. ''You sound like an expert on all this.''

''Rational, that's all.'' He laced his fingers over her ribs and kissed the side of her neck, her nape, each shoulder blade. Only the fullness of her breasts stopped the sweater from falling completely.

Page arched her body. Rational. She didn't feel rational anymore, didn't want to.

"I'm not sorry for wanting you," Ian murmured against her ear. "But I want it to be a two-way thing. Is it?"

He rubbed his fingers back and forth beneath her breasts. Then he covered them gently, supporting their weight, touching his thumbs lightly to her nipples.

Page closed her eyes before she said, "I think it's what I want."

Ian turned her, eased her arms free of her sleeves and enfolded her, stroking, pressing his lips to a hundred small, erotic places. When he drew back they were both breathing hard.

Page loosened his tie and pulled it away, pushed his jacket from his shoulders and took off his shirt. And while she worked, Ian planted kisses designed to make her task more difficult...and more tantalizing. She smiled, evading him again and again until she finished.

She felt no awkwardness. They stood, inches apart, absorbing each other, touching. It was Page who broke first. She reached for him, pressed aching breasts against the provocative roughness of the dark hair on his chest.

Slowly, Ian moved them both backward, glancing behind him until he sat on one of the straight-backed chairs by the table with Page on his lap.

"You are something," he told her and brought his lips a whisper away from hers. "But I'm sure I'm not the first man to tell you that."

The statement-cum-question registered, nagged a

little, but did nothing to stop what was happening in Page's body. "What's that supposed to mean?" she asked and ran the tip of her tongue along his lower lip.

His eyes lost some focus. Their mouths came together, and the kiss was deep and searching. Ian spread his hands behind her head and neck, and she clung to him, her nerves and skin, every part of her, open, raw, close to pain with the longing for release.

Ian bent his head to catch a nipple carefully in his teeth. And with the contact of his tongue came a deeper longing. His hand was on her leg, smoothing from knee to thigh, then gripping tight where the lace edge of her panties made a ridge through her hose.

"I'd like to be with you this way a lot, sweetheart," Ian said, moving his mouth to her other breast. Insistent pressure between her legs shocked and excited her, and she shifted, pushing her fingers beneath his belt. The rough hair continued over his belly.

"Let's go upstairs." Ian's voice was thick. He put a knuckle beneath her chin and kissed the spot between her eyes. "My bed's been too empty lately."

She turned cold.

Ian slid her to her feet and stood, wrapping an arm around her.

His bed had been too empty lately. Surely he didn't mean that the way it sounded, but he must expect her to have been sexually active. He must think... It was too soon for this.

"Ian...oh, Ian, please listen to me a minute." She ducked from his arm and struggled to pull her sweater back into place. "You and I are..." She couldn't finish, couldn't look at him.

"What, Page?" The clear note in his voice surprised her, and she turned her face up to his. The passion was still there, the evidence of arousal, but no anger. He took several long breaths. "Tell me what's wrong."

She wanted to cry and laugh at the same time, and she wanted the uncontrollable shaking in her legs to stop. "I don't want to do this now. I've let everything go too far, and I shouldn't have. I'm sorry." His bed had only been empty lately? The implication was there and she hated it.

He pulled free strands of hair that had caught beneath her neckline and picked up his own shirt. "Are you going to refuse to see me again?" The question was matter-of-fact.

"Will you want to see me again?" she said. Nothing had ever been as difficult as this.

"You just won't accept how badly I want you." He gathered his jacket and tie, but didn't bother to button his shirt. "Yes, I'll want to see you again, and again. The only difference from here out is that there's no pretense, is there? Just now you were as ready to make love as I was. I'm not sure what changed your mind, but I've always believed a man or woman's body was private property, only shared if the person was sure the time was right. All I ask is that when you are sure the time's right you let me know."

He wasn't angry. Yes, the frustration was there in the tight lines on his face, but no anger. She had no experience with men who didn't get angry when what they wanted was denied.

Page had to go home, to think. Ian made no attempt to dissuade her.

In the car they kissed before they pulled away from Ian's house, and then once more when he stopped the car in front of Page's apartment.

He saw her to her door, but gripped her elbow before she could slip quickly inside. "Don't think I'm not going to try again."

Her heart resumed its heavy beat. "I think I hope you will." She was glad the dim light hid her blush.

"Then we'll have to do something about it sooner or later, won't we?"

"I suppose so."

"I know so, sweetheart."

IAN LEANED ACROSS HIS DESK and pressed a button on his conference phone. "Faber here," he said without enthusiasm.

"Ian, it's Martin. What the hell are you doing at the office on Sunday?"

"What the hell made you think of trying to reach me here?"

"Quit answering questions with questions. I couldn't get you at home, so I decided to take a shot there."

Ian spread a series of glossy photographs in a line across the desk. "What do you want, Martin? I'm busy." And he wanted to stay that way. He was making progress as he never did during the week with phones constantly ringing.

"You're going to make this tough on me, aren't you, friend?"

"Spit it out," Ian said. "We've got a big presentation coming up and I don't have time to chat." Tomorrow Daniel Max would make their final decision on an advertising firm. Ian felt confident, but he wanted to be well prepared.

"Okay," Martin said on a sigh. "I'm sorry."

Ian waited.

"Did you hear me, Ian? I'm sorry for the way we interrupted you and Page last night."

Now it was Ian's turn to sigh. He was trying not to think too much about last night, and so far he'd been fairly successful. "Forget it. It wasn't important. Now—"

Martin laughed. "I realize it wasn't important. She's not your type, but she is a beauty."

Slowly, aware of flexing muscles in his jaw, Ian put his face closer to the speaker. "What do you mean, not important?"

Again Martin laughed, nervously this time. "I was just repeating what you said. No offense intended."

"Of course not. But for the record, friend, Page Linstrom is a hell of a lot more my type than the Deirdres of this world. Page is one special woman, and I don't ever want to hear you suggest otherwise again."

"Ian, I—"

"Goodbye, Martin. See you around." He broke the connection.

Damn Martin Grantham. Damn all the others like him. Ian reached for a mug of cooling coffee and took a deep swallow, narrowing his eyes to look over the rim at the photos. They were good. Lots of color, fine wool...classic style. These lines, presented his way, would be a hit all over the country.

He set down the mug and lifted a photo of a woman with long, glossy brown hair. She wore a brilliant green tartan skirt with a green cableknit sweater and a soft woolen hat pulled low over her brow. Were her eyes brown or blue? He studied the photo more closely.

Page's eyes were so blue.

This wasn't working. His attention couldn't keep being divided this way. Page's eyes were blue, her hair was wonderful, so was her body...but she wasn't ready for the kind of relationship he wanted. He didn't dare push her too hard.

The model in the photo had brown eyes.

Disgusted with himself, Ian tossed the shot on top of the others. Was something different happening to him? His reaction to Martin's comments about Page still hung in his head. Did a man lose his cool that way over a woman for whom he felt nothing more than liking and desire?

He wasn't sure he was ready to face the answer.

IN FRONT OF PAGE on the kitchen table lay her business accounts. She made it a rule to keep up the books. It would be nice to have a professional take over some of this one day, but that was a long way off. Fortunately bookkeeping was one of her strong areas, but she couldn't concentrate today. Ian, the memory of the way he looked at her last night, the way he'd touched her, repeatedly made the columns of figures senseless. She wanted to hear his voice but wouldn't allow herself to call him.

Regardless of what had happened between them, their parting message to each other had been implicit: they would continue to meet. She'd have to do some thinking about how to handle all the possible ramifications of total involvement with Ian. How would she cope if, as seemed inevitable, they became lovers but only for a while?

The sound of the doorbell was an intrusion she didn't need. But people had been known to ignore visitors.

With Ian's business and a steady increase in Waldo's, together with several other new accounts—two generated by referrals from Ian—profits looked good. The mopeds she hoped to buy were beginning to be clear pictures in her mind, and decent operation quarters, and computerized dispatching.

The doorbell rang again.

Damn. She looked awful, and she wasn't going to waste time being polite to someone selling something she didn't want.

But whoever was out there wasn't going away.

Page stood up, resting her hands on the table. Her black velour sweats had holes in the knees and she looked down at furry slippers shaped like elephant feet.

So what. She didn't have to dress up for door-to-door salespeople.

Muttering, she scuffed down the hall and threw open the door. "Ye—"

"Page! You are home. May I come in?"

Rose Faber, swathed in glossy chinchilla, gave Page a dazzling smile as she swept into the apartment.

CHAPTER NINE

A WAFT OF SHALIMAR remained where Rose had passed. Page realized her mouth was open, closed it, and the front door.

"What an *interesting* little apartment," Rose was saying by the time Page followed her into the kitchen. "I've always thought Russian Hill was charming. When I was a little girl I had a friend who lived not far from here."

Not, Page bet, in a run-down apartment. "Really?"

"Yes." Rose slipped off black leather gloves, then her coat, to reveal a white suit Tanya would have described as a "smashing little number."

Page waited for Rose to say something more, like what she was doing here.

"I bet you wonder how I knew where you lived."

The thought hadn't come to her until now. "How did you know?" she asked.

Rose waggled a finger and tossed the chinchilla down as only someone who could afford one would. "I find out things I want to know." The words held no malice or threat, yet Page's stomach tightened. She glanced around the kitchen wishing she'd done her housekeeping stint and cleared away the papers, but most of all dressed in almost anything but what she had on. Had she even combed her hair?

"Well, Page. Come on, ask me how I found out. Intrigue isn't much fun if nobody cares about it."

Rose's cajoling tone began to grate. "How did you find out?" Page asked more tersely than she intended.

"Oh, you're cross because I didn't call first." Rose sat down. "Is it all right for me to come? I found out where you live, because Bob told me you were doing some work for Faber. I called shipping for the name of your firm and an address."

Why? was the first thought Page had. "You're welcome to come. It gives me the chance to thank you for having me to dinner. Somehow I don't seem to get to some of the things I should do. Like write thank-you notes."

"We loved having you." Rose looked around. "You must have a...shop, would you call it?"

"For the bikes and dispatching, I suppose you mean." Page propped a hip against the sink, trying not to visualize the way Rose must see her. "There's a garage at the back of the house. You know the way lots of these houses have them at the end of an alley? That's where my operations area is. That—" she indicated the table "—is my office, I'm afraid. Not very glamorous but the best I can do for now."

"Bob and I think what you've done is wonderful." Rose settled herself more comfortably. "It gives older people hope to see that there are still some youngsters with imagination and courage."

Page pushed at her hair. Rose made her sound like a child prodigy rather than one more struggling workaholic. "Thank you," she said, then remembered the importance of diplomacy. "I really appreciate the confidence Faber and Faber has shown in us. We'll prove we're worth the risk.''

''Yes,'' Rose said. Her smile became fixed. ''I'm sure you will. You know, you could be more to Ian than a business proposition.''

Page blushed and bristled in unison. ''I respect Ian as a businessman. I hope he's equally impressed with me.''

Rose's face set in a serious mold. ''Bob tells me that Ian considers you someone to be encouraged.''

Someone to be encouraged. Page was sure Rose meant well, but there was still that ring of patronage: the inventive little woman should be encouraged—provided she doesn't go too far....

Page longed to be blunt and ask Rose exactly why she'd come. ''Would you like some coffee or tea? Or there's some wine, I think.''

Rose flapped a dismissive hand. ''Tea if you have it. Preferably herbal, but anything if you don't.''

Page filled the kettle and put it on to heat. ''Let's go into the sitting room,'' she said. ''It's more comfortable.'' *Even if it is equally tatty.*

Installed in the sitting room, Rose loosened the buttons of her suit jacket. A matching silk shirt fell in soft pleats from neck to waist. ''Did you and Ian have a good time last night?''

Page's heart slipped away, and her stomach and everything else within her. ''Ian told you we went out?''

Rose's hesitation, the vague deepening of her color, fascinated Page. ''Well, no. Not exactly, that is. I kind of patched things together. Clemmie told me he'd asked for the number of Ruby's, then he wasn't at home. And, of course, Bob saw you in his office and found out about the arrangement for you to work for the firm. And believe it or not, my Bob has an eye for these things. He told me he thought Ian was really interested in you—personally I mean—and he was right, wasn't he?''

The heat in Page had little to do with Rose's words. While the woman talked, every second of last night's encounter replayed in living color. And again came Ian's promise: they'd have to do something about the way they felt sooner or later.

''Do you feel well, Page?''

''Of course.'' She nodded at Rose. ''Ian did take me to Ruby's last night. It was lovely.'' The straightforward approach would be easiest in the long run.

''Ruby's?'' Rose sighed. ''So romantic. He must really think a lot of you. And Bob and I think he has good taste.''

What exactly was this woman trying to accomplish? Page was convinced that Rose had a mission other than a polite, Sunday afternoon visit.

''You and Ian have known each other for some time now.''

Page slowly brought her concentration back to Rose. ''Several weeks,'' she said.

The kettle whistled and Page jumped up to assemble the best of her teacups and saucers. Fortunately her mother had taught her how to make tea correctly, and she warmed the pot with boiling water for a few moments. Even Rose's choice of Tanya's herbal tea, which Page detested, should taste better made this way.

She returned to the sitting room with a tray and

poured. ''I must admit I'm surprised to see you,'' she told Rose honestly. Looking down at her worn sweats she added, ''I would have changed if I'd known you were coming.''

''I know you would have,'' Rose said heartily. ''And that's the main reason I didn't call. I thought we should meet as we are. No artifice.''

Except the chinchilla and the smashing suit, Page thought, and immediately regretted her small-mindedness. What the woman wore was natural for her. If Rose Faber could reach out the hand of friendship, so could she.

Rose sipped Orange Pleasure tea with obvious approval and rested her head back on a blue armless chair that spilled stuffing from every seam. ''Your apartment is charming,'' she said, ''and Bob and I do so admire your inventiveness in business.''

Page went on alert. The woman had said the same thing in various ways several times now. ''Thank you,'' she said.

''You're going to be one of those women who become absolute powerhouses.''

''Powerhouses?''

''In their communities, dear. It's always the women with vision who turn into leaders.''

Page was becoming increasingly lost. ''I don't see myself as ever having time to become a community leader.'' She stopped herself from adding that there was nothing she wanted less.

Rose smiled comfortably. ''That'll change, you mark my words. There's nothing like a husband and children to put a different slant on everything a woman does. She stops caring so much about things she doesn't *have* to be bothered with anymore.''

''What sort of things?'' Page's grip on her saucer tightened.

''Oh, you know. Making money, or developing new friendships, all that stuff. Once there's a husband in the picture, his friends become yours and he takes on so many of the tiresome responsibilities we women were never cut out to handle.''

Page was smitten with a sense of déjà vu. Weren't these the messages she'd grown up with, only slightly differently phrased?

''I do think we've managed to pass on our values to Ian.'' Rose's expression was serene and distant now. ''Oh, he's had his little flings, but his head and heart are in the right place. He just has to find the right woman and he'll be the happiest man on earth.''

An aura of unreality descended about Page. Rose Faber looked like a society matron from a *Town and Country* article who'd wandered into the wrong room. She kept on talking, but intermittently Page heard words like home, family, settled, values, provide...

''Don't you think so, dear?'' Rose said, sitting forward.

Page had to respond. ''I...oh, I expect so.''

''Have you ever seen Ian with children?'' The query was crooned in Rose's luscious voice. ''You probably haven't had the opportunity. Lots of our friends have grandchildren, and if one of them is brought to visit us while Ian's over he just takes charge. I swear you'd think he'd been playing with babies and throwing balls to toddlers all his life. He has to be a natural, because of course he was an only child."

Beneath the chinchilla coat and mohair suit, Rose Faber had set out with the determined heart of a matchmaker. Page couldn't believe it, yet she couldn't deny the evidence. Ian was being presented to her as the perfect husband and father.

Rose sighed, evidently oblivious to the lengthy silences that greeted her little speeches. "Confidentially, Ian's admitted to me that he's ready to settle down and—this has to be strictly between you and me, Page—but he has hinted that he's becoming deeply attached to you. Isn't that lovely?" Her delighted laugh had a tinkling, girlish quality that set Page's teeth on edge.

"Really?" It was the best Page could do without telling the woman to stop meddling.

"Yes, yes. I can't tell you what it means to me to know that. And to his father. Ian's going to be one of those perfect fathers. Can't you just see him with his children?" Her eyes took on the appearance of one seeing a miraculous vision. "The woman who gets my Ian will be blessed. She'll never have to worry about another thing as long as she lives."

Page set down her cup, bowing her head to hide her face. She had to say something. "Ian's thirty-six, isn't he?" She didn't give Rose time to respond. "I'm surprised he hasn't, er, settled down before now if he's such a natural for the role."

"He's been waiting for that special person, Page. And until now she hasn't come into his life."

Page saw it all. The frustration Rose must have suffered watching her friends with their children tidily married and a batch of grandchildren tidily produced. And Ian was the odd man out, the one who hadn't slipped obediently into the expected pattern. For an instant she allowed Ian a little pity. Only for an instant. His mother was one smart lady. She'd categorized Ian's female companions to date and discovered some constants, the main one being that no woman had managed to get his wedding ring on their finger. But Rose, clever Rose, had sighted Page as something different and decided there was nothing to lose by closing in for the kill. First, much as she must abhor what Page did for a living, approval and admiration must be poured on to pave the way for what would follow: the carrot of an easy life dangled until the subject bit and held on.

Rose had made one fatal miscalculation… Page wasn't biting. What was supposed to sound to her like a dream was loaded with potential nightmare qualities, exactly the elements Page was determined to avoid.

Somehow she got through another half hour of Rose's "ode to Ian" without being rude, and when they parted it was on the note that Rose would look forward to their next meeting.

Page closed the door on her uninvited guest and tottered into her bedroom where she flopped, face down, onto the futon

She closed her eyes, determined to sleep before it was time to go back on duty.

Ian could be in on it.

Now she was getting punchy. She maneuvered herself beneath the comforter and started a relaxation exercise.

What if Ian was sick of his parents harping on the subject of marriage and children and he'd decided to find a suitable candidate? Perhaps he thought she was suitable because she turned him on—no question there—and he couldn't believe she'd be fool enough to turn down an opportunity for a leg up the social ladder and a cushy place in his family's bosom, his kitchen, his nursery…and his bed. And then—and this she mustn't forget—she'd get a chance to become civically prominent.

She groaned and pulled the pillow over her head. There was no choice. Cool the relationship at once.

Her nose itched, and then all of her skin. Her *teeth* itched. Damn it, why did she have to want the man so badly?

"PAGE, wake up."

Her triplets were crying. She'd run out of disposable diapers and the car wouldn't start. "Go 'way."

"Page!"

The babies were useless on bicycles. All her clients were complaining about late deliveries. Ian said if they had more babies it would be easier because then she'd have more riders.

The warm softness was snatched from her head and light hit her eyelids.

"Page, will you wake up, darn it. It's after five. You've got to go to work."

"What?" She squinted up into Tanya's face and felt her brain slowly clear. The images faded into fragments, then disappeared. "What!" She leaped up, staggering a little, and looked at her watch. "Oh, no. I'm going to be late."

"I'm glad I came home," Tanya said. "You were mumbling and tossing, but you would probably have slept until tomorrow. You don't get enough rest."

Page stripped off the sweat suit, preparing to deliver a broadside on Tanya's nerve to talk about insufficient rest. Then she glanced at her roommate and stopped rushing around the room. "You look... different." Tanya's eyes had their old glow.

Smirk was the only description for the expression on Tanya's face. "You know what they say, kid. Love is the key."

"Yuck," Page said, incredulous. "I think I'm going to be sick."

It had been several days since the incident of the bruises and Page had seen Tanya on a number of occasions since. Thinking back now, a subtle change had been evident each time.

"You're just jealous," Tanya said. "You need to be more of a romantic, like I am."

Page thought of Ian. Then she very deliberately tried not to think of him. "I take it this means your love life has straightened out?"

"You've got it."

"I'm glad." She smiled and gave Tanya an impulsive hug. "Any man who had a chance to be loved by you and didn't take it would be mad."

Hadn't Rose said something like that, only about Ian?

BUSINESS WAS ESPECIALLY BRISK that evening. And Waldo's mood lifted as the night wore on—to the point where he insisted on paying Page more for each drop. She arrived home exhausted but satisfied and was met by a ringing telephone.

She answered without thinking. If she had she'd have expected to hear Ian and she might have chosen not to talk to him.

"Hi, sweetheart," he said.

A little twist, part longing, part the remembrance of her decision to be strong, tightened her throat. "Hello, Ian."

"That took a long time. Don't you feel like talking?"

She wished she didn't. "I just got home. My brain's probably on overload."

"That's one of the things I wanted to talk to you about."

"My brain?"

"No, this nighttime working. You've got a lot more work in the day now, sweetheart. And you'll get more if you want it. But it's time you gave up this night nonsense."

Just like that. Time for her to give it up. Then it would be time for her to give up the rest because Mrs. Ian Faber could hardly ride bicycles all over San Francisco delivering intercompany messages and packages.

"Did you hear what I said?"

"Yes. I'm not giving up any part of my business, Ian. I appreciate the extra work you've generated for me. It's been enough for me to be able to start thinking about more employees."

"So why—"

"But I'm *not* giving up a thing. Growth is going

to be the deciding factor for me. The faster the better. I thought you understood that.''

She heard him sigh. ''I don't see how this one job can be worth what it does to your social life.''

At least he was honest about the real reason for his concern. How could he intensify his campaign if theirs was to remain a Saturday-night-only courtship? ''I'm satisfied with my social life.''

''Are you?'' He sounded hurt and Page felt regret.

''Maybe we've been concentrating too much on each other.'' The words were painful to say and she wished they weren't. ''You don't need me to give you permission, but why don't you see other people? We don't have any hold on each other.''

After a long time he said, ''I see.'' And the rest of the message came without saying—he'd thought he did have some hold on her.

''Ian, I'm sorry to be short, but this has been a tough night. Could we talk some more about this another time?''

''If that's what you'd prefer.''

''It is. I'll give you a call.''

IAN RESISTED THE TEMPTATION to smack the receiver down. Instead he replaced it carefully in its cradle.

She was backing off. Why? He hadn't imagined her reaction to him last night. Without knowing the reason for her drawing back, he still believed she'd wanted them to make love and that she hadn't stopped wanting it.

So why the complete turnoff?

He got up from the couch in the salon and poured a stiff Scotch on the rocks. All night he'd waited until he was pretty sure she'd be home, anticipating that she'd be pleased to hear his voice. And while he'd waited to talk to her he'd done some thinking. Without reaching any final conclusions, he'd identified a subtle change in his feelings for Page. He did like her, a lot, but he was beginning to want her on a deeper level. That scared him, but he was ready to go on and take a chance at whatever might lie ahead.

Pushing her to give up night riding had been a mistake. That must be the answer. He already knew she hated being told what to do. The urge to call her back and apologize came and went. She definitely hadn't wanted to continue the conversation.

With the drink in hand, he wandered into his bedroom. He didn't turn on the light and felt his way to a love seat by the window.

Over there somewhere—he looked in the direction of Russian Hill—Page was probably already in bed. His own bed held no appeal. He wasn't tired. His needs were for something other than sleep, and he gritted his teeth against his body's answering leap at the thought.

He closed his eyes, willing quiet inside, but saw Page as she'd looked, semi-naked, her mouth soft and kissed...and on her face an expression that mirrored the desire he'd felt, felt now.

The Scotch made his nostrils flare but he welcomed the surge of warmth in his veins.

"QUIET. ALL OF YOU!" Page yelled over a lunchtime argument raging in the garage. "I said, be quiet."

"Tone it down, guys," the Zipper said, waving his

arms like a baseball umpire signaling a successful steal. "The boss is trying to say something."

Gradually the din ebbed.

"Thank you," Page said. "Can we take this from the top?"

"I've had it," Ken said immediately and dropped to sit on the floor.

Page ignored him. For days business had been conducted with no interference from the phantom riders. But she'd been contacted midway through her morning ride with a request that she call Lilian. It appeared the truce was over and now she really had trouble.

"I just came from the hospital." Total silence let her know she finally had full attention. "Perkins has a mild concussion and a broken ankle, but he's going to be fine. They wouldn't let me ask him any questions, but I understand you know what happened, Buzz. Describe the guy and the bike involved, please."

Buzz popped a huge gum bubble and plastered her body to a wall. Between her hands she snapped a length of gold ribbon.

"Buzz. I'm waiting."

"I didn't see the guy."

Page frowned. "But the message I got said you witnessed the, er, accident."

Lilian came forward. Jemima had another cold and clung to the hem of her mother's sweater. "Buzz didn't see the guy, but she did see Perkins crash. He went up on a curb, hit a bike rack and did a forward somersault."

"He made a mistake, then," said Page. "Or someone got in his way. It was just an accident."

"The hell it was!"

At Ken's roar, Jemima started to cry, and the Zipper swept her into his arms. "Keep it down, Ken," he said, his eyes narrowed. "You're upsetting the kid."

Page waved for silence. "Ken," she said, "what point are you making?"

"The police took the bike away before Buzz could get a real good look at it, but she reckons the brake cable was yanked out." He rested his forehead on his arms as if he'd delivered final sentence.

"And what do the police say?" Hope flickered in Page. If the police were suspicious of foul play they might do something.

Buzz paced to the door and back. "They say what they always say. We're careless. We don't maintain the equipment. The bike was just plain mangled from the crash. In other words, nothing. But I know someone pulled that cable. It didn't look right."

"She could have something," the Zipper said quietly. "I'm not panicking, but I do think we'd better get into the habit of doing better checks."

Page nodded. "Okay. But you're gone, huh, Ken? You want out?"

"I'm thinking about it. Nothing's worth dying for."

Cold sweat shot out on Page's back. "Don't talk that way."

"You might not be so willing to brush it aside if someone tried to break your body permanently," Ken persisted. "And that's something else that's off about all this. Why are you the only one who hasn't been hit?"

"I don't know." Page wished she did. She certainly thought enough about it, and couldn't come up with a solution that made sense.

Jemima cried again, and the Zipper nuzzled her face into his neck. "Nobody's going to die," he said. "We're just going to work together—look out for each other."

"With one less rider," Ken commented, raising his eyes to Page's face. "How do you handle that one, boss lady?"

"Perkins won't be out for good," she said. "And I was going to hire some more people anyway. This just means I'll do it sooner." She glanced at Buzz who was still making cracking noises with the metallic ribbon. "I wish you wouldn't do that, Buzz. You're making me more nervous than I already am."

Buzz tossed the ribbon down, and Page noticed that it looked like one Tanya had worn a few times. She wondered where Buzz had found it, but Ken's voice boomed out again before she could ask.

Another half hour of bickering, and Page was back on the road. Lilian was contacting employment agencies and placing ads for new riders. With luck they'd be back to full complement, plus at least one, within a day or two.

At five she wheeled the Schwinn into the garage ready to take her break before going to work for Waldo.

Instead of the usual gaggle that heralded the end of the day, she was met by Lilian and the Zipper. Jemima was curled up on a small cot Page hadn't seen before.

"Page," the Zipper said. "You'd better sit down."

She closed her eyes. "Not more problems."

Lilian put an arm awkwardly around Page's shoulders. "Nothing we can't work out if we stick together."

Her head ached, and her shoulders. Her legs felt like lead. "Just get it out." She checked an impulse to say she couldn't take any more. Giving up was a luxury she couldn't afford.

"Buzz had an accident and Ken quit."

CHAPTER TEN

IF NOTHING ELSE, Chinatown was cheerful. Even in sheeting rain, the lights and fragrant smells were irresistible. Almost.

Page headed along Frank Street. She was delivering to a private address on Joice.

Her hair clung to her neck, and from time to time she wiped water from her eyes and face. This would stand out as the worst Wednesday of her life.

She made the drop at an apartment over a dingy variety store on Joice and contacted Waldo on her radio. "Move it," he said. "We're really cooking."

Without bothering to respond, she switched off and started to retrace her path. Coming out of Joice she swished through a deep puddle, blades of water shooting on either side of her bike.

She didn't sight the other rider until the spokes of his wheels glittered in a streetlight. Swathed in hooded oilskins, his head down, he didn't see her. Page slammed on the brakes, braced for collision and went into a skid.

"Watch out!" He wouldn't be able to hear her scream over the street noise.

Another cyclist did hear. He came fast from her left, miraculously passing inches in front of Page. "Idiot," he yelled.

Page came to a stop, the bike slewed, but her feet hit the ground firmly and held. Her heart beat in giant erratic bounds while she watched the irate interceptor, still shouting, ride out of sight.

Breathing deeply through her mouth to quiet her nerves, she scrubbed at her eyes and turned to deal with the other cyclist.

He'd gone. She fought down waves of sickness. Earlier Ken had asked why she hadn't been the victim of an attack. Well, she had now, or almost, she was sure of it.

She pushed off again and rode more slowly. If she could, she'd quit for the night. All her reflexes felt sluggish. She turned her thoughts to Buzz.

Buzz wasn't in the hospital, but she had sprained both wrists. When Page talked to her, the girl's determination to get back to work as soon as possible had come as a surprise. Rather than thinking of giving up, Buzz wasn't about to be beaten by a couple of "bum wrists." But there had been that same story. Failed brakes. And this time Buzz had a pretty watertight theory. She'd gone into an office to make a delivery. Right before that she'd used her brakes and they were fine. Afterward, on a downhill flight, they were gone. Buzz's contention was that someone had watched until he had a minute or two, when Buzz was away from her bike, to pull the cable loose but not completely free. It would look okay, but wouldn't hold when used.

Why was this happening? Where was the sense in victimizing a little outfit that was no real threat to anyone?

Farther down the street a group of people staggered

from a lighted doorway onto the sidewalk. Page kept an eye on them as she approached. As so often happened, one man walked into the street without looking. She heard his loud laughter. ''Rider on your left,'' she called, but still had to swerve to the opposite side of the road to avoid him.

The rain was even heavier. On nights like this, it wasn't too hard to agree with Ian's opinion of this facet of her business.

He hadn't called on Monday night, but on Tuesday she'd picked up the phone just as she'd been about to get into bed. ''How about getting together Saturday night?'' he'd asked. ''I don't have any fantastic plans yet, but I'll come up with something.''

She'd refused, and he hadn't tried to persuade her to change her mind. That shouldn't have rankled, but it did. She muttered under her breath, berating herself for being indecisive. If she'd decided the man was a complication she couldn't handle, she'd better find a way to stop mooning over him.

Maybe he'd call again tonight.

''Page Linstrom, wise up,'' she said aloud.

She started uphill again, her thighs and calves straining. With the slick streets came added tension, and she checked from side to side constantly, expecting trouble any moment. *Relax,* she told herself. *Be alert but loosen up.*

Ahead a traffic light turned bleary red. She was moving slowly, too slowly. When she returned to the deli, Waldo was likely to have one of his yelling attacks, and she wasn't sure she wouldn't yell right back.

At the junction, beneath the signal, she stopped and

rested a foot on the pavement. She rarely got cold, but she was chilled now. Rain gear was something she avoided, always believing she should travel with as little extra clothing as possible holding her back. A hot shower as soon as she got home usually made her feel fine—though tonight she wasn't sure she wouldn't need a lot more than a shower to warm her.

Something shimmered to her right. The light turned green and she leaned on the pedals, pushing while she checked the side street she passed. Was the glimpse of metallic sheen caused by reflection on a wet blue slicker?

She shook her head, brushing again at her eyes. For an instant she'd got the impression of a cyclist holding himself and his machine close to the wall, his head hooded and held as out of sight as he could manage. Hiding? Watching?

Riding faster, she ducked her own head and pumped hard. Now she wasn't only cold and depressed, she was jumpy. The appearance of a bus helped. And a taxi. Gradually the foreboding dwindled, and she reached the deli.

Waldo hadn't been kidding when he said things were cooking. She set out from his shop again, this time carrying eight small orders in her basket and three more in a knapsack on her back. Her destination was the Nob Hill area. No long distances this time, and for that she was grateful.

While she pedaled, she mulled over what had happened and was in the process of happening to Pedal Pushers now. Lilian already had three possible riders lined up for interviews early the next morning. With luck they'd scrape through somehow. The main thing was to find replacements who knew the city.

Page blessed her good fortune that she made the first eight deliveries in record time. Switching and doubling back on small streets between Pine and Bush, she accomplished the transactions quickly and smoothly.

As she headed for an address close to Union Square, she recalled the best news of the day. The Zipper, with sweetly funny shyness, had told Page that he and Lilian had decided to "give it a try." Remembering her own serious suggestion that they not go into a relationship thinking it might not be permanent brought a smile to Page's lips. The picture of Lilian and the Zipper, Jemima in his arms, protesting that they *did* intend to be together permanently made the rain and cold lose their bite.

Another red light impeded her progress. Page swerved onto the sidewalk and sped into a small alley that would take her where she wanted to go as fast as the route by the main street.

A small lamp attached to a wall at the far end of the alley made a misty arch. She leaned down, pulling a Velcro tab on her shoe more snugly across her foot. Then she bent the other way to repeat the adjustment.

Silver threads. Spokes. Her forward thrust carried her on while she strained to see.

Page felt an upward clawing in her stomach. Someone was leaning against the wall, almost totally obscured except for that brief flash from the spokes of his bicycle wheels.

She applied the brakes. There was time to turn around. There had to be.

No time. She was almost beside him now. And the space was too narrow.

Speed was her only chance. Why had she slowed? What did he want—to kill her, rape her?

Page opened her mouth to scream. At the same time she opened up, pummeling the pedals, driving with legs that had no feeling.

She heard what he did before she identified what it was.

Metal, shrieking as it buckled, the acrid smell of jammed rubber. He was ramming something rigid into her wheel.

Sheen on blue oilskins. Low laugh.

Her feet stayed with the pedals. Then she hit, pitching, flying. The top of her helmet cracked on cobbles before the bike piled on top of her.

All the air went out of the night.

Page closed her eyes, scraped her hands beneath her to press her aching belly.

The stones were wet against her face.

CHAPTER ELEVEN

"TELL THEM TO let me out of here," Page said.

"You're going to have to be patient. I'll get them to spring you when they're sure you're as okay as you think you are." Tanya sat beside her in a small hospital room. Curtains were drawn around the bed to give some privacy. Another patient lay only a couple of feet away.

Page tossed, drawing up her knees and turning on her side. "I'm bruised. My ribs hurt. But that's it, I tell you. I don't have time to lie here, Tanya. Make them understand that."

"They want to make sure you don't have any internal injuries. Please stay calm. If they see you're all upset they may keep you even longer."

Page glared and covered her eyes with the back of a hand. She did hurt all over. But she didn't need to be here. "They had all night to watch me. It's already eleven in the morning. I've got—"

"I know, I know. Did the police talk to you?"

"Twice. In the emergency room and about an hour before you got here."

"What did they say?"

She looked at Tanya again. "They asked bunches of questions and said they'd examined my bike. And yes, they agree that somebody probably jammed a crowbar or something into my wheel, then took off. But I needn't expect the guy to be found.''

''Well, I guess that makes sense.'' Tanya played with the edge of a sheet. ''How would you find someone like that in a city this big?''

''You sound like the cops,'' Page commented, exasperated. ''A random attack. Probably never be repeated. And they weren't even interested in the fact that three of us have had crashes in two days. They think mine was probably something isolated and the other two were accidents. Accidents! Two bikes belonging to riders from the same firm lose brakes and it's an accident?''

''Did you argue about that?'' Tanya asked.

''What do you think? Then they got all high-handed and talked about bicycle wars like we were a bunch of Hell's Angels. I tell you, Tanya, I just want out of here so I can get my business back on the road while I still *have* a business.''

The squish of soft-soled shoes interrupted whatever Tanya might have said. ''How are we doing?'' The curtain swung aside and a nurse, thermometer in hand, approached Page.

''Nurse, I want—''

The thermometer was slipped beneath her tongue and a bony thumb applied beneath the chin. Her teeth snapped against glass. Page breathed heavily through her nose and caught Tanya's grin before it could be smothered.

''You're very popular, Ms. Linstrom,'' the tall, thin nurse said. Her name tag read S. Ribbenstraat. ''You have two other visitors waiting outside, and there've been several telephone inquiries.''

Once the thermometer was removed Page scooted up, shoving at her pillows and straightening the sheets. She'd show them how alert and well she felt and they'd be forced to release her. A plain white hospital gown did nothing for the image but she couldn't help that.

"We allow no more than two visitors at a time." S. Ribbenstraat spoke to Tanya. "Since the other two people are together, perhaps you'd like to change places with them for a while."

Page cast a glance toward an acoustical-tiled ceiling. "Anyone would think I was in critical condition."

"I know." Nurse Ribbenstraat sounded human enough for Page to smile at her. "Rules, rules and more rules. Some hospitals allow visitors to run in and out all the time, but we're not one of them, I'm afraid."

"I'd better go home," Tanya said. "Would you like me to call your folks?"

"No." Page sounded too emphatic. "No," she repeated more gently. "I talked to them a few days ago and they think everything's great with me. I'd rather keep it that way." All they'd do, Page thought, was repeat their opinion that a woman had no place trying to run a business alone in a big city.

"If you're sure," Tanya said. "Call me as soon as you can leave. Okay?"

When Page nodded, Tanya leaned over to peck her cheek, then slid through the gap in the curtains, leaning back once to waggle her fingers.

Page smoothed her hair. She had been able to comb it early this morning and wash her face. Any other effort at beautification would have been a waste of time. The skin beneath her left eye was discolored, and her cheek was covered in scratches and little purple dents from grit.

"Page?"

Her mouth dropped open and her eyes widened. She tried to reverse her reaction, but knew it was too late. Lilian, dressed in a white blouse, gray woolen skirt and cardigan, came into the curtained enclosure. She wore hose and plain black pumps, and her hair was restrained by twin tortoiseshell combs.

"Um...Lilian," Page managed when she found her voice. "How lovely of you to come to see me." In the eighteen months Lilian had worked for Page, she'd never appeared in anything other than jeans and sweatshirt, with tattered tennis shoes on her feet and her curly hair untamed.

"James, jr. is outside. He wanted me to ask if he could come in, too." Lilian bent closer. "He's trying to be cool, but I think he's scared by all this."

"He's not the only one," Page muttered. "Bring him in. And, Lilian, you look wonderful, but you didn't have to dress up for me."

Lilian's expression clearly suggested pity. "My mother brought us all up to wear our best to the doctor's. I don't remember much of what she used to say, but that makes sense."

Page didn't bother to ask why.

A couple of minutes later James preceded Lilian to the bedside. He stared hard at Page's face. "SOB," he said and blushed. "I mean, well...yeah, that's what I mean. Here." He dropped a bunch of brown chrysanthemums wrapped in cellophane on her stomach. "I don't like these much, but the grocery store didn't have anything else."

"Thank you, James." She was holding back, trying to be polite when she really wanted to bombard them, particularly Lilian, with questions.

"Sit down," she offered. "There're two chairs for the two visitors they allow at a time in here."

Lilian sat. James remained standing.

"I checked every bike in the place this morning," he said, and his grimy nails proved it. "All the new guys' machines, too. There isn't a screw out of place."

New guys?

"James is right," Lilian said, sliding forward on the chair. "We know the equipment is tip-top. And you'd be proud of our James. He gave everyone a lesson in spot checks. No rider leaves a drop location without making sure his machine is the way he left it."

Page held up a hand. Excitement swelled through her veins, but she had to take things slowly. "New guys? Did we get some more people already?"

Lilian laughed, shaking her head. "Gee, I'm sorry. The Zipper says when I talk I always start at the end and work back. There were three messages on the machine this morning. Two from employment agencies and one from a guy the Zipper spoke to at the Hotel Utah." She paused and clasped her hands in her lap. "We called the hospital and they said no visitors before nine, so we figured we'd go ahead and interview and try to get some riders on the road. Was that okay, Page?"

She wanted to jump from the bed. "Okay? Of course it's okay. You interviewed?"

"Yes."

"And you found a couple of people?"

"Five." Lilian flinched as if expecting a verbal blow.

James came a step closer, his face flushed. "They're all okay, Page. Honest. I was there, and the Zipper and Lilian grilled them like in one of those TV hearings. By eight-thirty they were all on the road. The Zipper's covering the radio while we're visiting you. He'll come later if you're still here."

"I don't intend to be— Ouch!" A pain shot between her ribs and she pressed a forearm to her side.

Lilian leaped to her feet. "What is it? Should I get the nurse?"

"No," Page whispered urgently. "They'll lock me away if I can't convince them there's nothing wrong with me."

"But there is," James said in his mature voice. "You've got to take it easy or you won't get better so fast."

Page wrinkled her nose at him. "Thanks, doctor."

"Page, James is right. We can keep going. You've got everything so well in place that it's a breeze. Or it is now that we've got new people. And Buzz called this morning, too. She says another week and she'll be ready to go again."

"Let's hope we'll have enough business to need this new army," Page said, not completely joking.

"We will," Lilian assured her. "You talked about someone to take on more night deliveries—and then there's that idea you had for expanding to Sausalito.

We can handle it all. Wait and see. Another year and we'll be one of the biggest in town. I couldn't pass up any of those guys—there's a woman, mouthy but wise. I took them all because I know you're gonna need 'em.''

Page couldn't help grinning. ''Maybe we will. I sure hope so.... James! Why aren't you in school?''

He backed away. ''I'm going now. Lilian called the school and said I had an appointment at the hospital.'' They all laughed.

An hour later Page was less euphoric than she had been when Lilian and James left. Professionally things looked rosy, but a brief visit from a doctor had punctured her bubble enough to cause a slow leak of enthusiasm. Her ribs were severely bruised, and there was a trace of bleeding from a kidney. She wouldn't be released for at least another two days, and definitely not until the doctor was satisfied there was no significant renal damage.

Nurse Ribbenstraat popped her head around the curtain, a sympathetic gleam in her eye. ''The doctor told me about your urinalysis. Don't let it get you down. It's very common after the kind of fall you had, and by tomorrow your tests will probably be clear.''

Page wasn't encouraged.

''There's a man here to see you. If you're too tired, I'll ask him to come back later.''

Ian, Page thought. Then a cold place came into her heart. Ian wouldn't even know what had happened, and after the cool way she'd treated him lately he wasn't likely to come here.

''Shall I tell him you're tired?''

Page sighed. "No. I'll see him." It was probably the Zipper, and if anyone could cheer her up it was good old Zip.

Instead of the Zipper, Waldo Sands strode in, deposited a showy white azalea on her bedside table and pulled a chair close beside her. "You look like hell." He eyed her critically, peering at her face, lifting a hand to examine the scraped palm.

Page pulled the sheet up to her chin. "How did you know I was here?" As soon as she asked she knew it was a foolish question.

"When you didn't come back in or radio, I tried to reach you. Then customers started calling on orders that hadn't been delivered, so I got in touch with Tanya and she'd already been contacted by the police. You were lucky the next guy through that alley wasn't a wino with empty pockets."

Good old Waldo. Always the pragmatist. "It was a couple and they were great."

"I'm sure they were. Is your bike a total write-off?"

"From the way it sounds. My people will make sure I have the equipment I need by the time I'm ready to go. Which reminds me, Waldo. My knapsack's in the closet over there. I don't know what's in the deliveries, but something might be salvageable." She paused, remembering something else. "The envelopes. Oh, Waldo, I forgot about the money. I bet that guy took it."

He grimaced. "Don't give it another thought. How long will you be here?"

His nonchalance over the money surprised her. But then, Waldo Sands didn't need to worry about funds the way she did. "I'll have to stay at least a day or so. And I think they're leading up to saying I've got to lie low for a little while after that." She prayed he wouldn't say he couldn't keep the work available for her.

"Looking at you, I'm not surprised." He hitched at the knees of his pants and crossed his legs. His suit was of fine tan wool, his silk shirt the palest blue, his tie burgundy. The deli business must be booming, Page thought.

Waldo smoothed a manicured thumbnail as if deep in thought. "I feel badly about this."

Before she could regroup from surprise, Page's brows shot up. "You don't have to. Danger goes with the job." And she thought of Ian.

"You were working for me," Waldo said. "I've always been very pleased with your performance, and as soon as you're ready I want you back. I'm sure you don't have medical coverage, so I've arranged for all your bills to be sent to me."

Gratitude, and guilt for having misjudged him, sent tears brimming into her eyes. "Waldo, I—"

"You're grateful. Yes, I know. But as you'll already have worked out, I'm a selfish man and I don't let useful things go easily. You've been very good for me. Like I told you recently, if you want to put another rider on at some time I think we could expand our little night trips. That is—" he hesitated "—that is, if you haven't decided against continuing."

"No, I haven't." Page was emphatic. She held out a hand and he shook it. "It may take a week, two at the most, but then I'll be back at it. And, Waldo, thanks a million for thinking of the medical bills. I'll repay every dime, I promise. That'll take time, too, but you'll get it back."

He stood up. "We'll talk about it another time. Get well and get back to work."

At the door he stopped and turned. "Where did you say the knapsack was?"

She pointed to a narrow closet, and he removed the red pack. "We had some disappointed customers last night," he commented, wrinkling his nose at the crushed box he held up. The next thing he held up was a pile of payment envelopes. "Voilà, my dear. One less thing for you to worry about." He smiled and made for the door again.

He was wrong, Page thought. Those envelopes were one more thing to worry about. At least if they'd been missing, she could have considered theft as a possible motive for the attack.

The day crept by, punctuated by the delivery of little paper cups containing pills and regular checks of her vital signs. Rather than easing, the pain in her ribs got worse, and she learned this was to be expected, but that within a day or so it would be better. She was grateful no bones had been broken.

She slept for a while in the afternoon and later enjoyed a brief, lighthearted visit from the Zipper, who arrived in time to make horrified faces at her dinner.

Then the long evening set in. Earlier in the day the woman in the next bed had gone home, and Page was relieved to have some solitude.

She lost track of time. The lights in her room were turned off, and she lay watching figures pass outside her door. Occasionally a nurse came in to peer at her, but Page kept her eyes closed and feigned sleep.

The sound of the door clicking shut startled her out of a doze.

A faint and eerie glow from the window washed the room, silhouetting the tall figure of a man.

Page opened her mouth to scream, sat up and thrust her feet from the bed.

"Be quiet." Ian's voice, different again than she'd heard it before, but definitely his. He put a hand over her mouth as he spoke.

Page moaned. She hurt all over, and where his hand rested the skin felt raw.

"They wouldn't let me in here," he whispered. "Some mouthy bat said it was too late. I had to wait in a stairwell till I could sneak past."

She wanted to lie down.

"If I take my hand away you won't scream?"

She shook her head and sucked in a breath.

"I called when I thought you'd be home from work and your roommate answered. She told me what happened. Damn it, Page, why didn't you have someone get in touch with me?"

The pain in her side was intense now, and she couldn't turn to lie down.

"Say something, will you? Why didn't you tell me?"

"Ian," she murmured. "Help me, please."

"Oh, my God." He loomed over her. "What is it? What's happened to you?"

"Nothing. My ribs, that's all. I can't lift my legs to lie down. I want to lie down."

She heard him fumble and the lamp above the bed came on. "Oh, no. Look at you. I knew something like this would happen. Damn it all, why didn't you listen to me?''

''I hurt.'' She doubled over, close to tears.

''Sweetheart, I... Shall I lift you?'' He sounded suddenly frightened.

Without waiting for an answer, he picked her up gently and placed her on her back. He was sliding her legs beneath the covers when the door opened and the overhead lights glared.

''What is going on in here? Ms. Linstrom, do you know this man?''

''Yes—''

''You must leave at once, sir. Our patients are sleeping.''

Ian faced the small, wiry nurse who stood, hands on hips, in the middle of the room. ''This patient isn't sleeping.''

''We have rules—''

''This is my, um, fiancée. I just got back into town and found out she'd had an accident. We need to be alone, if you don't mind.''

Page watched the woman's face and felt closer to laughter than she had in days. Ian had audacity, she'd give him that.

The nurse drew up to her full, short height. ''That's all very well, sir. But this is irregular and I can't allow you to stay.''

''Oh, nurse.'' Ian sank onto a chair and rubbed a hand over his hair until it stood endearingly on end. ''If you only knew what a shock this has been. I'm sure you understand what I mean. I can tell a sensitive woman when I meet one. Would it be so bad if you pretended I wasn't here for half an hour or so, just until I can be sure Page is all right? Then I promise I'll go without another word.'' He smiled and the effect on the woman was predictable.

''Well...yes, I suppose that would be all right. But only half an hour, mind you. I'll be back to check.''

The instant the door closed again, Ian stood over Page again and she stopped smiling.

''I repeat, why didn't you let me know about this?''

''I—''

''No.'' He gestured dismissively. ''You don't have to try to explain. We both know the reason, don't we? You didn't want to admit that I've been right all along. A woman has no place in the business you're in. And I don't only mean at night.''

Just like that. Page glared into his dark eyes. She'd learned the hazards of speaking first and thinking later. ''Ian,'' she said very quietly, ''your little manipulation with the nurse was amusing. Obviously you've had a lot of experience at putting women in their places. Don't try it with me.''

He stuffed his hands into the pockets of his jeans and after a moment returned to the chair. Several times he said, ''mmm,'' chewing on his lower lip while he thought.

Formulating the next offensive, Page decided. Then, with something close to anger, she acknowledged that he did really care for her and that she wanted him to, but not on his terms..

''What are your injuries?'' He was curt, abrasive.

''Bruised ribs and a few scratches. I'll survive.''

''How about the next time?''

''There won't be a next time.''

He pushed his hips to the edge of the chair, stretching out his legs. His glare was aimed at his shoes. "You aren't thinking straight. Just because you're the product of an overbearing father, you feel you have to prove something by finding the hardest thing you can do."

Page snorted, disbelieving. "Can you hear yourself? Overbearing father? Boy, you could give lessons in that department. And you don't have any right. I didn't look for something hard. I looked for something challenging, which I might be able to get going without a lot of capital. Not having a bundle of money waiting like a magic carpet for you to ride on is something you wouldn't understand."

"Page—"

"Please. You've said your piece. You always do, no matter what anyone else feels. You're so used to being in charge you think you can take over wherever you are. Watch my lips, Ian. You have no say in what I do."

He covered his mouth and the hard light in his eyes turned anxious. "I know I don't, but I still wish you'd get out of this."

"You aren't listening." She sat up and winced. "This isn't a situation you can control. I have a living to make and this is how I intend to do it. Also, there are people who depend on me for their livelihood."

"Who, apart from you?"

Her patience snapped. "I have a staff of people who rely on the jobs they have with me. This accident is a setback, but that's all. As soon as I possibly can I'll be riding again. I'm not your mother, Ian. I don't need a man to make me feel whole. I don't want to get my kicks from telling a man how wonderful he is. Please, would you leave?''

He shot to his feet. Rage didn't suit him, and the vibes he sent out made Page sink low in her bed. ''Who do I think I am? I think I'm someone who cares about you, you idiot. And I think I'm someone you care about—a lot. We've already established that, and I don't change my mind easily. And what the hell's the stuff about my mother and not needing a man supposed to mean?''

''Nothing.'' Despite Rose's interference, Page liked the woman. She didn't intend to come between mother and son.

''Don't give me that.'' Ian bent over the bed until his face was inches from hers. ''You made a statement and I deserve an explanation.''

Page thought as fast as she could with the clean scent of his breath on her cheek...and his mouth moving much too close to hers. ''All I meant was that I make decisions and act on them based on my background and experience. So do you. Your mother is happy being a support system for your father and nothing more. I think that's great for her because she's happy that way. But it's not fine for me.''

''I see.'' The twitching in his cheek betrayed the effort restraint was costing him. ''Well, I haven't said I expect you to become a doormat for me, only that I don't like what you do. And I'm never going to change my mind about that.''

Page closed her eyes, visualizing the loss of Faber's business.

A big hand, brushing back her hair, didn't relieve

the anxiety, but it did touch something wanting in her heart.

"Is it so wrong for me to worry about you?" he said.

"It's flattering." There must be no backing down. "I'm very grateful for your friendship."

He withdrew his hand. The hardness was back in every line of his face. "You're welcome. And I suppose I have to respect your right to choose what's most important to you."

"Thank you."

Ian didn't look at her again. "I was a fool to hope you might feel the same way I did. And I really did think you might."

"And how was that?"

He spread his hands in the air. "Like we could have a chance at something worthwhile together."

"As in my becoming more important than a means to keep your bed warm."

"That was a rotten thing to say."

"I..." He was right, she thought. "Ian, I didn't mean—"

"Drop it," he said, and strode from the room.

How was she supposed to feel? Did he really think he was being fair? "Choose what's most important," he'd said, as if there could be no middle ground, no making room in her life for both him and her business.

Page pulled the sheet over her head. The overhead light was still on, and the cotton was luminous.

Ian had behaved as if there'd been some unspoken commitment between them. How did a woman deal with a thing like this? With wanting it all, the man *and* her independence.

"I'M FRUSTRATED, LILIAN. Do you blame me?"

Lilian made a sympathetic noise and set a cup of tea on the table beside Page's futon.

"How long have I been off work?"

"Only ten days. And you are working. Have some of this." Lilian pushed the cup closer.

"Paperwork is all I've done," Page grumbled, "and I get tired too easily. I want to get up to full steam—now."

"Give yourself a few more days," Lilian said in what Page thought of as her sickroom voice, low and croaky. "I've got to get back to the garage. Go through the stuff I brought up, and I'll be back later."

Left alone, Page looked at the pile of papers awaiting her and closed her eyes. She didn't feel like juggling numbers this morning.

The sound of the front door opening brought her eyes wide open again, and she sat up. Lilian must have forgotten to tell her something. Maybe there was a problem. Things had been going smoothly for Pedal Pushers recently, almost too smoothly, and she couldn't get rid of the premonition that peace wouldn't last.

Someone tapped on her bedroom door.

"Come in." She lay on top of the comforter in her favorite black sweats and elephant slippers, but she wasn't concerned. The only people who came to see her were used to her wardrobe.

"Are you decent?" Ian popped his head into the room and Page's blood left her veins.

"I'm always decent." Decent, but close to cardiac arrest at this moment. "Why don't you go into the sitting room. I'll be right out." When she'd recovered some composure and found something respectable to wear.

Undeterred, he came in, glanced around and, finding no chair that wasn't occupied with things Page didn't want to think about, sat cross-legged on the floor beside her. "Lilian let me in. She said you should be kept quiet because you're still recuperating."

He spoke as if there hadn't been a ten-day silence between them.

"I'm not an invalid," Page said. There was no elegant way to get up. "Another week and I'll be back to full output."

He smiled with the usual effect. "You sound like a generator."

She smiled back. The infuriating prickling came in her eyes. He was so wonderful to look at...and to be with. When he wasn't ordering her about. She tried to harden her heart. No doubt he'd be issuing those orders again any minute.

"I like your elephant feet," he said. "They have a certain...panache? No, that's not right. They give an impression of authority."

She sniffed. "That's what I think. I've considered having sneakers or cycling shoes made in the same style. Should impress the customers, don't you think?"

He bent forward. "Anything you do impresses me. I've spent the last nine days wishing it wasn't true. A couple of times I thought I might be getting close to persuading myself, but it won't work. I've got to have you in my life, Page.''

The top of his head was within reach, and she ruffled his hair until he looked up. ''How is it ever going to work out with you and me?'' she asked him. ''I don't want to sound selfish, but I'm afraid of getting hurt. Even now it's bad when you're not around. But at least we're still at a point where we can get out without being too emotional. If we keep going, it may not be that easy—not for me at least.''

''We're not going to hurt each other.''

''How can you be so sure?''

''I just am, that's all. And I'm sorry about the way I came on at the hospital,'' Ian said. ''That was unforgivable, and I shouldn't have waited this long to apologize.''

Sorry, but had he changed his mind about anything? ''When you're a strong person it's hard to back down,'' Page said. ''We're both strong. Have you thought about what that means?''

''That life with you will never be dull.''

Page crossed her arms. He was so positive, and he automatically spoke as if their future lay together. She wasn't sure she was ready to believe that. Most of all she wanted the confusion to go away.

''Does your face still hurt?''

''No.'' A greenish tinge remained below her eye, but her cheek had healed completely.

''How about your ribs?''

''I'm not hurdling yet, but as long as I don't do anything too wild they feel fine.''

He got to one knee and put a hand on each side of

her on the mattress. "Then I'm going to kiss you. Very gently. Nothing wild—okay?"

Without waiting for permission, he settled his mouth on hers, and the sweetness of him made Page feel formless, a malleable thing beneath the persistent pressure, the parting of her lips.

He pulled back a little before he kissed her again more urgently, then withdrew altogether. When she opened her eyes he was sitting beside her on the futon, and there was no mistaking the tense set of passion in his face.

"I brought you something." His laugh was unconvincing. "Take a quick look and tell me what you think."

From the envelope he gave her, Page took a stack of photos. White beaches, palm trees, lush tropical settings and what looked like a small, white plantation house on a bluff overhanging a turquoise ocean.

"I think they're beautiful. I didn't know you were into photography."

"You don't know everything about me yet. But we'll try to take care of that. Do you like the setting in the pictures?"

"Fantastic," Page told him. "Where is it?"

"Hawaii. Maui. I stay in that house quite often."

She looked again at the shots. "Lucky you. I've always thought I'd enjoy Hawaii."

So far so good, Ian thought. But he wasn't kidding himself that the hardest part wasn't still to come. "It is lovely. And easy to get to—Maui, that is. They have direct flights out of San Francisco now, and in a few hours we can be there."

He watched her face for reaction, but she hadn't

really heard what he'd said. She was studying the pictures.

"The drive up the road to Hana. That's where we'll have to go. It's pretty hairy. It's all switchbacks and one-way bridges. But you can smell mangoes and breadfruit, and it feels like the jungle."

"Does it?" She sounded wistful. A view of the house held her attention now. "It's hard to imagine. Like something out of the movies."

"We could leave tonight." He stopped breathing.

"Oh, sure." She laughed. "I'm always doing things like popping off to Hawaii on a few hours' notice. You do like your little jokes."

He was...he thought he might be falling in love with her. "I'm not known for my sense of humor," he said with mock seriousness. "In fact, most people are afraid of me."

Page chuckled. "So I've heard in your mail room." She sobered. "The people who work for you say a lot of flattering things, like how they respect you. They also say you're one nice guy, Mr. Faber."

He felt uncomfortable. "You mean members of my staff talk about me for no particular reason?"

Her blush relaxed him, and he leaned to kiss her brow. "You asked about me, didn't you?"

"Uh-huh. Does that make you mad?"

"Not as long as you don't do it again. In fact, I kind of like thinking you did that. The plane leaves at nine thirty-eight."

She stared. "What plane?"

He crossed the fingers of the hand at his side. "The plane we're taking to Maui, so you can swim in the ocean and relax for a few days before you get completely back into work.''

She didn't speak for so long he felt panicky. ''Say yes, Page. We'll have a great time and it'll be good for you. When's the last time you had a vacation?''

''I don't remember.''

''There you are, then. It's a date.''

''Oh, no.'' She scooted around him and stood. ''I've got to get back to my paperwork.''

He got up and blocked her path to the door. ''The paperwork will wait. Lilian said she'll get someone called James, jr. to give her a hand.''

''You talked to Lilian about this?'' Her voice rose to a squeak.

''Yes. I must say I like your employees. The Zipper's interesting. He told me he used to ride race horses, but he didn't like it because the horses had minds of their own. Bicycles only do what you make them do.''

She groaned. ''I can't believe you talked to my people about all this.''

''Why? You talked to mine.''

The parting of her lips, then the closing, let him know he was getting closer to his objective. She couldn't argue the last point.

''I can't go.''

''You can if you want to.''

''You don't understand that some people can't do what they want to do, do you?''

She was thinking of money as well as time. He went on, ''Lilian said you can't ride for at least another week. She said she and James would take care of the books and that your roommate would be here to watch over the apartment. The only reason I can think of for your refusing to come is that you don't want to be with me.''

''I don't have the right clothes,'' she mumbled. Nor could she afford to buy any. And despite Tanya's cheeriness lately, Page still worried about her and wasn't comfortable with the idea of leaving her completely alone.

Frustration made him flex his fingers. ''We can get what you need there. We'll only be gone a few days.'' She was blushing, damn it. She must be thinking of the expense. ''Oh, darn, trust me to forget the important thing. This vacation is my get-well present to you, so you can't refuse.''

''I can.'' She frowned. ''Things like this cost a lot, and I don't take expensive gifts from people.''

Behind her frown trembled vulnerability and, he was sure, longing. Carefully, afraid she'd sprout prickles or smack him, he took her in his arms.

''I'm not people, sweetheart. I'm the guy who thinks you're something more than special. And if you don't let me do this I'm going to feel like the kid Santa Claus missed. You wouldn't want that, would you?''

She shook her head.

''Then it's settled. I'll pick you up around eight. Wear something light but with a coat on top. We'll leave the coat in the car. Bring a suitcase, and we'll get the extra things you need when we arrive in Maui.''

He kissed her again, savoring the softness of her lips, then let her go. ''Do we have a deal?''

''I guess so.''

"Good. Rest a while if you want to. But be ready at eight." Inside he was terrified she'd try to back out, but he made himself grin. "By the way, the decor in here is something. I bet no one else ever thought of using bicycle parts as objets d'art."

Her laughter was what he'd wanted to hear.

CHAPTER TWELVE

THESE WERE *South Pacific* beaches. Just like the ones in the movie. Page turned her head to say as much to Ian before she recalled that the beaches in the movie had indeed been Hawaiian.

Ian had felt her glance toward him. "Comfortable?" he asked.

"Mmm. It feels funny to be warm like this in November. But I love it."

"So you're not sorry you came?"

She almost hadn't come. "No." Right up to takeoff in San Francisco she'd believed she would back out. But they'd been here three days now, and Page was beginning to feel very much at home in the white house on the cliffs above them.

From time to time she thought of Pedal Pushers, worried that something might happen to another rider while she was too far away to take immediate action. But the peace here, the beauty of it all, managed to keep her concerns at bay.

"You need more sunscreen," Ian said. "I don't want you burning. Lie on your stomach."

"Yes, sir." Obediently she flattened her chaise and turned over.

The chaise gave with Ian's weight as he sat by her

knees. "Did I say I think you should wear a bikini—or whatever this thing's called—all the time?"

She buried her face in her forearms and laughed. "You did—several times." The bikini was the most daring thing she'd ever bought. "The latest," the saleswoman in Lahaina had assured her of the tiny, flowered bottom and the bra, which was in fact two sections that adhered to her breasts.

Page would never forget Ian's expression the first time she'd joined him on the narrow beach below the house and taken off her wrap. Behind dark glasses his eyes were invisible, but she had no doubt where he was looking or that he liked what he saw.

"Aah. That's cold." A stream of sunscreen snaked across her back. But his hands were warm, and quickly slick.

He smoothed her body from neck to waist and down to the bikini bottom. Massaging in smaller circles, he covered her shoulders and arms, the backs of her legs. When he held her ankles and slathered the soles of her feet, she yelled.

"Important," he said, continuing until she wriggled. "If the bottoms of your feet get burned, I have to carry you everywhere, and gorgeous as you are, petite you aren't."

"Insulting—"

"Ah-ah. Don't say things you'll regret later. You need more here."

His fingers smoothed her sides and she shuddered, but he carried on, touching lightly the tender skin where the clusters of flowers didn't quite cover the fullness of her pale breasts.

He teased, nipped at her ear and bent over her until

the hair on his chest met her bare back. Then he got up and waited until she rolled over onto her back and propped herself on her elbows. The sun was behind him, turning his already tanned body, the muscular arms and long, tensile legs, into a wavery dark form.

"On second thought I wouldn't want you to wear that all the time." The words were light but his voice thick.

Since their arrival on Maui he'd done this again and again—come close enough, touched or talked in a way that brought her desire for him tingling to life, only to draw away while she still ached. Was he really playing with her? Or did he keep reminding himself that he'd billed this trip as purely for her health? Page sighed and dropped flat on the chaise. Her health wouldn't tolerate many more exercises in frustration.

"You'd get cold. Probably catch pneumonia."

"What?" She shaded her eyes and squinted at him.

"Wearing the bikini all the time. You'd turn blue on that bike of yours in midwinter." He sat on the sand and picked up a stick.

"Very funny, Ian." His ability to turn sensuality on and off unnerved her.

He tapped her tummy with the stick. "Are you eating enough?"

"Yes, of course." His questions went off in the strangest directions sometimes. "Why would you ask a thing like that?"

"Oh, I was wondering if I should make some chicken soup or something. You've got the flattest stomach I've ever seen."

And then, between the aching moments of sexual tension there were these times when she felt more relaxed than she ever had. "I think you're suppressing fatherly instincts." She closed her eyes at once, remembering Rose Faber's visit. Some subjects had to be avoided.

Ian didn't answer at once. The stick continued its light tattoo on her belly. "Maybe I am a frustrated father. But that's not what I'm feeling right now, anything but. How are your ribs?"

Page's turn to be silent. His route to what he was really thinking might be tortuous, but it wasn't hard to follow.

"Page, do your ribs still bother you?"

"No. I feel like a whole human being again."

He cleared his throat. "You look like a very whole human being. Hey, how about driving the rest of the way up the Hana road?"

He bounced to his feet and hauled Page up.

"I guess we're going to Hana," she said, and smiled widely up at him. He seemed different here, carefree, irrepressible.

He only gave her time to find a pair of thongs and put on her wrap while he pulled shorts over his abbreviated swimsuit and shoved his feet into tennis shoes.

They'd flown into Kahului airport, where Ian had picked up a rental car for the long, twisting drive toward isolated Hana. The house—Page hadn't asked directly but she assumed it belonged to Ian—was twenty miles along the narrow, pockmarked highway. On their first full day, he had insisted they go west into the busy old whaling town of Lahaina with its cobbled streets crowded with tourists, its trendy bars and restaurants and a plethora of boutiques.

Page's necessary clothing had been bought, more than she thought necessary, but Ian, relaxed and happy and determined to shower her with things she didn't expect to wear again once she left Maui, kept suggesting and adding items. He'd refused to let her have the bill, but she intended to start paying him back as soon as they got home.

Yesterday and today had been spent relaxing, but Ian had let her know repeatedly how much he was looking forward to taking her to the end of the famous fifty-mile-long road to Hana. He hustled her into the car and shot from the driveway, only to slow to a crawl at once to negotiate the first of a hundred sharp curves.

"A person could get sick with all this winding back and forth," Page remarked as they bumped around a bend and dropped into yet another dip.

"You feel sick?" He glanced at her anxiously.

"No. Just making a comment."

The car windows were down and pungent scents wafted in. Shafts of sun pierced the dense trees and vines that enclosed the road like a tunnel.

Wet drops hit Page's arm, resting along the window rim. "It's raining again. This is the strangest place. Sun, rain, everything all mixed up together."

The car crested another rise, dropped again sharply to a bridge and Ian pulled onto a slim turnaround strip. "Let's get out."

"It's raining."

He stared at her. "So? Aren't you the woman who rides around San Francisco in midwinter wearing ballet tights?"

Mumbling that her work gear had nothing to do

with ballet, Page climbed from the car. Immediately she was glad she had. Ian joined her and led the way along a tiny pathway beside a steep drop, which the bridge spanned. A few feet from the road they entered a fragrant grotto molded of giant, trailing philodendron leaves, spiky lauhala trees balanced on their tepees of straight air roots, ferns and myriad other specimens. Ian pointed out one after another, giving names she knew she'd forget.

"Listen," he said, holding up a finger.

Page tilted her head. A steady pitter-patter sounded, rain hitting the roof of foliage overhead. The air around them was moist and heavy with the scent of fruit and flowers, but no drops penetrated the green cave.

"Like it?" Ian's voice sounded funny again.

Page felt funny. "Yes." She swallowed, aware of how alone they were, how close. "Are these orchids?" Sprays of tiny, purple blossoms sprang from a mossy bed.

"Uh-huh."

"They just grow anywhere here?" While she outlined a flower Ian came to stand beside her.

"I've started needing you, Page."

She took a breath, held it, closed her eyes when she walked into his arms. "I know," she said against his warm chest. She needed him, too. He must know that.

"Don't go away from me again."

"I wasn't the one who went away," she said and held her bottom lip in her teeth, not wanting to spoil the moment.

"You're right." He loosened the belt of her wrap

and pulled her close. "I was the one who went off in a sulk, wasn't I?"

"You were upset."

"So would you be if you walked into a hospital room and saw someone you… It was a shock to see you like that."

Someone you what? What had he almost said? "I should have let you know about the accident, but after our last telephone conversation I wasn't sure you'd want to know."

"You aren't always very smart."

"Thanks."

"I only meant that you should be able to read my signals better by now. You know how much you mean to me."

Her body was all exposed nerve ends. His hands were beneath the wrap, ranging over her back. Pressed to him she felt naked, wished that she was, that they both were.

Sun had faintly gilded the hair on his chest. She ran her fingers over it, looked at his tanned skin beneath her palms and kissed each spot she touched. He stood very still while she bent to brush her mouth across his flat stomach.

When she straightened he slowly opened his eyes. "We'd better not stay here," he said hoarsely.

Page smiled, watching his mouth before she guided his face down to hers. "Why?" she said and parted his lips with her tongue.

The noise he made came from deep in his throat, and she felt him quicken against her. He framed her face with his hands, and the control was no longer hers. The kiss he gave was urgent. Her legs shook and she clung to him, wanting to slip to the leaf-strewn ground and take him with her.

He lifted his head so abruptly she gasped. ''Damn it.'' His chest rose and fell rapidly while he closed her wrap and hastily tied the belt.

Page caught his hand, ready to protest, when she heard what he must have heard. Voices.

''That's what I meant when I said we shouldn't stay here,'' Ian said, fashioning a smile and leading her back to the path. They exchanged nods with the two chattering couples they passed, reached the car and slumped into their seats.

''I feel like a teenager who got caught parking,'' Page said, scrunching down.

Ian leaned over and kissed the corner of her mouth. ''Yeah, fun huh?''

''Depends on what you call fun.''

''You sound irritable...and frustrated, maybe?''

She pulled up her knees and rested her face so that he couldn't see it. ''Neither. Embarrassed, that's all. I got carried away, and that's not like me.''

''Isn't it? That's too bad. I kind of enjoyed it.''

He started the car.

Kind of enjoyed it? He *was* playing with her, putting her in situations where he could test her reaction to him. And she'd fallen completely into the trap again.

''Do you still feel like going all the way to the end of the road?''

Why did he ask? Because he expected her to insist on rushing back to the house where they could be sure of solitude? ''Absolutely I still want to go. I wouldn't miss it now.''

The last time they'd gotten really close she'd been the one to call a halt. She didn't think Ian was small-minded enough to deliberately turn the tables, but it was possible he'd decided to allow her to set the pace between them. Unfortunately she wasn't sure what she wanted the pace to be.

Many curves later they reached the Heavenly Hana Inn and stopped the car long enough to peer through its Japanese screen gate, flanked by stone lions, to a luxuriant garden. The town of Hana was nothing more than a scant collection of aged but picturesque buildings. Page made appropriate noises of awe, but her mind was elsewhere. It was still elsewhere when they parked by a breakwater to watch the wild sea rush in, and when Ian pointed out what had been Charles Lindbergh's final home.

Two hours later they arrived back at the house and drove down the short, steep driveway.

"Do you want to live it up tonight?" Ian asked as he let them into the entryway with its shiny, red, koa floor and stark, white walls. "We could go into Lahaina or Kaanapali if you like. You haven't seen the hotels there. Quite something."

"That would take hours."

"We can go if you want to. I don't mind driving."

She felt irritable. "I do," she said, and walked past him.

The main room in the house had a fireplace, which looked much used—Page wondered why in this climate—and clusters of elegant bentwood furniture with downy cushions in shades of pink and gray and mauve. Beyond, through French doors, was a wide lanai, where the same colors had been used on the cushions of white cane chairs and chaises grouped around glass-topped cane tables.

Page went outside and dropped onto a chaise. She should shower and change, but she didn't feel like it yet.

Half an hour later she lost interest in the rushing, roiling surf, colored the palest lime green as the sun set. Ian hadn't joined her.

She shifted restlessly and felt annoyed with herself. Mature women shouldn't expect people to be nice to them when they were rude.

''Pupus!''

Ian had approached noiselessly on bare feet. He set down a tray bearing two tall glasses of something golden, each topped by a wedge of pineapple speared by a tiny red umbrella. The *pupus*, which he'd already explained was the local term for hors d'oeuvres, were macadamia nuts and a plate of tiny egg rolls.

''You're much too good to me.'' Page eyed the egg rolls. ''I know you like to cook, but how did you whip those up so quickly?'' Had he been up even earlier than she'd thought that morning?

''Miracles of convenience food, m'dear. You, too, can learn to love microwave fare. Feel any better?''

She rubbed at the arms of her chair. ''I was pretty snippy. Sorry. I don't know what made me like that.'' At least she wasn't about to tell him.

He regarded her thoughtfully. ''Have some of your *mai tai*. It'll relax you a bit. You're still convalescing in a way. The old nerves are bound to get pretty racked up by the kind of thing you went through.''

They hadn't discussed the details of the accident, but she had no doubt that Lilian had filled him in.

"You're probably right," she agreed. "I hope I never have another night like that."

"You won't..."

Page had lifted her glass. She paused with the rim against her lips, watching him. His features were taut. Then, gradually, they softened, but his chest expanded slowly and she heard him exhale. Without speaking he'd said it all. He hadn't changed his stand on Pedal Pushers one bit. He was only trying to time his next attack more diplomatically. She took several sips of the drink. It was excellent. Diplomacy should be her motto, too. Given time, if she didn't explode every time he did what came naturally to him, she'd win him over to her side. If she wanted to—and she was definitely beginning to think she might.

"Um, Page, remember telling me we operate from the base of our experience?"

"Yes."

"I can't seem to put mine completely away. But I want to. I don't want to cramp your style."

Not reminding him that he had no right to do so was hard. "We don't have to go into that. There isn't any need."

"Maybe not now. But there could be later on."

In other words he was beginning to see her as someone who might become important to him—very important. "It was nice of you to suggest going out tonight. I wasn't very gracious. But it's so lovely right here and we've got plenty of food." They'd bought supplies before coming to the house.

"You mean you're offering to cook me a gourmet meal?" He grinned, and she leaned to punch his arm lightly.

"Smart mouth. I meant we can throw something together and sit out here and enjoy the most beautiful place I've ever seen."

He parted his lips, then bowed his head before saying, "I've always thought of it that way, too, but it wasn't quite this beautiful before."

The territory was becoming dangerous again. Page got up. "If you don't mind I'd like to take a quick shower and put on one of those creations I'm not going to get to wear if I don't start changing four or five times a day."

"You'll get to wear them."

She'd reached the doors.

"We'll come back one day if you want to," he added.

Page sighed and went inside. Trips to idyllic settings were ordinary events to him. To Page this one time was a dream to be treasured, remembered, and probably never repeated.

The house was long, one storied, and two large bedrooms, each with its own lanai, faced the ocean. A third was smaller and had windows with a view through the palms that fringed the property on three sides.

Page showered and washed her hair quickly. She worked hard with her blow-dryer, brushing, shaking, until the heavy mass was shiny, falling straight but bouncy around her shoulders.

When she left her room and passed Ian's, his door stood open, and she heard running water. The shorts and swimsuit he'd worn lay on the floor where he must have dropped them on his way to the bathroom. She smiled before she headed for the kitchen. The small insights she was getting into his habits brought a certain intimacy and satisfaction. He wasn't totally organized. He also wasn't careful of such niceties as modesty. What if she'd walked by while he was flinging his clothes on the rug? Page's smile broadened. Of the two of them, she would probably have been more affected—much more affected.

While she worked in the kitchen, she learned something else about Ian. Like her brother and father, he took outrageously long showers. She'd found a wok, chopped vegetables, shelled and de-veined shrimp and assembled everything else she needed for the meal she planned before she heard the shower turned off.

After testing the air outside and finding it still deliciously warm, she set two places at one of the tables and took a single bird-of-paradise blossom from the sitting room to complete the arrangement.

She was standing back to admire her efforts when a pair of arms encircled her. "Mmm. You smell as good as you look," Ian said.

Turning in his arms, she hugged him back and pecked his cheek. "You smell pretty good yourself. And look pretty good." A khaki shirt, open at the throat and tucked into pleated cotton pants of the same color, gave him an island look that was fashionably casual. His hair was wet and his feet bare. Page studied his toes. "I see you dressed for dinner."

He put his hands on her shoulders and held her away. "Never mind me. Did you know that from where I'm standing that dress is transparent?"

Instinctively Page crossed her arms. "It is not."

But it was—or almost. Ian took his time following

her outline inside the loose, white gauze dress that brushed the straps of flat, white sandals. Her hair, glossy and full, took on a burnishing from the flames of torches he'd lit before going to take his shower.

"Dinner's ready to go."

"I'll help." He followed her to the kitchen. Her usually smooth gait was jerky. He'd made her self-conscious. Odd that a woman who must know only too well the effect she had on men could still seem like an innocent sometimes.

They spoke little while they ate. Inconsequential comments about the food, which he hardly tasted, and the wine.

This wasn't working out as he'd hoped. He picked up his glass, then set it down without drinking. What exactly had he hoped for? That completely removed from everything and everyone involved in their day-to-day lives they'd find out what they truly felt for each other? Yes, that was it.

He stood up abruptly and walked to the steps at one end of the lanai. He had discovered what he felt—that he wanted Page with him for good. And he was pretty sure Page might want the same, but there were strings attached—on both sides.

"I'm going for a walk. Coming?"

She stood and picked up their plates. "I don't think so. I'm tired. I think I'll clean up these things and go to bed. You go ahead and I'll see you in the morning."

He considered helping with the dishes, but he thought she'd prefer to be alone.

The meandering route he took through the palms was familiar. He'd played in this garden above the sea as a child when his parents first bought the place, and had returned at least two or three times a year ever since. The house was the original structure, improved bit by bit over time. Once it had been the home of a sugar-plantation manager and his family. Ian recalled the black metal stove, replaced by a modern descendant now, that had been fueled by ironwood cut from casuarina trees on their own property.

Tonight the magic wasn't the same. He'd imagined all this with Page at his side, but something was planted solidly between them. Oh, the so-called chemistry was right—they both knew that very well—but going for a commitment between them presented a hazard because of the obstacle he couldn't accept and discard yet. He laughed, a short, mirthless sound that jarred him. He'd finally met a woman he could imagine spending the rest of his life with, and what held up the proceedings? A lousy bicycle, for God's sake. At least, that was the symbol of the obstacle, that and her crazy notion that she had to confront danger day in and day out to prove how independent she was.

This was their fourth night on Maui. Two more and they'd be San Francisco bound.

Ian propped a shoulder on a broad palm trunk and crossed his arms. He might as well face his immediate problem. For three nights he'd slept—if that's what it could be called—in a bed only feet from her. Each time he'd closed his eyes he'd imagined he heard her turning, breathing. He couldn't stand thinking of going back for more of the same.

The ocean fussed at the shore below, but he heard a different sound and turned. The white dress showed clearly as she picked her way over what was strange ground to her. Page had come in search of him.

His heart gave a thud. Had she seen him yet? Instinct stopped him from calling out or going to meet her. He wanted to watch her look for him...and find him.

"Ian, is that you?" She was still yards away, but she'd paused. He realized his light clothing must also show in the darkness.

"Yes. Over here. Watch out for roots."

He went to meet her and blessed the absent moon. Keeping a smile on his face was getting tougher by the second.

"Wow, it's dark." Her voice was breathy. "I thought I'd get lost out here."

She found his hand and he almost pulled away. Instead he twined their fingers together and held himself rigid.

"What's the matter?" She was sensitive. She hadn't missed his tension.

"Nothing. I thought you were going to bed."

She didn't reply immediately. Her grip on his fingers slackened and she removed her hand. "I'm sorry. I wasn't thinking. You want to be alone." She cleared her throat. "I'll go back."

"No!" He caught her wrist before she could turn away. "I don't want to be alone. That's the last thing I want."

"But you seem...you seem..."

"Don't go." He wanted to say so much, declare so much, but the words formed a maze in his head.

His chest felt tight. "Let's walk." He put his hands in his pockets and moved on. "Step where I step."

With everything in him he wanted to hold her, to take her with him, but he didn't even trust himself to touch her.

He made his way to the place where a Japanese teahouse had been built between the palms. "Come in here," he said, climbing two steps and going inside. Benches lined latticed walls, which allowed the breeze to pass through.

Ian sat sideways on a bench, put his feet up and wrapped his arms around his legs. He rested his chin on his knees. There had never been a time when he felt less sure of how to deal with a situation.

For a moment he was afraid Page hadn't followed. He straightened and looked over his shoulder. She stood at the base of the steps to the teahouse. He couldn't see her face.

This was it. Either they confronted what was between them or they gave the whole thing up. "Page—"

"I know, I know. We've been fencing too long. I'm sick of it, too."

He breathed deeply, but his chest was still tight. "So what do we do about it?"

"Stop being scared, I guess."

"Scared?"

"Of letting go and taking a few risks."

"I don't think..." Hell, no he didn't think there were any great risks, because he believed she'd be happy as soon as they were together, really together. But she wasn't there yet and he had to give her time to catch up.

The moon had chosen that moment to appear. Silver gray crept from above to cast Page as a statue inside swirling gauze. She was waiting for him to go on talking.

"Sweetheart, I don't think we're going to risk anything if we decide to love each other."

He joined her and smoothed her hair back from her face.

"Is love something you decide to do?" she asked.

Her eyes glistened, and he thought he saw moisture on her cheeks. His thumbs confirmed the suspicion. "No, it's not." The tears were salty when he kissed her face. "I don't think we have any say in the thing at all. Darn it, *I* sure don't have any say at the moment."

"Hold me, Ian."

In his arms she felt small and shaky. She was vulnerable now, possibly more vulnerable than at any other time in her life. But so was he. The difference between them was that her weakening made him strong. Energy surged through him, and desire. She was fragile in some ways and he'd always remember and revere that in her, but she was also passionate and ready to share herself with him.

"Is it too cold for you out here?"

"No. I'm warm. You're not holding me tightly enough though."

He crushed her to him in a reflexive action and heard her make a small noise. "I'm sorry. Damn, I'm sorry. I forgot the ribs."

She giggled. "The ribs are fine. You winded me, that's all."

"Guess I don't know my own strength." With her still-damp face cradled in the hollow of his neck, he felt he could snap large trees if necessary. "I'm going to come right out and say something. Is that okay?"

She was unbuttoning his shirt and his stomach pulled in sharply. "Depends on what you intend to say," she murmured. Now she pulled the shirt free of his pants and kissed his jaw and neck again and again while she ran her fingers through the hair on his chest. When she raised her face her eyes were bright. "Say it," she ordered, putting her arms around his shoulders, "whatever it is."

"I'm in love with you."

"Kiss me."

He closed his eyes and did as she asked for a long time. Somewhere during the kiss his shirt fell to the ground. He knew that under the white dress, she wore a bra and panties of some pale color and it was time he saw what the color was. The edges of his mind dulled, but there was something else he knew he needed.

"Is there anything you'd like to say to me? Anything at all?"

"Like I love you, too? I do, Ian. Whether I want to or not, I do. And I sure didn't get to decide about it."

She slipped from his arms and pulled the dress over her head. Then she reached behind her back for the fastening of her bra.

"No," Ian said. "Let me look at you like that first." He touched the narrow bands of satin across her hips, slid his hands around to cup her bottom. "Peach, is that what this color is?"

Her laughter caught and faded. "Yes, does it matter?"

"Everything about you matters. I want to know all the things you like, including colors."

Keeping a forearm around her waist, he took off the rest of his clothes. When he was naked he urged her to him, and the smooth satin aroused him in a way only her flesh could improve on.

As if she read his thoughts she slipped the straps from her shoulders and leaned against him while she worked the bra to her waist, her breasts rubbing tantalizingly at him with every twist of her body.

He bent to kiss first one then the other nipple. She moaned and eased his head up until their mouths came together with fierce tenderness. When he reached for her hips again she was stepping out of the panties.

Soft grass covered the area where the teahouse had been built. He dropped slowly to his knees, passing his lips and tongue between her breasts and ribs until he reached her stomach. Her fingers were in his hair. He used his thumbs, his mouth, felt the trembling...

"Ian," was all she said before she pushed him to sit on the grass. Kneeling between his thighs, she kissed his brow, his nose, his mouth, all the time smoothing his body, every part of his body, with her hands, until at last she stilled, holding him.

For an instant passion flared unchecked, but at the center of the white heat came the sense that Page wasn't deciding what to do because she was a practiced lover.

The heat grew. He couldn't hold on. "Sweetheart, let me, okay?" He wasn't really asking permission to take over.

In a simple motion he moved her astride him. She

closed around him, drawing him in until all conscious thought faded, and his being did what it had to do—be a man with this woman.

Page's head felt light. She still pulsed from the first release. Now it was happening again, this time as she'd longed for it to happen, with Ian filling her.

His movements grew stronger and stronger, and her own strength grew with each push. She braced her weight on a hand on each side of his shoulders. He covered her aching breasts.

Then it built once more, the searing that was sweet in its intensity, and she threw herself back against his raised knees.

He dropped his hands to his sides. She saw the gleam of sweat on his body and upturned jaw. Carefully, desperate to lie with him, she moved and was instantly enfolded and rolled to the grass.

"Thank you, my love," he said against her neck. "You are so wonderful."

She didn't know what to say. Heaviness seeped into her limbs and her eyes wanted to close.

Ian leaned over to peer into her face. "Sleepy, sweetheart?"

"Happy," she told him, and nuzzled his neck and jaw.

Above them, palm fronds clicked in the breeze. Later, when they'd returned to the house, that same flower-scented breeze wafted through the open windows of Ian's room to cool Page's heated skin.

BELOW THEM the ocean off the coast of Oahu stretched, sometimes emerald, sometimes turquoise, streaked with the gray shadows of hidden coral. On the return journey they'd had to change planes in Honolulu, but Page hadn't minded. In the six-hour layover Ian had taken her to Waikiki where she'd walked on the beach, made him take her photograph to prove she'd been there and announced she didn't need to return to anywhere in Hawaii but a lovely white house on the road to Hana, Maui.

They flew first class and Page had no doubt that Ian had never flown any other way. Without asking if she wanted any, he ordered a bottle of champagne as soon as the seat-belt sign went off.

The attendant filled their glasses, and Ian turned to Page. "We're flying back to the rest of our lives, so I think it's time we toasted a few things."

She smiled at him and lifted her glass, but felt apprehensive for the first time in days. "Well, I can start," she told him. "Here's to you."

He waited until she drank. "Thank you. Now I get to give a list. Here's to you, and us, and a great marriage and as many kids as we decide we can handle. And—" he put a finger on her mouth as she tried to speak "—last but not least to someone you wouldn't think of drinking to now—my mother, who is one smart lady."

He drank. Page didn't.

The elaborate arrangement of flowers on a serving table smelled cloying. "Why is your mother one smart lady?"

"I told her you'd probably never agree to go with me on this trip, but she kept insisting you would and she was right."

"It was your mother's idea for you to invite me to Maui?" In the past two days she'd forgotten Rose, forgotten almost everything but how good it felt to be with Ian.

"No-o, not exactly. I asked if they minded my using the house because I was thinking of inviting you to go, and she thought it was a great idea."

The air conditioning was too cold. And Page's brain seemed to be cooling, too. "The house isn't yours?"

"No, it belongs to my folks. I thought I told you that."

"You didn't."

His parents' house and he'd pushed her to join him there because his mother had encouraged him. A setup to further the marry-Ian-off campaign?

"We should set a date, Page. These things take time."

He hadn't even asked her to marry him. Not actually *asked* her.

"I think we'll open the rest of the house. You'll have a ball decorating."

Decorating. He was mapping out her life, and whatever plans she'd had before didn't enter into his calculations. A woman who was decorating and having as many babies as she and her husband could handle might have some trouble fitting in a business that usually left her four hours a day for sleep.

"You're quiet, sweetheart. What are you thinking about?"

She looked at him. Her declaration of love hadn't been a lie—she did love him, so much that at this moment it hurt.

"Page?"

"I was thinking that you'd better hold off on the wedding plans."

CHAPTER THIRTEEN

"TAKE THINGS MORE SLOWLY," she'd said. They were to back away from each other and spend time thinking about what they really wanted.

Ian stared into the refrigerator, forgot what he'd been looking for and slammed the door. In the three weeks since they'd returned from Maui he'd seen Page twice and talked to her on the phone a couple of times. On the two occasions when she'd agreed to meet him it had been for coffee between the end of her day shift and before the nap she needed to get ready for her damned evening shift. And he was sick of it.

He sat at the kitchen table and rested his brow on his forearms. One minute everything had been wonderful, perfect, a go from here to eternity. The next she'd turned cold fish on him.

As he had dozens of times before, he went over their conversations, hunted for the exact moment when he might have said something to turn her off. And he came back to the same one—on the plane when he'd mentioned that his mother thought the trip was a good idea.

But that made absolutely no sense. Page liked his mother—or at least, she didn't dislike her. And what difference did it make one way or the other? She wouldn't be marrying his mother.

Marriage. He got up and paced around the room. She had said she wanted to marry him, hadn't she?

Her business was the stumbling block. She didn't want to admit she could live without being responsible for her own fate—totally responsible, that was. He didn't want a wife without a mind of her own. Page's individuality and guts had been what first attracted him to her.

Well, hell, she could have her business. A bicycle should keep her really warm at night.

He checked his watch. Martin might still be at home and glad of some company. They'd patched up their differences over lunch, and some of the old rapport had returned.

Since he hadn't gotten around to installing a phone in the old kitchen, he'd have to go upstairs. He glowered at the ridiculous blue wallpaper. And he'd been dumb enough to think Page would want to help redecorate this place. He strode up to the salon. He'd actually talked to her about it. What a fool she must think him.

At the desk he found Martin's number and lifted the telephone receiver. Slowly he punched in digits, his skin growing clammy.

The ring droned in his ear, once, twice—ten times. She wasn't home. But of course she wasn't. Page was already out there in the dark and cold. He'd known it would be Page he tried to call even as he'd found Martin's number. He let the phone slip back into its cradle.

Didn't Page know what this was doing to him?

Wasn't she suffering just as much? Half-hour dates for coffee every week or so wouldn't cut it for him, not when he knew, knew so very intimately, what they could have together.

A walk might help him straighten out his head. Dressed in a heavy, wool greatcoat but with his head bare, he set off. At the first corner he stopped beneath a streetlight. Misty rain sheeted down.

She was out here somewhere. His stomach turned as it did every time he thought that some other nut, or the same one, might be tailing her, waiting for another opportunity to attack.

He bowed his head and trudged on. She was her own woman. Page had made sure he understood that. His best bet was to work on accepting their relationship on her terms—at least for now.

"QUIET NIGHT," Waldo said, handing over two boxes. "Typical middle-of-the-week stuff."

Page did her best to smile before she set off. Tanya was behaving strangely again. She either had nothing to say or snapped monosyllabic answers to Page's remarks. Waldo Sands was undoubtedly the cause of Tanya's recurring troubles, and Page longed to say something to him about her friend. If there had ever been any doubt about Tanya's involvement with the man it no longer existed. Earlier in the evening, as Page approached the delicatessen, she'd seen her roommate get out of a taxi and enter the shop. When Page followed only seconds later there was no sign of Tanya.

Both of the orders Page carried now were for her own area, Russian Hill. She pedaled slowly. Since her return from Maui she'd noticed she tired more easily. The result of the accident, she supposed.

The rain was getting to her. She'd broken her rule tonight and put on oilskins. The restriction around the arms and legs irritated her.

Every light turned red as she approached. At an intersection she planted her feet, waiting, hardly seeing colors through eyes that saw things in a blur. The rain on the road to Hana hadn't gotten to her. But that had been warm rain…and Ian had been with her.

Green. She was off again. Being tired had nothing to do with the accident. There were no lingering side effects from a few bruises. The truth was that she was sick of being out here at night, worrying about who might be waiting in every doorway and alley she passed while she longed to be with Ian.

Instead of taking the shortest route, she detoured down Laguna past his house. No lights in the windows. He didn't go to bed this early so he must have gone out. Not that it was her business.

A few more blocks and she unloaded the second box. Unfortunately Waldo had radioed to say there was another order. It was past one and she wished she could go home. Instead she rode doggedly back to the deli.

Laguna and Green. Page read the address as soon as Waldo put the box in her hands.

"Something wrong?"

She looked at him unseeingly. "No, nothing."

"We haven't heard from Mr. Faber in a while. I thought we'd lost him."

"Evidently not quite," Page said, keeping her

voice level. Inside she was jumpy, excited, apprehensive.

The box was heavy—more champagne?

She traveled fast until she was within a block of Ian's house. Then she stopped. Despite the hood pulled over her helmet, rain had driven in and the hair around her face was wet. With almost numb fingers she poked the strands back. He'd been angry the last time they spoke. According to him she was avoiding him, deliberately making him miserable. He didn't understand, he'd said. Yes, she was avoiding him, but she'd never consciously hurt him. Would he...? No, Ian wasn't a vindictive man, he wouldn't deliberately subject her to another scene like the one she'd encountered the night they met.

Page walked the bike the rest of the way. This had to be his way of getting to talk to her. She wanted to talk to him, too, but she was afraid of letting her emotional need for him influence decisions that mustn't be lightly made.

Lights were on in the house now. Hauling the bike up the front steps was harder than she remembered. She propped it against a pillar and knocked.

The door swung open. Ian stood just inside.

Page jumped.

"Hi," he said. "Rotten night."

"Yes. How are you?"

"Cold and wet...and lonely." He wore an overcoat and his hair was wet. His arms were crossed, his hands pushed inside the sleeves.

So was she, so very very lonely—so ready to forget everything but him. But she wasn't a fool. She'd seen what happened to a woman after a few years of being a nonperson.

"I've got your order from Touch Tone." No exchange of words had ever been this awkward.

"I don't want it."

She'd lifted the box. "I didn't think you did."

"Can you come in?"

"I shouldn't. I'll probably be called out on another job."

"Is that the only delivery you've got now?"

Circles getting smaller. "Yes." Page held the box tighter. He wasn't closing the web about her without help. She wanted to be there.

"Well, you'll have to get your receipt, won't you? And it's warmer in here than it is out there."

Page stepped inside. "I'm dripping, Ian. I'd better not walk on any rugs."

He took the box from her and set it on the floor. "Sweetheart..." He bowed his head and she saw drops glisten in dark curls.

"Why are you so wet?" she asked. Suffocation must feel like this.

"I went for a walk. For two hours, or three, I don't remember. I was trying to stop thinking about you, and all I did was see you everywhere I looked." He kept his head bent and she touched a cold hand to his hair. Before she could withdraw, Ian trapped her fingers and held them. "This is no good, Page. You aren't happy, either. I can see you aren't."

But what could she do to heal the situation if she didn't know how to make him understand that she had needs separate from his and would always have those needs?

"Please stay and get warm."

She let him unsnap and unzip the oilskin jacket, and she turned while he pulled it from her arms. The helmet and pants she removed herself, then her sodden gloves. The radio was attached to the neck of her leotard, the silver one Ian liked. She went to press the button and call in, but he stopped her. "It's one-thirty and it's foul out there. Couldn't you ask whatever his name is to let you call it a night?"

"I still have to take the receipt back."

"Let me talk to him. I'll tell him I'll bring it by myself in the morning."

His meaning was implicit. He not only wanted her to stay a while, he was inviting her to spend the night.

Page signaled Waldo.

"Yeah?" He sounded tired.

"Would it be okay if I called it a night? I'll drop off the last receipt in the morning."

After a short, crackly pause Waldo said, "Sure, kid. We don't have anything else to go out. See you in the morning."

He switched off without waiting for a response. Page unhooked the radio. "If I'm going to stay for a bit I'll bring my bike in."

"I'll bring the thing in." She didn't miss the anger in his voice. How could they overcome their differences if he wouldn't give at all in her direction?

Page sat on the bottom step of the stairs and pulled off her muddy shoes. Then, with the bike making puddles on Ian's Italian marble and her oilskins spread over the top of the machine to drain, she walked beside him up to the salon.

Once in the room he fell silent, sitting, still wearing the damp coat, on his beautiful leather couch.

Page waited awkwardly in the leotard and cycling tights, her feet bare since she'd taken off her socks.

She coughed.

Ian rested his head back on the couch and closed his eyes.

"Stay and get warm," he'd suggested. The atmosphere in this room was frigid.

The fire was laid. She picked up a box of matches from the hearth and lit the paper. The instant leap of flames was a relief, as much for the sound as the warmth.

She looked at Ian over her shoulder. His eyes remained closed. He'd retreated to his "your move" position. Page opened the door and walked up the hall until she found a bathroom. With two towels in hand she returned to the salon.

Ian was on his feet. "I thought you were running out on me again."

A great rush of anger powered her. "Knock it off, Ian. You're punishing me because you don't feel so good. Well, I don't feel so good either. Here." She tossed him a towel. "Get off the wet coat and dry your hair. And stop feeling sorry for yourself. Maybe then we can see if there's any point in trying to talk."

He stared, slowly taking off his coat. "Yes, ma'am. Anything you say."

As usual, her rage was short-lived. She couldn't help laughing at his comical surprise. "I've got a terrible temper, you know. I'm famous for my rages."

"How about your fibs?"

"You don't believe I've got a violent temper?"

"No. Dry your own hair."

She considered telling him to save his orders for subordinates. Instead she knelt in front of the fire and tossed her hair forward. "Smart people don't tramp around in the rain if they don't have to." The towel muffled her voice.

"Smart people don't *ride* around in the rain if they don't have to."

He was behind her.

"Ian, we've been over this so many times. This is part of my job. In time I hope I'll be able to do very little of the actual messenger duties myself, including any night jobs. But for now—"

"I know. For now I either accept things the way you want them or you'll walk out of my life."

Page stopped rubbing. She took off the towel and pushed her hair back. The fire was bright now and the smell of woodsmoke pungent.

"I'm not issuing ultimatums," she said. "And there's a lot more to discuss than how you feel—or don't feel—about Pedal Pushers."

He knelt beside her. "Discuss away."

She looked sideways at him and giggled. He grinned back. "Lovely pair, huh? Your hairstyle kind of suits you—primitive." He ruffled her tangled hair. "I probably look like a wild man."

"I like it." Unfortunately she liked him wet, dry, mussed up, tidy, awake, asleep—any way he came. She sat on the rug. "I think expectations are the question. Right or wrong, I feel you have certain expectations of me that I may not be able to handle."

"Like?"

"Oh, no." She shook her head. "I'm not making

it that easy for you. You tell me what you see for the two of us in the future.''

He sat beside her, his hip touching hers, and grasped his knees. ''Okay,'' he said slowly. ''From the beginning then. But afterward it's your turn.''

''My turn will get mixed up with yours.''

''Fine. Did you or did you not agree to marry me?''

Page sighed. He was one of those people who attacked in order to defend. ''You didn't ask me.''

''What?'' A chilly finger and thumb yanked her chin around. ''We spent days together as close as a man and woman can be. And I distinctly remember saying we had to—''

She jerked her face from his fingers. ''It's coming back to you? That's right. You said we had to get on with wedding plans because they took time.''

He wasn't quick enough to hide his exasperation. ''Women,'' he said. ''I didn't actually say: Ms. Linstrom, would you do me the honor of becoming my wife? That's it. You're something. Total emancipation until it comes to the old-fashioned stuff.''

''Wrong.'' She did have a high boiling point, but it could be reached. ''Absolutely wrong. Certainly I would expect you to ask me to marry you, but that's only a small part of what's going on here.''

Their faces were inches apart. Page finished speaking with her lips slightly parted.

He'd seen many beautiful mouths, but none as beautiful as hers. Ian roused himself, moving his attention to her eyes. No relief from the spell there. ''Page, will you please marry me?''

She closed her eyes, and he grabbed her before she could resist, kissed her with all the pent-up desire of three weeks' separation from a woman he'd come to need as much as he needed air.

When he raised his head they were both gasping. "That wasn't fair," she whispered. "Don't do that to me, please. We both know there's nothing wrong with our physical reactions to each other."

If he was supposed to feel guilty, something must be missing from his sense of right and wrong. "That silver outfit you wear feels good. It feels really good."

"Ian!"

There was no missing the warning. "Okay, okay. I asked you to marry me. What's the answer?"

"That we have a lot of ground to cover before I can answer."

If he suggested they continue their discussion in bed she'd undoubtedly walk out. Nevertheless, the notion made a memory of the chill he'd been feeling.

He stared into the fire. "Maybe I'm too uncomplicated, but I thought we'd made a commitment in Hawaii. But something changed by the time we left, didn't it?" At least she'd let him know they still had something to build on.

"I don't think anything changed," she said. "We didn't go beyond feelings, that's all. Good sex doesn't necessarily make a good marriage."

He winced. Her directness occasionally caught him off guard. "There's a lot more between us than sex. Not that it isn't a part of what's good for us. I'm glad it is."

"I'm not prepared to give up my work," she said, and he felt her tense beside him. "That means I wouldn't be able to be the kind of wife you want."

He didn't know exactly what to say. Her job did bother him, or rather some aspects of it. "I never said I expected you to give up your business for me. We'd both have to make some life-style changes, but marriage is bound to mean that."

"What changes would you make?"

"Well..." Now that he thought about it, he wouldn't have to change much. "I guess the main thing would be that home and family would take the place of most social activities I used to have. Not that I'll miss them." An understatement. "In fact I began to drop out of that scene some time ago."

Page rested her chin on a fist. He looked at her and bit the inside of his cheek. Gloomy was the only description for that look.

"Did I fail the test?"

"No. You wouldn't have to do anything else to make me happy. And coming home to you, being with you for part of every day would be bliss for me." She met his gaze squarely. "Do I fail the test?"

She was a puzzle. "I don't know what you're saying. As far as I can tell we want the same thing—to be together."

Her sigh was pure frustration. "You want me decorating your house and having your children and cooking meals and being a social success for you. To do all that I would have to give up everything else, and I'm not ready."

That was it. How could he be such a fool? "I...I don't expect you to do that."

"Yes, you—"

"No! Not immediately anyway." He must be careful. "You do like kids?"

"I love them. But not—"

"But not now. Fine. We'll wait until you're ready. As long as that doesn't mean I'm on social security before I get to hold our first baby."

"I don't want to wait too long, either." Her voice broke.

"So we don't have any more problems?" He reached for her, but she shrugged away.

"Don't try to go too fast, Ian. It's not that simple."

Ian got his own taste of frustration. "All right. Tell me where we go from here—in your opinion. I've got to be comfortable, too. You do understand that?"

She wiped the corner of each eye, but he made no attempt to touch her.

"I understand. This is how I think it goes. For the time being I continue exactly as I am. I may even get a bit busier for a while, because we've taken on new people and I'll have to do some street beating to drum up more customers."

He didn't like the idea of her knocking on doors. "Have you done much selling? It's tough."

"How do you think I got started? I'm not crazy about it, but I'm articulate and I make a good presentation."

"Maybe I should—"

"No, Ian. You shouldn't do anything, please."

"I was only thinking about a mailing."

"We already do mailings. Listen—" she faced him, and despite damp lashes her eyes shone "—things are clicking for me. I'm starting to see what looks like success way down the road somewhere. You've got to know how that feels." She paused, one hand rammed into her hair. "Maybe you don't know. It's got to be different when you go into an established business.''

Her enthusiasm brought tenderness welling up in him. ''I do know what you mean.''

''Do you, Ian? When we get a new customer, I've been known to yell and jump up and down like a kid. I feel invincible.''

''We do understand each other.'' He had to hold her. ''We're more alike than you know.''

''Maybe.''

He put an arm around her waist and she rested her cheek against his neck.

''Sweetheart, I was wondering if there was something about my family, my mother perhaps, that bothers you. On the plane you seemed to freeze me out when I mentioned her.''

She chewed a fingernail, something he'd never seen her do before.

''There is something,'' he said. ''Has my mother talked to you?'' He couldn't believe she'd go that far, desperate as she was for him to settle down. ''Has she?''

''Your mother is a lovely lady. I like her.''

''She *has*.'' He made to get up but Page swung around and held his shoulders.

''Rose came by to see me. She was charming, totally accepting of the fact that I'm very different from any of the people she's used to dealing with.''

Irritation made keeping still a feat. ''Was this before or after our trip?''

''It isn't important.''

''It is to me.''

She kissed his chin, but he wasn't about to be deflected. "Before or after?"

"Okay. Prior to the trip."

"About the time when you were giving me a hard time every time I called. Before your accident."

"Let's drop this."

Like hell. "Did she tell you what a wonderful husband I'd make...and father maybe?" Blood throbbed into his cheeks. A downward sweep of Page's lashes confirmed his worst fear. "Oh, no. And that's what made you turn off me."

"Don't be embarrassed." She smiled up at him and held his face in her hands. "Mothers like to do things for their children. And they want them settled. Particularly when they're as ancient as you."

He couldn't laugh. "Watch it with the ancient."

"Ian, we'll probably be the same with our children."

She'd slipped and now he did smile. "Our children? As in yours and mine?"

"Eventually. Probably." She let go of him and turned to the fire once more.

"When I mentioned my mother on the plane, you thought the vacation had been one more part of the plot to snare you, I suppose?"

"Let's just say I felt a bit manipulated."

So did he, but he wouldn't say so now. "Would you mind if I told my mother off?"

He was rewarded with a glare. "I'd never forgive you."

"Then I won't. Can we get back to where we were?" Logic was taking a back seat to what had been steadily building in his body and brain—desire.

"As long as we understand each other."

He was having difficulty thinking at all. "Understand?"

"We'll meet as often as possible and you'll accept that? You won't give me a hard time?"

"I'll never give you a hard time again." He nuzzled his face into her neck.

She moved her hair aside for him and pressed closer. "And we'll go slowly on the marriage thing?"

"Not too slowly." Her neck was so smooth and it smelled of a light perfume and wind and rain...and he was crazy about her.

"Mmm. We won't worry about details for a while."

Sounded good to him. Her mouth was soft and firm at the same time and tasted like mint. Did she chew gum? Irrelevant thoughts. She kissed him back with enough pressure to send them both into a heap on the rug.

The silver stuff clung, slippery, a second skin. Ian wanted to feel the real thing. Page had already undone his shirt and started her favorite kissing game over his chest and stomach.

"This thing you're wearing—help me." But she was too busy with his belt.

She shifted as he wriggled the ankle-length tights off.

"Okay. Time out." He pinned her beneath him. "Are you interested in my feelings?"

Her face was flushed. "I'm very interested."

"Good. I feel like a starving man faced with his first whole lobster. I want you out of this thing."

She stared, then covered her mouth and laughed.

"I'm glad you find this funny."

"Oh, no. Not funny, Ian. I'm insulted. I remind you of a lobster?"

"Don't tease me," he moaned.

Her laughter ceased abruptly and she sat up. "I'm not teasing. I don't ever want to tease you."

She eased the leotard from a shoulder, pulled out her arm, repeated the process until she was naked to the waist.

Ian's lungs refused to expand. He knelt beside her and tilted her head up to meet his kiss, gentle now, before he smoothed her body.

Leotards were a snap.

CHAPTER FOURTEEN

"THEY WENT *WHERE*?"

James, jr. bounced Jemima in one arm and flourished a wrench with his spare hand. "I told you. Niagara Falls. They were catching a seven o'clock plane."

Page left her helmet strap hanging and sank onto Lilian's chair. "Why didn't they tell me?"

Red splotches popped out on James's face. Jemima wriggled and he put her down. "Don't touch anything," he ordered and was rewarded with a pout. "Zip said he and Lilian were too old to make a big fuss out of a thing like getting married. They decided to fly to Niagara Falls tonight, get married and be back in time for work on Monday morning."

"And you're in cahoots with them, you little crook."

"I'm helping, that's all," James said, sounding perturbed. "We all know you're working extra hard so you can...so you can..."

Jemima had arrived at Page's knee and she picked the little girl up. "Yes, James? So I can what?"

"Get married," he blurted and attacked parts of a dismantled bike with gusto.

Page rocked Jemima and kissed her shiny curls. "How is it that my employees know everything about me and I don't know the most important things about them?''

James yanked the wrench harder. ''You do know about us.''

''Answer my question. How do you know I'm thinking of getting married?''

The splotches became one total red face. ''Lilian says that Mr. Faber calls all the time and sends flowers and stuff, and she says she can always find you at his house if you're not upstairs. And she says you'll probably marry him around New Year's.''

It was Page's turn to blush. ''A bunch of spies,'' she said, but without rancor. ''And you could just be right. But I still wish Zip and Lilian hadn't sneaked off without telling me. I'd like to do something for them.''

''You can. When they get back, tell them it's okay for Jemima to be here in the daytime.''

The suggestion caught Page off guard. ''She very often is. I've never complained.''

''No. But they worry you don't really like it and Lilian wants the kid with her.'' He let out a whistling breath as if he'd done something difficult in saying his piece. ''She's smart, y'know. Even if Lilian can't afford for her to go to preschool right now, that kid'll pick up a lot being with all of us.''

Page hid her face in Jemima's hair. If they weren't careful the child would pick up more than she should. ''I'll tell Zip and Lilian it's fine for her to be here,'' she said. The little one felt soft and smelled clean, a small-child smell that started an ache deep inside Page. One day… ''James, how are you going to look after Jemima all weekend? What will your grandmother say?''

Mention of his grandmother always produced a blank expression. ''Jemima'll be with me while I'm here in the garage. Buzz will take her at night. And I'm going to get her out for a walk every afternoon.''

Page smiled. ''You sound pretty organized.'' She couldn't think of a less-likely pair of baby-sitters than James Amwell, jr. and Buzz, although she was now completely recovered from her accident. ''But it's time she went to bed now. You'd better call Buzz. I've got to get going.''

Page set off, a warm sense of well-being fueling her. The thought of Lilian and the Zipper making a home together with Jemima brought an involuntary smile. And the business was really going well.

A month had passed since the start of her truce with Ian. As James had suggested—and Lilian would have to be told to stop monitoring private calls or keep her mouth closed—they were planning a wedding around the New Year.

As with all nights now, this one went too slowly. While she worked she kept her thoughts trained on the next day, which was Saturday.

For several days fog had taken the place of rain. A misty fog that rolled off the bay and slunk through the streets in eerie streams.

Page wore a down-lined jumpsuit over her leotard and tights. Ian's idea, and a good one since the suit was intended for cross-country skiing and was very light.

Friday was usually a busy night and this Friday was no exception. By one-fifteen in the morning, twelve satisfied customers had been dealt with and she'd been given enough to do to keep her out until past her two o'clock cutoff. She stopped at a phone and called her apartment. Tanya never went to bed this early, and fortunately she was at home. Ian now made a habit of getting some sleep and setting his alarm so that he was awake to speak to Page at two. She didn't want to disturb him early, but neither did she want him to worry if she was late home. Tanya promised to give him a message.

Another new dimension to Page's operation was a man called Gary, one of the recently hired riders who had opted to take on extra hours at night. He started at eleven, and when Page had met him on her last return to Waldo's he'd told her he was as busy as she was. The dream was finally becoming real.

Her radio blipped. "Hello, Waldo!"

A voice she didn't recognize answered. "He's stepped out. How many boxes do you have left?"

Page frowned. Waldo's radio was his private pet. "Two."

"Give me the addresses."

"One's for a place on Larkin, the other's Market. You want street numbers?"

"No. It's the Market one that's wrong. From what's written here I thought it might be. Somebody must have copied an address from the next column. Take it to Shipley. Instructions say there's a turnoff just before Rich. Keep your eyes open or you'll miss it. Some guy who lives in a studio apartment over a warehouse. You'll have to go through an abandoned junkyard."

"Sounds charming," Page said, but the dispatch had been terminated.

Twenty minutes later she pedaled slowly toward her last drop. This was a rough area of town, not one she'd ever been sent to before.

There were almost no streetlights. She passed one standard and glanced up. Broken glass reflected a glitter. Knocked out with a rock...or a bullet?

Street names were tough to locate. Fourth. She'd gone too far. An unpleasant thrust speared her stomach. The city was never this silent, particularly this section, from what she'd been told. The drunks and down-and-outs must be asleep...or tucked up in jail.

She wasn't sure exactly where she was, and by a dingy storefront she stopped to look for numbers. Gold paint peeled from glass above the door, and she bumped her bike onto the sidewalk for a closer look.

"Get the hell out!"

She reeled back, stumbling on her own wheels.

A lumpy heap rose, turning into a shambling figure that approached with weakly flailing arms. Page smelled liquor and sweat...and heard a stream of obscenities.

She leaped on the bike and rode on, sweat running down her own icy back.

"Man's place..." were the last words she heard as she hurtled around a corner and sighed her relief at the sight of the word Clementina on a sign. Only a couple of blocks away.

The dispatcher had been right. Missing the alley before Rich would have been easy. But Page's sharp eyes picked out a darker slit in a solid wall of darkness and she rode in. Her heart and lungs vied for her attention. They thudded and hurt in unison, and her throat burned. Ian was right. This could be madness.

She found the yard easily. The beating in her ears lessened and she breathed more easily. Not for long. Making out exactly what the junk consisted of was impossible, but it lay in hulking masses all around her. She couldn't see a warehouse.

This was one task she probably shouldn't try to complete. Waldo wouldn't expect her to go through anything this frightening.

Fear.

Page breathed through her mouth. Apart from the night of her attack she'd never felt afraid while she was doing her job—until now.

Her front wheel hit something and she braked hard. Careful where she trod, she dismounted and made her way on foot, peering ahead. There had to be a building here somewhere. She hated to give up. A flashlight would be a blessing. She'd never needed one before, but in future it would be standard equipment for any night-rider she employed.

"Hello?" She grimaced. The only person likely to hear that puny effort was herself.

Perhaps she should call Waldo and make sure of this. Her eyes were adjusting slowly. Rather than junk, the piles looked like tarp-covered boxes, or stacks.

A soft swipe against her legs almost stopped her heart completely. "What...?" Another sweeping rush and a feline yowl, and she was left trembling but smiling. All the indigents in the area weren't two-footed.

There was no warehouse. No studio apartment. The yard was just that, a big storage yard. Now she felt too sick to go on or turn back. Something was very wrong.

Shaking so violently she could scarcely make her hands work, she leaned her bike against the nearest shrouded pile.

She unzipped her suit far enough to reach her radio. Instinctively, she crouched and bowed her head before starting to press the switch.

Her thumb never made contact.

The arm that shot around her throat and jerked her upright had metal things on it that crushed into her windpipe.

The white light that met her eyes blocked out the world.

SHE'D NEVER TOUCHED more than the edge of the existence that belonged to these people. Page walked through the receiving room at the police precinct house with the disjointed sensation that she'd entered a nightmare. Someone else's nightmare.

Her wrists hurt. The policeman who'd handcuffed her in the yard and reeled off a lot of words about her rights shoved her ahead of him between rows of men and women, some lolling with blank faces, some arguing, some crying.

"I'm a bicycle messenger," she tried again. Like all the other times, the officer wasn't interested.

"You'll get your chance," he said. "Be a good girl and don't make a fuss, and things will go easier for you."

Go easier. He'd talked a lot of nonsense about bets. She was supposed to know about it all, but she couldn't think straight.

In a cubicle enclosed by frosted glass she was pushed to sit on a shiny wooden chair and told to wait.

Minutes passed. Gray metal file cabinets. Gray shelves. Spilled papers. Chipped desk littered with Styrofoam cups and empty sandwich wrappers.

She wanted Ian.

The door opened. ''Miss Page Linstrom?'' A pudgy man with hammocks of fat beneath his eyes entered, reading her name from a sheet in his hands. He looked at her, saggy jowls wobbling. Not unkind, Page registered vaguely. Tired, bored, disinterested, nothing more. She was another stranger accused of… what?

''I'm Detective Sloane,'' the man said flatly. He opened the door again and yelled something. The policeman who had arrested her came in and took the handcuffs off her wrists before withdrawing again.

Sloane balanced on the edge of the scarred desk. ''Says here you were picked up in a storage yard off Shipley. Care to save us all a lot of time and tell the whole story? Shorter the better. More names the better.''

Feeling returned slowly to Page's fingers and she gripped the seat of the chair. Underneath it was satin smooth. How many other fingers had rested there, held on to something tangible while their owners sweated?

''Miss Linstrom, it'll be easier on you if you talk.''

''I…I don't know what this is about.'' Her voice was high and squeaky. ''I'm a bicycle messenger. I was trying to make a delivery.''

''Hmm.'' He took a plastic packet from his pocket

and emptied it on the desk. She recognized payment envelopes for Waldo, the ones the policeman had taken from her. "How long have you had this job?"

"Er—"

"Two years. We already know."

So why had he asked?

"Who is your contact?"

She felt faint. "I don't know what you're talking about. I want Ian."

"Is he your contact?"

Dimly she remembered scenes like this from movies. She wasn't supposed to answer questions until she understood what was going on. "Ian is my friend. I don't know why I'm here and I'm not talking to you till I do."

He got up and walked behind the desk, sat down and clasped his hands over his belly. "Lady, I don't think for one minute that you're as dumb as you'd like me to believe. We know what you've been doing and now we've caught you in the act. You were read your rights, so why not just come clean."

"There was something about a lawyer."

"Yeah, yeah." Still no anger, only resignation. "I thought you might be smart enough to finger whoever's making the big money out of this, that's all. Your lawyer would have been happy to walk in here and find half his work done for him. And we'd come off smelling like roses. But if you want it the hard way..." He picked up a phone on his desk. "Sloane here. Send a matron. I've got one for beauty portraits and prints."

Page shot forward in her chair. "What am I supposed to have done?"

He smiled and the effect wasn't reassuring. "You were given the charges when you were arrested, but I don't mind repeating them for you. Off-track betting is an offense in this state. You are a runner for an off-track betting organization."

CHAPTER FIFTEEN

HOW LONG had she been there? The cot she sat on was hard, covered by an olive-green blanket. For what seemed like days she'd remained motionless, listening to other prisoners coughing, swearing, shouting at passing guards.

Earlier they'd said she could be released if someone posted bail. She didn't have enough money of her own.

After she'd been booked, a woman had informed her of her right to make one telephone call. Her lawyer had been the suggested recipient. She didn't have a lawyer. One would be appointed for her if that's what she wanted. Her insistence that she didn't need one, that she wasn't guilty of anything, had caused a few unpleasant and knowing laughs.

The call she'd made was to Tanya. Ian had been her first thought, but she couldn't make herself dial his number. He'd told her so many times how much he hated the night work and shown his disapproval of her occupation in general. This fiasco would squelch any argument she'd ever made against his opinion.

Tanya had sounded distant, horrified. Page was not to worry, Tanya insisted, but nothing in her voice or what she said gave reason to expect help.

That had been hours ago. Page's watch had been taken away and put in a bag with her name and a number on it, but she still knew it must be midafternoon Saturday by now.

"Linstrom, get ready." A female guard, clipboard in hand, shouted into the cell without looking at Page.

Ready for what? She had nothing with her. A comb and toothbrush, a few basic needs had been provided, and she'd already done what she could for her appearance.

Sickness came in waves, and with it cold sweats. A tray of food, brought a long time ago, stood untouched on a chair.

The clack of heels returned. Page got up from the edge of the cot and stood with her fists clenched at her sides. She wouldn't think. Just go through the motions, do whatever they told her to do, wait for the hell to end.

Keys jangled and the door swung inward. "Move."

She moved. Into the corridor, through an electronically controlled door, reversing all the procedures she'd been put through early in the morning.

Her small possessions—watch, gloves, a gold chain she wore around her neck—were spilled onto a counter, and she was told to check them, then sign "on the line" to indicate that they had been returned.

Putting the chain on again was impossible. Her fingers refused to work the clasp. At last she was ready, back in the down suit, although she probably wouldn't need it, and with her helmet and gloves clutched in front of her.

"Right." The guard didn't smile or make eye contact. "You can go. I'm sure you've already been told not to leave the area and what any violation of bail restrictions would mean."

Page nodded. "Yes, thank you."

With the woman holding her arm she walked into a hall where the burst of noise and activity made her cringe.

Then her arm was released and she stood alone in the midst of chaos.

A different hand touched her lightly between the shoulders. "Are you okay?"

She looked up into Ian's face, and the tears she'd suppressed flowed unchecked. "I'm scared," she said, leaning against his chest and holding on. "I don't know what's happening to me."

He spread his fingers on her back. "It'll be okay."

"Ian, did they tell you what they think I've done?"

"Yes."

She raised her face. Fatigue grayed his features and dulled his eyes.

"Tanya called you?"

"Yes. Why didn't you?" He wore jeans and a parka and hadn't shaved.

"I knew what you'd say if I did." How long had he been waiting? "I wanted to talk to you, but—"

"We'll discuss it later. I want to get out of here." He eased her arms away.

The slight warmth that had seeped into her, the relief at the sight of him, ebbed away. There was something different about Ian and she didn't think she liked it.

They left the huge, gray stone building and crossed to a parking lot on the other side of the street. Ian opened the door of the Mercedes for her, shut her inside and walked around to slide behind the wheel.

He wasn't saying anything.

She should thank him for coming. And posting bail...he must have done that. He drove from the lot without glancing at her.

"Was it you who posted bail?" She touched his arm and felt muscle contract.

"Yes."

She removed her hand. "Thank you." The sick feeling overwhelmed her now. "They impounded my bike and radio. I don't understand—"

"Standard procedure, I imagine. They'd need to go over those things." His voice was level, but his knuckles showed white on the steering wheel.

What is it? Page longed to ask. *Why aren't you making me feel safe like you always do?*

Ian's chest felt as if giant hands compressed it. After Tanya Woodside's call he'd dashed down to the jail and demanded Page's release. There had been no mistaking the expressions on the faces of officers who listened until he'd finished railing: pity. They considered him a sucker for a beautiful woman who'd been living a double life for months. Then he'd been told the details of the arrest, the prior events. He didn't know exactly what to do next but there were questions of his own to ask—of people the police hadn't mentioned—and regardless of what happened he would never stop loving Page.

He was exhausted. No sleep. Only hours of waiting and wondering while he balanced attempts at logic with the facts he'd been presented.

"Ian?" She sounded as tired as he felt and something twisted inside him. "You don't believe I did what they said, do you?"

"How can you even ask me that?" he shouted, and when he looked at her tears shone in her eyes. "I'm sorry, Page. I'm uptight. Frantic. I don't know what to do first." How true. He'd been told there was evidence to incriminate Page but not what that evidence was. It had even been suggested that she could have engineered her own accident in an attempt to deflect any official interest in her illegal activities. He had never felt so impotent, or angry, or confused.

"Can we talk for a while?" Page asked.

He wanted to, but he didn't dare take the time. "I've got to ask some questions—try to make sense of all this. The sooner I get on it, the better."

She was quiet for a moment, then said, "I don't want to go home."

He closed his eyes fractionally. This was the hardest thing he'd ever done, to try to remain objective while all he wanted was to get her away from this mess—regardless of whether or not she'd done something wrong. Wrong? Hell, he must be cracking up. Page wasn't capable of what they'd accused her of doing.

"Ian, would it be all right if I waited at your place? I could call my staff from there and see how things are going."

For both of them he had to be strong. "I don't think that's a good idea. If the police want to talk to you they'll expect you to be at your own apartment. Get settled in there, and I'll talk to you as soon as I talk to someone who knows more about this sort of thing than I do."

Outside her apartment, Page watched Ian come around to open her door. She got out and stood in front of him.

"I'll come in and get you settled," he said.

He was anxious. Page sensed his tightly constrained nervousness, his desire to leave.

"No need," she said, needing him more than he'd ever know. "Do whatever you have to do."

His eyes showed uncertainty. "Are you sure you're all right?" he asked.

She made herself smile. "Sure." That he cared for her Page didn't doubt, but nothing in his life to this point could have prepared him for what he'd been through in the past few hours.

"Good," he said, backing away. "Talk to you later, okay?"

"Okay." But it wasn't. Couldn't he feel that?

Without waiting to see her inside, he walked swiftly to his side of the car and got in. Page stayed at the curb until the Mercedes merged with other traffic.

She went, not into the house, but to the garage and pushed open the door. That it wasn't locked surprised her. After what the police had said, she'd expected padlocks and chains to guard their precious evidence.

"Page!" Tanya, whom she'd never seen in the garage before, leaped up and rushed to fold her in a tight and shaky embrace. "Oh, Page, thank God you're back."

"I told those SOBs they were nuts." James came forward, more disheveled looking than usual. Behind him stood Buzz with Jemima on her shoulders.

"Page, Page," the child said around the thumb stuffed in her mouth.

"Shhh," Buzz said, jiggling. "Come and sit down, Page. Geez, we've been frantic around here."

Page ached with gratitude for these special people. With Tanya's arm still draped around her, she sat in the chair James set in the middle of the floor.

"What happened?" Buzz asked. She swung Jemima down, and Page promptly found her lap invaded by the sweet-smelling bundle.

She cuddled the child close and felt some of the tension slipping away. "You see before you a hardened criminal." The quip didn't have the right ring.

"Did they hurt you?" Tanya stayed close.

Page looked at her and noted that the pinched appearance had intensified. "They didn't hurt me—physically, that is. The damage happens up here." She pointed to her head. "Are you okay, Tanya?"

"Fine, yeah. Terrific. Tired, that's all. I couldn't sleep after you called." That made sense, but it didn't account for the new bruise on Tanya's temple.

Page decided to wait until they were alone to pursue that topic. "Thanks for calling Ian. I guess you did that?"

"I had to. I couldn't think where else to get the money, and I figured he'd want to go down there anyway." She glanced toward the door. "Didn't he bring you back?"

"Uh-huh. But he had to leave and check out some things." She thought about what Tanya had said, that she hadn't known where else to go for the bail money. More proof that there was no wealthy Woodside family she supposedly was always able to turn to.

James stood beside Page rubbing his bony hands together. ''Do you know what those turkeys say?''

She felt the rage he was trying to hold in. ''You mean the police?'' Jemima had turned her face up to hers, and Page kissed a soft cheek. ''What did they say that I haven't already heard?''

''How should I know?'' Truculence didn't suit James. He shoved his hands in his pockets and paced to the window.

Buzz hunkered down in front of Page. ''They came in here before James arrived this morning and found all kinds of money stashed around the place. Did they tell you that?''

They'd told her. She nodded.

''Page. I was here last night to pick up Jemima. James was here, too. We'd have seen bundles of notes packed in black boxes if they were here.''

Page became very still. Black boxes? She spoke carefully, keeping her voice level. ''The police didn't mention boxes to me. But, according to our men of the law, I'm very good at tucking away bucks. Rolled up and stuffed inside bicycle frames, they said.''

James snorted. ''There wasn't any money in any bicycle frames yesterday.''

''How can you be sure?'' She had to be sensible and ready for the contentions the police were bound to make.

He shrugged. ''I just am, that's all. The weight would be different. The sound. I'd notice something.''

''Yeah,'' Buzz agreed.

Tanya sat on the floor and crossed her legs. ''James and Buzz know what they're talking about. And surely Ian will help you out. They'll listen to him.

Pillars of society always carry more weight than the rest of us.''

Page silently rocked Jemima. She couldn't second guess what Ian might decide to do. ''We'll have to wait and see what happens. I know I haven't done anything wrong and that's the main thing. I've got to believe that there is justice.'' And she had to try making sense of something vague but insistent forming in her brain.

IN THE EARLY EVENING Ian called. He said he was still making inquiries and couldn't see Page tonight. He wanted her to sit tight until they could work everything out. Nothing would ever be so bad that they couldn't face it together. Was he saying he assumed her guilt but would stand by her?

Tanya, who had drawn a discreet distance away without leaving the sitting room, came to put an arm around Page as soon as she hung up the phone. ''Is something wrong between you two?''

Page would have liked to be left alone to cry. ''I don't know. And I'm not sure I care.''

''You don't mean that. Give Ian a break. He must be shocked like the rest of us are.''

But the rest of them had shown their support with something more precious than money—their faith in her.

She turned to Tanya. ''Forget about me for a minute. What did you do to your face? You've got a bruise.''

Tanya touched her temple. ''I don't know,'' she said, but color rose in her cheeks. ''I guess I bumped it without noticing.''

The doorbell stopped Page from replying that Tanya must have *felt* the blow—just as she'd felt her fall a few weeks earlier.

Their visitors—or rather Page's visitors—were two policemen.

A middle-aged officer pushed in front of a younger man and stood on the doorstep with his feet spread. "Page Linstrom?"

She nodded. A little sound let her know Tanya was behind her left shoulder.

"Detective Sloane wants you down at the station."

She found her voice. "Why?"

He shrugged and the other man leaned forward. "A few questions, ma'am. We should get going."

"Couldn't you ask me the questions here?" The inside of her throat hurt and she could barely swallow.

"That wouldn't be convenient," she was promptly told. She knew arguing would be useless.

Detective Sloane, looking even more tired than the night before, was already installed behind his ugly desk when Page entered his office.

"Sit down." He waved to the slippery chair. "Sorry to bring you in again. We need to clear up a few more points."

At no time before had she been given a chance to plead her innocence, and she didn't expect any change in policy now. But she was going to try to make this policeman listen anyway.

"The man who called me on my radio last night..." She paused until Sloane looked up. "The one who told me to go to a different place. Do you know who he was?"

"No. But I'm sure you do."

She drew in a shaky breath and pressed on. ''I never heard his voice before. Waldo usually gives me my instructions. Talk to him, he'll tell you.'' She'd tried to call Waldo herself earlier but there'd been no answer.

Sloane laughed shortly. ''I'm sure Mr. Sands would tell me if I asked him. We aren't concerned with him now, only with the outfit you were working for.''

''I don't know what you're talking about,'' Page muttered.

Sloane shuffled papers and mumbled, then burped and didn't apologize.

''Sure you do. You ready to give us some names?''

The helplessness intensified. ''What names am I supposed to give you?''

''Okay. A quick synopsis to help your memory. We got a tipoff last night, and the information we received checked out. The caller said you'd be making a drop in that yard and you were there. Our mistake was not waiting long enough to get whoever was supposed to take that box from you.''

''Box?''

''Don't be coy with me. The box you were supposedly delivering. We found more of them at your garage. They were useful, weren't they?''

''You're not making sense.''

''No, of course not.'' He gave her a thin smile. ''You didn't use those deli boxes to pick up bets and deliver payoffs, did you? What made someone turn you in? How long have you been stockpiling money in that garage of yours? Is that what happened? Did you steal from your head honcho until he got mad enough to take you off the street? Are you sure it isn't time to let whoever your boss is take some of the heat? We'll give you all the protection you need if that's the hang-up."

He was mixing her up. "I'm a bicycle messenger," she said, feeling like a parrot. "I've got my own company and I work all day, as well as at night. Waldo Sands is just one of my customers. I don't know what happened last night, or how there came to be money in the bikes or in those boxes—"

"And in the box you were about to deliver at the storage yard. And in the envelopes you hadn't yet emptied of incoming bets."

Page stared. "In the envelopes?"

"Surprise, surprise." He sounded bored. "Yeah, in the envelopes. Not that you knew about it, of course."

"Sure I did. Payments for goods."

He laughed unpleasantly. "Lady, there aren't goods in any deli that bring the kind of bucks you were carrying. You want to talk about it now?"

She only stared.

Many more abortive questions followed before she was treated to another unwelcome ride in a police car. Back to her apartment.

Page sat behind the two officers, so wide awake she doubted she would ever sleep again. The whole thing was coming clear to her now.

Page pressed a fist against the cold window and rested her brow on top. She had it. All of it—or almost all. Although they didn't say as much, the police understood the basics too, but expected to get at more evidence. She was supposed to supply that evidence. That's where they'd slipped up in their calculations, because she wasn't guilty of any crime. But she would be able to give them some of what they needed.

Page rolled her head against her fist. Why had it taken so long to remember about that box?

Before she could go back to Detective Sloane to tell him what she'd figured out she must talk to at least two people.

One of them had set her up last night.

CHAPTER SIXTEEN

"YOU KNOW THEY'VE arrested Waldo Sands?"

Ian exchanged glances with his father and looked back at Walt Isaacs. "I didn't know. What does that mean?"

The lawyer sank lower in his chair, tipped back and crossed his feet on his desk. "It means that unless the guy says your lady friend's innocent you'd better buy a commuter pass to the local pen."

"Ian," Bob Faber said as Ian leaped to his feet, "we've got to stay calm if we're going to help Page."

"I don't like the way he talks about her." Ian leveled a finger at Isaacs. "I'm here because we were told you're the best in town. I expect you to be on our side."

Isaacs studied his fingernails. His jeans were the designer variety and his blue sweater was cashmere, but even slouched in his chair he exuded slick, all-pro city lawyer and Ian didn't like him.

When he spoke he stared at Ian with hard blue eyes. "Ready to get down to this? If you are we'll talk. Otherwise I've got better things to do. In case you haven't noticed, this is Sunday and the reason I'm here is because you hounded my household staff half the night and I didn't want you to keep it up today."

Bob Faber's hand shot out to grip Ian's arm. "Sit down, son. We know you're doing us a favor, Isaacs, but I expect your bill to reflect that. Where do we go from here? Or should I say, where do we start?"

Isaacs swung his feet down and opened a folder in front of him. It contained a single sheet of paper. He read quickly and pushed the folder aside. "She isn't in custody?"

"No." Ian hated this cold bastard. If he hadn't come so highly recommended he'd tell the man to get lost.

"That's strange. She should be."

"What the hell do you mean?"

"Ian." Bob Faber's voice held a note of pleading. "Cooperate. Hear the man out."

"I don't know why she isn't behind bars," Isaacs continued, unperturbed. "What I'd like to suggest up-front is that we go for a plea bargain. It's her best shot."

"The hell—"

"Ian! For God's sake. Start thinking with your head." His father's thin face turned red. "We're up-set, but we can't do a thing for Page if we don't keep our heads."

"Right," Ian said tightly and subsided into a chair. "I apologize, Isaacs."

"Forget it. The police are being tight-lipped. But from what I got from a source of mine, she looks guilty as hell. She had money on her and they found more in her garage. The story is that she's working for a big-time operation in competition with Sands. She's a plant."

''Knock off the present tense,'' Ian said, then shrugged. ''Go on.''

''Yeah. Okay. She's supposed to be a plant whose function was to feed back information about Sands's activities. The police believe she double-crossed whoever she was working for and they turned her in as a way of getting rid of her and taking Waldo Sands out at the same time.''

''Crap,'' Ian said through clenched teeth.

His father cleared his throat. ''I agree with Ian. If all this is true why hasn't she, er, fingered her boss?''

Isaacs's laugh chilled Ian. ''This is big time, guys, big crime for big bucks that's likely to pull in a bundle of names we'll all recognize.''

''I figured out that much,'' Ian commented.

''Good. I guess you've also heard of honor among thieves. Forget that one. Try fear among thieves. She's not singing because she wants to stay alive. She knows they'll take her out if she opens her mouth.''

Ian massaged his temples. ''I don't believe a word of this.''

This time Isaacs didn't laugh. ''You'd better hope we get a judge who doesn't believe a word of it.''

WHEN WOULD THE POLICE show again? Page made her way slowly back to her bedroom. She'd been there most of the day. Wind rattled the window and she jumped. Her nerves were shot. She had to talk to Ian before she was picked up again. Where was he? Last night his phone had been steadily busy and today he wasn't answering. She didn't have the energy to go looking for him. The clock in the sitting room chimed six. How much longer did she have?

She stretched out on the futon without putting on the light. Each time she got up she felt dizzy, and the fear that she might really be sick grew. There was no time for illness now.

The phone rang and she reached for it, hardly able to breathe.

"Page? This is Ian." He didn't wait to be sure who had answered. "We'd better get together."

"Yes." But she couldn't ride to his house, not feeling as she did.

"If I come to your place can we have some privacy, or is your roommate around?"

The urgency was there, the suggestion that he felt panicky. "Tanya isn't here." A headache joined Page's other symptoms.

"I'll be right over."

He hung up. Page slowly did the same and put on the lamp beside her bed.

IAN RAN DOWNSTAIRS and outside, pulling on his raincoat as he went. The young evening snapped about his ears as he opened the car door. No dampness softened the air, and he felt winter's tightening grip.

The drive to her apartment took minutes. He parked in front, leaped the steps in one bound and rang her bell. Then he turned his back. A darkening sky touched trees and rooftops. Each breath he took carried brittle air into his restricted lungs. Please let him find the right words…and have enough strength for himself, and Page, if necessary.

The lock rattled behind him and his resolve wavered.

Hinges creaked.

"Page. Oh, hell, Page."

Ian walked inside and pulled her into his arms. He crushed her to him, kissing her hair, her closed eyes, her cheeks. At first she responded, then as abruptly, she pushed him from her and went into the kitchen.

He called her name and heard her say, "We've got to talk."

"I know," he shouted, waving his arms, his carefully hoarded control fleeing completely. "So talk. But for God's sake make me understand what's happening." That wasn't what he'd intended to say, or at least, not in that way.

He followed her into the kitchen. She wasn't there. More slowly he entered the hall leading to the rest of the apartment. "Where are you?"

"Sitting room," she said clearly and he found her huddled on a shabby blue couch in a cluttered boxlike room.

He leaned against the wall just inside the door and crossed one foot over the other. His careless comment had already made this harder than he'd feared. "I love you, Page. I'll always love you."

"I know. But you also think I'm a criminal. I'm not."

The pounding in his chest eased, but only slightly. "The police have some strong evidence. We have to come up with a way to combat that."

She wore jeans and a blue sweater. Her face was pale and there were dark shadows under her eyes. They'd both been through too much.

"There is a way to combat it," Page said. "First we have to be honest with each other."

"What do you mean?"

"I know the whole story now. I worked it out."

He saw her look at her socks. They were mismatched, and she hitched her jeans farther down. He walked to stand in front of her.

"You mean you can prove your innocence?" The thrill of hope seemed unreal.

"I didn't do anything wrong, Ian. Obviously you wouldn't have any way of being sure of that, given the way we met, but honestly, until Friday night I don't think I'd ever as much as thought about betting. Why should I? It's not something that's ever touched me before."

"Go on."

Page pushed back her hair and kept her fingers against her scalp. Her legs ached, and her arms. When Ian went home she'd take her temperature.

"Page, speak to me."

She took a deep breath. "Something the police said last night—or something they didn't say—made everything clear. There *is* no unknown betting operation I'm working for, or anyone else in this case, although the authorities think there is. Those envelopes of Waldo's for his so-called deli clients are the way he collected and paid on bets. I was just a pawn who carried them around. On Friday something went wrong. There have to be a lot of rival operations and one of them managed to get a call through to me. They sent me to that yard and tipped off the police. Then they planted money in my garage. All very tidy. First Waldo used me as a runner. Then one of his competitors used me to eliminate him."

"What was it the police didn't say?"

"That Waldo is in custody. And he has to be, or they'd be searching for him, because he isn't at his place. When I asked them to talk to him they pretended they weren't interested. That didn't make sense."

She laughed without mirth. "They believe I'm a kind of double agent, a crook with her feet in two camps. And their theory is right except I didn't know a thing about it. Now by suggesting the only way I can stay out of prison is to implicate these people I'm supposed to know, they hope to get more information out of me. They'll take me in as soon as they're tired of waiting for me to make a move. This all seems like something that only happens to other people."

Just voicing it all brought wobbly excitement, the start of relief. She knew her theory was right.

"Okay," Ian said. "So why didn't you tell this theory of yours to the police and defend yourself?"

She got up and rested her hands on his chest. "You were frightened when I was arrested."

He looked into her eyes. "Wouldn't you have been if the position were reversed?"

"No. I'd have believed it was a mistake and expected everything to be cleared up."

"I did. But I was still frantic when nothing positive happened."

Her mouth dried out. "We met when I was making a delivery for Waldo. Your name was on the envelope. Ian, were you one of Waldo's clients? It doesn't matter to me if you've placed a few bets here and there. But it's going to come out if I tell the whole story from beginning to end. A lot of names are going to come out."

At first she thought he was taking her in his arms. Instead he gripped her shoulders and put her away from him. ‘‘You…you think I’d let you suffer to protect myself?’’

‘‘Ian, I—’’

‘‘I love you. I want to marry you. And I’ve been through hell over this. Where are you coming from? Can’t you see what it’s like for me? I saw a lawyer today, and he thinks the evidence against you is solid. You’re going to have to prove you weren’t involved with Waldo or someone like him. You can’t use holding back out of loyalty to me as an excuse for not giving whatever evidence you’ve got.’’

She was crying now. ‘‘I couldn’t risk hurting you.’’

‘‘I haven’t done anything.’’

She gulped and the tears stopped. ‘‘I believe you if you say so. But neither have I.’’

‘‘You were caught with evidence that suggests otherwise.’’

‘‘You sound like a policeman.’’

He moved away. ‘‘I know I’m not involved with this. I’ve spent all afternoon interviewing some of my ‘friends’ and I found out what I needed to. If you’d thought hard enough about that first night you came to my place you might have remembered a comment that the order had been placed in my name. I didn’t place it. I’d never heard of Touch Tone Gourmet before.’’

‘‘One of the others called Waldo? Of course. I do remember now. So one of them was a betting client of his?’’

‘‘Does it matter to us? The police will get around to that. But it doesn’t alter the fact that you were employed by Sands, and at this point you're under suspicion."

"I'll do something about that."

"Do it now. I'll come with you."

She could hardly see him through a blur of tears. "Thank you. But you have to trust me. There's one more thing I have to do first."

"What?"

"I can't tell you."

He pushed a hand into his hair. "That sounds like another way of saying you can't trust me. Or you won't. I don't buy that, Page. If you've got everything under control and you're in the clear, why not finish this now?"

"I'm tired," she told him. "I think I need to be alone for a while." Only an hour ago she'd longed to see him. What was he making her feel now? Did he doubt her innocence even though he insisted otherwise?

Ian's face set in rigid lines. "You don't want me here?"

"I didn't say that."

"Oh, but I think you did and maybe you're right." He went to the sitting-room door. "I'll look forward to hearing how things work out for you. Let me know if you decide I can do something to help."

"Ian!" She leaped to her feet to follow him, but stopped when she heard the front door close. The car's engine sounded as a muffled roar before tires squealed and the noise quickly faded.

Page walked back down the hall. Holding her eyes wide open seemed to help the dizziness. She stumbled and caught herself against the wall. When she reached her bedroom she took the phone off the hook. Ian was unlikely to call and there was no one else she wanted to talk to. She thought she would vomit soon.

EARLY THE NEXT MORNING after drinking tea—the only thing that sounded good to her—she checked in at the garage and found the morning routine clicking.

"You doing okay?" the Zipper asked on his way out. He and Lilian had returned the night before.

"Sure," she lied, waving as he left.

Jemima sat on Lilian's knee while she worked the radio. "Hi, Page," Lilian said and continued filling in dockets. "Things are hopping around here."

"And you're coping okay?"

Lilian glanced up and moved her mouthpiece aside. "I'm coping fine. Zip's mad enough to take on the whole San Francisco police department but I'm coping with that—not that I blame him. You look like hell."

Page grimaced. "I know. That's how I feel, too."

"Did you hear any more from the police?"

"Nope." She was surprised they hadn't come to get her by now. Not that she cared much now that she felt estranged from Ian. "I think I may have the flu. Will the place fall down if I go upstairs again? I'll try to make it in again this afternoon."

"It'll be fine." Lilian frowned, and Page saw her chest expand. "I don't think you've got the flu. Once this stuff with the cops is sorted out you'll be okay. Go get some rest."

Page smiled and trudged down the alley beside the house, then around to the front steps. Lilian wasn't to know that she'd never feel completely okay again. Oh, she'd heal, but nothing would ever be the same.

She went into the apartment, closed the door behind her and locked it. No need to postpone the inevitable any longer. She put on the chain.

"Are you locking me in?"

Tanya's words pounded into Page like a blow. She spun around. "I thought you were still out."

"And you were making sure you'd know when I got back?" Tanya's hair hung in uncombed tangles around her pale face. She wore a long coat over a brown, checked shirt and jeans.

"What makes you say that?" Page's heart beat harder.

Tanya walked, tennis shoes scuffing, into the kitchen, with Page close behind.

"I got back a little while ago. I was going to try to get away without seeing you." Tanya indicated a suitcase and a large duffel bag near the door leading to the rest of the apartment. "You know, don't you?"

"Love makes people do crazy things," Page said softly. "I don't think you wanted to hurt me."

"But I did. I hurt you a lot." She sniffed and looked at the ceiling. "I loved him so much, Page, so much."

Page pulled out a chair and sat down. "Why Waldo? Of all the men you could choose, why pick one...?" What was she saying? Wasn't she the one who'd told Ian you couldn't decide who to love?

"I didn't love him at first." Tanya hunched in a corner. "See, I don't have a rich family waiting to hand out bucks like I told you I did."

Page made a sympathetic noise, but she didn't say

that she'd figured out for herself that the wealthy Woodsides were a myth.

"Waldo gave me things. He gave me everything. And he treated me like someone special."

"You are special. When did you know what he was into?" She was going to get through this with Tanya and help her make some decisions. After that she'd start picking up her own scattered pieces.

Tanya slid down onto the floor. "I knew a long time ago. He used to brag about it...all his money. I was a safe pair of ears, because he'd bought me."

Page visualized the box of money in Tanya's drawer. "When did Waldo start hitting you?"

A small noise came from Tanya's throat.

"Why would you keep going back for more of the same? You could have walked away."

"Walked away to what? I know what having nothing feels like, and I couldn't face it again. Wrong, I know. Weak, I know. But that's the way it was."

"What made you...frame me?"

Tanya covered her eyes. "I'm sorry, Page. He didn't want me anymore. I was supposed to get lost while he took up with someone else. He gave me a bunch of money as a payoff and told me to take a walk."

"But you wouldn't stay away."

"I couldn't. On Friday I went to him again. He was with her—the new woman. He hit me in front of her."

"Then you came back here. And when I called to let you know I was still out and would be late you decided to get back at him through me." She was tired, but there was no stopping now.

"I thought the police would go straight for Waldo and find out you were for real."

"They had Waldo figured, Tanya. But I was framed tight enough for them to believe I was in it, too." Page took a crumpled wad of gold ribbon from her pocket. "When did you drop this in the garage? On one of your secret visits to check my movements in the job book?"

"Page—"

"The other night you contacted a rival outfit and gave them my call number?"

"Yes," Tanya whispered.

"The call number was easy to get from Waldo's, right?"

"Yes. I got it a long time ago."

"And it didn't matter that I would end up in jail and scared to death?"

Tanya hugged herself. "I wasn't thinking anymore. I'd tried to warn Waldo that I meant business weeks ago with those accidents—"

"With those 'accidents' my riders had?" She sighed, wanting desperately for this to be over. "You never talked to Ken about my problems because you didn't have to. You already knew because you'd given your rival outfit information about us and then you saw what happened. My God, Tanya, they put both Perkins and me in the hospital. No wonder Waldo was so quick to pay my medical bills. He really needed me back at work and thinking nice thoughts about him. Boy, did you make a patsy out of him."

"He asked for it. But I didn't expect you to get hurt." Tanya lifted her chin and her eyes were filled with tears. "I never thought anything would really happen to you—or anyone. The man I was dealing with said he only wanted to slow Waldo down by frightening him."

One more thing. "If you didn't intend me to be seriously implicated why did you plant money in the garage?"

"I couldn't think straight anymore." Tanya covered her eyes. "I just wanted him to get what he deserves. He never believed I'd do anything to hurt him. He could always bring me to heel, he said."

Page thought of something else. "When I was in hospital I wondered why the envelopes hadn't been taken from my backpack when I was attacked. Now I know. Your friends didn't need them."

Tanya had stopped listening. "Waldo said I was a loser. He said I was useless and should creep away somewhere."

And she would have crept away if Page hadn't caught her. "If you want to run I won't stop you," she told Tanya. "But I am calling the police, and they'll find you."

"Call them. I'm not going anywhere."

"I won't press personal charges against you," Page said. "You'll have to answer for some things, but at least this way you'll eventually get to start over again."

"In jail?"

"Maybe not. I know a police detective who likes to make deals."

WHAT A DIFFERENCE A DAY MAKES. Wasn't that the way the song went?

Page propped herself against a wall in Union Square and watched a man in a clown costume making animals from skinny balloons.

"And an elephant for the boy with red hair," the man said, crouching in front of a freckle-faced toddler to offer a pink masterpiece with a foot-long trunk.

Two women accompanied several children, who watched the clown with the single-minded intensity Page had so often seen in the very young.

In her hand she held a rolled copy of a newspaper. She opened it again, turned to an inside page and read an insignificant article most people would miss: San Francisco had one less off-track betting outfit. Her own name wasn't mentioned. She was "an informed source." There had been arrests and would be more.

And an hour ago on this Monday in late December she'd spoken with another informed source. A doctor.

In about seven months Page would become a mother.

CHAPTER SEVENTEEN

THIS WAS ONLY the second time Page had visited Ian's suite at Faber and Faber. She walked from the elevator to his secretary's empty desk.

An oak-framed clock on the wall showed four-thirty. Ian was in the building. Page had checked the parking garage and found his car in its marked slot. She would wait until his secretary returned and ask to see him.

The pills the doctor had given her earlier in the day for nausea worked. She'd taken the first one as soon as she'd gotten back home to change for work and felt better already—physically. Once she'd seen Ian and told him what he had a right to know it would be business as usual for her.

The intercom on the secretary's desk buzzed, buzzed again, and again. Page looked at the control panel. The signal came from Ian's office. He must be in there and not know, or remember, that his secretary was away from her desk.

There wouldn't be a better or an easier time to say what she'd come to say.

He didn't look up when she entered his office. "Clemmie, what the hell's with you today? I rang half a dozen times. Take this stuff and get someone to run it down to the art department. Then I want you to keep trying that number I gave you till there's an answer."

Page closed the door. "Hello, Ian."

His head jerked up, but he remained crouched over the papers on his desk. "Page! I've been trying to call you. Your phone's been busy since last night."

"I took my phone off the hook."

"All night and all day?" He sat back, a pencil braced between the fingers of both hands. "I went over this morning and got no answer. And that watchdog of yours in the garage said she didn't know where you were."

She wouldn't be pushed around by him just because he'd had some sort of guilt attack about the things he'd said to her. "Lilian didn't know where I was."

"And she didn't tell you I was searching for you?"

"She hasn't seen me yet," Page said, and sighed. Buzz had been covering the radio when she went to the garage for her bike. "And she won't hear from me until I leave here and report in, not that you have to concern yourself with any of this. You must be very busy, so I'll make this short."

"Please—" he got up and skirted his desk to stand in front of her "—sit down. We were idiots last night."

She gave a grim laugh. "We seem to have a talent for saying the wrong things to each other."

He looked tired, so tired. "I did try to call last night, but like I said, I couldn't get through. I figured you were asleep so I didn't try to come over. Then today I still couldn't reach you. I read—"

"The paper." She completed his sentence. "I didn't come about that," she told him.

"Let me get you some coffee?"

The pulse in his throat was visible and strong. If she put a hand on his chest she'd feel the same beat. How was it that he didn't have to touch her for her to feel that he had? "No coffee, thanks. Ian, I'm pregnant. This morning a doctor told me I should deliver in about seven months."

She made herself look at his face. His lips were slightly parted. He stared back at her, but she couldn't read the expression in his dark, dark eyes.

"I'm not sorry," she went on. "Don't ever think that. And don't think I'm here because I expect help." She paused, and he continued to stare. "Getting pregnant may not have been very smart, but I do like children. I'm going to love this one, and I'm not a kid myself anymore, so it's time I started a family if I'm going to have one.

"The thing is that I kind of assumed I might not be ovulating because I'm so active I don't have many periods. So I'd put it out of my mind and that's why it happened."

He was utterly immobile and silent.

Page took a deep breath to finish her piece. "I'll have the baby and return to work as soon as possible. You haven't made any secret of how keen you are on children, and that's why I'm telling you this. I would have anyway, because I don't believe in depriving another human being of his or her rights. You have a right to know, and if you want to see the baby, or be a part of its life, we'll work it out.

"That's all I wanted you to know."

She backed away. He opened his mouth wider, and muscles worked in his jaw, but he still didn't speak.

Page found the doorhandle behind her and slipped from the room. By the time she reached the street she was running and fastening the chin strap of her helmet at the same time.

She was also crying. When was she going to accept the message that love was not only something you couldn't decide, it also didn't go away when you wished it would?

WHERE WAS SHE? How had she gotten away so fast? How could he have let her get away at all?

Ian dashed to the street. No sign of a red leotard and tights or white helmet...or a bike that resembled a pile of junk.

Rushing back into the building he ignored greetings from colleagues and employees and snatched up the phone on the information desk.

''Pedal—''

''Ian Faber here.'' He interrupted Lilian. ''I don't know what instructions your boss has given you about letting me have information, but I want to know where she's headed and I want to know now.''

He heard the dispatcher swallow. ''Um, Mr. Faber, will you hold?''

She clicked off on him before he could reply, and he gripped the receiver in both hands, rolled to the balls of his feet and bounced. How could he have stood there like a statue while she gave him the most important news he'd received in his life? Shock. The only plausible excuse was that she'd thrown him into shock.

"You still there, Mr. Faber?"

"Yeah, yeah."

"Ms. Linstrom just called in for her next drop."

"You didn't tell her I—"

"No, I didn't tell her you were on the line. She's headed for Jeffry Sidds on Drumm. That's—"

"I know where it is, Lilian. Thanks." He hung up and shot from the building. Drumm was close and he'd do better on foot than in his car.

He wasn't in such terrific shape. Two blocks of running flat out, and his breathing sounded like something out of a scene in an Alfred Hitchcock movie.

When he passed Slattery he peered ahead, searching for anything bright red—and he saw it. Shiny red, and a bicycle, but it immediately slipped from sight. Just about where Drumm would be.

Women in New York wore tennis shoes to work and carried heels, or whatever else they wanted to use indoors. The trend had spread throughout the country's major cities. Who said men in slippery leather-soled shoes were better off than a woman in high heels?

He skidded to a stop at the end of Drumm Street, just in time to see Page walk slowly from a building and mount the bike again.

"Page!"

His yell was lost in the hubbub.

She pushed off, head down, gaining speed.

Ian ran full tilt. His lungs screamed for relief.

He saw her make a left at Halleck Street. Now his shirt stuck to his body, and he yanked his tie down until he could work the button at his neck free.

"Page." Around the corner, and he barreled into

her as she climbed off the bike, an envelope in hand. "Thank God. I couldn't keep this up much longer."

She was, he realized, holding him while he trembled and fought for breath. "Ian, are you all right?"

He rallied, lifted his chin and ran a finger around the inside of his loosened collar. "Great shape," he said, fashioning a smile that couldn't possibly look as phony as it felt. "Need..." He still hadn't caught his breath. "Need to talk to you, that's all."

She let her hands fall from his arms, and he felt he'd lost something desperately important.

"I'm sorry if I dropped a bomb on you," she said, apparently reading the address on the envelope. "There didn't seem to be a better way to deal with, um, it. You really don't have to worry. I'm very much in charge."

He bridled. "The hell you are. Not on your own."

Page took a step backward and the uncertainty he'd seen on other occasions came into her eyes. "I know what I'm doing," she said. "And I'm a capable woman."

Ian's breathing had returned to normal. People brushed past, hurrying on their appointed daily tasks, but he ignored them, reaching for and gently taking Page's arms in his hands. He eased her nearer. "I know how capable you are. But could you let me be capable for a change?"

Her marvelous blue eyes darkened, and she didn't stop him from taking off the crash helmet and tossing it into the basket on her bike.

"Everyone needs to be capable sometimes." Her voice had that breathy quality he was so crazy about. "But, Ian, don't worry about me or about doing the right thing. I'm really happy about this baby and I wouldn't change a thing. We'll be all right, really we will."

He couldn't remember the last time he'd cried, but he felt very close right now. "You sure will be all right."

"I know...I knew you'd start worrying about your child. That's something I can accept. I would, too."

"Please, could we stop this. I said we'd both been foolish, and if you'd given me a chance I'd have said what I've been trying to say to you since last night."

She bowed her head. "Say it."

"Okay, okay. I shouldn't have flown off the handle at you the way I did yesterday. I was stressed out."

"And now the truth is out in the papers you're over that nagging little doubt you had about me?"

"Damn it, Page, I..." He let out a soundless whistle. "Sorry. I keep doing that, don't I? But you keep driving me to it. I hadn't even read the paper when I was trying to reach you last night. As you'd notice, if you stopped to think, the news only broke late this morning."

He was right, and she was tired and beginning to feel weak again. "You talked about how much evidence the police had against me."

"I know. And I didn't handle it well. But I was terrified they had you cornered and would lock you away. I came to you last night ready to work out a plan of attack. Then I overreacted when you asked if I'd been betting. I'm sorry. I was wrong."

"So was I. But that doesn't alter the fact that I'm not into shotgun marriages."

"Oh, Page." She didn't stop him from drawing her

to him. "Couldn't you stop being superwoman just for once. I sure don't feel super-strong right now, and I'm happy for you to know it. What I feel is... I feel a million feet high and happier than I'll ever be able to explain. And I'm not only interested in the baby. It's the baby and you as a package that drives me wild. A package attached to me. Don't you feel that? Don't you know what I feel? It's got to be the same for you as for me."

There was a moment's pause, a moment when he saw her mouth tremble. Then she placed a hand on each of his shoulders and looked into his face. He felt people bump into them but didn't care.

"You've got to think carefully," she said. "Is what you're feeling now something to do with guilt? If it is, Ian, then it's misplaced."

She had the bluest eyes he'd ever seen. He hoped the baby would be a girl with the same color eyes. When she curled her fingers around his lapel, staring downward, he realized he'd put a hand on her abdomen. He laughed self-consciously and hugged her again.

"Sorry if I'm familiar. But I do have a vested interest, you know. There's no guilt in this, Page. I think I started loving you the night we met."

She didn't appear to be listening closely. Her face settled against his neck and he locked his knees. This wasn't the moment to crumple to the sidewalk.

"Page, did you hear what I said?"

"Yes."

"Will you please marry me?"

Page registered another bump from a passerby and moved closer to Ian. "I don't know. I don't know about anything. Do you understand yet that I won't give up my business?''

He looked fantastic, a slight sheen on his brow, his collar loose, his hair curling in the light fall of San Francisco's misty rain.

''I understand,'' he said. ''But you come home to me. Today, you come home to me. And every day.''

''You're reacting, not thinking. It's the baby.''

He shook her, but gently. ''No, it's not only that and you know it. We covered all this ground before, then got sidetracked. Think back to where we were with each other a week ago.'' He brought his face very close. ''I can't live without you because I don't want to. But there are one or two things that ought to be said.'' One dark arched brow rose higher than the other.

''Name 'em,'' she said.

''No more late-night deliveries of champagne and truffle pâté.'' His lingering kiss made a quiet place around them until he raised his head. ''And you'll agree that as a pregnant woman, maniacal bicycle riding is out.''

''I have a question or two first,'' Page said.

''Make them fast.'' His impatience showed and it amused her.

''You want us to get married?''

''I already said that.''

''Okay. That's fine. And I promise to be kind to your parents and try to make you proud. But you won't expect me to play bridge every day or serve on committees for the rest of my life, will you?''

His fingers were making holes in her arms. ''I don't want you to be anything but yourself. I don't want you to change. But we will have some compromises to face, you know that?''

"I know that."

He passed his tongue over his lips, frowning. "Does that mean you will marry me?"

"Yes."

He shook his head, smiling, and folded her close. "Thanks a lot for the enthusiasm. You are such an incurable romantic."

POSTSCRIPT: Three years after their marriage, Page and Ian Faber have two children, a boy Robert—named for Ian's father—and a girl, Zara, now nine months.

In addition to Jemima, Lilian and the Zipper have a two-year-old boy, Mark.

Pedal Pushers continues to operate under Lilian and the Zipper's management with Page's careful guidance and never diminishing interest.

Page and Rose Faber are close friends although Rose has given up on persuading Page to own a fur.

Tanya Woodside plea-bargained and received a suspended sentence for her part in Waldo Sands's operation. She is now happily married to a professor of economics at a Californian university and studies computer graphics.

MISSING MOLLY

Janice Kay Johnson

CHAPTER ONE

THE CURVE OF THE FREEWAY ahead was so familiar, Nora Woods felt the grip of terror.

A rest stop—there was a rest stop just around the bend. She'd pull in, get a grip on herself before she drove the remainder of the short distance home.

Home. Clutching the steering wheel with sweaty hands, Nora made a bitter sound that couldn't have been a laugh. Not home. Not anymore. Her parents lived in White Horse. She didn't.

So why had the word come to her so naturally? As if no place else could ever be home?

She knew the answer: because no place else ever *had* felt like home. She hadn't tried to do anything but exist, wherever she'd been.

Nora pulled into a parking slot in front of the rustic building that housed the rest rooms and turned off the car engine. Surreptitiously she looked at the few people strolling between rest rooms and cars or peering at the map and information posted on large display boards. She didn't recognize anyone, thank heavens. Which was hardly surprising—in her entire eighteen years of living in the small town off the next freeway exit, she'd never stopped here. Why would she, when she'd be home in a few minutes?

Home. The word and the images it conjured brought a wave of nausea this time. She leaned her forehead on the steering wheel.

Why was she doing this? Nobody would want her back, nobody but her parents. Here she was, dreading even the approach to White Horse, with the river, low at this season, and the dairy cows grazing on the flat land that flooded every winter and the town crowning the bluff at the head of the valley. How would she feel the first time she walked into the grocery store and came face-to-face with a former classmate or a teacher or a parent who had known her from her skinny, gap-toothed youth to the Stanford-bound valedictorian she'd been twelve years ago?

This wasn't Seattle or even Everett, where people moved frequently. The people she'd known growing up in White Horse would still be here.

Stoop shouldered and ancient seeming even when she was a kid, Mr. Halsey would still be tending his garish rows of dinner-plate dahlias and fair-entry tomatoes and pumpkins just down the block from her parents' house. It was now late afternoon. He'd have had his nap and be out in his garden, hoeing rich brown dirt that couldn't possibly sprout a weed after all these years of regimentation.

The Evanses would still live next door to him, their seemingly endless brood infuriating him with Frisbees that sailed into his rows of corn or decapitated his dahlias, softballs that thudded into the walls of his house or shattered windows, or the lawn mower that sat idle while dandelions grew delicate silver seed heads that blew into his yard. Mrs. Evans, a plump aide at the elementary school, would probably have had three more babies by now. The kids Nora remembered would have grown into teenagers who gunned their car engines at all hours and finally left home so that the girls' bedroom only needed two bunkbeds instead of three or a younger brother could move from the couch to the boys' room.

The same clerks would be checking at the local Thrifty grocery store, still tossing remarks to each other over their shoulders as they chewed gum and fluffed their dyed blond hair. The town librarian had seemed old to Nora then, but she'd probably been no more than fifty, which meant she undoubtedly still presided over the books and the after-school crowd who wanted a place to hang out. The FFA kids were probably working their parents' dairy farms, while Joel McMenamin would now be a partner at his dad's auto body shop.

Hardly anybody left White Horse. Only the few transients who lived in the half-dozen apartment houses in town. The kids who were college-bound, ambitious, ready to take the world by storm.

And the screwups.

Nora's stomach took another sickening lurch, but she made herself lift her head, take a deep breath and start the car again. She'd made the decision to face her past, and she wouldn't chicken out now.

Very carefully, she backed out of the slot and accelerated onto the freeway.

Just before the exit for White Horse, she was jarred by the realization that time hadn't stood still after all. The gray snag that had stood beside the river her whole life, providing a perch for bald eagles, was gone. Sometime in the past twelve years, it had become too brittle or rotten and toppled.

The loss of the stark silhouette bothered her more than it should have. Nora supposed it was a symbol. Mr. Halsey might not be out working in his garden; he might have had a heart attack and died last year, or the year before. His house might have sold to a young family who wouldn't have the time to keep up his garden. Mr. Evans might have gotten a vasectomy. The librarian might have retired.

Part of Nora wished she wouldn't meet a soul she knew, and part of her longed to believe White Horse hadn't changed. She didn't belong, and never would again, but she liked to think of life here going on forever the way it always had.

Maybe that's why she'd never come home. Not because she feared what people would say to her, but because so long as she was far, far away, she could believe her absence was the only change. Along with the thump of softballs striking Mr. Halsey's house, the squeaks and wails of discordant music from the fifth-grade band concerts and the little girls in ballet costumes proudly twirling down Main Street in the Fourth of July parade, teenagers would be hanging out at Tastebuds after school, chattering at football games instead of watching the incomprehensible action on the field, singing in *Fiddler on the Roof* or *Hello, Dolly!* on the auditorium stage, parking after dates at the end of Sternberger Road where no streetlights touched the darkness.

The teenagers would be people Nora had known,

their twosomes dissolving and reforming, the friendships sometimes catty but mostly loving, the complaints about parents halfhearted. Time would have formed a bubble, allowing her to age outside it but freezing everyone inside.

Rob would be there, maybe taking a girl to Homecoming or the prom but never really having a girlfriend, because he was waiting for her, Nora.

And Molly would talk all the time about what Nora had written to her or said on the phone. She'd be dreaming about going away to college but secretly frightened of leaving home, grateful when somehow, mysteriously, the departure date never came. Because how could she go anywhere without Nora? They were inseparable.

Had been inseparable.

Molly had gone alone to the cemetery that overlooked the river, where she lay beneath a stone that read simply, Much Loved.

Because her best friend Nora had killed her.

Don't think about it, Nora told herself grimly, her hands locked like claws around the steering wheel. She saw the road ahead of her, but not really. She was too dizzy from the eddies of remembrance and emotion that spun her from one whirlpool to the next.

Don't think about Rob's face the last time you saw him, when he asked, "Do you know how much I loved my sister?" Don't think about the sight of his back as he walked away and you fought not to fall to your knees and scream, "But don't you love me, too? You said you did!" Then you would have been sobbing. "Rob. Please love me anyway."

The litany became the clank of the train on the railroad track. *Don't think. Don't think. Don't think.*

The 7-Eleven was still on the corner, the Mexican restaurant where her family—and most others in town—had gone for every celebration sat unchanged but for a fresh coat of whitewash on the stucco, and the town's one traffic light was red although no traffic came from the other direction.

Main Street could have been used as a movie backdrop for a film set in the 1950s, the traditional false-fronted buildings shabby but still inhabited by businesses that hadn't yet been forced out by national chain retailers. A marquee down the block listed an—almost—current blockbuster, suggesting that the town's single-screen movie theater hadn't closed its doors. It was after five now, and stores had closed, but parked cars clustered around the five-lane bowling alley and the several taverns.

As if her car knew the way, it made the turns that took her up the hill from downtown. A few new houses had been shoehorned into vacant lots. Remodeling had changed the facades of others. But the big old trees were showing tiny green buds for spring, and the sidewalks still buckled over their roots. There was Timmy Svenson's house, the same—or a nearly identical—disemboweled pickup sitting on blocks in the driveway.

She'd quit breathing by now. Rachel Montoya's house had a new front porch, Jessica Gibbs's was the same white with black trim it had always been, except that a tricycle sat on the sidewalk in front. Had the house sold, or did Jessica have a toddler who visited Grandma?

Another car passed, and Nora stared straight ahead, too shell-shocked to risk recognition. A shout had her turning her head despite herself, but she didn't know the small gang of ten- or twelve-year-old boys clustered on the street corner with skateboards shifting restlessly under sneakered feet.

Another block up the hill and the houses grew in size, the lawns became greener, smoother, the small-paned windows glittering from spring cleanings. Once she would have turned on Cedar so that she would pass Molly's house on her way to hers, only six blocks away. It had been as automatic as breathing from the moment she got her driver's license.

That day she'd stopped there even though it was almost dinnertime and Dad had sighed. But she'd had to turn into Molly's driveway and tap the horn. When Molly raced out the front door, Nora had been sitting behind the wheel of the family car. "I got it!" she'd exclaimed in delight. "I can drive now."

"Pick me up to go to the library tonight?" Molly asked, her grin huge even though she should have had her license first, if she'd been able to get into fall quarter drivers' ed.

Nora had wished so desperately that Molly's big brother Rob was home, but of course he wasn't on a Wednesday. Three years older, he was attending the University of Washington in Seattle. He came home weekends sometimes, keeping alive the huge crush she'd had on him for years and years. Just last weekend, she'd have sworn he was flirting with her, that for a moment his hand lingered when he touched her shoulder as he edged past her into the kitchen.

Yeah, what were the chances of that? she'd jeered to herself, but she had been right. He *was* flirting. Only a few weeks later, he and she had been out on the front porch, her perched on the railing and him leaning beside her, just talking quietly or listening to the frogs sing hoarsely to the night while Molly went to make popcorn and get sodas for them all. Laughing at…she didn't remember, just a joke, Nora had wobbled on the railing and Rob grabbed for her. Heart beating hard, she steadied herself against his chest, then looked up. He muttered something under his breath and kissed her.

Sixteen-year-old Nora thought she'd died and gone to heaven.

Thirty-year-old Nora continued straight, crossing Cedar and jogging instead two blocks farther along. Not that Rob would be home—no, that was silly, he wouldn't live there anymore, probably hadn't since she'd gone away, unless he'd come home for a while to keep his parents company after Molly had died. He did live in town, Nora's parents had told her, but he would likely have his own place. Still, she didn't want to see the house, and she dreaded meeting his parents.

Molly's parents. Who had once been the next-best thing to her own. She'd half lived at their house, just as Molly had half lived at hers. From kindergarten on, she and Molly had been inseparable, childhood and early-teen tempests causing rifts that never lasted over twenty-four hours.

She had a flashback, remembered herself stomping

home. She would never, never, *never* be friends with that Molly Sumner again. She didn't even care that her dirty sneakers were smacking down on the cracks in the sidewalk. So *what* if her mother's bones broke! She didn't care. She was so mad!

She had kicked at a pebble and sent it careening across the street. Flinging open her own front door, she'd stormed in and up the stairs, ignoring her mother's called "Nora? Is that you? I thought you were staying at Molly's for dinner?"

Like she'd eat at that...that *traitor's* house. She hated Molly! Why had they *ever* been friends? It had made her even madder that tears were running down her cheeks by this time, and that her nose was all snotty and her chest wanted to burst with pain. She hated Molly!

So why did she miss her so bad, too?

It wasn't fair. None of it was fair!

In the bizarre way of the most vivid memories, right this minute she was a child again, lying on her bed with her face in a pillow, feeling miserable. All because... Nora didn't remember. That was the funny part. Whatever heinous crime Molly had committed wasn't memorable enough to stick. Only her own hurt and fury had branded themselves on her psyche.

As had the timid knock the next day, the murmur of voices downstairs, her mother's call, "Nora! You have a visitor!" And Molly, who had burst into tears at the sight of her and flung herself halfway up the stairs until they hugged and cried and said they were sorry ten million times.

Damn. Dragging in deep breaths, her adult self

didn't move her foot from the brake to the accelerator, even though no cars came on the cross street. Her nose burned and a lump clogged her throat, as if she were eight or ten or however old she'd been and forgiveness was hers.

Saith the Lord.

Molly couldn't forgive her, and neither would anyone else. Nora didn't even try to forgive herself. She knew the Lord wouldn't.

But she had been a coward all these years, running from the condemnation and pain that she had brought upon herself. If Molly's parents wanted to spit in her face, they should have that right. She'd stolen from them any closure. Any chance to say, *Look into our eyes and see what you have done to us.*

Oh, how she dreaded seeing that. She knew from the desert of her own life precisely what she had done to them.

It even hurt to breathe as she made herself start the car forward again, the last two blocks. She saw more changes, more houses that were the same. There was the Evanses', the lawn as ragged and worn in spots and weedy as ever, bikes and soccer balls and baseball gloves tossed wherever on the driveway.

On an almost painful rush of happiness, she saw the rich brown beds of earth and the neatly tied frames for the raspberries and Mr. Halsey himself, more stooped, white hair tonsured, but still it was Mr. Halsey sprinkling seeds on the mounded rows, pausing to tenderly push them down into the soil.

And then, and then, she was home. Turning into the driveway, hearing the crunch of gravel as she parked in exactly the spot designated for her car since the day she'd had her very own.

Home.

And she knew that tonight she would lie on her bed with her face in the pillow and weep, aware there would be no reconciliation, no forgiveness, no friendship, because none was possible.

COLLEEN SUMNER TURNED HER HEAD so fast, the hairdresser's scissors snipped air. "What did you say?"

She met the shocked eyes of Delia Ramsey, a woman who was a friend in the way of people who had gotten to know each other well while sitting together for endless hours on bleachers at baseball games and soccer games and swim lessons, watching their children star or hunch unhappily on the sidelines or grin triumphantly at some then all-important athletic feat.

With her hair dripping and the ugly plastic drape around her shoulders, Delia did not look her best. "Colleen, I'm so sorry. I thought you knew."

She did sound as if she meant it, as if she had not been meanly playing for reaction.

"Nora Woods is here, visiting her parents?" Colleen asked, rephrasing what she had actually heard to make the news bearable. She did not yet feel anything except the stunned awareness that soon, any minute, emotions would crash over her like an unexpectedly big wave at the beach.

Neither hairdresser moved. Both stood back, Janet with the scissors still poised, Renee with a towel ready to wrap Delia's hair. Colleen saw them only as backdrop, as still life, reflected in the huge mirrors that revealed herself as harshly.

"What I heard—" the other woman cleared her throat, as if in advance apology "—is that she may be back to stay. That her parents asked her to move home again."

No! How could that be? Would they have been so insensitive?

The shock was striking her not like a gigantic wave at all, but more like an earthquake, trembling the ground beneath the salon chair, sounding an oncoming boom in her ears.

She thought of Nora as dead, as buried as Molly was. That made it possible to be kinder in her thoughts, to avoid the sin of hate. Even after all these years, Colleen didn't think she could feel compassion for her daughter's killer if they came face-to-face. No matter what came before.

Running into one or the other of Nora's parents once in a while was hard enough.

They had come, together, two days after the accident. When the doorbell rang, she'd found them standing on the front porch, stiff and solemn, tears awash in Fran's eyes. It was Nora's father who had cleared his throat and said awkwardly, formally, "We wanted to tell you how sorry we are. We will miss Molly as if she were our own daughter."

Her insides were as barren as a recently cooled lava bed, still she had flinched in pain. "Thank you for saying that," she had told them in a monotone. "I know you mean well."

She had closed the front door in their faces and flicked the dead-bolt lock, knowing the thunk of it striking home would say to them, *Please do not come back.* She could not bear it if they did.

She and Allen had talked a thousand times about moving away. Going anywhere but here, where they lived with a constant barrage of reminders. Someplace hot and dry, better for her allergies. Eastern Washington, or even Arizona. Allen was a contractor; he could work anywhere. She knew he would be willing if she opted to go.

But Molly was here. Not just in the graveyard, although Colleen did visit there weekly, after services on Sunday. She was *here,* where penciled marks on the wall beside her closet door measured her growth, in nicks and scratches in the house. In her bedroom, where the quilt her grandmother had made her still covered the bed, in the kitchen, where she had sat on the counter, drumming her sneakered heels, munching carrot sticks and chattering endlessly while she watched her mother cook. In the hall, where her father had placed a wing-backed chair so that she could hang her legs over the arm while she talked by the hour to friends.

To Nora.

Molly was everywhere, a presence who might pop up in the next aisle of the grocery store, begging, "Can I buy this?" In the line in front of the movie theater, at the high school, at Mario's where she'd been a waiter for two years.

Colleen would feel as if, in leaving White Horse,

she was deserting her daughter. As if she were losing the last essence of Molly.

And yet she knew that in clinging to her daughter, she had given up living herself. Sometimes she longed with clawing desperation to start over, to let Molly go.

But then she'd think that Molly might be lonely, or she would imagine a stranger painting Molly's bedroom, covering those faint marks on the wall, sandblasting the brick corner of the garage where Molly had put the Buick into Drive instead of Reverse, taking down the absurdly big mirror in the front bathroom, in front of which Molly had danced and preened and despaired.

No. She couldn't do it. Colleen knew she could never leave.

She came back to herself with a bump, a fifty-six-year-old woman getting her hair cut and gossiping idly with the beauticians and other customers. She had no idea how long the tableau had been frozen in the beauty shop, with the three women staring at her.

"I hadn't heard," she said carefully. "I'm glad somebody told me. I'd rather be...prepared."

"I'm sorry to be the one to give you the news," Delia said with contrition.

Then Colleen let Janet turn her chair again so that she faced the mirror.

Snipping, the young woman asked, "Is Nora the one who...?"

A lump in her throat, Colleen nodded.

Mercifully, the hairdresser didn't ask any questions. After cutting in silence for several minutes, she began to chatter about a trip to Maui she and her husband planned.

"My mother volunteered to take care of Chelsie." She laughed. "In fact, she's dying to have her all to herself so she can spoil her rotten!"

Colleen made a sound. Any sound, just to encourage Janet to talk about herself so that she wouldn't notice that Colleen wasn't listening.

Nora. For the first time in many years, she made herself picture Molly's dearest friend.

Nora wasn't as pretty as Molly—no one was—but she'd had a quiet incandescence that earned a second look. With dark auburn hair, thick and wild, went milky pale skin that was almost translucent. As a young child, she'd been not so much shy as guarded, those huge brown eyes wary and thoughtful. With her hair pulled back in a braid or ponytail, she could and often did look washed-out. Only a close observer saw the delicate bone structure of her face, the pretty curve of her lips, the intelligence in her gaze.

As a teenager, she'd developed a certain style, with Molly's help, of course. Makeup brought color to her face and the chic, simple clothes she'd chosen gave her flair and even sophistication. People noticed Molly first, but Nora was no wallflower. Molly was the one elected Homecoming Queen, but Nora hadn't lacked dates, even before...

Rob. Colleen almost gasped. Poor Rob! How would *he* react to the news that Nora was home? That he would see her around, whether he wanted to or not?

She had hurt him badly. All of them, of course, because her horrible judgment had cost them Molly.

But Rob, most of all, because he'd loved Nora, too. To have the girl he cared so much about kill his beloved sister had devastated him.

Perhaps they'd have grown apart. They'd been so young. Colleen couldn't believe her son would actually have *married* his little sister's best friend. Once she'd headed off to California to college, they both surely would have begun dating other people and drifted apart. But twelve years ago, when Nora was just graduating from high school and Rob was finishing his junior year at the university, he had imagined himself passionately in love with her.

Of course he'd come home to see Nora and Molly graduate. On the mantel at home was a photo of him, grinning, his arm around Molly in her cap and gown. There'd been others, too, of him with Nora and with both girls, but they were shoved in boxes in the basement with every other reminder of Nora Woods. Where they belonged.

Furious suddenly, Colleen wondered if Nora had thought about anybody else when she decided to march back into White Horse as if she hadn't killed anybody in a drunken driving accident, as if she hadn't gone to prison instead of college, as if she had a *right.* Had she thought about how seeing her would make Rob feel? How, for the people who had loved Molly, the sight of her would bring back memories so sharp they'd splinter and slice flesh like shards of glass?

Had she *thought* at all? Or did she assume that after twelve years, everybody would have forgotten bright, bubbly Molly Sumner, just because *she* undoubtedly had?

Colleen sat with a rigid back in the salon chair as Janet blow-dried her hair. Under the plastic cape, her fingers clenched the arms of the chair. Tension quivered through her and her muscles ached as if she'd been working out instead of forced to sit here. She stared blindly at the mirror, not caring whether this cut was good or somewhat careless, as the last one had been.

Out of charity for the child she had known, she would ignore Nora's presence in White Horse as long as she could. Unless they met. Until. Then, her daughter's killer would find out that not everybody had forgotten.

That bygones were *not* bygones, and never would be.

CHAPTER TWO

THIS DAMN HOUSE WAS HAUNTED.

When Rob's mother went to the kitchen to pour coffee, without a word his father stood from the table and wandered like a sleepwalker into the entry hall. A moment later came the sound of the den door shutting.

Rob stood and went to the window of the dining room. He hated coming here for dinner. When he had his parents to his place or met them at a restaurant, he could almost forget how deeply they still mourned. Here… He made an inarticulate sound and slapped his palm against the window molding.

Dad would stay in his den for the rest of the evening, alone. Mom might chatter to Rob, but she'd suggest moving into the living room, where her gaze would stray constantly to the mantel and to the wall that was covered with framed photographs.

To her shrine.

Meantime, Rob would sometimes swear he heard the quick, light thump of his sister tearing down the stairs. Or he'd turn his head and for an unnerving moment imagine she stood there, in the foyer, looking at him. Sometimes she'd be the beautiful, not-quite-assured teenager she'd been when she died. Other times, he'd see her as a child, as if he himself were still one.

He never went up to her bedroom. He never sat out on the big, covered front porch where he had kissed Nora the first time, that night when the lilacs were in bloom, their scent heady and seductive.

No; he got the hell out of here as soon as he decently could.

But tonight, how could he? His mother was upset, and he didn't blame her. His own stomach churned, and he realized with quiet rage that he was staring out the window thinking about Nora, as if she might emerge from the darkness any minute as she had a thousand times, leggy in jeans, hands tucked in the pockets of a down vest, vibrant hair carelessly braided.

''To be out of my way,'' she'd say, with an indifferent shrug, not seeming aware that her hair was glorious, that if she'd worn it loose and shimmering she'd have had every boy in the school gawking.

Stepping back from the window, his frown deep, Rob thought incredulously, *Nora is home.* All these years, all those tortured imaginings of what her life had become, and now he could ask her. If he dared. If he could live with the answer.

He wished he could hate her with his mother's single-mindedness. Somehow she'd managed to block out every memory of the little girl who'd had her own place at their table as if she were Molly's sister, of the valedictorian speech where the radiant young woman had thanked both sets of parents, ''all shared with my best friend Molly.''

Rob remembered his mother's stir of pleasure, the

tears that had sparkled in her eyes when she'd hugged Nora afterward.

But to his mother, the one terrible mistake had erased everything that came before. He had tried once, a few months after the funeral, to talk to his mother about his own agony and guilt.

She had risen from her chair with great dignity, said, "She is dead to me" and walked out of the room.

Rob had never spoken Nora's name aloud again in his parents' hearing. Nor had they in his.

Until tonight.

"Here's the coffee..." his mother said. "Oh, dear. Your father doesn't want his?"

Rob turned. "I don't know. Do you want me to take his cup to him?"

"You know he doesn't like to be disturbed when he's working." That was their fiction. Dad was always "working" when he vanished into his study to hide from his wife's grief or his daughter's ghost or his own regrets.

Rob shrugged and accepted his cup. "You and Dad should sell this house," he said abruptly. "Go somewhere sunny."

"You know we can't." Her face tightened. "And I certainly won't be driven away by *her*."

Despite his turmoil, Rob had to be fair. "Why would she try?"

"Why else is she here but to flaunt herself in front of us?"

"To see her parents? To say she's sorry?" He shouldn't be arguing. He wished Nora hadn't decided to come home to White Horse, either. But he couldn't seem to help himself. Yeah, Nora Woods had gotten falling-down drunk and chosen to drive anyway. Yeah, in her colossal arrogance she'd killed his little sister. But Nora wasn't petty or cruel.

His mother stared at him, aghast. "You're not going to try to see her?"

A muscle in his jaw jerked. "I don't know," he said quietly.

"Rob!"

He reached for his mother's hand and squeezed, his grip strong and reassuring. "Not in the way you're thinking. Just...maybe to lay my own memories to rest. To see what she's become."

To realize that she was a stranger, not the child who had alternately irritated him and called to him, nor the teenager, an awakening beauty, who had kept him coming home weekends, who had fascinated and enthralled him more than any girl or woman before or since.

Maybe, finally, he could shut that door, once he'd seen her.

"I don't know if I will," he said, letting go of his mother's hand and trying to sound indifferent. "I may not have any choice."

Face tormented, his mother asked, "Why couldn't she leave us in peace?"

Peace? he thought, jarred. His mother hadn't known an hour's peace since that phone call in the middle of the night twelve years ago. Did she kid herself that she was at peace?

"She may leave town without any of us seeing her," he suggested, and took a swallow of his coffee as if he'd dismissed thoughts of Nora Woods. He was dismayed to discover how much he hoped she didn't leave before he saw her.

His mother reached for her cup, as well, but her hand shook so that she tucked it back in her lap. Her voice trembled as well when she said intensely, "Make her go away, Rob. Call her and tell her to go."

He stared at her, appalled at the corrosive hatred in her eyes. "I can't do that, Mom. She served her time. She has a right to come home and see her parents."

"She should be dead, too."

The idea repulsed and horrified him. How many times had he imagined Nora's face mangled and bloody as Molly's had been? Her body crumpled and shattered, too? How many times had he wondered if he had been able to choose which girl would survive, would he have chosen his sister?

"No." He shuddered and pushed back from the table. "How could you want to make the tragedy worse?"

Her eyes widened; she flinched. "Rob..."

In the face of her distress, he made himself sit down and say with surface calm, "I know you don't mean that. I'm sorry she's here, I'm sorry you're upset. But I won't call and harass her. Chances are, you heard misinformed gossip and she's home for no more than a visit with her parents."

His mother took a deep breath and gave a tiny nod. "Yes. Of course, you're right. I don't have to see her."

Maybe it would be good for her if she *did* see Nora, Rob found himself thinking. Something had to shake her out of her obsession with Molly's memory and the way of her death. Her mental state was unhealthy, and he didn't know what to do about it. His suggestions over the years that she consider counseling had been rebuffed. Sometimes Mom seemed fine, involved in some of her usual activities, out and about doing errands, complaining about some city council decision or a neighbor boy's obscene rap music played at full volume.

Dad, too. At work, or when he and Rob played their occasional round of golf, he seemed to be a different man than he did at home.

Hell, maybe the house *was* haunted.

But Rob didn't believe his sweet if sometimes mischievous sister would choose to linger where her presence caused pain. No, the ghosts here belonged to the living; they were shadows cast by his parents' misery. And he hated knowing there wasn't a thing he could do for them.

Rob stayed another half an hour, drinking the coffee he didn't want, trying to steer his mother into talking about something besides Molly and Nora. But he knew when he left that, even as she puttered around the kitchen, she would have enclosed herself in her obsession as surely as his father had shut himself into the den.

The early April night was so clear, the stars glittered with a diamond brilliance. Rob shivered in the below-freezing air. He climbed into his BMW, started it and waited for warmth. Looking at the Craftsman-style bungalow where he'd grown up, small-paned windows golden, porch light spilling onto the well-tended lawn, he wondered whether the neighbors or his parents' friends had any idea how little Allen and Colleen Sumner had healed from their loss.

Without making a conscious decision, he backed out of the driveway and turned toward Nora's house. Despite the fact that it wasn't more than five or six blocks from his parents', he couldn't remember the last time he had driven past it. He wouldn't say he went out of his way to avoid it, but somehow another route always seemed more logical. He had no intention of stopping tonight. He just wanted to see it, to know she was home again, that she might pass in front of a window or be curled on her end of the sofa, watching television, or be sitting at the kitchen table nursing a cup of tea while she talked to her mother.

The lights were on there, as well, almost every one in the house, as if the Woodses were having a party. But only one car sat in the driveway, off to the side of the garage, where Nora had always parked. The car was small and ancient and battered, he could tell even under the yellow streetlight. It didn't seem to suit her, neither the Nora he remembered nor the successful, sophisticated, smart woman he had imagined her becoming.

His foot tapped the brake and he turned his head. He saw movement in a front window, but the blinds were pulled. Something between exhilaration and anguish filled his chest, and his fingers tightened on the steering wheel.

Would she forgive him? Had she thought of him at all once she got over the first pain? Did she ask her parents about him?

He forgot to breathe. God, what if she was married, had children?

"Damn, damn, *damn*," Rob muttered, his foot coming down hard on the gas. What the hell *difference* did it make whether she was married? All he wanted from her was to know that she was all right, that she'd gone on with her life. Maybe that she'd forgiven him.

Or maybe what he really wanted to know was how *he* felt about her. Whether he still carried a hot coal of anger over everything she had destroyed; whether the mere sight of her laughing would still swell his heart; whether he could meet her as an old friend and no more.

He made himself brake at the corner and turn sedately without a glance back at the house.

Soon enough, he might have his answers.

WHEN NORA CARRIED her empty cereal bowl into the kitchen, her mother opened the dishwasher and smiled. "Why don't you pop it right in?"

Nora did so and smiled, too, unable to resist her mother's delight at seeing her morning, noon and night. "Done. Is the coffee ready yet?"

"I think so." Her mother opened a cupboard and took out a couple of mugs.

As always, she looked like catalog copy in pressed chinos and a russet sweater over a white oxford-cloth shirt, her dark red hair cut stylishly short. Her face seemed to get more interesting with the passing years. Almost homely in her wedding pictures, she approached beauty now, Nora thought. Funny. She had this vague memory of enviously wishing that *her* mommy was as pretty as some of the other mommies.

As a budding preteen, she'd anxiously studied herself in the mirror and prayed that her cheekbones weren't as strong as her mother's, that she didn't really look like her, the way relatives always said she did. Now she almost smiled at the realization that she should be so lucky.

Her mother continued, "I was just making a grocery list. What would you like to have for dinner tonight?"

"Lasagna," Nora said without hesitation. She could see it, taste it. Nobody's lasagna tasted like her mother's. "But you don't have to cater to me forever."

Her mother reached out and stroked her hair, the lightest of touches, but her mouth trembled before she turned away. "I'm pleasing us both," she said, in an almost-steady voice. "And your father eats anything. You know that."

Nora laughed at the reminder of her father's reputation as the leftover man. Put it in front of him and he'd eat it. He swore everything was better the second time around.

Did she qualify? Nora wondered. Was she somehow a better person for her suffering, or had the suffering she'd caused marked her forever, as if with the scarlet *A*?

She pushed the self-pity from her mind. If only for her mother's sake, she was trying to be upbeat. To pretend that she actually *was* the Nora Woods who had once lived here.

She was stirring milk into her coffee when her mother asked, "Like to go to the grocery store with me?"

"No, I feel lazy," she said. Too quickly. "I might take a walk later."

"You've been home three days."

She plastered a look of mock surprise on her face and turned, leaning a hip casually against the counter edge. "And you're pushing me out of the nest already?"

Her mother's expression was troubled. "You're hiding."

"I'm here to see you and Dad. That's what I'm doing."

"Is that the only reason you agreed to move home?" her mother asked shrewdly.

"I..." Nora closed her eyes. "No. You know it isn't." Taking a cleansing breath, she forced a twisted smile. "You win. It's time to quit being chicken. I'll come with you."

Her mother's answering smile was warm with approval. "Good girl."

An hour later, Nora was as scared sitting beside her mother in the car as she'd been as a child on the way to the dentist the time she'd had to have two teeth pulled. She tried to look composed while her insides twisted with terror. *Anybody* could be at the store this morning. It was Saturday. Lots of people shopped on the weekend. Most people did.

People like the Sumners—mother, father and son.

What if they didn't know she was back in town and they just rounded the corner to head down the canned soup aisle, and met *her?*

She swallowed. Maybe she should write them, say, *I just thought you should know I'm in White Horse, in case we should accidentally meet.* Except, she wanted to meet them eventually, didn't she? To say things she should have said twelve years ago, and let them do the same, however it hurt? So perhaps she *should* write. She could say that she was hoping to talk to them. *May I come by?*

Just the person they wanted knocking on their door. Nora's mother had told her about her and Dad's visit, after the accident. They hadn't known what to expect, but cold rejection wasn't it. Not after all the years they'd shared daughters, Fourth of July picnics and fireworks with the two families lying on big blankets on the middle school field, looking up at the glorious explosions in the black sky, not after the exchanges of Christmas gifts and the two mothers sewing together to surprise the girls with Halloween costumes.

"I hope," Mom had said sadly, "that I could have kept loving Molly, if it had been the other way around." She stopped, paused for a long moment, then said on a sigh, "But it's hard to know, until something happens to you, how you'll react."

Staring out the car window, Nora thought, *Too late.* She hadn't written the Sumners, and she and Mom would be at Thrifty any minute. Short of her staying in the car, slumped low so no one could see her, she was risking meeting people she'd known.

"Busy place this morning," Mom said cheerfully, pulling into a crowded parking lot.

Nora was almost catatonic. She couldn't do this. Couldn't. Couldn't.

But somehow she did. She found herself following her mother across the parking lot, grabbing a shopping cart, pausing to examine the pansies as if she cared which color Mom put in a window box.

Fingers locked on the handle of the cart, she trailed her mother through the produce section. It felt frighteningly open. Her panicked gaze darting from one shopper to another, Nora longed for cover.

"Hmm. These bananas don't look great today," her mother said in disappointment. "Unless..." Her face brightened. "Why don't I make banana bread? I haven't in ages. Does that sound good to you?"

Guessing that a response was required, although she hadn't the slightest idea what her mother had just asked, Nora nodded.

"Your dad loves banana bread. He'll be so pleased."

She kept chattering, as if every display of apples or onions or cauliflower called for comment. Nora knew she was doing it to distract her.

It didn't work.

They left vegetables and fruits behind to pick out milk and mozzarella and cottage cheese for the lasagna. Shoppers pushing carts kept passing them. Nora eyed them covertly. Strangers. Or people she'd known who had changed unrecognizably.

Maybe no one would know *her,* she thought on a brief surge of hope that died stillborn. Of course they would; who else would she be, shopping with her mother and looking too much like her?

Momentarily absorbed in the hope, she didn't notice the young mother coming down the aisle toward them until their carts almost bumped and she heard a gasp.

"Nora?" At his mommy's cry, the little boy in the child seat turned to stare at the strange lady, too. "Nora! It *is* you!"

Nora was blank for a moment. Although the young woman looked familiar—her eyes, anyway—Nora couldn't quite place her. But if her cheeks hadn't been quite so plump, and her hair was longer…

"Rachel?" she said uncertainly.

"I can't believe it's you!" Rachel rushed forward and enveloped her in a hug that Nora returned awkwardly. "Oh, I've thought about you a million times! I ask your mother constantly…oh, Mrs. Woods, hi!" She actually had tears in her eyes. "Nora. You're home. My goodness."

Rachel Montoya had been part of Molly and Nora's crowd in middle school and high school. Of course Molly was always and forever Nora's best friend, but she'd had good times, too, with Rachel, who was a little more studious, like Nora. They'd spent a week together at a marine biology camp up in the San Juan Islands when they were, oh, fourteen or fifteen. Molly had been jealous, but Nora had had a great time even though she felt a little disloyal, having so much fun with Rachel instead and doing something that didn't interest Molly at all.

"I'm home," Nora agreed. "Um…obviously you've gotten married and had children."

Rachel laughed. "I'm Rachel Buckley now. I met John at Western—that's where I went. Mom and Dad still live here, of course. John and I actually just moved back to White Horse the year before last. He's an assistant principal at the high school. Can you believe that?" she asked gaily. "I've taught second and third grades, but I'm being a stay-at-home mom right now for a couple of years. Ryan here and his four-year-old sister Lori are keeping me hopping! I don't know how mothers of preschoolers work full-time, too!'' She stopped. ''Wow. That's probably more than you wanted to know. But I'm just in shock. You're here.''

''Yeah,'' Nora agreed again, wryly. ''I'm here.''

''What have you done?'' The pretty, plump young mother flinched. ''I mean, besides...''

''Prison?'' Did she sound harsh for a minute? Nora didn't care, although none of it was Rachel's fault. ''I got my degree, too, at Central. Since then I've just been working.'' She shrugged. ''Not doing anything exciting. Not like tracking pods of whales.''

Her high school friend's face brightened again. ''That was fun, wasn't it?''

''Mmm-hmm.'' Even if it had happened in another life; if another Nora had been the one to grip the railing of the boat and feel the wind sting her eyes and whip her hair as she strained to see the individually distinctive markings on each slick black-and-white back as the orcas in the pod had arced out of the gray sound. ''But obviously neither of us became a marine biologist.''

Rachel made a face. ''I wasn't sure I wanted to spend my whole life wet and cold.''

''Really?'' Nora asked, surprised. ''You were the one who kept talking about it.''

''I was convinced that having a passion for something like that made me sound adventurous and deep. Which—'' she scrunched up her face again ''—only goes to show how shallow I was.''

Nora's laugh almost came easily. ''What fifteen-year-old is anything but?''

''I'm sure there are a few who have already fed

the starving in Ethiopia and invented a new whindig for the computer and raised their five younger sisters and brothers because they have no mother. Aren't they the ones who get the really great scholarships?"

"I always wondered if they weren't all bald-faced liars," Nora admitted.

Rachel's little boy tugged at her shirt. "Mommy, I'm hungry."

"And we've been blocking the cereal aisle for ten minutes." She smiled at Nora. "Can we get together and really talk?"

"I'd like that." Another surprise—Nora meant it.

"I assume you're at your mom and dad's? I have the number. I'll call you tonight." Rachel said her goodbyes and pushed her heavily laden cart forward again.

Nora said nothing as her mother tossed a box of cereal into the cart.

"I told you Rachel had been asking about you, didn't I?" Mom asked.

"Yes. I just..." Hadn't believed it. "I didn't expect her to be so glad to see me."

"Most people will be," her mother said quietly.

They met a couple of other acquaintances while they did their shopping, all of whom said hello pleasantly. Nora's tension ebbed, so that by the time her mother paid and they left the store, she was almost relaxed.

Until her mother said, in a changed tone, "Oh, dear. Is that the Sumners' car?"

Nora didn't know which car to look at.

"Give me your keys," she said urgently. "I don't want to run into them here."

Her mother didn't argue, popping open the trunk and then handing over the keys. Nora fumbled with them before she found the right one and got it in the lock. Shaking, she almost fell in, slammed the door and slumped down in the seat, her heart pounding hard. In the side mirror, she saw a dark blue car pass, but without sitting up, she couldn't see well enough to tell who was at the wheel.

A minute later, her mother slammed the trunk, disappeared to return the cart, then got in on her side once Nora had flipped the lock.

Mom took the keys, but made no move to start the car. "I don't even know if that was them, Nora."

"I'm just...not ready to see them."

"They loved you once upon a time."

"If they don't speak to you, how do you think they feel about me?"

Her mother was silent for a moment, lines between her brows. Finally she said, "I'm glad you don't want to cause them pain. But don't...oh, don't feel as if you have no right to be here. You do."

"Are you sure?" Nora asked. The truth was, she often thought she had no right to be alive at all. She'd been behind the wheel; *she* was responsible. Why couldn't she have been the one to die? Why had God been so unjust as to punish the innocent and save the sinner?

Or had he saved her so that she would truly suffer for her wrongdoing?

"You spent two years in prison. You paid."

"Molly is gone forever." Nora's voice shook. "I can never pay for that."

Even her mother could think of nothing to say in

rejoinder. Face sad and worried, she started the car and backed out.

Unexpectedly, about halfway home, she asked, "Have you had any counseling?"

"Why would I need counseling?"

"Nora, you made a mistake." Mom sounded mad. "A bad one, as it turned out. But you didn't do anything eighteen-year-olds don't do all the time, heaven help them. Yours had tragic consequences. But it was a dumb teenage thing. No more." She jammed on the brakes so hard at a stop sign, Nora had to grab at her seat belt. "You're too smart, too kind, you have too much to offer, to spend your whole life punishing yourself."

She'd tried to tell herself the same, but she'd never been able to believe it. She had killed Molly. She could never take back what she'd done. When you made a mistake, you could say "I'm sorry" and be forgiven. How could this be a simple mistake, when even a repentant "Sorry" would never be good enough?

"Mom," she said drearily, "I've tried to get on with my life. I went to college, I work, I've even made a few friends. What else can I do but try?"

"Forgive yourself," her mother said, as if she'd read Nora's mind.

"I can't." Her voice thick, Nora realized that her cheeks were wet with tears. "I just can't," she whispered.

Right there in the middle of the street, her mother stopped the car again, unbuckled her seat belt and reached for Nora.

She sobbed out her anguish on her mother's shoulder, soaking her sweater, grasping for comfort in the familiar, murmured "There, there. It'll be all right. You'll see. It will."

Mommies always believed everything would be all right. Huddled in her mother's arms, crying for the first time in years, Nora desperately wanted to be a child again, who could believe.

But she couldn't time travel. Nothing would allow her to snatch back the years and regain her faith that everything would always be all right.

It wouldn't be. Not for her, because she didn't deserve it.

CHAPTER THREE

DR. BERGSTROM LEANED back in his office chair, contemplated Nora for a long, unnerving moment, and then said, "When can you start?"

"You mean, um, when *could* I start?" Nora asked. Of course that's what he meant. He was probably interviewing a dozen other people for the clerical and bookkeeping job at the White Horse Veterinary Hospital.

"No," he said patiently, "I mean when *can* you start."

Nora stared. "You're giving me the job?"

Amusement glinted in his eyes. "Yep." He tossed her application onto a heaped in box. "I think you'll suit us just fine."

"But...don't you have a partner?" *Oh, good,* she thought, trying to hide a wince, *make him take back the job offer, why don't you?*

A rangy man with close-cropped blond hair and penetrating gray-green eyes, he grinned. Raising his voice, he called, "Theresa? Joan, is Theresa in?"

A voice floated back. "She's out front, talking to a client. Want me to get her?"

"Please."

In an effort to look serene, Nora had clasped her hands together on her lap when she sat down. Now they were locked in a death grip. She didn't know if she'd be able to unlock them.

"How are your parents? I haven't seen them in a while," the veterinarian said conversationally.

"They're fine. Good." What else could she say? she wondered desperately. "Um, Jackson—our dog—died a couple of years ago. Mom and Dad haven't replaced him."

He nodded. "I put him down. Ripe old age."

"Oh. Yes. I guess he was old." In fact, she could hardly remember a time before they'd had the small terrier mix. He must have been, oh, seventeen or eighteen when he'd died. "I remember Dr. Hughes's daughter. She must be..." She frowned, calculating.

"In graduate school, getting a master's degree in chemical engineering. Theresa's son, Mark, is a senior at Reed this year."

"Really?" She flushed at the amazement in her tone. "I'm sorry. It's just that White Horse always seemed frozen in time to me. You know?"

He nodded. "How long has it been?"

"Twelve years," she admitted. Almost. Twelve years this June. Once the spring leaves had unfurled, the tulips and lilacs bloomed and the senior prom was past.

Before he could comment, the other veterinarian in the practice, Theresa Hughes, appeared in the doorway. In a white lab coat, a stethoscope around her neck, she looked much as Nora remembered, a petite, slim woman with thick dark hair in a ponytail. Only her face showed a few more years with a fan of tiny lines beside her eyes, her skin slightly more weathered.

"Nora!" she said with apparent delight. "I'm so glad you're home again. And to stay! I saw your mother just a couple of weeks ago at the library and she told me you were coming."

Nora had hardly known the new veterinarian in the practice, although she'd had a jazz dance class with her daughter, Nicole Burkett, then a sulky young teenager unhappy about the move to a "hick" town and the fact that her mother was dating Joe Hughes, a logger.

"I...thank you," Nora said inadequately.

"I've just offered Nora the job," Dr. Bergstrom said. "She seemed to think I should clear it with you."

"Are you kidding?" Dr. Hughes beamed. "I saw your résumé. We're lucky to have you."

"But..." She had an infuriating lump in her throat. "I do have a felony on my record."

Theresa Hughes's mouth firmed. "Ridiculous. Cracking down on drunk driving is one thing, charging a good kid with homicide for a onetime mistake is another."

"More than a mistake," Nora felt compelled to say.

"In any case," Dr. Bergstrom interjected, "it was twelve years ago. Unless you have a drinking problem..." He paused delicately.

"No!" Embarrassed at her vehemence, Nora tried to relax the tension in her shoulders. "No," she said more quietly. "I've never touched alcohol again. I never will."

He nodded, his eyes kind. "Then I fail to see what your conviction has to do with this job."

"It's..." She stumbled, swallowed. "It's made it hard to get work before. Once I admit to being an ex-con."

Eventually she had taken to lying. But no matter how good a job she did, once her employer found out, she was fired.

"But we know you," Dr. Hughes said, her own voice gentle. "You should have come home sooner."

"Thank you." She was humiliated by the tears burning her eyes. "I'll do my best."

Dr. Bergstrom rose and pushed back his chair. "Then let me show you around, introduce you to the rest of the staff."

Theresa Hughes wrinkled her nose. "Is it too soon to reveal the mess that's been piling up the past month since her predecessor quit?"

"We'll save that for tomorrow," he said in the same bantering way, as both pretended they hadn't noticed Nora's incipient tears.

Joan, the receptionist, was an older woman whom Nora didn't know. She seemed friendly, as did the young vet tech who was prepping a dog on the stainless steel surgery table in back.

"Teeth cleaning," Dr. Bergstrom said, nodding at the retriever mix. "I just finished my appointments for the day and am going to start surgeries. Theresa is picking up the last few office calls."

Nora nodded and peeked into the narrow hallway lined with shelves that held the medications. It seemed cramped to her, as did the surgery area where an X-ray machine was squeezed between a surgery table and a bank of cages. She'd never been back here before.

As if reading her mind, Dr. Bergstrom said, ''We need badly to add on. Theresa and I are tripping over each other, and the practice is so busy we've brought in another vet, which is compounding the problem. He's out doing farm calls today. I'll introduce you to Rick Spencer tomorrow. We're actually breaking ground in July for a major addition that will triple the square footage and allow us to add an equine area. You'll have an office then. In the meantime—'' he led the way toward the front ''—you'll be wedged in here, where you're in earshot of reception in case they need you.''

The narrow built-in desk held a computer. In trays were completely full and other piles buried the keyboard. Below were file drawers and, above, some shelves that held letterhead, what looked like order forms and binders.

Nora had known she'd be filling in when the waiting room got too busy or if someone called in sick, but she was uneasy to see that she was not only in earshot but in sight of clients standing on the other side of the counter in the waiting room. She'd envisioned herself holed up in a small private cubicle, hunched over a computer, sending out billing notices, typing letters, preparing orders. Safely anonymous.

Forcing a smile, she said, ''This is fine.''

''Concentrating may be hard here,'' he said apologetically, ''but it's the best we can do for now.''

''Really.'' This smile was more genuine. ''It'll be great.''

''Okay.'' He held out a hand. ''We'll see you in the morning, then?''

''Nine o'clock,'' she agreed.

"Ah, good." He glanced past her. "Rob! Did you run into a problem?"

Rob. Nora's heart stopped.

Turning in slow motion, she told herself it wouldn't be him. The name was common. This would be some other Rob.

But it wasn't.

He hadn't noticed her yet and was saying amiably to Dr. Bergstrom, who half blocked her, "Just a quick question. I was over at Smith & Ralston's, so I thought I'd stop by instead of calling when I got back to the office."

"Ah. You just caught me before I started a teeth-cleaning."

He had changed, and he hadn't. She would have known him anywhere, but the young, cocky Rob she'd known had filled out and matured into a man. Dark, wavy hair, shaggy back then, was cut conventionally short but still wanted to curl, she saw with an aching heart. Eyes that were blue in some lights, gray in others, had acquired crinkles at the corners. His tall, broad-shouldered but lanky body had gained bulk, from what she could see above the counter. His face still lit with a crooked smile that always felt like a gift. His cheeks had grooves she didn't remember, and lines seemed permanently furrowed between his brows. He looked better than he had twelve years ago, but not as happy.

And the very sight of him still made longing cramp in her belly and her chest.

She must have moved, because he suddenly saw her. He stopped whatever he'd been saying midsentence, his eyes locked with hers.

She wasn't breathing; she knew that. She only stared until her ears rang and spots swam before her eyes. *Oh, Rob, Rob,* she cried inside. She couldn't tell what he was thinking, only that he was shocked.

"Nora," he said finally, in an oddly quiet voice. "I heard..." He gave his head a little shake, as if clearing it.

Dr. Bergstrom laid a warm hand on her arm. He must have felt her trembling, but he gave no indication. "We've just hired Nora to bring order to this place. I'd forgotten your history. I'm sorry to spring you on each other this way."

"I should be going," she said, backing away, grateful that her feet worked. "If you'll excuse me."

In her turmoil, she knew vaguely that Joan was gawking, that Dr. Bergstrom looked worried. She backed into someone—Dr. Hughes—mumbled an apology, and fled.

She'd come in the front door, but had noticed a back one. Hurrying past the vet tech and the sleeping dog, the sound of barking from the kennels following her, she hurried out the rear and around the building to her car.

She tried the door and whimpered when she remembered locking it. Habit from city life. Of course her groping hand couldn't find her keys in her purse. She had to set it on the hood and root through it before she found them at the very bottom, hiding beneath the book she'd stuck in it just in case she had to wait for her interview. Hand shaking, she was finally unlocking the car door when she heard his voice say urgently, "Nora! Don't go!"

Her hand stilled and a small sob escaped her lips.

She wasn't ready for this. She never would be. Why had she thought facing her past might help heal her?

Nora drew a shuddering breath and turned, pride lifting her chin high. "Hello, Rob," she said.

He was hurrying toward her, those furrows in his forehead deep. In well-cut dark slacks and a pale blue dress shirt, his tie just loose enough to suggest confidence, he was formidably handsome.

"You were running away."

With dignity, Nora said, "I assumed you'd prefer not to see me."

"Why would you think that?" He winced. "Don't answer. I remember what I said." His mouth twisted. "All too well. But, damn it, Nora, you have to know I didn't really mean it!"

Her laugh would have corroded steel. "Do I? You mean, I've spent twelve years thinking you hated me, when all the time you were hunting for me to say you were sorry?"

He had the grace to flush. He'd always known how to reach her if he wanted to. He hadn't wanted.

Voice deep, ragged, he said, "I've regretted the…heat of what I said."

"But I deserved every word, didn't I? I killed Molly."

"It was an accident."

"Everybody keeps saying that." Her own bitterness made acid churn in her stomach. "Nobody said that twelve years ago. The judge and jury didn't say that. Molly can't say that."

"But Molly would if she could."

She wasn't the only one surprised by his simple

statement. Some emotion shifted in his eyes, which she suddenly realized were vividly, startlingly blue.

"Molly would hate..." He stopped.

Her throat choked with tears, Nora said, "I would give anything, *anything,* to take it back. Please believe me."

He took a step forward. "I do. I know you loved her."

Feeling crowded, she groped behind her to open the car door. Edging around it, Nora said, "I have to go."

He frowned. "Go where? Will you have lunch with me, Nora?"

"Why?" she asked baldly.

She'd taken him aback.

"It just...seems as if there are things we should say to each other. That should have been said a long time ago."

Wasn't that what she'd come home for? But she was already close enough to tears. She'd already heard more than she had ever hoped to hear from him. *I know you loved her.* And, *It was an accident.*

"I wish I'd died instead."

"Nora!"

"I wanted you to know that." Her eyes blurred and she ducked into the car.

His hand kept her from closing the door. "Can we get together?"

She bit her lip so hard she tasted blood. "Maybe. I don't know. Not now."

"When?" His eyes were alive with a kind of urgency she didn't know how to answer.

"I don't know." She hesitated. "Your parents..."

His expression changed, became shuttered. After a moment, his hand dropped from the door. "I'll call."

She knew what that meant. The reminder of his parents had killed any desire he'd briefly harbored to—what?—reminisce about old times? Reawaken the embers of their teenage passion? Settle hurt feelings?

She didn't know. Told herself she didn't care. They couldn't go back. She had wanted only to see him once, and she'd done that. He had cleansed something in her when he said, in a way, that Molly would forgive her.

Was it true? she wondered, as she closed the car door and watched Rob walk away. If Molly could send a message from beyond the veil, what would she say?

Nora didn't like to think of Molly dead. What if she was in some dark, cold place? Bewildered, not knowing what had happened, why everyone she loved was gone?

Shuddering, Nora started her car.

She tried, oh so hard, to think of Molly as an angel, floating on fluffy white clouds, listening to celestial harps and smiling seraphically.

But Molly, in incessant motion, wouldn't like lounging around on downy clouds. She'd listened to grunge at full volume in her car, so that you could hear her coming a block away. And she'd had this wonderful, bawdy laugh that would shock the gentle, serene angels inspirational artists liked to paint. Molly was good, kind, funny, but not saintly at all. She just didn't *go* with conventional images of heaven.

In the first year, Nora had begged Molly to appear

to her. Whispering under the covers at sleepovers, they'd promised each other they would if they could, never imagining that death wasn't fifty or sixty or seventy years away. But Molly had never come. Nora had taken it as a sign that Molly hated her.

Realistically she knew that maybe Molly *couldn't* appear to her. If it was that easy, wouldn't everyone pop back to reassure their loved ones? There'd be ghosts everywhere you turned. Even assuming there was a heaven, it was likely that Molly had no conscious self, no awareness of who she had been and who she'd left behind. No desire to project herself into Nora's bedroom some night.

But…oh, it would have been nice. To talk to her again, just once. To know that she was all right, whoever, whatever, wherever she was.

In a way, that was why Nora had come home to White Horse. Maybe Molly was still here. Maybe Nora would sense her, find comfort.

So far, all she'd found was memories, and they couldn't offer forgiveness.

STUNNED BY THE POWER of his reaction to her, Rob strode back to his car. Damn it, he'd *known* she was in town. How could he have been so unprepared? So shocked to see her?

Hell, he'd been as shocked as if Molly had been standing there! Mom said she thought of Nora as if she were dead. Well, apparently he had thought that, too. A bittersweet memory, not a living, breathing woman.

He glanced back to see her car disappearing up the

block. If she glanced in the rearview mirror, he couldn't tell.

His own car was in the Smith & Ralston lot a block up Olympic Avenue. He was working on half a dozen jobs right now, including the expansion of the veterinary clinic and a brand-spanking-new building for the legal partners. Their current mustard brick building, left from the fifties, was not only small but squat in appearance. Ellis Smith had won as the defense counsel in a big murder case a few years back, and as a result business had poured into the tiny firm.

As he'd said with an aw-shucks grin, "We're big potatoes now. We talked about moving to Everett, setting up business near the courthouse to save ourselves the drive every time we have to appear, but then, hell, we'd be driving to work every day. We figure people can come to us. If they quit coming someday, well, we were doing fine back when we mostly wrote wills and handled divorces."

The fancy new two-story redbrick building with a tile roof and arched windows that Rob had just designed for Smith & Ralston wasn't for two lawyers who planned to do nothing but write wills. Bulldozers were clearing the rubble of the old feed and seed store today. Rob had earlier met the contractor there to see how the site preparation was going.

Right this minute, he didn't give a damn about the new building. Brows drawn together, he brooded.

Nora had changed. Well, of course she had. She was twelve years older. But it wasn't just that. The Nora he'd known had been confident. Not brassy, in-your-face like his sister, but sure of her views and values and worth. And why not? She was the smartest kid in school and everyone knew it. She was the star of the High-Q team and the debate team and a shoo-in as valedictorian. Aside from that, she was pretty enough to be elected to the Homecoming Court, athletic enough to be a good tennis player, and kind enough to volunteer at the food bank. Which made her sound like a Goody Two-shoes, though she wasn't. She was smart, funny and—to him—heart-stoppingly pretty as she grew into her ridiculously long legs and thick red hair.

She'd had a temper, too. Not the infamous redhead kind that flared unpredictably, but she stood up for herself and her friends. She had great cheekbones, warm brown eyes and a face full of life.

Today she had looked worn, wan and thin. Too thin. The old Nora wouldn't have run at the sight of him, afraid of a painful confrontation.

He swore under his breath, picturing the one moment when the dullness in her eyes had lifted to reveal anguish and a plea for him to believe her.

I wish I'd died instead.

Did she really? Was she, like his mother, caught in the sticky sap of grief that would petrify them both, like bugs in amber?

He hadn't finished his sentence, but he thought again how Molly would have hated to see them both made so miserable by her death! His sister had loved life and she would never have wanted her best friend and her parents to be emotionally crippled by her loss. He couldn't be sure of much, but he did know that.

Maybe what bothered him most was to see Nora grateful for a clerical job here in White Horse. She'd been interested in so many things: computers, biology, psychology. Articulate, poised, quick on her feet, she'd been a hell of a public speaker. So, okay, she'd gone to prison instead of Stanford University. But hadn't she gone to college when she got out? What was she doing, wasting her abilities on a job that couldn't pay much above minimum wage?

He still remembered her expression when he'd lashed out that last time he saw her. The blood had seemed to drain from her face, leaving her so pale her eyes had looked huge and dark and stricken. She'd had a goose egg on her forehead and a bruise discoloring one cheekbone. The way she'd looked at him, as if he'd just struck her, had haunted him for twelve years now.

In his worst dreams, she'd come back looking like that, and he would know he had hurt her beyond repair.

Well, it looked as if that worst fear had come true. The defeated, tired, timid woman he'd seen today was the product of one terrible mistake—and the price society and people who should have loved her had exacted.

He stopped at his car, flattened his hands on the sleek blue roof and bowed his head.

Why *hadn't* he ever tried to get in touch with her? A letter, saying, *In my pain, I was cruel, I'm sorry. It happened, we miss Molly, but it was one of those things that go down when teenagers think they're immortal.* He'd driven drunk a few times when he was young and idiotic. Molly had gotten mad at him once, made him stop the car and had marched home in the middle of the night, at least a mile, with him creeping along beside her in his car pleading with her to get in and not tell Mom and Dad. Had he been drunk enough to fail to make a corner and crash headlong into a tree? *There but for the grace of God...* Why hadn't that occurred to him, before he accused Nora of murdering his little sister?

Or had it? Had his viciousness come from the guilty awareness that it could have been him?

He groaned and swore again.

Would she ever talk to him again? Did he blame her if she didn't? Should he even ask? What would be served by rehashing the past?

But he knew he'd be calling, that he had to see her again. That he had to know she wasn't as unhappy as she had looked today.

At last he drove back to his office, detouring only to get an espresso and croissant from a stand on the corner. Given his state of mind, he was dismayed to see his father's pickup truck parked in front.

Problems at the development, where he had designed houses and his father was building them?

"That's all I need," he muttered, slamming his car door.

"Mr. Sumner is here," the receptionist chirped. "He's in your office."

"Thanks." He bared his teeth in what he hoped passed for a smile.

His office was stark, not so much an advertisement for his skill as a blank slate. Oak woodwork and crown molding edged white walls and framed tall windows. A few sketches of buildings he'd designed and a few photographs of completed ones hung simply on the expanse of white. His broad maple desk occupied one end. At the other was a conversation area with a coffee table and several leather chairs. His father sat in one, flipping through a magazine. An imposing man when he strode around a construction site, he looked out of place here in dusty jeans, work boots and a chambray work shirt, his big calloused hands dwarfing the slick magazine. These last years he'd gotten a little soft around the middle and his dark, wavy hair had begun to gray.

"Ah," he said in apparent relief, dropping the magazine onto the table. "Your secretary said you'd be back soon."

"Problems out at the site?"

His father hesitated. "No-o. Not exactly."

"Not *exactly?*" Rob set down the cup of espresso and the croissant.

His father sighed. "More at home. Your mother is...agitated."

"I noticed," Rob said with a grimace. He sat in one of the comfortable chairs and pried the lid off the cup.

"She doesn't think you listened to her."

"I always listen. I just don't always agree."

His father nodded, rotated his shoulders uneasily, and sat in silence. He never had been comfortable talking about feelings. He had said "I'm proud of you, son" on appropriate occasions, but always awkwardly, his relief obvious when Rob said "Thanks" and changed the subject. Rob worried that his father had held his mother in the early days and patted her back when she cried because that's all he knew how to do. To him, it would be natural to hide his own tears and never express his grief, leaving her alone with hers. His nightly disappearance into his study seemed symbolic of their silence and isolation.

"Your mission?" Rob prodded. His mother must be desperate, to send Dad.

"I'm not sure." Forehead furrowed, his father sounded genuinely uncertain. "To talk to you."

"Consider it done."

Dad grunted. Jerking his head toward the croissant, he said, "Want to go out for a real lunch?"

"Are you hungry?"

"Ate already."

"Then this is fine. It's been a hell of a morning."

His father raised his brows.

"I ran into Nora."

Dad's eyes rolled like a spooked horse's.

"She looks like hell. Like—" Rob frowned "—a shadow of herself. As if light should shine through her."

His father gazed toward the windows, apparently absorbed in the slow movement of clouds. Silence stretched, as if he didn't intend to respond at all. Finally he said, "She's been through a lot."

"The accident was twelve years ago." As if Dad didn't know; couldn't name the days since he'd buried his youngest child.

That knowledge thickened his voice. "Some things you never leave behind."

"Dad..." Rob stopped. How the hell did you say *You and Mom* should *leave Molly behind, except as a fond, sad memory?* He settled for "I'm worried about Mom."

"Hearing about Nora has brought it all back for her."

In frustration, Rob said, "Brought it back? She's never laid it to rest!"

"No," his father said heavily. "No, she hasn't."

"She needs help."

Dad shook his head. "She won't take it."

"Make her!" Rob snapped.

His father stared at him as if he had gone stark, raving mad.

Rob made himself speak more gently. "Dad, it's been twelve years. Molly isn't coming back. What's the sense in living as if she might? Or not living, because she won't? You and Mom are in your fifties! You've got a good thirty years ahead of you. Do you want to spend it in that house, listening for Molly to come down the stairs, for her car to pull up in front, for her music to vibrate the pictures on the wall? You get out during the day, but Mom does the errands she has to do and no more. She needs new interests. Damn it, she needs to say goodbye!"

Grief settled onto his father's face, aging him before his son's eyes. "Parents aren't meant to bury their children."

"But sometimes they do." Rob felt callous, but it needed saying. "Are you going to spend the rest of your life at her graveside?"

His father made a rough noise in his throat and bowed his head. God, was he crying? Rob wondered apprehensively.

When he looked up, his eyes were dry but so sad he might as well have been. "You're right, son." His voice carried the grief with the same familiarity as did his face. "You're right. I'll talk to her."

"If she sees Nora..."

His father rubbed a weary hand over his face. "I don't know what she'll do."

Rob stood and went to the window. His back to his father, he said, "Today Nora told me she wishes she'd died instead of Molly." He turned, asking a question that had no answer. "Why couldn't we keep everyone's lives from being destroyed by Molly's death?"

Not an introspective man, his father tried anyway. "We were so absorbed in our loss, we didn't look around."

Nobody in his family had bothered to mourn for everything Nora had lost, although they had claimed to love her. It had been so damn easy to let grief become anger. To blame, because you didn't want to think something so terrible could happen for no reason at all.

His mother still clutched the anger as if she were a frightened toddler and it her blankie, a bulwark against the emptiness that swirled inside her, that echoed in her house. But the anger, Rob thought, was also the festering bacteria that kept her wound from healing and slowly fading into a faint scar.

But he had no idea how to convince her to let it go. No idea at all.

And he could tell, from the defeated lines of his father's carriage as he left, that Dad didn't either.

His mother and Nora, both hurting, were bound to meet. Nora, he had a feeling, would bow her head and wait dumbly for the death blow.

He could only hope to God that his mother would come to her senses in time and not deal it.

CHAPTER FOUR

"IT'S *SO* GOOD TO SEE YOU." Rachel laughed. "And nice to have time to talk without the kids constantly interrupting, dearly though I love them." On this Saturday afternoon, she had planned a "play date" for her two so that she and Nora could really talk, she'd told Nora ahead.

"Do you have pictures?" Nora asked, glancing around. With the builder's favorite cream-colored carpet and white walls, the living room of this very new house in a development that had sprung up from a cow field was sparsely furnished, making her suspect Rachel and her family actually lived elsewhere in the house and couldn't afford rarely used wing chairs and end tables that would be mostly for show.

Her friend—how odd to think of her that way, when Nora hadn't thought of her at all in so many years!—lit up. "Do you really want to see them? I warn you, once you get me started, we may be poring over albums for two hours! I'm one of those doting mothers who takes a camera everywhere."

"That's okay." Nora smiled. "I'd like to see your husband and daughter. And your parents."

"Great!" Rachel leaped to her feet. "Would you like coffee? Or, better yet, cookies? I just baked raisin-oatmeal ones."

"That sounds wonderful."

Rachel fetched the first album and left Nora to set it on her lap and open it randomly while she poured coffee and brought it with a plate of cookies. Then she disappeared and returned with an armful of other albums, all labeled.

She was one of those people who loved putting together photograph albums. The pages, Nora saw, were beautifully decorated, comments written in a careful, flowing script beneath the photos.

Nora flipped back to the beginning. The very first page stole her breath and plunged her into the past. In an impromptu snapshot, she, Rachel, Molly and another friend of theirs, Jennifer Wisniewski, smiled jubilantly at the camera in their graduation robes, gold tassels dangling. Molly's was falling over her face and her eyes were comically crossed as she peered at it.

They looked so happy. "Free at last!" Rachel had crowed, making them all laugh. Nora felt it rising in her, the delight at officially crossing the threshold to adulthood, the anticipation of her future, the freedom from the dull requirements of public school, the excitement about tonight's party and the celebration dinner and show Rob was taking her to tomorrow night since he wasn't allowed at the official graduation party.

So happy, and so few hours from tragedy.

Eyes burning, glad Rachel had briefly left the room, Nora dragged in a breath and turned the page. There was Rachel, still in graduation robes, with her mom, then her dad and finally with her younger brother. Other students and families milled in the background.

All those faces who peopled the small world Nora's imagination had frozen in time.

But those people changed slowly in the pages that followed. The few photos from the summer after graduation showed teenagers subdued by a death that had shadowed the whole community. Nora remembered the previous summer, when her whole crowd had hung out whenever they could at the river, swinging on a rope from the big maple that overhung it, splashing and wading and sunbathing and gossiping. If her friends had continued the tradition, Rachel hadn't taken pictures of them. Perhaps too many people were gone, leaving early for jobs and college.

Or prison and the graveyard.

Rachel sat beside her again on the flowered sofa, setting the albums on the glass-topped coffee table. She focused her eyes on the open album, and said, "Oh, there I am, moving into my dorm room." Her laugh was rueful. "I was terrified!"

Molly, for all her outward confidence, had been scared about heading off to Washington State University in Pullman, on the other side of the state. She hadn't been the student to make it into a top private school like Stanford, but she'd decided she should go farther away from home than her brother had, only an hour away in Seattle, or an hour the other direction in Bellingham, where Rachel had gone.

"I want a brave new world!" she had declared, posing dramatically.

But one night when she was spending the night at Nora's, her voice had come out of the darkness, small and quiet. "Nora? Are you excited about Stanford?"

Surprised, Nora had turned her head on the pillow.

"Well…sure. Aren't you excited about going to college?"

False bravado rang in the voice Nora knew better than her own. "Of course I am!" She was silent for a long time. "I wish we were going together, though. Think how much fun we'd have, sharing a room."

Nora had rolled on her side, propping her head on her hand. Smiling at the idea, sad at the thought of going months at a time without seeing her best friend, she said, "We would, wouldn't we? I wish…"

"Wish what? That you were going to WSU?" Her friend made a rude noise. "You don't belong there. You're too smart. Besides, we'll see each other during breaks. And summers. Remember, we've got to get jobs in the same place next summer! It's a pact."

"Sworn in blood," Nora agreed.

Molly's voice went small again. "You won't tell anyone, will you?" She didn't wait for a response; she didn't have to. Of course Nora wouldn't. "It's just that sometimes I'm scared. I've never gone anywhere! Your family travels, at least, but we never go anywhere. And I didn't go to summer camp. Or even that marine biology thing you did."

"You went to cheerleading camp."

"For four whole days. And that was in Tacoma. Big adventure."

"But you had fun," Nora reminded her.

Molly didn't say anything for a minute. "Yeah," she said at last. "I guess. I think I lied about how much fun I had. I was homesick at night. Really homesick. I missed you so much, and I missed home, and my mother, and your mother…" Her laugh was half-sob. "What if I hate it there?" she ended piteously.

Nora groped under the covers until she found Molly's hand. Her friend squeezed so hard her bones creaked.

"You won't," she promised: Molly? Not make friends? Not having boys calling constantly? Not being the life of parties? Impossible! "Anyway," she added practically, "if you do, you can transfer. Go to Western or the U, like Rob. Then you could come home if you want to."

"But you won't be here!" Molly wailed.

"I will at Thanksgiving, and Christmas, and spring break..." If theirs were at the same time. "And we'll have a great time next summer! I think we should apply to work at Kalaloch. Nobody can make a bed better than we can, and we could go to the beach every day when our shift is over." Nora's parents had let her take Molly one summer when they went to the resort in the Olympic National Park. They'd stayed in a log cabin, had beach fires at night, climbed on driftwood and seen humpback whales breeching toward the endless horizon. Molly and Nora had wanted to go back ever since.

Covers rustled as Molly rolled over. Her voice quickened. "Yeah, Kalaloch would be fun. I could be a maid. Mom'd think that was hysterical."

"My mom, too," Nora agreed, relieved that her distraction had worked. Was Molly really scared about going to college? Nothing scared her! She was the brave one, Nora the worrier.

Now, in the present, Nora said, "I'll bet all kids are scared when they move in."

"My roommate admitted she was, too." Rachel was silent a moment, her gaze on Nora's face. "What was prison like? Was it like living in a dorm?"

Nora didn't, couldn't, look up, not without revealing more than she wanted to. "No," she said in a voice devoid of any emotion. "Oh, in a way, of course. Sharing with other women. Putting up with their foibles. But…you don't have the freedom."

Rachel's eyes held unexpected compassion. "I read some books about women in prison. Because of you going there. But somehow I never quite pictured *you*…" She stopped. "I hoped it wasn't really like that."

"It was," Nora said shortly.

Rachel stunned her by reaching for her hand, which lay on the photo album, and squeezing it, her grip warm and unexpectedly strong. "I wrote you."

"I didn't get mail for months at a time. It's used as a carrot." The couple of Rachel's letters that she had gotten, Nora hadn't read. She couldn't bear to. Just the round girlish handwriting on the envelope, the return address—Western Washington University—had been enough to shatter the fragile shell she was growing. She didn't want to hear news of home or chatter about classes and sororities and football games.

"You never wrote back."

"No. I…" Nora hesitated. How to explain? Rachel didn't appear hurt, not anymore, if she had ever been, but Nora found she wanted her to understand. "I couldn't. I had to become someone else to survive. Reminders of home hurt so bad I couldn't encourage them." She tried to smile. "I'm sorry."

"No. Don't be." Rachel squeezed her hand again and let go. "You did what you had to do. Sending you to prison was wrong. It made two victims instead of one."

"I was drunk and I killed someone else. Shouldn't I have been punished?"

"I suspect you punished yourself adequately."

Adequately? No self-flagellation could make up for what she'd done. But she understood what Rachel was saying.

"How do the police and the courts know who's really sorry and who's just pretending?" she asked. "I don't think sending me to prison was wrong. What *is* wrong is what goes on in prisons. They destroy people. They grind them down and steal their confidence and their ability to make decisions. They do nothing to solve the problems that led the women to commit the crimes in the first place. The alcoholism, the abusive marriages, the poverty or lack of job skills." Her voice crackled with anger. "If a term in prison is to serve any purpose, it should build character, job skills, education. Women should receive counseling, attend AA, have a chance to stay connected to their children and families. They shouldn't be made to feel..." She bit off the rest. She would never, ever, tell anyone what she had been made to feel.

"Vehicular homicide should be for drivers who have had DUIs before. Not for a teenager who makes a mistake once."

"I drank other times. I even drove a few times."

"We all did." Rachel still had that same unnervingly gentle expression. "What teenager doesn't?"

"There must be some." She prayed there were. "Plenty. Kids who don't think they walk on water."

"You didn't. We used to laugh at you when you just *knew* you'd done so horribly on a test, or your paper stank, or...remember after you took the SATs?"

Nora smiled. She'd been positive she had done so badly she'd be lucky to get into the community college. She had always gone into tests feeling positive and come out sure she'd failed. "I remember," she admitted.

"You were one of the least arrogant people I knew," Rachel said quietly.

"Okay, I was a mix. Mostly, I knew I was smart, I had the best boyfriend in the world, *I* was going to Stanford." Her mouth twisted. "Inside, I think I *was* arrogant."

"Confidence isn't the same thing."

How to know one from the other anymore? She'd lost the ability to be either.

When she didn't answer, Rachel said, "Now, if either of you was arrogant, it was Molly."

"Molly?" Instinctively Nora fired back, "Molly was one of the sweetest people ever!"

"Sure she was. But she was also Miss Popular. She never had any question in her mind that she was the most beautiful, that the guys all would choose her, that she was the center of attention. She was kind because she could be."

Nora stared in shock. "You didn't like her."

"I did like her. How could I help it? She was funny, with that great laugh." She fell silent for a moment, as if to pay tribute to Molly's wonderful, raucous laugh. "I was lucky she liked me enough to include me in your circle. I always felt...grateful."

"Really?" Nora said in astonishment. "I never knew..."

"Of course you didn't. You were her best friend. And, in your own way, you were as blessed as she was. Don't get me wrong. I liked Molly. I mean that. I mourned her. But you were the one I admired and really wanted to be friends with."

Still stupefied, Nora began shaking her head. "You didn't really know her. Not well enough. Or you wouldn't say any of that. Molly pretended, just like all of us did. It hurt that she wasn't as good a student as you and I were. And she was scared about going to college. Really scared. I promised never to tell anyone." But it seemed important now that Rachel see Molly's feet of clay and know that she hadn't always been the laughing, flirtatious Homecoming Queen. "The one time she went to that cheerleading camp—remember?—she was so homesick, she almost called and asked her mother to come get her. I think she applied to Washington State because going farther from home fit the image everyone had of her, even though, inside, that's not who she was."

Rachel had been gazing down at her hands. "I suppose I should have realized that," she said, her eyes meeting Nora's. "What teenager doesn't agonize in front of the mirror?"

"The ones who can't stand to look at themselves at all?"

They both laughed, but ruefully.

"Our coffee is stone-cold," Rachel said, rising. "Let me get fresh."

They finally drank some and nibbled on cookies. Nora looked through albums with Rachel providing a running commentary.

She squawked at the sight of herself in a hospital gown cuddling her newborn daughter, her hair stringy but her face glowing as she gazed down at the homely red infant with the thatch of dark hair.

"Which all fell out," Rachel said. "I started seeing it on her crib sheet. She ended up bald. I was in a panic until the nurse-practitioner patted my hand and assured me it was normal. I taped a pink bow to her head while this paler fuzz grew in."

Photos showed small, shabby apartments furnished with sagging couches and mismatched chairs from garage sales, but also a husband who seemed to be touching Rachel whenever the shutter snapped. Clearly Rachel thrived on motherhood. Page after page showed her kneeling in a sandbox with one of her kids, pushing her son on the swing or catching her daughter, who was shooting down the slide. It seemed she was always laughing.

Nora felt a pang of envy that surprised her. She'd regretted so much: the education she didn't get, the career she might have had, the admiration and pay and respect. Rob.

But somehow she'd never imagined the family she might have had—herself as a mother, Rob as a father.

Now that she had, longing clutched her in painful fingers.

Blindly she turned the page again. She had known that coming home might hurt, but she had been numb for so long that she'd expected any thaw to come slowly.

If she was going to endure even a few months in White Horse, to satisfy her parents, she would have to learn what she could safely feel and what she couldn't.

She tucked her regrets away, in their safe box, and laughed and commented on Rachel's pictures.

Nora was surprised to realize she'd enjoyed the visit when Rachel glanced at the clock above the mantel and said, "Oh! I'm going to have to pick up Ryan and Lori in a few minutes."

"I promised to make dinner tonight anyway, so I'd better get cracking," Nora said, moving the pile of albums to the coffee table and rising. "This has been fun."

"It has." Rachel smiled. "I'd like you to meet John. You'll come to dinner, won't you? Maybe next Saturday?"

"I'd love to."

"I also had an idea." She was accompanying Nora to the front door. "If you hate it, I won't even raise it with John."

Nora stopped, her hand on the knob. "Hate it?"

"Well." Her plump, dark-haired friend looked uncertain for the first time. "John has been having speakers at the high school who have HIV or are recovering alcoholics or, recently, a young woman who was raped by a guy she'd been dating for a while."

Nora tensed. "Yes?"

"I thought maybe you'd speak at an assembly. About drinking and driving."

"Speak?" she echoed.

"You were a great public speaker." Rachel studied

her face with anxious eyes. ‘‘But, like I said, if you hate the idea, let’s forget I ever mentioned it.’’

‘‘You want me to talk about what I went through.’’ She did hate the idea: it was unimaginable. Rachel might as well ask her to strip naked in front of fourteen hundred high school students and talk about a woman’s body, pointing out her flaws. She had a weird, fleeting moment of imagining herself patting her buttock and saying, ‘‘Now, stair steppers are a great way to avoid this kind of flab.’’

Rachel’s gaze was worried but...purposeful. ‘‘I thought you might keep somebody from making the same mistake. I could tell them I drank and drove, but it wouldn’t have any impact. From you...’’ She hesitated. ‘‘They know who you are.’’

‘‘Nora the infamous?’’

‘‘Not like that. Just...some of the kids knew you. Since you baby-sat and you volunteered at the hospital and...’’ She trailed off. ‘‘I’m sorry. I shouldn’t have asked.’’

‘‘No, it’s okay,’’ Nora made herself say, although the words came out gruffly. ‘‘Really. I’ll do it.’’

Her friend’s expression lightened. ‘‘You will?’’

She was going to hate herself for agreeing. ‘‘If even one kid listens to me...really listens...’’ She sucked in a breath. She’d said enough, didn’t have to finish aloud: *It would give some meaning to my survival.*

Tears sparkling in her eyes, Rachel hugged her impulsively. ‘‘Thank you. I’ll tell John.’’

Nora stood with her arms at her sides, not sure if a response was called for. She’d become—not uncomfortable—*unfamiliar* with physical affection. "Okay."

"John can talk to you when you're here for dinner." Rachel gave a sniff and a wavery smile. "I'm so glad you came home, Nora."

"Um...thank you." Nora backed out the door, tripped over the jamb, righted herself. Awkwardly she said, "Thank you for the coffee and cookies."

Rachel laughed. "You're welcome."

Driving the short distance home, Nora realized that she felt...eased by the visit. As if, perhaps, somebody from her past actually did like her. As if, maybe, her mother was right, and most people would welcome her home.

COLLEEN SUMNER STOOD to one side of her front window and peered out like some detestable neighborhood snoop. She hadn't recognized the sound of an approaching car engine. Nor did she know the car, a bright yellow Volkswagen Beetle. Straining to see the driver, she wished she'd thought to ask somebody what that girl drove.

Would she have the nerve to come by, like some sightseer? Colleen quivered at the thought of her slowing, perhaps even pulling to the curb as she sighed with pleasant memories of romantic moments with Rob or silly ones with Molly.

All she could make out was that the driver was a young woman with dyed blond hair. The Beetle was going too fast as it passed. Colleen was sure she heard, even through the glass and walls of the house, a deep bass beat of music played at a ridiculous, inconsiderate volume. It seemed as if the windows shivered for a moment, and then the music—if you could call it that—faded.

These young people would all be deaf by the time they turned thirty. What she couldn't imagine was why they thought other people wanted to hear their music as well. Or did they play it so loud in a deliberate attempt to be offensive?

Hearing herself, she let out an irritated breath. She was sounding like an old fuddy-duddy! She'd certainly listened to loud music herself. How her father had hated Cream and the Rolling Stones and especially Bob Dylan, with his dreadful, nasal whine. She *had* enjoyed annoying him, she had to admit. But he was her father. She hadn't been so arrogant as to flaunt herself or her tastes the way these kids today were.

Or the way Molly had. Her loud music had been a bone of contention. But Colleen wouldn't think about that now.

Peering down the empty street, she stood, indecisive. She should be starting dinner. As if Allen would care. It seemed these days he must eat big lunches out. He'd pick at his dinner and then vanish almost immediately into his study with no more than a murmured apology or excuse. As if they didn't both know why he was hiding out from her.

Watching the Altbys' black-and-white cat cross the street and saunter up their front walk, Colleen made no move to go to the kitchen.

What if Allen asked for a divorce? Would she care? Even as tormented, as single-minded, as she'd become, she thought she would. Their silver wedding anniversary had come and gone. She still loved him.

Occasionally she even felt a stirring of some sexual interest, although they hadn't slept together in a long time.

Those first couple of years, they had grieved together, united in their pain and anger. She had cried on his shoulder, huge, agonized, bitter sobs tearing her even as she felt his wet cheek against her hair.

Then, somehow, they had drifted into a kind of silence. The tears were past, and there seemed to be nothing left to say. The things they used to talk about were too trivial to merit conversation. He had his work to be absorbed in. She had Molly.

They'd become almost comfortable in their silence, she thought. Too comfortable, maybe. Over the past few years, Allen had become more and more reclusive and she had quit pretending. He didn't often suggest they do anything together, and she didn't fabricate a day's worth of activities to convince him she was filling her time.

She couldn't blame him if he did divorce her. She'd abandoned him in many ways. In as many ways as one could, without physically moving out. And yet, she hoped he didn't.

A pickup truck came around a corner down the street and she stiffened. But almost immediately she recognized it as the beat-up, faded blue Chevy belonging to the Gilmer boy. He'd turn—yes, he did—at the next corner.

Colleen stayed out of sight—as if anyone was looking—beside the window, an appointed sentry who wasn't allowed to leave her post. She retained enough common sense to know she was being ridiculous.

She hadn't left the house in days. She was certain

she'd encounter Nora if she did. Working right here in town, at the veterinary clinic, she might run out on a break at any time—to the grocery store, the library, the dry cleaner. Who knew?

Her getting a job meant she was staying. Colleen didn't think she could stand much more of this. She'd been made a prisoner in her own house! She was going stir-crazy. How else to explain this insane need to monitor all the passing traffic? But she hadn't told either Allen or Rob that she was afraid to go out for fear she'd run into *her*.

She hugged herself and stared out the window at nothing. Seeing nothing. She shouldn't let Nora Woods have any influence on her whatsoever. She didn't deserve so much as a passing thought!

But her very existence, now that she was right here in White Horse again, rubbed at Colleen like a blister that swelled under the skin until any more pressure would pop it. She could not put it out of her mind for one single minute. She hated and feared the idea of meeting Nora. If she were civil, she'd hate herself afterward. But she dreaded as much the idea of what would happen if she let loose her hatred. She, who had never done a violent thing in her life, knew herself capable of tearing at Nora's skin and eyes in a desperate wish to obliterate her, as Nora had done to Molly. But other people would never understand how her rage and grief had festered. She would be shunned or, worse, pitied. As if there was something wrong with her because time hadn't healed, as everyone had promised it would.

Not even Allen, who shared her deep, abiding sadness, would understand if she broke and attacked

Molly's murderer. And Rob...Rob might look at her with revulsion and even anger, because he still harbored some secret tenderness toward his sister's killer. And she couldn't bear that. Who else did she have but her son?

But it wasn't right, her trapped in this house as if she wore one of those electronic shackles, while *she* worked and shopped and maybe even flirted with Rob, as if she were the prodigal daughter returned.

Colleen's rage grew and flourished, a few unfurled leaves at a time, as it had grown every day in the hothouse of her misery.

She did not want to meet Nora Woods.

But she might never find any relief from this fury and anguish until she did.

CHAPTER FIVE

OUT OF RESPECT for his mother, Rob did his best to stay away from Nora.

His fingers tightened on his drafting pencil. Oh, hell, who was he kidding? What really kept him away was the memory of the expression on Nora's face when he'd asked to see her again.

He couldn't seem to blank from his mind the way she'd stumbled; "Maybe. I don't know. Not now." She'd looked...confused, as if she didn't understand why he was interested. And perhaps a little bit afraid.

Of him? Because of the brutal way he'd rejected her after the accident? Remembering his cruelty and rage lashed him now, biting deeper into his flesh since he'd seen his vibrant, smart-mouthed Nora reduced to a wan facsimile of the girl he'd known.

When? he'd wanted to beg. *Next week? The week after?*

Or did she mean never?

Rob had hoped that his mother would get used to the idea of Nora back in White Horse, but that wasn't happening. He'd had his parents to dinner once and dropped by to see his mother a couple of times since the night when she had asked him to call Nora and tell her to get out of town. These days Mom pretended to be interested when he talked about work, but he knew pretence when he saw it. And he felt her intensity when she asked, as she invariably did, ''You haven't seen her, have you?''

He always knew who she was talking about. Her eyes glittered and her fingers would bite into his arm when she reached out as if to compel him to tell her the truth.

''No, why would I?'' he'd said the last time, hating the implied lie.

Why would he? Because he wanted to. Because he needed to. Because he couldn't close the door on the past as easily as he'd hoped.

Because Nora Woods, however damaged by that one horrendous night, still drew him as no other woman ever had.

His mind made up, he abruptly stood, shoved some papers into his briefcase and said to his secretary on the way out the door, ''I'll be at the vet clinic.''

''Sure thing,'' she said cheerfully.

He parked in front of White Horse Veterinary Hospital and then sat behind the wheel for a minute, girding himself as if he were facing a grueling presentation for a multimillion dollar job.

What if he didn't happen to see her? Did he have the guts to ask for her? Now that Bergstrom and Theresa Hughes had remembered the history between their new employee and their architect, they might not appreciate him pursuing her.

Well, to hell with them, too, Rob thought irritably. It wasn't any of their business. If Nora wanted to tell him to take a hike, he'd listen.

On the way in, he politely held the door for a rottweiler dragging its apologetic owner out. The waiting room was jammed. A young couple was absorbed in a fat brown puppy on the woman's lap. Toddlers slammed blocks together in the corner play area. Several dogs waited, panting anxiously and drooling on their owners' pant legs. The couple of cats in plastic carriers must be wondering if they were going to be fed to the surrounding pack.

The receptionist smiled. "Mr. Sumner! I'll tell Dr. Bergstrom you're here."

"Tell him I just have a few quick questions." He glanced around. "I guess I should have called."

"It's a madhouse today," she said with a laugh, and disappeared through the narrow room that currently served as dispensary and office for the bookkeeper. Nora.

Aiming for casual, Rob eased a couple of steps to the side so that he could see her desk. His heart jolted at the sight of her, auburn head bent over a sheaf of papers.

As if he'd willed her to look up, she did, head turning like a deer's when it senses danger.

"Nora," he said, with what he hoped was an easy smile. "How goes the job?"

After the first startled, wary look from her big brown eyes, she smiled tentatively. "Fine. Although it's taking me a while to catch up. They'd been without a bookkeeper for six weeks."

"While the piles of bills and invoices teetered?"

Her smile widened, showing a momentary spark of humor and life. "Something like that."

He leaned against the chest-high counter. "You figured out how to read Eric's handwriting yet?"

Now Nora laughed, a musical sound that rippled

over his skin like a zephyr. "Most of the time. I did try to pay Pro-Vet a thousand more than they were owed until I studied the invoices."

Rob grinned. "Eric wrote out a list of requirements for the addition. I could have sworn he was demanding a sugary peppermint, for reasons that mystified me. I had to ask." Encouraged by the merriment in her eyes, he translated, "Surgery preparation area was a little more understandable."

She gave a gurgle of laughter. "I should think."

Joan, the receptionist, reappeared with a smile. "Eric will be with you in just a minute." She scanned the room. "Tom? You can bring Pyro into the examining room now. Dr. Hughes will be with you in a minute."

An obviously elderly golden retriever, Pyro shambled resignedly beside his geriatric owner into a room instead of out the front door, as his one wistful glance suggested he had hoped for.

"Rob!" Eric Bergstrom appeared beyond Nora. "Come on back."

Rob circled the counter and passed Nora, who had returned her attention to the papers in front of her. In Bergstrom's office, he discussed several options for dividing space and made a recommendation.

The vet frowned, studying the sketches. After only a moment, he gave a decisive nod. "Works for me."

"Good." Rob closed the notebook and stood. "I should have called, but seeing the drawings can help you envision the space better."

"No, I'm glad you came." Bergstrom gave him a hooded look. "You and Nora have a chance to talk?"

"Briefly."

"Good, good. She's accomplished miracles since she took over."

"She was supposed to go to Stanford with damn near a full ride," Rob said. "She has the ability to be a CEO, if life had gone the way it should have."

"I know." Frowning again and staying put in his chair, Bergstrom steepled his fingers. "I feel guilty."

"Guilty?"

"As if I'm taking advantage of her troubles. I shouldn't be able to afford her."

"She applied."

The vet grunted. "And I snapped her up. But..." His frown deepened, then smoothed out. "Oh, hell. She probably won't stay."

Rob was the one to frown now, although he turned away to hide the expression. She could do that, up and move away. He could never see her again.

A part of him had always thought Nora would come back into his life. Now that she had, he didn't want her to go.

"It sounds as if she likes working here."

"She's good with the people and the animals." Rising, the vet clapped him on the back. "I'd better get back to work."

Rob promised to be in touch and followed Bergstrom back toward the front of the hospital. His heart sank when he saw that Nora's desk was empty.

She wasn't out in front helping clients, either, and he found he didn't have the guts to ask where she was. He'd seen her, they'd talked, and it seemed to him she'd loosened up a little. He'd find a way to run into her by accident one of these days soon, even if it meant he had to loiter down the street and follow her from work.

He nodded goodbye to Joan, held the door again for a woman with two kids, two cat carriers and a harried expression, and headed down the porch steps toward his parked car.

He'd almost reached it when he saw Nora. She sat on a bench outside the employee entrance like a smoker taking a break, except that her fingers were threaded together on her lap and she was watching him walk toward her. Her lab coat, a bright fuchsia printed with cavorting, crayon-colored cats, clashed with her hair.

"Hi." He approached as if she were as skittish as the wild deer he'd imagined earlier.

"I was hoping to talk to you." She sounded poised, but she was too still, too straight backed, as if she made herself face him.

"You know you can call me anytime."

Sure she did, he mocked himself. *After all, he'd been there for her all these years, hadn't he?*

She didn't say anything.

"Can I sit down?"

"Oh!" Faint color leaped to her too pale cheeks. "Of course."

He sat on the garden bench flanked by rhododendrons and facing the parking lot.

"I wanted to consult with you about something. I'd like to talk to your parents," Nora said in a rush. "To say I'm sorry. I know they must hate me, but just once..." Her voice choked, caught. "Just once, I want to say it."

He hadn't expected this. "I told Dad what you told me. That you'd give anything to take it back."

They both remembered what she'd really said: that she wished she had died instead. It was in her eyes when she looked at him with something approaching hope.

She swallowed. "What did he say?"

He hesitated. "I don't think Dad has ever thought it was anything but an accident."

She heard what he didn't say.

"But your mother does."

"She's..." He hesitated, torn between two people he—not loved, he certainly didn't *love* Nora, not with so many years separating them from their past—*cared about* might be the right choice of words. "Mom has never gotten over losing Molly. She misses her every day. Some of her grief has turned to anger."

Nora bit her lip and looked away, staring with what he guessed were unseeing eyes at passing traffic. "I don't blame her," she said in a soft, stark voice.

"I think, if she'd talk to you, it might help her recover. But I don't think she'll do it." He moved his shoulders uneasily. "I haven't even told her I've run into you."

Nora nodded but said nothing.

Studying her profile, he was struck again by how pale she was, how still, as if she'd lost the ability or desire to project any emotion but sadness.

"You weren't happy to see me," he said. "Why this sudden desire to meet with my parents?"

She let out a tiny puff of air. "It isn't sudden. Or I don't think it is. I told myself I was coming home to White Horse to make my parents happy. But I'm beginning to see that I…oh, needed to quit running away. That maybe I have an obligation to *see* the pain I caused. It seems…wrong to spend my life so far away that no one knows what I did.''

He thought he understood more than she was saying. ''Where no one really can love you, because they don't know you.''

She gave him a startled look before bowing her head. ''Maybe,'' she said, so quietly he had to strain to hear.

''I'm glad you came home.'' Rob was surprised to realize how much he meant it.

''Thank you.'' Lifting her head, Nora's smile twisted. ''Will your dad see me, at least?''

''Yeah, I think so.'' He'd *make* his father meet her and bestow whatever forgiveness he could wrench from his wounded soul.

She rose to her feet, her purpose achieved. ''Then…if you would…'' Her decisiveness wavered. ''Or should I call him?''

''No!'' He rubbed the back of his neck. ''No. Let me set it up.''

''Thank you,'' Nora said again, her pansy-brown eyes holding his steadily.

''I'll call you.''

''Okay.''

She walked away before he could say, *Wait!*

He could have stopped her, of course. She would have turned with puzzled gaze, silently asking again, *What do you want?*

He still didn't know. Her? Maybe, but the past was a mighty obstacle, a mountain range so dangerous it would have stopped the westward settlers. Even assuming he and Nora could put it behind them, what about his mother?

Then, of course, Rob thought wryly, there was the question of whether Nora was interested. Which she had given no indication of being.

In his car, he grabbed his cell phone.

His father was on-site. Rob could hear the roar of heavy machinery in the background, the squeal of a dozer raising its blade, voices shouting above the racket.

"Let me get in my truck," his dad yelled. The noise became muffled following the slam of the door. "That's better. What's up?"

"Did I get you at a bad time?"

"No, I needed a break."

From further sounds, Rob guessed his father was rustling in the cooler, popping open a soda and taking a long drink. "So?" his dad asked finally.

Rob didn't beat around the bush. "Nora wants to meet with you."

This silence pulsed.

"Dad?"

For a moment, he thought he wasn't going to get a response at all.

At last, his father asked, "With your mother, too?"

"I told her I didn't think Mom would listen to her."

"What is it that she has to say?"

Rob leaned his head back against his seat and closed his eyes. "'I'm sorry.'"

Another thick silence. "This means something to her." It wasn't quite a question.

"Yeah. She feels as if she's been running away from your anger and pain all these years."

"So she wants forgiveness."

"Actually..." Rob frowned, thinking it over. "I suspect what she really wants is for you to give her hell. She thinks she deserves whatever vile things you choose to say."

His father understood. "A hair shirt."

"Something like that."

Dad grunted. This pause suggested he was thinking it over. "All right. Say, lunchtime tomorrow?"

Half-surprised, Rob said, "Shall we meet at Facelli's?"

"I won't stay for lunch. Your mother would never forgive me. But I'll listen to Nora, for what it's worth to her. Noon?"

They agreed, and Rob pushed End, dropped the cell phone on the seat and considered going back in. No, he decided at last, too eager. He'd call later.

When he got through to the vet hospital at four, Joan passed his call right through to Nora.

"Hello?" she said tentatively, as if she couldn't understand who would call her.

"It's Rob. I talked to my father."

"Oh." Her voice was small. He imagined her squaring her shoulders, because her voice firmed. "Will he see me?"

"He says yes. Can you have lunch tomorrow? At Facelli's? Do you know it?"

"I've seen it." She didn't sound quite steady. "It's new."

"Dad can't eat with us, but he'll stop by."

"Oh." Her voice got lower. "Okay. I understand."

"But I'd like to take you to lunch."

"You don't have to, Rob."

Knowing the wages of honesty, he'd been tempted to let her assume his father would be having lunch with them.

"I want to."

This silence was less easy to interpret than the others that had preceded it today. He was apparently throwing a lot of people for a loop.

"All right." She spoke like someone nerving herself to face a firing squad. Not like a woman who was pleased at an invitation. "It was nice of you to arrange this," she said, her voice stilted and polite.

And therefore she felt compelled to subject herself to an unwelcome interlude with him, he realized, heart sinking.

"Lunch would be nice," she concluded.

He had to grit his teeth against the repetition of "nice," clearly a message. He'd been nice; she couldn't be rude enough to say "no thanks" in return.

The sad part was, he was desperate enough to keep her on the hook. "Great," Rob said heartily. "Tomorrow, then."

By the time the phone hit the cradle, he knew how it felt to despise himself.

STANDING ON THE SIDEWALK, Nora gripped the straps of her purse as if it were a rope keeping her from plunging over Snoqualmie Falls.

"Breathe," she whispered, and made herself do it. Her heart was drumming, her fingers were getting slippery with sweat, and she felt sick.

Nora hadn't felt so terrified since she'd walked into

the Washington Corrections Center for Women in Gig Harbor eleven and a half years ago.

She drew a deep breath. What was the worst that would happen? Mr. Sumner would let her see his anguish and tell her flatly that she was responsible for it. There was nothing he could say that she didn't already know.

She made a ragged sound. It was just...hearing it from him wouldn't be the same. He had tucked her in sometimes when she was little, along with his own daughter. His hand would crawl across the bedcovers toward them as he said, always with that same glee, "Don't let the bedbugs..." his hand would pounce "*...bite!*"

They'd giggle and giggle, as if he didn't do the same thing every time. Every night, according to Molly. "Daddy thinks he's so funny."

"He *is* funny," Nora argued.

She still remembered the night when she and Molly were about twelve. Mr. Sumner started, "Don't let the bedbugs..." and Molly interrupted with a snap in her voice, "Oh, Dad! We're not little kids anymore!"

His hand and face had both gone still, and then he had given a small, crooked smile. "No," he said quietly. "Sometimes I forget." He'd told them goodnight and left with dignity.

Molly hadn't even seemed to notice his hurt feelings, but Nora had, and had ached for him, although she was too loyal to Molly to say anything.

Mostly, though, she'd admired Molly for her willingness to defy her parents. At thirteen, both had chafed against being treated like children, and sometimes Nora just wanted to scream at her mother or father, "I'm not *stupid,* you know!" or "I wish I could move to Molly's house. *Her* parents treat me like *my* opinion counts!" But she mostly bit back her irritation, because she knew they loved her even if they couldn't seem to see that she was all grown up.

"The truth is," she moaned to Molly, "I'm too *nice.* Why can't I ever just tell them the truth?"

"You are too nice," her friend assured her. "They've conditioned you. Parents *deserve* to hear the truth once in a while."

The truth, of course, evolved as they matured. Still clutching her purse, still standing twenty feet down the sidewalk from the Italian restaurant, Nora had one more memory of a sleepover at Molly's, of her father flicking off the bedroom light and standing in the doorway, a dark silhouette.

"Night, girls," he'd said casually, and started to turn away, pulling the door closed behind him.

Seventeen-year-old Molly had said suddenly, "Daddy?"

"Hmm?" He'd turned back.

"Do you remember how you used to pretend your hand was a bug? And you'd say, 'Sleep tight, don't let the bedbugs bite'?"

He stood without speaking for a minute. "I remember."

"I always loved that," Molly said sleepily. "When did you quit doing it?"

Nora's eyes were adjusting to the darkness and she saw the sadness and pleasure both in the smile that was just for his daughter.

"When you started to grow up," he said, and again, "Good night."

Weirdly, Nora had to blink away tears as she started forward toward Facelli's.

New to her, although her mother said it had opened at least seven or eight years ago, the Italian restaurant occupied a narrow brick building that had once held—she had to think—a fabric store. The front window now said Facelli's in gilt script and the door was heavy, dark and elaborately carved. The interior wasn't as dim as she'd expected. The back wall had unexpectedly been replaced by French doors that led to a tiny patio with tables. She was vaguely aware of padded booths along a wall that had held bolts of fabric, of Italian movie posters framed above the tables, of rich earth colors and a host approaching her inquiringly.

But everything else faded when she saw them, father and son, sitting at a booth halfway down. Their heads, one dark, one streaked with gray, turned toward her, and past took a dizzying tumble with present.

Mr. Sumner hugging her at graduation. "Two girls graduating today," he'd said, his voice a low rumble for her alone. "I'm a proud man."

"Don't let the bedbugs bite."

And his face when she saw him in the corridor at the hospital, disbelief and grief etching years into it. Revulsion twisting it when he caught sight of her.

Ignoring the restaurant host, she found her feet carrying her forward, toward the two men who stood as she approached.

Rob would look like his father someday, she thought, thicker around the waist, heftier in the shoulders, gray adding distinction to a face creased by the years. But when she was close, Nora had a moment of shock, because Mr. Sumner had aged so much. There was gray in his hair, of course, but it wasn't so much that as his face. She remembered mostly smiles, small ones lit by a spark of mischief. Now, it seemed that grief had weighed on the flesh, tugging it downward, deepening lines that had nothing to do with smiles, creating pouches beneath eyes that were bluer than his son's. His shoulders were rounded, as if he hunched from a burden too great to carry.

She had done this to him, to a man she loved like a father.

Nora's feet rooted to the floor and she wanted to flee, as she'd never wanted anything in her life.

Except to bring Molly back.

"Hello, Nora," Mr. Sumner said, his eyes searching her face.

Tears blurred her vision. "Thank you," she whispered, "for seeing me."

He inclined his head in acknowledgment.

Rob took her elbow in a warm, strong hand. "Sit down, Nora."

He slid in first and tugged her afterward. She reached out dumbly and he took her hand, gripping it firmly against his thigh under the table, giving her some of the strength she'd always known he possessed.

Mr. Sumner slid into the booth facing her. His expression was...watchful, but not grim. "You don't need to be afraid of me."

She blurted, "Was I... Do I *look* scared?"

"Terrified."

"Oh." She gripped Rob's hand tighter. "I'm not

afraid of you. Only of seeing what I did to you, I suppose."

He frowned. "Aren't you taking too much credit?"

"What?" she asked, startled.

"We're all responsible for how we handle what life throws at us."

Nora felt a quiver run through Rob, but she didn't look away from his father.

"I killed Molly."

"You were behind the wheel that night, sure."

"I was drunk," she said desperately.

"So was Molly."

"But...I was driving." She felt as if she'd wandered into a dense fog that distorted her surroundings. Nothing he said was what she'd anticipated. Determined to make him see more clearly, she explained as if to a slow child. "Molly wasn't."

His gaze pinned hers. "Had you planned ahead who would drive?"

"Only...only when we left for Gavin's house." They had been at a parent-sponsored graduation party when Gavin declared it too tame and invited all his friends to his house.

"The parents are out tonight," he'd announced with a sly grin. "They think I'm safely accounted for. We can go hang out there for a few hours."

Somebody else had a couple of kegs ready for a good time.

"You want to drive or shall we take my car?" Molly had asked Nora, assuming they'd go as a team.

Nora hadn't really wanted to go at all. It was that good-girl thing again. She'd told her parents she would be here.

But…she was eighteen now, and a high school graduate. An adult, she'd thought defiantly. She didn't *have* to account for every second to them anymore. In a few months she'd be off at college. She wasn't that big on parties, but if ever an occasion called for one, this was it, wasn't it? Liberation! The official crossing of the divide between childhood and adulthood.

"I'll drive," she'd said impulsively.

Her offer to take her car had been a declaration of her willing participation, not an acknowledgment of responsibility for getting them home safely. Neither girl had ever once thought of her as a designated driver.

But *she* should have thought of herself that way. They'd taken her car. She was behind the wheel.

Not Molly.

"What if she'd driven instead?" Molly's father asked now, relentlessly. "Would she have refused to drink?"

Nora stared at him, mouth opening, then closing. *Yes!* she wanted to declare. *Maybe. That isn't the point.* I *was drunk.* I *drove.*

But a slide show forced its way before her reluctant inner eye. Molly, head thrown back in a hearty laugh as someone—Jay—squirted champagne on her. Who had brought the champagne? Nora didn't remember. Molly tipping up her glass and swallowing with gusto. Molly lying on the couch with her head on Nathan's lap while he fondled her breast.

Molly staggering when they weaved their way out to the car. The two leaning on each other, laughing helplessly. Partway home, Molly whispering, "Ooh,

I'm going to be sick,'' and Nora stepping on the gas to hurry.

''No,'' Nora whispered now. ''No. We...neither of us...we never thought about driving safely. We just...we never thought at all.''

''She could just as well have been behind the wheel.'' Her best friend's father looked now as if he were marching lockstep to his own death, going with dignity, never hesitating, but knowing what was to come. ''She could have killed herself, or you.''

Rob's fingers bit into Nora's, but she didn't even flinch.

''No,'' she said, shaking her head, unable to stop, a metronome. ''*No.* I was driving. What she might have done... How can we speculate? I offered to take my car. She trusted me. I was the...'' Nora stopped. Closed her eyes.

''The steady one? The reliable one? The one who never got drunk?'' Mr. Sumner made a noise that hurt even to hear. ''I knew my daughter, Nora. I loved her, and I knew her. She liked to party. She didn't look ahead, not the way you did. She was good-hearted and impulsive and sometimes... What is it the Irish say? Feckless.''

''But if she'd been driving,'' Nora whispered, ''everything would have been different. We would have made it safely home.''

''Maybe. Maybe not.'' Looking even older, he slid out of the booth and stood as if his back ached. His eyes seemed wise, and ancient. ''Don't throw away your life in penance, Nora. That's just more waste.''

''But...what I've done to your lives...''

''The waste of our lives is our fault.'' He sounded

clipped, even angry suddenly. "I've regretted all these years that we didn't stand beside you. We all carry our own guilt."

She gaped.

He gave a small, crooked smile. "Your own is heavy enough. Leave me mine."

With that, he gave a slow, civil nod and walked away.

Pulling her hand free from Rob's, Nora twisted in the booth to watch Mr. Sumner go.

How could he just *leave,* after saying things like that? As if...as if any of the tragedy was *his* fault!

"I'm sorry," she whispered. "I didn't get to say it, but...I'm sorry."

CHAPTER SIX

"HE LEFT!"

Looking at the back of her head, Rob said, "Yeah. I told you he couldn't stay for lunch."

"But..." She spun to face him, her expression a mix of outrage and bewilderment. "Doesn't he *hate* me?"

Rob kept his tone calm. "I told you he doesn't."

"He should!"

Hair shirt. His father had been right. She *wanted* Molly's parents to hate her, because...why? It would reinforce her opinion of herself?

"No." Rob shook his head. "Dad shouldn't. Damn it, Nora! You were part of our family! What if one of your kids accidentally kills a sister or brother? Do you hate your own child?"

Distress widened brown eyes. "But I'm not..."

"As good as. Dad's right. We should all have been at your side. We should have been in court, sitting right behind you."

"No." She shook her head. "No. It was Molly that counted. It was..."

"Molly was dead," he said brutally. "Do you think she would have *wanted* us to desert you?"

"Why are you being so nice?" Nora stared at him with genuine bafflement. "I don't understand."

"Because..." He stopped. *Because I love you.* No! Because he'd loved her then. Because... "I hope," he said, picking his way through the thousands of words he could have chosen as if they were delicate wildflowers he might easily trample if he misstepped, "I hope because I'm a just man. Because I've had twelve years to realize how wrong we all were. Obviously, Dad feels the same."

Nora bowed her head abruptly, and he understood that she must be hiding tears.

"Did you know...?" she asked, voice thick, muffled.

"What he would say?" God, he wanted to touch her. To pull her against him and let her soak his dress shirt with tears. To stroke his hand over the thick, springy silk of her hair, a memory so vivid he could *feel* it. "No," he said roughly. "He...surprised me, when he talked about guilt. He must know that he and Mom haven't handled Molly's death well."

Nora looked up, with tears in her eyes. "How do you handle a child's death well?"

"I don't know," he said, low, "but it's sure not by spending twelve years obsessively fixated on her memory. Mom has a goddamn altar set up at home! And Dad..." He grunted. "Dad has no idea how to help her, so he's gone into hiding. I just didn't realize that he knew why he was doing it."

Her forehead furrowed. "So...he feels guilty because he hasn't helped your mom more?"

"Apparently."

They both turned at the click of heels on the tile floor. The waitress smiled. "Have you had time to decide on your order yet?"

"Oh!" Nora was startled. "I don't know if I can…"

"Stay and eat." Both women must know he was begging. He didn't care. "Please."

Nora looked at him with those wide, blind eyes, then reached for the menu. "I'm sorry. If you'll give me just a minute…?"

"Of course," the waitress said warmly, and retreated.

Nora gazed down at the open menu. "This all looks good." She sounded too bright, too perky. She'd promised to stay to lunch, and she wouldn't be a grudging companion.

Rob clenched his teeth on a wave of frustration and hurt that was completely unjustified. They had a history. *He* was the one who'd let her down, not the other way around. He had no right whatsoever to expect anything at all from her, and every reason to assume she'd have no interest in resuming a relationship.

But the way she'd reached for his hand, as if instinctively, and held on to it. That must mean something.

Or not. He mercilessly squashed his own fantasy. He'd been next to her. She might have been completely unconscious of taking his hand, of who he was. He'd been there, that's all. He was an idiot to think anything else.

"No." She suddenly slid out of the booth.

He jerked. She was leaving.

But she circled to the other side and sat. "We ought to be able to look at each other."

He bit back a ragged sound. "Sure."

She aimed a smile toward the hovering waitress, who approached again and this time took their orders.

When she was out of earshot, Nora said, "Your dad meant to make me feel better, but I feel even guiltier instead! He seems so unhappy."

"I think he is." Rob grimaced. "I guess I've known he was, but not how much." He fell silent for a moment. "I don't think of him as introspective. I figured he just hid out from Mom without realizing that he was...oh, giving her permission to keep grieving."

"Can you just...wrench someone out of mourning?" Nora asked doubtfully.

"Maybe not. But you can try. Or he could have forced the issue by insisting that she take steps herself."

"Counseling."

"Yeah." He pinched the bridge of his nose. "I wonder if he's just...become aware of his failings, or whether he intends to do something."

Nora watched him worriedly. "How would your mother take it if he put his foot down?"

Rob grunted. "I don't know. I just don't know."

But he had an idea. His mother had always been the dominant force in his parents' marriage. Not that his father was a weak man. On the job, he was forceful and decisive, and even at home he sometimes became stubborn. That's what Mom called it: stubborn. Every once in a while, he'd refuse to do something or go somewhere, and it exasperated her to no end. But most often Dad went along with her decisions. He apparently believed that women were in charge of the home, or else he was just too easygoing to butt heads incessantly with his wife. Rob's memories from growing up were that Dad had always seemed content with the relationship.

If Mom got strident, he'd shrug, a smile in his eyes. "That's your mother. Wait her out," he would advise.

Perhaps reacting to the expression on his face, Nora moaned. "Now I feel worse. It's like I'm creating some kind of chemical reaction just by my presence."

"Maybe you are." Rob reached across the table and touched her hand. "And maybe that's a good thing."

"Is it?" she asked, fixing him with a fierce stare. "What if your parents end up divorced? Or your mom tries to kill herself? Or just becomes sadder?"

All those fears were already weighing on him, but he still said steadily, "Change can go either way. I know that. But if her world gets shaken up a little, she might also decide to take some positive steps. We can hope."

She hadn't mentioned one fear that niggled at him. His mother was fixated on Nora. What scared him was the depth of her anger and the irrationality of the blame she cast. Did she hate Nora enough to act on it? He couldn't imagine she'd hurt anyone, but he could almost see her vandalizing Nora's car or throwing a rock through her window or just creating an ugly scene.

Mom sure wasn't going to be happy when she found out Dad had met with Nora.

Rob shook his head impatiently, refusing to believe the mother who'd sewed Halloween costumes and served as president of the parent-teacher group and snatched him out of a swim lesson after the sadistic teenager instructor had tossed him into the deep end and scared the crap out of him would become a hate-monger.

No. It just wasn't in her. It couldn't be.

"Let's talk about something else," he suggested, ignoring the band of tension that squeezed his skull. "Your job. How's it going?"

"Fine." Nora shrugged, then turned a smile on something—someone—past his shoulder.

He turned his head to see that their salads were arriving.

While they ate, they chatted like two old friends. He brought her up to date on the lives of people they'd both known from high school and town.

"I did see Kathy Putnam the other day," Nora commented, her face as vibrant as he'd seen it since her return. "She came to the hospital with a goat in the back of her pickup. I swear, she had this swarm of kids with her. They couldn't possibly all be hers, but—"

"They were hers," he interrupted. "I think she and Drew have five."

She gaped. "Five?" Then, on a rising note, "Drew?"

"Yep." He grinned. "Didn't get a chance to talk to her? Or did she not want to admit to having married the biggest nerd in the history of White Horse High School?"

"He was...yuck." Then she blushed. "That's mean. He was nice! It's just that he had such a horrible complexion, and he *smelled,* and I swear he always said the wrong thing at the exact worst moment."

"That was our Drew," he agreed. "A social misfit." Drew Falkner was actually between Rob and Nora in age. Rob tried to remember if Drew had been one year behind him or two.

"What does he do now?" Nora looked unwillingly fascinated.

"Apparently he dreams up computer games. You know, the elaborate sword and sorcery kind. I guess he's hugely successful. In fact—" Rob smiled "—I designed a house for them. Hell of a place, if I do say so myself."

"Wow." Nora laid down her fork. Her laugh was pretty on her face. "What does he look like now?"

"Uh..." Like any man, Rob didn't pay much attention to those things. "Well, he's taller," he said unhelpfully. "Almost my height, I think. No pimples."

"Well, duh!" She gave him an exasperated look. "Does he have scars?"

"You mean, from the pimples? No." Rob shrugged. "I guess he's not a bad-looking man. He and Kathy got together when he came home after graduating from MIT. Took a job with some software outfit in Lynnwood, but he rented a place up here."

"And they have goats." Nora was obviously still trying to reconcile the teenagers she'd known with the adults they'd become.

"And cats, dogs and horses. They have ten acres and a couple of barns. Nice place."

"Wow," she said again. "Sometimes I think I've entered a time warp."

"You have." He pushed his plate away. "That's what you get for staying away too long."

"Mom kept me up-to-date on a few people. Mostly my best friends."

"Have you gotten together with anyone?" he asked, trying to sound casual. He didn't know whether he'd be glad or depressed to find out she'd jumped back into old friendships without a hesitation. *Damn it,* he thought again, *I don't deserve her trust.*

"Rachel Buckley. Um, Rachel Montoya then. Her husband's an assistant principal at the high school."

He dredged through his memories and came up with a fuzzy picture of a reasonably pretty, brown-haired girl who'd hung around with Nora and Molly sometimes. "I remember her vaguely. I didn't know she was in town."

Nora began picking at the fringe on her napkin, her gaze lowered to it as if it were an absorbing sight. "Rachel talked me into something I know I'm going to regret."

Rob waited.

"I'm going to speak to a high school assembly next week. About drunk driving, and the consequences."

"You're kidding." He was sorry for his reaction the minute the words were out. "I don't mean that."

She overrode him. "Unfortunately, I'm not. Is it such a horrible idea?" Her eyes were big and beseeching. "She took me by surprise when she asked, and I thought that maybe I could do some good."

"No, it's not a horrible idea." He opted for honesty. "It just sounds…traumatic. What does the high school have now? Twelve, thirteen hundred students? Can you talk about what happened with half of them not paying any attention…"

"And the others pitying me?" Her attempt at a

smile went awry. "I used to be a pretty good public speaker."

"I remember." How could he not? When she'd given her valedictory address, she'd spoken eloquently and with passion, as if her way was clear. She'd known where her parents, Rob and his parents were sitting, and her gaze kept straying to them. Looking right at him, she had talked about the future, about having children and the world she wanted to bequeath to them. Oh, yes, she was articulate. But in those long-lost days, she had believed her world was predictable, that nothing could prevent her from seizing the opportunities dangling like brass rings on a carnival ride.

With the new topic, her face had lost its vibrancy, as if somewhere along the way she had learned how to make herself become invisible. Even her tone was colorless. "I have to do it. If even one kid in that gymnasium listens, it's worth any amount of public shame for me."

More of the hair shirt. He wondered if she *wanted* to do this as a sort of public self-flagellation, or whether she genuinely felt driven only because she might make a difference. Rob didn't know how to ask such a question.

"Good for you," he said. "I'd like to come, if my being there won't make you more uncomfortable."

"No-o." She drew the word out uncertainly. Apparently having decided, she said more firmly, "No. But don't feel as if you have to—"

"I want to," he interrupted. "You aren't the only one whose life changed that night."

Her gaze shied from his. ''Yours didn't so much. You went back to the UW in the fall, didn't you?''

''Yeah, after a hellish summer.'' He waited until she met his eyes again before saying with quiet force, ''I missed you, Nora. God, did I miss you.''

She blinked quickly, as if to ward off tears, but said only, ''You knew where I was.''

He didn't even know how to explain. ''I was... conflicted.''

She shook her head hard. ''It doesn't matter anymore. Really. I'm grateful you've been so nice. Thank you for setting this up with your dad.'' She gathered her purse and made getting-up motions.

Nice. There was his favorite word again. That, coupled with the sight of her scrambling in retreat.

''No,'' he said, as she got out her wallet. ''Let me take care of lunch.''

''Oh! You don't need to...''

''Nora.'' He spaced every word through gritted teeth. ''I will take care of it.''

Her widened eyes told him she heard his frustration. The beginnings of curiosity had her searching his face for answers.

''Okay.'' Instead of backing away, she continued to study him. ''Thank you,'' she added, almost absently.

He threw some bills on the table and slid out of the booth. ''Shall we?''

''Um? Oh. Sure.''

She kept sneaking looks at him as they left the restaurant. ''I'm parked this way,'' she said, gesturing.

He turned to go north on Cedar, although his car was in the other direction.

"I want to see you again," he said.

"Rob." Nora stopped in the middle of the sidewalk, right in front of Milt's Auto Parts with its big plate-glass window. "Do you think we would have gotten married, if not for the accident? Or did we just have a high school romance?"

They turned to face each other. He ached at the familiar, delicate curves of her jaw and cheekbones, the velvety patina of a redhead's skin, the chocolate-brown depths of her eyes. His thumb tingled with the desire to touch her full lower lip, find out if its cushiony softness had changed. He couldn't kiss her in full view of Milt and any customers—she'd probably slap him anyway—but, God, did he want to.

Hoarsely he said, "It was more than that for me. I would have waited for you."

She nodded consideringly. "I wanted to die when you walked away from me that day. Not just because of Molly, but because I'd lost you."

Sucker punched, he almost doubled over from the pain in his gut. "I would give anything to..."

"No." She stopped him with a surprisingly strong grip on his forearm. "Don't say it. We can't go back." Very slowly, with meaning he couldn't evade, she repeated, "We can't go back, Rob."

He swore. In a voice that sounded raw to his ears, he said, "We can start again."

"No." Panic flared in her eyes and she did back away now. "No. I can't! I just...I can't."

Terror roughened his voice. "I don't do it for you anymore?" he asked crudely.

For an instant he might have imagined, he saw something in her eyes, a longing to match his own.

"Don't ask," she whispered, and fled.

He let her go. What else could he do?

"YOU ... *WHAT?*" The paring knife dropped from Colleen's suddenly nerveless hand to clatter on the tile counter.

Allen was deliberately expressionless. He had put up what she thought of as his brick wall. When he decided to resist or do something he knew she wouldn't like, he got like this: impenetrable and blockish, refusing even to give her the satisfaction of a fight.

"I got together with Nora Woods today," he repeated, with no more inflection than the first time he had said it. He might just as well be telling her he'd stopped at the grocery store to pick up milk.

"Why?" she whispered.

"She asked for a hearing, and I gave her one. I thought she deserved that much."

Colleen stared at him with loathing. He'd done this knowing how she would feel. He might even have done it *because* of how she felt.

"By all means," she said venomously. "Let's be civil to our daughter's murderer."

"She isn't a murderer." For the first time, his face showed some emotion: exasperation. "Darn it, Colleen! You know better. In your heart, you have to know better. It was an accident. A stupid, idiotic thing, but sometimes that happens. They both should have known better, but they were teenagers."

"They?" She felt as if dry ice were engulfing her

chest, stinging and freezing it at the same time. "Molly wasn't driving!"

Her husband, who never raised his voice, shouted, "She was drunk as a skunk!"

"But she wasn't the driver!" Colleen screamed back. "That...that *girl* was!"

"Girl." His voice had gone quiet again, low and soft and implacable. "Listen to yourself, Colleen. She was a kid. For God's sake, it's past time to forgive if not forget."

"Why not just forget, too? Isn't that what you're asking? That we just take down the pictures and pretend we never had a daughter?"

"I'm not saying that," he said wearily, as if he was tired of *her*.

"Aren't you?" Chin thrust out, she faced him. "When was the last time you visited her grave?"

He flinched, but she felt no regret at the knife thrust.

"Molly isn't there. Some bones are in that coffin, not our girl. I think about her."

"You don't," she said in astonishment, realizing it for the first time. She had known an abyss was dividing them, but she'd believed they shared at least their grief. "You want to...to let Molly go."

He leaned toward her, cords standing out in his neck. "*Yes.* She's dead, Colleen. We buried her twelve years ago!"

"It won't be twelve years until June! You don't even remember the anniversary of her death."

"I remember." He looked at her with dislike or even disgust. "How the hell could I not? You've turned it into Christmas and Thanksgiving and all our birthdays and every saint's day rolled into one!"

Colleen gasped.

But he wasn't done. "You spend six months crawling into a black hole to meet that day, and the next six months crawling out. You don't even let the goddamn sun touch your face before you're scrambling back down." He said an obscenity then, one that shocked her, coming from the mild-mouthed man she knew. "Sometimes I think I buried my wife that day, too. The both of you are nothing but bones under the earth, side by side."

"I make you dinner." Agony balled in her chest, a dry sob she would not let burst loose. "I get my hair cut and grocery shop and vacuum and weed the flower beds. What more do you want me to do?"

"Live." He took a step toward her, his blue eyes so sad they hurt to look into. "Colleen, there has to be something better than this."

This. Their home and her, he meant.

"Then find it," she spat, the pain and anger inside her rising like a geyser, burning and spewing and blinding her. "You're free to go looking anytime."

He didn't react with the shock she desperately wanted to see. He'd known where this conversation was going, set her up so that he could believe and even tell other people, like their son, that *she* was the one to end their marriage.

He looked at her with perplexity and shook his head. "You don't even hear me anymore."

"I have heard every word."

"No. You've heard what you meant to hear. Not what I said."

There was only one inalienable truth. "I cannot forget my child to make you happy."

He sighed. "I have never asked you to forget her. Only to remember her with love and sadness and acceptance."

"She didn't have to die! She shouldn't have died!" Colleen cried, hugging herself. "I want to go back. I want..."

"You can't." His face twisted with emotion she didn't even try to read through tear-blurred eyes, Allen reached for her. "You can't go back. Only forward."

She lurched to evade his familiar, strong hands. "You never loved her the way I did, or you'd understand!"

His hands dropped to his sides. "Colleen, will you see a counselor and try to work through this? For my sake."

Furious at herself for crying, she straightened proudly. "Is that an ultimatum?"

The weariness returned to his face, weighed down his shoulders. "Yes," he said. "I guess it is."

He sounded like he had the night he'd answered the telephone when it rang late, then come into the bedroom and told her Molly had been in a car accident and was dead.

"Then go." Colleen tasted bile. "I will not leave the house where I raised my children."

"I don't expect you to. I'll pack a few things."

When she said nothing, when she didn't move, he just nodded and left the kitchen. She had heard his footsteps on the stairs a thousand times, but never with the knowledge that she might not hear them again. Each tread was the sonorous tolling of a bell, a farewell.

Tears pouring down her face, Colleen saw them in church on their wedding day, dashing out to the ringing bell and the flurry of rice. She had tossed the bouquet and turned to see her laughing groom holding open the car door for her. The christenings of their children tumbled through her mind, too, and the terrible day of the funeral, the church, the graveyard, the empty, empty house that had never felt as if it held a whole family again.

But the divorce wouldn't take place in church, she thought, as she stood frozen in disbelief and pain. No bell would toll for her. And the house, oh the house, would be emptier yet, with only her and her memories.

When she heard him coming downstairs again, even slower, even heavier, she pushed off from the cabinet and ran to the living room. The silence told her he had paused behind her in the entry, but she was curled on the couch cradling a framed photograph of Molly, beautiful Molly laughing as she was meant to laugh forever, when she got married and held her firstborn and watched her own children graduate from high school.

Rocking, rocking, Colleen pressed her wet cheek against the framed glass, as close as she could be to Molly. She hardly heard the front door open and close.

CHAPTER SEVEN

EVEN IF SHE'D BEEN BLIND, Nora would have known where she was. The clatter of bleachers, the thunder of feet, the din of voices, the smell of floor polish and sweat...all were as familiar to every schoolchild as the smells and sounds of her own home.

This gymnasium, like the rest of the high school, hadn't changed at all.

"We did resurface the floor last year," Rachel's husband had told Nora a few minutes before with some pride. "But we've failed to pass a bond issue to build a new high school. Your parents have probably told you. With the economy the way it is..." He'd fallen silent, apparently brooding on the deficiencies of the 1950s-era campus, inadequate even with rows of portables for the numbers of students.

How vividly Nora remembered filing into the gym for assemblies with her friends, searching the bleachers for others, squeezing her way up to sit beside them. She could close her eyes and imagine a note, folded into a tiny wad, being pressed into her hand when the speaker was dull. Mostly she kept thinking of the campaign speech she'd given when running for junior class secretary and, finally, her valedictorian speech, delivered from the podium that had been set up only a few feet from where she hovered today, in the doorway leading to the administration offices. She'd survived those talks even though she was nervous. She'd survive today's, too.

Her parents were here. She kept turning her head to where they sat on the bottom row of the bleachers nearest the microphone, as if they might have disappeared. She didn't know if Rob would come, or was even aware she was speaking today. Not after the last thing she'd said to him.

We can't go back.

But oh, how desperately she wished they could. With the gym rapidly filling, the white noise of the teenagers' whoops and laughs washed over her. She would give anything, anything at all, to go back to graduation, to be waiting in her robe to file in procession with her friends between rows of beaming parents in folding metal chairs. To finish her speech, to declare, "Let's get started!" as she had, and to walk out to a life unencumbered by guilt and grief and punishment.

What scared her was that, more than anything except her grief for Molly, she wished she had never lost Rob, or that somehow they could recapture magic that had felt like love, even if she was too young then to know for sure.

She had never imagined loving another man. Never thought she'd have the chance to love him again. When he had looked at her with naked emotion and said, "I want to see you again" and "I would have waited for you," she had crumbled inside.

But she could not take this second chance, assuming that was really what he was offering. How could she? She didn't deserve that kind of happiness. She would destroy any relationship by the rot of guilt. Every leap of joy would be crushed by the agony of knowing her best friend was dead because of her. With the rules she'd constructed for herself, it was okay for her to live, have small triumphs and pleasures, but not complete happiness.

Society might believe she had paid with her term in prison, but Nora knew better. *This* was how she paid.

"They're quieting down," John murmured in her ear. "Are you ready?"

Panic clutched at her with sweaty fingers, just as it always had when the moment to speak came, but she made herself nod. He searched her face with kind eyes, smiled and said, "They're good kids. They'll listen," then strode past her to the microphone, a lone sentinel beneath the basketball hoop.

His amplified voice boomed. "Thanks for taking time from your busy schedules to come today." He waited for the ripple of laughter to subside. These assemblies were obligatory, just as they'd been in Nora's day. "We have a special speaker, someone who is going to talk to you about a decision she made when she was eighteen years old, one that can never be unmade. Students, welcome Nora Woods."

Stomach balled in terror, Nora walked the twenty feet from the alcove by the door toward the microphone and the vice principal, who was stepping back, leaving the floor to her. She felt tiny, minute and painfully exposed. She'd chosen to dress casually, in chinos, a white T-shirt and clogs. Not quite teenage, not quite so adult that these kids wouldn't listen to her.

But maybe she'd made a mistake. Maybe they would respect her more if she'd worn a suit and heels.

Or maybe it was thinking she could do this at all that was the mistake.

She looked toward her parents but didn't see them. They were lost in a sea of faces, one indistinguishable from the next.

She reached the microphone and realized it was too high for her. On tiptoe, she said, "Um...hello."

Through the sound system, her voice was tinny and small and uncertain. Students began to murmur. She hadn't even started and she was already losing them.

"I'm sorry, let me adjust that," John said, reaching past her.

"Let me just hold it," she said quietly to him.

The microphone screeched as he removed it from the stand and handed it to her.

That got their attention, at least. She saw hands clapped over ears and faces all turned her way.

Swallowing, she looked again toward her parents and this time made them out. Both nodded encouragement.

Nora took a deep breath, walked forward as far as the cord would let her, and into the microphone said conversationally, "Twelve years ago, I graduated from this high school. The graduation ceremony was right here in the gym." She looked around, as if remembering. "You've probably all seen friends graduate. You know, the folding chairs that are saved for parents and grandparents and little sisters and brothers, while you had to sit in the bleachers."

She heard rumbles of agreement.

"I was a valedictorian, one of three. Pretty full of

myself. I'd been accepted to Stanford University with a scholarship that made it affordable. I'd gotten a bunch of other scholarships, too. My friends were all going different places, mostly to college, but one guy had gone through the NT program and was going to work for Microsoft, and a couple of people hadn't decided what they wanted to do and were looking for jobs. That night was pretty cool.''

She looked from face to face, trying to read expressions, trying to make every kid there feel as if she was talking to him or her alone.

She admitted to being nervous about leaving home. ''But, hey, that was three months away! Graduation night, we were mostly excited. You know what that's like.'' She smiled wryly toward the bleacher that had traditionally held the seniors at assemblies. ''Free at last.''

Almost in chorus, they yelled, ''Yeah!''

At the other end of the gym, some adults stood along the wall, listening. Teachers, she presumed, glancing without interest. She wasn't here to talk to them.

But the sight of one tall, dark-haired man made her heart lurch and her voice falter when she tried to start again.

Rob had come. And beside him was his father, nearly as tall, broader, stolid. A kind man she had loved almost as much as she did her own dad, and never more than right this minute.

Damn it, she was close to crying! Nora blinked fiercely and took a couple of deep breaths. She could not look at them, could not let herself think about what it meant that they were here.

"My best friend Molly was planning to go to WSU. We'd grown up in each other's homes, closer than sisters. Heading to different colleges, that was hard." She made herself look around again, meet the eyes of kids no different than she'd been then. Hopeful, scared, cocky, all at the same time.

"That night, Molly and I started out at the parent-sponsored party. The one without alcohol." She expected boos and was surprised by the silence. They were listening, if not really putting themselves in her shoes.

"We decided to sneak out and go to another party. There were kegs of beer and bourbon. I think the beer had been spiked. We both got really drunk." She paused. "*I* got really drunk, and I was driving."

Now the silence was absolute.

She finished this part of the tale simply. "I drove too fast, didn't make a curve and hit a tree. I killed Molly."

Nobody in the audience stirred. She paused, both to collect herself and to give it time to sink in.

"Molly's life was over. But that wasn't the only consequence. Her parents...I don't know if they've ever recovered. Her brother misses her to this day.

"I'm here to remember Molly, but also to tell you what happened to my life, because that one night I got drunk and drove.

"I was nervous about heading off to Stanford. The thing is, I knew that I really would be free. At least, by my standards then. I'd be able to stay up all night if I wanted, skip class, eat pizza for breakfast and no vegetables for a month if I felt like it. I wouldn't have to ask permission to go out, tell anyone when I'd be home. I'd be an adult," she said, with the irony of someone who knows how cushioned the life of a college student is.

Nora deliberately let her voice become harsh. "I was convicted of vehicular homicide. I didn't go to Stanford. I went to the state penitentiary.

"In prison, you can't turn the TV channel without permission. You can't go to the bathroom without asking, you can't have seconds at dinner. You don't choose your clothes, your meals, the work they make you do. Every single thing you do is regimented. You can't laugh without getting into trouble." She fell silent, her chest made hollow by the memory of the never-ending humiliation she could never convey to anyone else.

She'd taken it harder than most of the other inmates, some of whom had been in before, many of whom had come from abusive homes where the men made the decisions, where the women hadn't felt respected or autonomous anyway. But Nora had been valedictorian, had been courted by top colleges, able to pick and choose. Everyone had known she had a golden future.

To go from that to being treated as if she were lower than worm castings, as if she were nothing, a loser who would always be a loser, had been devastating. She'd been in trouble a lot those first months, when she learned slowly and painfully, while she crouched cold and hungry in solitary confinement, that she *was* nothing, that her opinion had no value, that nobody was going to recognize that she, the high school princess, didn't really belong here, that she wasn't like the others, that she was special.

Always a fast learner, she hadn't been that time. She had had no idea that human beings were ever treated with such contempt, as if they were subhuman. As if they had no right to grieve for a lost friend or a lost future or a lost self.

But she had learned. Oh, yes, she had. And she would never be the same person again.

She tried to tell these students what prison had been like without admitting to the shame she would never shake. She talked about getting out, about trying to find a job and discovering that nobody hired an ex-con.

"I washed dishes and was glad to do it. I worked at a car wash. Finally, I went on to college, but a degree didn't matter. I was still an ex-con." She paused again, looked from kid to kid. "I *am* still an ex-con. I killed Molly, who I will miss every day for the rest of my life, and I destroyed the lives of her family. I destroyed my life. To this day, people say, 'Most teenagers drink and drive sometimes. You were unlucky. It was an accident.' But it wasn't an accident. I knew I shouldn't drive when I was drunk. I wasn't old enough to legally drink anyway." She drew a breath that felt shaky. Knowing that she was almost done, Nora became aware again that she was alone in the middle of the gymnasium, talking to a bunch of kids who were sure they were immortal.

She finished, "That's why I'm here today. To ask you not to make the same mistake. Your lives are full of hope. If you drink, don't drive. Simple. Don't kill yourself, don't kill your friend, don't kill a stranger, because you did something stupid." She hesitated, wanting to shuffle her feet, wondering if she should say something else: *Thank you,* or, *Okay, I'm done.* But in the end she just let the hand holding the microphone drop to her side and she gave a small nod.

What might have been five seconds of silence stretched excruciatingly. She braced herself for a patter of applause from the polite, ''good'' kids, like she'd been.

It started with one student clapping loudly, then another and another, spreading into a roar of sound. In astonishment, she saw that a few students were standing.

She lifted the microphone and said, ''Thank you,'' but doubted anyone heard her.

Someone—John—took the microphone from her nerveless hand and spoke into it as the applause died. Nora felt odd, as if she were standing outside herself observing. She saw a few teenagers stop to say things like ''It was cool you came to talk to us'' and ''Your friend, she'd have been, like, glad you did this.''

Would she? Nora wondered. *Molly?* she asked. *Molly, did I do the right thing?*

For all the world, she'd have sworn she heard her friend's voice, half mocking, half amused. *Yeah, we were really stupid, weren't we? Make an example of us, why don't you?*

Nora spun in a circle. ''Molly?''

''You were fabulous!'' Nora's mother enveloped her in a hug.

Her dad followed suit with a gruff, ''We're proud of you, kid.''

''Oh, Dad,'' she whispered into his shoulder.

Teachers thanked her, and a few more kids, and then Rob and his father were there, hesitating a distance away. She offered them a tremulous smile, and Rob came forward with a crooked, almost painful smile. His eyes were red.

She wanted him to hug her, too. She wanted so badly to lay her head on his chest, just for a moment, to hear the beat of his heart, feel the strength of his arms. To smell him and soak in his warmth and know a comfort nobody else could offer.

But he only held out his hand. "And to think I doubted you."

They shook hands, as if they were distant acquaintances. A lump in her throat, Nora said, "Thanks for coming, Rob." She looked past him. "And Mr. Sumner." Her own eyes seemed to be tearing up now, when it was all over. She couldn't think of the right words and knew the ones she chose were inadequate. "I really appreciate you coming."

He nodded and shook her hand, too. But then he faced her parents. "You have a fine daughter," he said gravely.

Equally solemn, they said "Thank you" in tandem, and then he nodded again and walked away.

Rob's eyes, blue and somehow electric, met hers. "Nora..." He shook his head, as if in frustration. "Never mind. I've got to go, but...you were great."

And then he turned away and she almost cried out with the pain. She might not see him again. He might have given up on her.

But she had no right at all to stop him.

She actually made a small, ragged sound.

As if in slow motion, he turned, although she couldn't imagine how he'd heard her from fifteen or twenty feet away.

His face looked ravaged, his eyes still red, the lines between his brows carved deep, the set of his mouth grim. His gaze locked on to hers, and then he made a sound, too, that might have been a groan. With long strides, he came back and she fell into his arms even as he snatched her into them. Distantly she realized he was shaking.

With her face buried in his chest, she couldn't see her family or his father or the vice principal. She only knew Rob—a smell she couldn't have named but hadn't forgotten, the way their bodies fit together, even the rhythm of his heartbeat, a heavy, fast thud beneath her ear.

"Thank you," he whispered, his voice low and unsteady. "Thank you for doing this."

She nodded convulsively, felt his mouth against her hair, as if he were kissing her head.

It seemed as if her heart was swelling until she could scarcely breathe. She had missed him so desperately, even when she refused to let herself think about him. *I need him,* she thought, in wonder and despair. *But I have no right.*

Molly, she wanted to cry. *Don't ask this of me!*

But of course Molly never had asked, never would have, not for this or any other punishment. Which didn't mean that Nora didn't owe it.

Rob released her. Nora felt his reluctance, as if he had to force himself to lift one hand, then the other, let his arms fall to his sides, step back. "Can I call you?" he asked in a rough voice.

His face blurred, and she swiped at her eyes. She could at least be friends with him, couldn't she? She felt like a pitiful small child, asking permission for a modest treat. Molly would want her brother and her best friend to stay close, Nora decided. She gave a watery sniff and a nod.

Even through the wash of tears, she saw the change in his face, the subtle relaxation, as if he'd been terrified and hiding it with grim determination.

"Okay." He backed away, his gaze not leaving her. "I will. Soon."

She kept nodding, like a bobblehead doll that couldn't stop after a nudge had set it in motion. *Please. Soon,* she wanted to cry.

But when he did call, when they did see each other, the temptation to want more would be so enormous, so much bigger than her, that Nora knew in her heart she should have said no.

Watching him walk away, she realized her mother stood beside her doing the same.

"Rob Sumner," Mrs. Woods said thoughtfully, "turned out just the way I hoped he would."

Nora turned her head. "Mom. It's not...we can't..."

Her mother smiled and squeezed her hand. "Don't be so sure," she said, before glancing around for her husband. "What do you say? Shall we go home?"

WHAT A WEEK.

Nora in the middle of it, seeming so small and fragile as she bared her soul for the benefit of teenagers who had, amazingly, appeared moved. Nora, fitting into his arms as if she'd never left them.

And his parents.

Rob parked to one side of the driveway in front of

the house where he'd grown up. His parents' house, except that his father didn't live here anymore.

He was still stunned. Dad had come straight to Rob's carrying a suitcase, and Rob had known.

A week later, Dad was still in the extra bedroom, but he was looking for a place to live despite Rob's insistence that he was welcome to stay.

"You're an adult with your own life," his father said with finality. "I'm hoping to have one myself."

In his more unworthy moments, Rob was angry at his father for deserting his mother. Damn it, he'd signed on for better or worse! But when Rob reacted like an adult and not a child who wanted his parents together no matter what, he didn't blame his father. Maybe he should have put down his foot years ago. Either way, who the hell wanted to live in the hushed misery of a funeral chapel forever?

Rob looked at the closed drapes in the front window and let out an unconscious sigh.

Apparently, his mother did.

He'd seen her briefly since his parents' split, but she'd been brittle and smiling and assured him that everything was fine, except that his father was obviously having a midlife crisis. If she knew Dad was bunked down in Rob's spare room, she didn't say and he didn't mention it.

Now, lucky him, he was here for dinner.

She met him at the front door and hustled him in as if she were a hostess expecting a dozen guests and delighted to be entertaining.

"I made a pork roast, your favorite, since it isn't worth cooking one just for myself and this way I'll have leftovers. Don't let me forget to send some home

with you! You might as well have sandwich makings.''

"Thanks, Mom.''

She swept right on as if he hadn't said a thing. "What a busy week! I had the garden club and I mowed the lawn myself—my gracious, your father had let it get long! Oh, and Patty Siegel stopped by. I hadn't seen her in ages!''

By this time they had progressed to the kitchen and she was briskly opening and closing the oven and cupboard doors while he stood and watched.

He tried a couple of times to get a word in edgewise, but his "Mom, how are you?'' brought a blank stare and an astonished "How would I be? Why, fine, of course!'' before she found something else trivial to discuss.

She'd wear down. She had to. Her hands had a fine tremor when she slowed enough for him to see it. Her cheekbones looked sharp, her skin stretched tight, her eyes unnaturally bright. Her movements were quick, birdlike; she never settled. Rob wondered if she'd been going like this since Dad packed his bag, not letting herself understand that anything had changed.

They sat at the dining room table. Every few bites, his mother was trying to offer him second helpings, commenting on the roast—"Is it slightly overdone, do you think? Gracious! I invite you for your favorite meal, and then I leave it in the oven too long!''—and mentioning how quickly a building he'd designed was going up in Everett.

Rob wanted to slam his hand down on the table until the dishes rattled and say, "God damn it, Mom! Talk about something that matters!''

But, coward that he was, he didn't want to talk about the things that did matter: the separation and Nora. What if Mom cornered him into admitting that he'd felt sorry for his father for so many years, he didn't blame him for moving out? God. What if she pushed him to admit that he was still in love with Nora Woods?

But guilt kept gnawing at him as he watched her across the table, pretending so desperately that nothing at all was wrong. She hadn't eaten more than a few bites, he saw with a glance at her plate, only pushed food around. Hell. Maybe that was why she looked so brittle. Maybe weight was falling off her because she wasn't eating.

He kept nodding and responding in the monosyllables she allowed him until she prepared to leap up and cut the pie she'd baked.

"Blueberry, your favorite! Not fresh berries, of course, but I did freeze a flat last summer."

"Mom." He reached out and covered her hand, felt it quiver under his. "You haven't eaten."

"Why, of course I have!" She snatched up her plate and tensed to rise, but he didn't let go.

"No. I've been watching. Have you been eating at all?"

Her eyes shied from his. "I sampled while I was cooking. You know I do that."

"Have you told any of your friends?"

For a fraction of a second, her face cracked and he saw raw pain and even shame. Then her nostrils flared and her chin rose proudly. "If you're referring to your father and me," she said frigidly, "I'd prefer to wait until things are more…settled."

He swore, shocking her, he saw. "Don't you have *anyone* to talk to?"

She gave a small huff. "I was foolish enough to think I could talk to you!"

"Then why don't you?" Rob suggested.

Her mask cracked again and she dropped the plate, not seeming to notice as it clattered and peas spilled onto the tablecloth. "What is it you want me to say? That I have no idea what your father expects of me? Well! Consider it said!"

No idea? Rob didn't know whether to believe her.

"Mom," he said as gently as he could, "you've stayed pretty wrapped up in Molly."

She wrenched her hand from his, eyes flashing. "You sound like him! What should I do, forget your sister?"

He tried again. "You've never been the same since she died."

His mother, who rarely cried despite the depth of her grief, had tears brimming in her eyes. "How can I be?" she asked—begged—in a voice that quavered like an old woman's. "Until I had you, I never understood what a mother's instinct is, how utterly you can love another person. I don't understand how anyone can recover from the loss of a child."

"Maybe you can't, not completely. I don't know," he admitted. "I haven't had my own yet. But sometimes I think you've forgotten the other people you love."

"You?"

The admission sounded so petty, but Rob made himself be completely honest. "Sometimes. After

Molly died, I felt...'' He moved uncomfortably. ''As if I didn't count.''

His mother's mouth formed a shocked *O*. ''Didn't *count?* Rob, that's not true! You always...''

He interrupted. ''I felt childish, but sometimes I wanted you to come back from your sadness for me. It's like, by dying, Molly became the favorite child, and I was left standing in the shadows, deserving only occasional notice.'' He shook his head when she started to speak. ''Mom, it's not that important. I'm an adult. I understand. I miss Molly, too, you know that. I'm just trying to tell you that I also understand why Dad gave up. He must have felt as if he didn't count, either.''

Tears ran down her cheeks and she didn't try to stem them. ''I never knew...'' She drew a shuddery breath. ''I love you. I've always cared about everything you did.''

When he could get her attention.

''I know you do,'' he said. ''But Dad...I don't think he's so sure anymore that you do love him.''

''He's expecting me to make choices that I can't make.'' Still she ignored the tears wetting her cheeks. ''Is that love? To even ask?''

''Can't you try?'' He was that little kid again, the one who wanted his mommy and daddy to make everything right, because that's what they did.

Her mouth worked. Tears dropped onto her hands, seeming to startle her. She looked down at them, then vaguely back up at him. ''I don't know.'' She pushed back her chair and stood, head high, as if she thought he hadn't noticed she was crying. ''Rob, I just can't talk about this anymore. Please, take some of the pork. And the pie. I doubt I'd eat it at all.'' She circled the table toward the entry and the stairs. ''I believe I'll go lie down. I must have a headache coming on. I'm sorry to abandon you...'' Her face convulsed as she heard her own double entendre. ''I am so sorry!'' she whispered, before she rushed toward the stairs.

Rob was left frozen, halfway between sitting and standing, horrified by his mother's disintegration and his own part in bringing it about.

What had he thought? he asked himself. That he could magically make her see reason? Put bandages on ancient, festering wounds and call them healed?

Despising himself, he grabbed the plates and went to the kitchen. The least he could do was clean up, so his mother wasn't left with it like a hangover in the morning.

After all, he thought, bitterly mocking, he was a good son, wasn't he?

CHAPTER EIGHT

THE VERY NEXT DAY, Nora got a call at work from a woman who introduced herself as Kathy Holmes and then said, rather apologetically, "You don't know me, but I teach at the high school and I heard you speak yesterday."

Wary, Nora said, "Yes?"

"What you did took a lot of courage."

Nora watched Dr. Hughes emerge from an examining room and begin rooting in drawers, muttering to herself, only a few feet away.

Very conscious of being overheard, Nora said, "Thank you."

"I don't know if you're aware that we're attempting to raise the money to build a youth center here in White Horse. We've bought land on the outskirts—maybe you know the vacant parcel kitty-corner from the hospital—and now we're beginning to plan a fall auction to start the next stage."

"Yes?" Nora said again, not having the slightest idea where this Kathy Holmes was going.

"The thing is..." There was a small pause, and Nora pictured this unknown woman taking a deep breath to prep for the kill, so to speak. Or perhaps she was bracing herself for a refusal. "We're rather short of volunteers," she admitted in a rush. "I desperately need some people willing to work on procuring items for the auction and planning it. I thought perhaps, since you cared enough to speak to the students yesterday, you might be interested."

Dr. Hughes had turned her head and was looking at Nora with raised brows, as if in silent question.

Nora shook her head and mouthed, "It's for me."

The vet nodded and went back into the examining room with a pair of dog nail trimmers in her hand.

"What do you mean, procure for the auction?" was all she could think to ask.

"Write letters, visit local businesses in person, and beg for a donation," the woman told her frankly. "Guilt them into giving."

"Tell me about the youth center."

As she listened, she wondered if she and Molly would ever have used a facility like this. Sure, White Horse had been—and still was, apparently—lacking in any place latchkey kids and teenagers could hang out without getting into trouble. But she and Molly had never been in trouble; they were good girls. They just had one foolish rebellion.

Still, this dream sounded good. "The skateboard park out back should solve a lot of problems," Kathy Holmes said enthusiastically. "We'll require pads and helmets, of course, but the kids will have someplace to go besides the grocery store parking lot. Inside, we'll have pool and Ping-Pong tables, Foosball, a gymnasium, locker rooms, an art room… We hope to expand the kids' sports available to include volleyball, and girls' basketball will have more access to practice time, and…" She rattled on.

Nora thought about kids she'd known, the ones

whose parents weren't willing to—or couldn't—drive them to soccer practices or dance lessons or Youth Symphony. Everybody in town could walk to this new location.

Would it prevent teenage parties and drinking? Probably not, but maybe, just maybe, it would make a difference for a few kids. Having adults that cared would help. And maybe a few teenagers would be too busy with sports or their art or even a summer job supervising the younger kids to go to a party.

"Okay," she interrupted. "You said you had a meeting planned? I'll come."

"Really?" Kathy sounded so amazed even she laughed. "Bless you. It's tomorrow night at seven at my house."

Thus Nora found herself on a total stranger's doorstep ringing the doorbell the next evening.

Kathy Holmes turned out to be a plump woman who looked to be about forty. Dressed in a red broomstick skirt and a loose white tunic, she wore her brown hair bundled in a knot at her nape, a few gray hairs unashamedly left natural. Something of a latter-day hippie, Nora guessed, following her in and noticing a Grateful Dead poster and a bead curtain across a doorway.

"I teach history," she told Nora over her shoulder as she led her toward the voices coming from a front room. "Which is sometimes thankless, I'm sorry to say. Kids these days get into computers. Hardly any of them care about the French Revolution."

"You must convert an occasional one," Nora protested out of politeness if not conviction.

Her hostess laughed. "Oh, I try. I try." She

stopped just inside the living room. ‘‘Everyone, this is Nora Woods. Why don't you each introduce yourself? Nora, pick a seat. Can I get you coffee or tea?’’

Three other people were already settled comfortably on the leather sofa and in deep armchairs. Trying to decide if any of them looked familiar, Nora gave a tentative smile and chose a wooden rocker.

The living room was cluttered but wonderful. South American textiles hung on the walls cheek by jowl with African statues and a Northwest Coast Indian mask. The furniture was richly colored, the dhurrie rugs on the oak floor overlapping and somehow harmonizing despite colors that should have clashed. Kathy Holmes, Nora decided instantly, was a woman of talents and interests far beyond the French Revolution.

Her own life suddenly seemed rather pallid.

The one man in the room did look vaguely familiar to Nora, and the two of them concluded that he had been a contemporary of Rob's at the high school.

‘‘I remember when...’’ He stopped abruptly.

When you got in a drunk driving accident and killed Rob's little sister, he meant.

Nora only nodded.

The other two women were evidently as involved in building this youth center from scratch as Kathy was. When Kathy reappeared with Nora's tea, they launched into a discussion of the hotels in the area they'd visited as potential sites for the auction and dinner.

‘‘Already booked,’’ Norma Costin said about one. ‘‘Unless we want to reschedule for November...’’

‘‘It'd be just our luck if it snowed, or we had a

blizzard and the power went out, or…" When Kathy paused, everyone sat in silence as they contemplated disaster. "No. I think October is as late as we dare go."

"Nora," she said finally, handing her a few stapled pages, "this is a report of what we've managed to procure so far. I'm afraid we're finding it frustrating. I don't suppose you've ever done this kind of thing before…?"

"I'm afraid not." Nora leafed through the three pages. Local restaurants had given meals, a few artists had donated pieces, somebody was giving a stay at their time-share condo on Maui—the one coup—and a gas station offered an oil change and lube.

What they had so far was not going to bring very much money.

"How do you intend to sell tickets?" she asked, looking up. "I mean, who will come to the auction itself?"

"We're hoping that part won't be a problem," one of the women answered. "The Rotary Club and chamber of commerce are behind us, of course. There is lots of enthusiasm locally. Unfortunately, that doesn't translate to people willing to work to make this happen. I do think it will translate to people willing to pay fifty dollars a plate for dinner and buy some nice things."

They talked about who had already been asked to donate and not yet responded.

"How about bed-and-breakfasts around the state?" Nora asked. "Or classy hotels? Could we put together some travel packages? You know, a night in Port Angeles and dinner? That kind of thing?"

"Oh, that sounds wonderful!" Kathy looked at her approvingly. "We've been thinking local, but maybe just because we knew White Horse businesses would give. But we could try others. Donations would be tax deductible."

Others threw out ideas. One woman admitted she didn't have the courage to ask anyone in person, but said she could write letters. Kathy was busy enough with her job and two kids, and was also writing grant proposals to cover construction costs. One of the women was in charge of choosing the hotel, meals, decorations and finding an auctioneer. That left Nora, another young woman named Kelly Siegel, who had arrived late, and the man to do procurement.

"We're *it?*" Nora asked, slightly incredulous. "You need to raise half a million dollars!"

"Well, we won't raise it all at the auction, but seed money would be nice. We're hoping, too, that we can get an architect to volunteer his services, some of the materials donated, and so on."

They all nodded with hopeful, eager expressions. Nora couldn't decide if she was the only realist, or if she'd just forgotten that dreams could come to fruition.

Despite being the newcomer, she found herself doling out assignments. "Kelly, you'll write or call Puget Sound area theaters, the opera house and so on and try to get tickets. See if you can figure out which are the best Seattle restaurants. Doesn't *Seattle Weekly* have a list of recommended ones or reviews or something?" Kelly nodded and scribbled notes. "Mark, you'll continue pursuing local businesses for now. Expand to Stanwood and Marysville and Arlington, too, why don't you? The skate park will attract kids from all around, for sure.''

He, too, nodded and made notes.

''I'll start writing letters to hotels around the state and in Oregon and see if I can't get some stays donated. If I can, I'll shoot for meals or even activities in the same areas.''

''Sounds wonderful,'' Kathy said briskly. ''Shall we meet again two weeks from tonight?''

Nora headed for home with a box of brochures and another one full of letterhead, and a task that appeared intimidating and even hopeless. Did people really just give away stuff because you asked? She knew vaguely that charity auctions were built on the principle, but she'd never actually attended one.

''That's my first order of business,'' she decided aloud. She would find an auction and attend. And then she'd ask all the businesses and people who had donated to give to this one, too.

Bemused to find herself involved in something like this, she also felt energized. As if she had a *purpose* at last.

THE FIRST TIME ROB CALLED he kept it light. He didn't even suggest they get together.

Nora was excited, telling him about the planned youth center and the way she'd jumped in with both feet.

''Do you know, I sent out thirty-five letters today, and they were all to bed-and-breakfasts in Ashland, Oregon?'' She laughed. ''I don't know whether to be terrified that no one will respond, or that too many of them will! Do that many people want to go to Ashland?''

''The Shakespeare Festival there is a huge draw,'' he said, leaning back in his desk chair and enjoying the humor and gentle self-mockery in her voice.

''Yes, but thirty-five?'' She sighed. ''I had no idea there were so many bed-and-breakfasts. I could write to hundreds of them just in Oregon, never mind Washington. And I keep thinking of other things. What about a rafting trip down the Skagit River to see bald eagles, or a trip on the Victoria Clipper, or a hot-air balloon ride, or...'' Apparently out of breath, she stopped and laughed again. ''Hey, you want to write letters?''

He was damn near tempted to say yes, just to have an excuse to see her and talk to her more often.

''No,'' she said suddenly, ''I have a better idea.''

Suspicious, he asked, ''Yeah?''

''We're hoping to find an architect to donate his work on the youth center. Is there any chance...?''

He grinned at the delicate pause. She had him, a big fat sockeye reaching with open mouth for the cruel hook disguised inside a delicacy. Unlike the sockeye, he knew what he was biting down on.

''I'll do it.''

''You will?'' Delight vibrated in her voice. ''Rob, thank you! I can hardly wait to tell the others.''

Suddenly serious, he said, ''You've gotten deep in this, haven't you?''

''I suppose I have.'' She was quiet for a moment. ''It just seems...important. Useful.''

He doubted she'd felt either important or useful in a very long time.

"I think it is," he agreed.

When he said goodbye he wondered if she'd seemed just a little disappointed. Because she'd wanted to keep talking? Or because she'd hoped he would ask her again to get together?

That, or he was deluding himself, Rob thought ruefully.

That week he either called his mother daily or stopped by home. It seemed to him that reality was sinking in. A slim woman to start with, she was definitely losing weight. She had moments of chattering gaily as if nothing was wrong, but more often she sounded subdued and sad. Rob couldn't decide if that was a good sign or bad.

"Have you talked to Mom?" he asked his father that night.

Allen Sumner lowered his newspaper. "A couple of days ago. We talked about paying bills and so on. I did a little yard work."

"She said she mowed."

A frown pinched his father's forehead. "Stubborn woman. She knew I wouldn't let things go. She's just trying to prove she can get by fine on her own!"

Rob gave a grunt of near amusement. "She probably can, on a practical level. When I was little, I thought Mom was superwoman. I know she's a better plumber than you are."

His father gave him an irritated look before lifting the newspaper again. "I don't want her hurting herself doing something she shouldn't have to do."

"Dad." Rob waited until the paper rustled and lowered enough to let his father peer over it and his reading glasses. "If you two divorce, you can't spend the rest of your life mowing Mom's lawn and oiling squeaky hinges on her kitchen cupboards.'' Rob didn't know if he was pointing out facts or playing a troublemaker. ''Isn't she going to have to learn to do the stuff she hasn't before?''

His father glared at him. ''We can afford a yard service.''

''You know what I mean.''

''Damn it, of course I do!'' Allen flung down the newspaper, which—to his obvious fury—fluttered toward the floor instead of slamming down. He stomped out of the room.

Rob watched him go with raised brows. Interesting. Did Dad feel guilt because he'd taken the marriage vows seriously, or was he being prodded more by hurt, regret and a sense of loss? Mom claimed she didn't know what she was expected to do to save their marriage, but Rob hoped she was lying. Deep inside, he just didn't believe his parents belonged apart.

He waited an endless two days before he called Nora again and was a little stung by her distracted tone when she came on the line after her mother fetched her.

''Rob?'' She sounded as if she barely remembered who he was. ''Oh, it's you.''

''Am I interrupting something?''

''Hmm? Oh, I was just doing some research online. It's amazing what you can find.''

''Like?''

''Addresses. Ideas. I just keep wandering.'' Her voice quickened. ''I'm hunting down specialty nurseries that might give gift certificates.''

Ah. The auction.

"And garden art. Surely everyone would like a great terra-cotta pot or a cool trellis or statue to sit in a flower bed. Yesterday I came across an auction preview page for a Seattle charity, and that gave me more places to start. The possibilities are almost infinite!"

"That's actually what I called about. There's a Fly-In Saturday at the Arlington airport. You might go down there and hit up the pilots for a lift somewhere, or a glider flight, or whatever."

"That's a great idea!"

He had all her attention now, but he doubted it was his manly charm that had done the trick. No, he was useful, Rob thought wryly.

"Um, Rob?" Suddenly she was tentative.

"Yeah?"

"This local no-kill cat shelter is having their charity auction next Saturday. I thought I'd go, just to get more ideas, you know. And I wondered...well, whether you might like to come with me."

He didn't like heights, but he'd have gone to the moon with her if she asked.

"Sure, that might be fun," he said casually. "Is it black tie?"

"Um..." Papers shuffled. "I think so. Oh, dear. I don't have anything to wear." She sighed. "I guess I have to go shopping. But I'll need something for our auction, too."

"I assume the tickets cost," he prodded.

"Sixty dollars a plate. The dinner is vegetarian, but it sounds good. You have to let me pay for them, though. You're being nice and coming as my guest."

A hundred and twenty bucks? She couldn't be that loaded. And if she had to buy a fancy dress, too...

"I'd like to take you," he said mildly.

"Rob. Don't argue."

He knew when to shut up, even though the awareness that she couldn't afford the evening settled like an unreachable itch between his shoulder blades.

"All right." He tried not to sound frustrated. "When shall I pick you up?"

They settled on a time, chatted for a few minutes and ended the call. If he hadn't been so bugged about her paying for the evening, he would have pumped his fist in triumph.

Yes! He had a date with his teenage sweetheart.

COLLEEN SUMNER SAT at the kitchen table to pay bills, as she did twice a month. She proceeded mechanically, because she'd done it so many times. Piles of the bills she had to pay right now, the ones that she'd put off until closer to the due date, and ones that required some attention. She'd have to scrutinize the Visa bill carefully; the amount they claimed she owed was way more than it had been last month, and she was sure she hadn't taken it out of her wallet. Allen never…

Without moving from her seat on the kitchen chair, she took a sickening tumble and had to blink to right herself.

He might be using the credit card now. And she could hardly ask him to explain or justify his expenses. Perhaps…perhaps she'd just pay the bill and not question it, she thought, lifting it gingerly and moving it to a different pile.

But the PUD bill—that one, she intended to study. Rates had gone up and up and up, and Colleen thought it was time customers balked. How much electricity could she be using, living alone in this house, doing scarcely any laundry or cooking? Even when Allen had been home, they were always careful about turning off lights when they left a room, not leaving an unwatched television on, and so forth. It was May, nearly June, for goodness' sakes! With the spring as nice as it had been, she wasn't even using the heat very often. How could she possibly owe—she peered inside the envelope again—$369.38? Ridiculous! Colleen thought again, indignantly.

Or, at least, with as much indignation as she could muster, considering that she kept finding herself gazing vacantly into space with the checkbook open and a check half written out. She had had to force herself to sit down this afternoon. She had succeeded only because her routine was her refuge.

She didn't *care* whether the bills were late or not. Grocery shopping held no interest. This morning had been her haircutting appointment, and she'd almost not gone. But pride had made her go, and smile and talk as if her life had not gone adrift like an abandoned dory with a rotten hull through which water seeped and seeped, until the weight of sodden wood would sink it. Terror of sinking utterly had made her stop at Thrifty and progress up and down the aisles as if she needed Cheerios or was truly considering cooking chicken divan for dinner.

Structure seemed to be a crutch, or perhaps something like a climbing gym on a playground. A solid framework on which she scrambled, sneakered feet slipping sometimes so that she had to clutch with panicky hands to stop herself from falling to the hard-packed sand beneath and having the wind knocked out of her.

Oh, dear. She had completely lost her train of thought. Colleen had to pick up the bill from the garbage company again and read the amount to finish writing out a check.

She'd only half filled a can last week. Perhaps she should change to service only every other week. That would save some money...

Her head reeled again, or perhaps it was her stomach. She felt horrifyingly as if she'd leaned too far over the wide stone wall at the edge of the Grand Canyon and nearly fallen, out of vertigo as much as carelessness.

Right now, she was paying bills from their joint account. She knew Allen wouldn't abandon her entirely, but would he—could he?—really pay enough alimony to allow her to stay in the house? He had to live, too. Most divorced women had to go to work.

Colleen knew quite well that she had no job skills whatsoever. She had been a secretary when she met the handsome young carpenter, fell in love and got married. Thirty years ago, secretaries in a state-of-the-art office used IBM Selectric typewriters and carbon paper. She had learned, at Rob's insistence, to use the simple word processing program on the PC in Allen's office. She could even go online and send and receive e-mail, although Rob was the only one who actually ever sent her any, except for pornographers and people who wanted her to refinance her house or play a game they had designed, although Rob said the latter were really trying to send a virus to her computer, something she truly didn't understand. How could machines contract illnesses and spread them to others as if they could sneeze?

Who would hire a fifty-eight-year-old woman who hadn't worked since before the age of computers? The idea of even looking for a job terrified her. She was used to feeling competent, well-to-do, even—she blushed to realize it—rather superior to the clerks at the grocery store or her hairdresser or those young, pimply creatures who wore the silly hats and served burgers and fries to her on the rare occasions when she deigned to buy fast food.

Now she would be lucky if a fast-food joint hired her.

She shivered and hastily tore out the check. She mustn't think about it. Mustn't worry. Not yet. Maybe...maybe Allen would come to his senses. Or at the very least pay alimony generous enough to allow her to continue in the style to which she was accustomed.

Hearing her own irony, she closed her eyes. If he did continue to support her, she'd feel just as pathetic as she would at the local McDonald's or Burger King! She hated the idea of him taking care of her out of a sense of duty. She wanted quite fiercely to tell him she didn't need his money!

A sob caught in her throat. Yes, and then what would happen to her? She was a...a middle-aged *relic.* Useless, unneeded, maintained out of pity or guilt. Even her son had made plain what he thought of her.

She sat sniveling until pride made her wipe her eyes with a napkin. Self-pity was a dreadful quality. She would not indulge in it.

Perhaps she'd go back to school. If the university would accept her long-ago bachelor's degree, she might be able to get a teaching certificate at Western Washington University in only a year or two. When she was young, she'd thought about becoming a teacher. It was never too late, was it?

Teaching...now that might give her life *interest.* Truthfully, if she didn't soon find a reason to get out of bed in the morning, she might not bother. It wasn't just Allen, either. Why had she never realized how empty her life was?

She was staring vacantly again, but didn't make herself return to the bill paying, not just yet. Why *hadn't* she realized how dull her day's routines were, how stagnant *she* had become?

Perhaps because she'd never had to look at herself across the dining room table. Allen had always been there to deflect any self-reflection. She'd had a purpose: him.

Now he was gone, and with him her very reason for existence, it seemed. Unless she found another one.

What if he did come to his senses? Colleen wondered. If he rang the bell this evening and said humbly, "I was wrong. I want to come home," would she be pathetically grateful?

Oddly, she wasn't certain. The house was so dreadfully empty now, but it had been before, too. Even when he and she were actually face-to-face—usually at the dinner table—they often had nothing to say to each other. They talked like strangers, in bursts, when one of them remembered some tidbit overheard that day or read in the newspaper. An excuse to say something. The other would remark politely, after which they'd lapse into silence again, avoiding each other's eyes. Allen would escape as soon as he decently could, leaving her more alone than if he hadn't been in the house at all.

They had become strangers.

So...would she want him back?

The cowardly part of her thought yes, so that she didn't have to face the terrifying possibility of having to support herself.

The more courageous part of her wasn't so sure. Not if he moved back in and they pretended nothing had happened. Not if they went back to the way they'd been two weeks ago, and two months ago, and two years ago. Not if they went back to the way they'd been since he quit grieving and she couldn't.

But she did miss him, the Allen she had married and whose children she'd borne and whose puckish smiles had always warmed this spot in her chest. She hadn't felt that burst of warmth and delight in a long time. Perhaps he hadn't smiled, not especially for her, in an equally long time.

An insidious thought crept into her head. Perhaps she just hadn't noticed, and after a while he quit.

Had he really come to believe she didn't love him anymore, as Rob suggested?

This was another subject she'd been trying to avoid by framing her life with routine, with activities, however meaningless. She didn't want to think about whether her son was right, and she had quit caring as much about him, her firstborn, because of the tearing grief at losing Molly.

Admitting that it was true would mean...oh, guilt,

of course, that he'd ever had to feel all those things he'd told her. Worse, though, was that she might have to concede that her never-ending sadness wasn't normal, that she was sunk in grief to the point where she had failed her family.

Her daughter's face flashed before her. Perhaps five or six, she had skinned a knee and her mouth trembled and her eyes swam with tears. Colleen's heart swelled with the desire to hold her and make everything better, but she couldn't. Not anymore.

The bills. She fumbled blindly for the checkbook. Paying them was something that really had to be done. She would focus, and not think about Allen and whether he missed her or was only relieved to have escaped.

She especially would not think about all these other things, these glimpses of herself, as if she'd caught a reflection in a store window and thought in dismay, *Who is that?*

Perhaps someday she would be willing to find out who that unlikable, self-absorbed woman was, but not now. Not until her feet quit slipping on the bars and the ground didn't look so far away and so hard.

CHAPTER NINE

"OOH," NORA BREATHED, stopping abruptly. "Rob, look."

Upper arm brushing her bare shoulder, he studied the pen-and-ink drawing of a cat flowing through the pale green fingers of a weeping willow, body seen here but not there, a whisker and eye noting and dismissing the presence of the watcher.

"I like that," he said.

"Mmm." Nora rarely felt covetous, but she'd seen a number of things on the tables of silent- and live-auction items that she wanted—some for herself, and some for the youth center auction.

How had they gotten those airline tickets, for example? Did airlines just give them away, if you wrote and asked? Or did you have to know somebody?

Her mind tumbled with questions. Everything here was packaged, so that you couldn't buy a thirty-dollar item. If there was a Starbucks gift certificate, it was in a basket with a pair of unusual mugs and some coffee beans and flavorings and perhaps a gift certificate to a rival espresso shop, so that somebody would have to bid a hundred dollars to get all of it.

She stole a glance around at the elegantly dressed men and women browsing the tables and sipping mixed drinks and champagne and clustering for delighted reunions. Did people not come to an auction if they couldn't afford to spend lots of money? Or were people more likely to bid if they thought they were getting a bunch of stuff and not just some single thing?

Would it be tactless to ask, if she could find someone who'd worked on putting all this together? Would they think she was here to steal their ideas and donors?

Which, of course, she was, but she preferred to think she was here to learn.

"What are you thinking?" Rob murmured in her ear.

She made a face. "That I'm green with jealousy, and that I want a whole bunch of this stuff. Like this drawing."

"I might bid on it." He took a sip of champagne. "I could hang it in the office."

She turned to him in surprise. "You mean, you might actually buy some things tonight?"

He raised his brows. "Well, sure. Why not? I have to fly to Boston in September for a conference, for example. I'd rather the money go to this shelter than the airline, if the tickets don't go too far over value."

"You're going to bid during the live auction? Honestly?"

He grinned at her. "You want to bid for me?"

"Can I?" She felt like a puppy dog with a wildly wagging tail. "But I might not stop when I should."

"I'll elbow you." He suited action to words.

Laughing, Nora evaded him. "It's a deal. Oh, this is fun!"

It was. She hadn't felt like this in...so long, she

couldn't remember the last time. For one thing, she knew she looked pretty. On a shopping expedition with Rachel, she'd found a full-length black dress that hugged her body like a second skin. Somehow the black made her own skin, exposed by the spaghetti straps and low back, look creamy instead of pasty white. With lots of makeup and diamond earrings borrowed from her mother and her hair pinned in an artfully disheveled do, she had hardly recognized herself in the mirror at home.

The expression on Rob's face when he saw her had stopped her breath. It was like the way he'd looked at her when she made him go to her senior prom and he picked her up, but it was different, too. More... adult. She'd seen a flare of hunger more purposeful and darker, somehow, than his twenty-one-year-old self would have felt.

He had shielded that hunger more quickly, too, so that she would have missed that moment of naked desire if she'd looked at her mother instead or paused to lift her skirt before she started down the stairs. Considering her determination to be friends and only friends with him, she should be perturbed instead of delighted, but she couldn't help herself.

She hadn't felt beautiful and desired and feminine in a long time, either. Just for this evening, she was going to let herself enjoy the experience.

Molly, she reminded herself, had loved dress-up more than anything.

"I like that glass bowl back there, too." Rob laid a casual but somehow proprietary hand on the small of her back. "Mom's birthday is in June. I think she'd like it."

Nora would just as soon not think about his mother, but she let him steer her to another table where the gorgeous handblown glass bowl sat between a gift basket from a local department store and a board with a picture of a beach at sunset and a description of a two-night getaway in Ocean Shores.

The bowl looked as if it deserved a pedestal, or a spot alone in the center of a gleaming cherry table. Subtle shades of teal swirled like the currents of a tropical sea somehow captured in glass.

Nora peered at the bid sheet. The value was $450. So far, the highest silent bid was $360. And the guaranteed bid was—she gulped—$525.

''I don't know how your mother could not love it, but...''

''I usually buy her earrings, but I thought right now she could use something special.''

If Nora had ever *not* been in love with Rob, at that moment she tumbled right back in. In a black tux, he was not only hands-down the sexiest man in this room, he wanted to do something special for his mother.

With the lump in her throat, Nora couldn't have said a word to save her life.

She watched in silence as he scribbled his bid number on the ''guaranteed bid'' line.

Her heart ached. *If only...*

He looked up at her, and his expression changed. ''Is something wrong?''

Somehow she found her voice. ''Wrong?'' It cracked slightly. ''Of course not. I'm just, um, moved that you'd do something so wonderful for your mom.''

He watched her with an intent, frowning gaze for a moment, as if he didn't believe her, then said, "Thank you. I think."

She summoned a teasing smile that felt less natural than her mascara. "You're welcome."

"Oh, fiddlesticks," someone said from behind him. "I knew I should go with the guaranteed bid!"

Rob turned with a friendly smile. "Did I ace you out?"

"I've had my eye on that darn bowl since it came in." The middle-aged woman sighed. "I suppose I'll have to visit the artist's studio and either beg for a donation for next year or just give up and buy a piece."

"Oh!" Nora couldn't hide her eagerness. "Are you on the committee that put this auction together?"

"Yes, two of us chaired together this year." She clasped a hand to her chest. "Tell me you haven't spotted some awful mistake."

"No, I've actually been dragged into handling the procuring for an auction to raise money to build a youth center in White Horse. I've never done anything like this, and neither has anyone else involved. We came tonight to see what we ought to be aiming for. I'm dazzled," she confessed.

"Oh, bless you." The woman smiled and held out a hand. "I'm Elizabeth Pearce."

Nora introduced herself and Rob.

"If you have something to write on, I'll give you my phone number. Feel free to call if you have questions, or we can even have lunch. After all—" she glanced around "—after tonight, I can call my life my own again. For a few months, until we start all over again.''

''Thank you so much!'' Nora groped in her tiny black velvet bag for her checkbook, which she'd brought in case she saw a modestly priced something she couldn't resist. Nora had her write her name and number on the register cover before Elizabeth was called away to consult on something to do with wine.

Nora did finally bid on a gorgeous gold-and-crimson shot-silk shawl from India and was delighted when she won and the shawl was hers.

Rob laughed at her childlike pleasure. ''You really wanted it, didn't you?''

''I don't know what I'll do with it, but isn't it beautiful?'' She took a last, pleased look at her possession before letting Rob steer her to their dinner table.

They joined in the conversation with their fellow diners, a couple who both worked at Microsoft, a Boeing executive and his wife and a couple of women who said they were regular volunteers at the shelter.

The live auction was exciting, with the auctioneer prowling through the crowd with his microphone to coax bidders thinking of dropping out. When the airline tickets came up, Nora raised Rob's bidder card and felt the force of the auctioneer's personality.

''I have $400.'' Other bid cards shot into the air. ''Okay, $450, $500, $600. Now we're talking, folks. You know these are good to fly round trip anywhere the airline goes. Do you have any idea what you'd pay for two of you to fly to the Yucatan Peninsula in Mexico? Well, I'll tell you. Close to $3,000. Yep.'' His commanding stare moved from table to table. ''So let's get cracking here, folks. Who'll give me $700?''

Nora raised the bid card; others did the same. To her disappointment, Rob did eventually make her drop out. "I don't want to go to Ixtapa," he said in her ear. "I just want to fly to Boston, and I can do that for a lot less than $2,000. Even if I go twice."

The auctioneer tried coaxing her, but when she laughed and blushed and shook her head, he gave up on her.

She watched in amazement as the bidding rose to $3,000 and above—$3,400, $3,500, finally closing at $3,700.

"Anything above value," one of the men at the table said knowledgeably, "is a tax-deductible donation."

"Really?" Nora made a mental note. *Don't assume we can only get value or less...*

Rob straightened beside her. "Here comes that pen-and-ink drawing. Got the bid card?"

"Don't you want to do it?"

He shook his head, his eyes very blue and warm. "I like watching you."

She knew color was flaring in her cheeks again. "Oh, thanks. Now I'm going to be self-conscious."

He leaned forward and said just for her ears, "I haven't taken my eyes off you since you came down the stairs at home. Do you have any idea how beautiful you are tonight?"

She stammered and flushed and blew it utterly, saved only by the auctioneer who opened bidding at $200. She raised Rob's bid number again and again, waiting for his elbow in her side.

At $600, she said, "Should I stop?"

Before he could answer, the auctioneer was at her

side. "This beautiful lady must be a real cat lover, folks. She lost those airline tickets, but she's determined now. She's not going to let someone steal that painting out from under her nose for only $650, now is she?" He shoved the microphone toward her.

The audience laughed sympathetically, and Rob's grin was fiendish.

"Um, I don't know, I..." She cast him a desperate glance that became narrow-eyed when he didn't come to her rescue. Turning back to the auctioneer, she said firmly, "Certainly not." And held up the bid card.

Applause rippled through the ballroom. The auctioneer went to pick on the other remaining bidder, who stood—or sat—firm.

At last the auctioneer proclaimed, "To the beautiful lady in black, at $700!"

Nora sagged in her seat, her heart pounding at what she'd done. What if Rob didn't want it? Could she come up with the money?

"Why didn't you stop me?" she whispered.

"Because I wanted the drawing." With the faintest quirk of the mouth, he expressed wicked amusement. "And because I was having fun."

She tried to feel indignation. "At my expense!"

"With you," he corrected, the smile only in his eyes now. "Come on. Don't lie. You enjoyed that, didn't you?"

Nora succumbed. "Yes. I've never spent that much money in my life on something so...so..."

"Trivial?"

"Indulgent."

"I think I'm insulted."

"Don't be. Everyone is entitled occasionally."

"You're right." His voice had gone low and husky, his gaze intense. "Everyone is. That includes you, Nora Woods."

Unable to look away, she was torn between hope and the full knowledge that hope was illusory. Was she entitled to indulge her wants and not just her needs? Nora wondered wistfully. If only sometimes?

Perhaps that was what tonight was about. She had felt rather like Cinderella from the moment she bought the beautiful dress and hung it in her closet, imagining the night when she would put it on and walk down the stairs to her prince, waiting at the foot.

So far, it had all been magical. He had looked at her just as she'd imagined he would, when she let herself imagine such things, in weak moments right before sleep. She'd sipped bubbly champagne and drifted among elegantly dressed people with Rob's hand securely at her waist. She had bought something pretty for herself and had the fun of winning a live-auction bid with all eyes on her, as if she was someone.

She would have liked a dance, but it was just as well there was no band and no dance floor. If Rob had wrapped his arms around her, she might have had to flee, like Cinderella when the clock struck midnight. Because that was more than she was allowed.

Oh, yes, she could indulge herself...but only a little bit.

"Maybe I am entitled," she said softly, but even she heard the sadness in her voice, too, before she made herself look away from Rob's eyes and pretend to be interested in the bidding for a ride-along with a K-9 police deputy.

NORA SEEMED SUBDUED after that, and Rob cursed himself for saying something so pointed.

Damn it, he thought in frustration, she was as bad in her own way as his mother was. Molly would be disgusted with both of them. His sister had been remarkably unsentimental for a teenage girl. She had boyfriends, but never pretended even to herself to be in love with any of them. She had loved their family cat deeply, but when Olly died of old age and they buried him, she cried once and not again. She'd never mooned over sad songs, and she'd razzed Rob unmercifully when she caught him lying in bed doing his own mooning over a picture of Nora stolen from his sister's room.

"You like Nora!" she'd exclaimed in satisfaction. "I knew you did."

"What are you talking about?" He'd tossed the photo at her. "This was sitting here on my bedside table. What, are you trying to set me up?"

She just grinned like a Cheshire cat and sank down at the foot of his bed. "You love Nora Woods, you love Nora Woods," she chanted.

Growling, he lunged at her, but she rolled off the bed and plopped onto the carpeted floor.

"What's wrong with liking Nora?" she asked. "Nora's cool. And pretty, too. I'll bet you don't have a single girl in any of your classes who can hold a candle to Nora."

He didn't, of course. "She's okay, I guess."

"Uh-huh." His sister propped her elbows on the edge of the bed and contemplated him with knowing eyes. "Why are you embarrassed about liking Nora?"

"Even if I did like her...jeez! She's sixteen!" he burst out. "She's my little sister's best friend!"

"So what? You're only nineteen. Mom and Dad are five years apart in age," Molly pointed out. "Three years is nothing."

It felt like something to him. What would his college friends think if he started dating a sophomore in high school? *They* were getting in their girlfriends' pants. *He* wouldn't even be able to try, especially not since she'd probably tell Molly everything.

He glared at his sister. "You haven't told her you think I like her, have you?"

"Of course not." She gave that grin again. "Yet."

"If you know what's good for you, don't."

"You know—" she picked up the photo and waved it in the air between them "—you should make up your mind. What's the good in having some secret crush? I mean, either you like her enough to do something about it, or you don't." She shrugged, as if his agonizing was stupid.

That was Molly in a nutshell: decisive, clear about what she wanted, unlikely to wish for what was out of her reach—and impatient with the maunderings of others.

So, okay, *life* was beyond her reach now, but he could easily picture her shrugging about that, too. Her bumper sticker had read, Shit Happens. Mom hadn't appreciated it.

Mom and Nora both, Rob thought, needed to soak up some of Molly's philosophy. Molly had never been passive. She had always tried to influence her fate, but she had also never wasted time or energy regretting spent opportunities.

"So? I'll find a better job," she'd said with determination when a teen boutique where his clothes horse of a sister had really wanted to work hired an older girl instead.

The Molly he remembered would be astonished if she could see her mother and her best friend now.

Too bad they didn't seem to realize that.

Rob tuned in to realize the auctioneer's place had been taken by a young woman who was thanking everyone for their generosity. A glance at his catalog told him the week in Yachats, Oregon, had been the last item for auction.

"Time to pay the piper," he said.

The line to pay went fast. Many of the auction-goers had chosen the prepay option, it seemed. Rob went to get the car while Nora waited with her scarlet-and-gold silk shawl wrapped around her shoulders, the glass bowl packed in a box in her arms, and the drawing leaning against the wall beside her.

Pulling up to the curb, he saw her through the floor-to-ceiling glass, an exquisite, slender woman in black velvet that flowed over her body like dark water. That long piece of silk wrapped around her shoulders picked out hints of fire in her auburn hair, and left only her slim, white throat exposed. She didn't notice his arrival. Perhaps the brightly lit room reflected in the glass made the night outside impenetrable. She was clearly oblivious as well to the glances others in the lobby gave her. She might have been all alone.

He almost expected her gaze to pass disinterestedly over him when he went through the doors, proving that this was all a dream, that she waited for someone else. A few times over the years, he'd seen a woman who could have been Nora. He remembered once in particular, when he was in downtown Seattle on business, and this leggy woman in a sleek, dark suit had been coming toward him, walking up Fifth Avenue. He'd stopped dead, even though people bumped into him and a teenager growled something obscene. The woman was shrugging into a raincoat as she walked. Her cap of auburn hair defied the gray day, and her face was intelligent, beautiful, distracted. "Nora?" he'd said hoarsely.

She'd looked right through him. Even as he realized she wasn't Nora, that her mouth wasn't right and her eyes were gray or hazel, he had felt a stab through the heart as vicious as if she *were* Nora. Would she look at him like that, if they met on the street? Would she choose not to know him?

Unconsciously he braced himself as he pushed open the swinging glass doors and Nora turned her head. But a smile lit her face, and relief punched him in the gut.

He carefully loaded the artwork in the trunk and then held open the passenger door for her. He smelled her hair as she bent to get in. Tonight she had a spicy, exotic fragrance that went with the diamonds and sleek velvet.

Once behind the wheel, Rob said, "You've grown up since the prom."

She turned a laughing face to him. "That's a surprise?"

"I was just thinking about the last time I saw you in a formal dress with your hair up."

"Mmm." As he turned onto a dark street, she gazed through the windshield. In the flash of streetlight, her profile was delicate and reflective. "The dress is still in my closet. It looks so young and... sweet."

A reminiscent smile curved his mouth. "You looked damn sexy in it to me."

"Yeah, but you were young, too."

"Young?" He pretended outrage. "I was a junior in college! A man among boys!"

Her giggle was infectious. "Well, I thought you were, too. I was positive all my friends were painfully jealous, because you were so much hunkier and more mature than *their* boyfriends."

Rob deliberately said, "All your friends except Molly. You know what she told me?"

They were on the ship canal bridge, heading north in the express lanes. The freeway was dark. He caught only a fleeting impression of her face.

After a long pause, she spoke. "No, what?"

"She said I looked like Charlie Chaplin. As if I didn't fit my tux."

Nora couldn't seem to help the giggle. "It was a little big."

"It was Dad's. I couldn't afford to rent one."

She was still laughing. "I wondered, but...oh, dear! You looked so handsome anyway."

"I took pleasure in being a head taller than Molly's date."

"Molly's...? Oh. Poor Griff."

"I made sure to remark on his pimples when I saw her at the aquarium, too."

"How mean of you!"

"Charlie Chaplin." He shook his head. "I was

George Clooney in *Oceans Eleven.* Suave, worldly, irresistible.''

''Did you really think things like that?''

A grin stretched his mouth as he remembered his youthful self. ''Oh, yeah. Girls aren't the only ones who spend a hell of a lot of time studying themselves in mirrors, you know.''

''Actually, I did know. Molly and I used to spy on you.''

Despite himself, he turned his head. ''You *spied?*''

''Uh-huh. And eavesdropped,'' she added conversationally. ''If you put your ear to the heating vent in her room, you can hear conversations in your bedroom pretty well.''

Rob muttered a profanity and Nora laughed.

Under his breath, he muttered, ''I don't think I want to know what you heard.''

''You and your friends did a lot of...bragging,'' she said delicately.

He groaned.

''You were remarkable studs. I'm pretty sure every girl in your graduating class had been deflowered six or eight times, if the notches you all claimed to have on your bedposts were accurate.''

He groaned again, but laughed at the same time. ''What were we, sixteen? We were all virgins ourselves!''

Her laugh joined his. ''Somehow, even Molly and I guessed that. Although,'' she added reflectively, ''I was horribly jealous even so. It *might* have been true. I had an awful crush on you about then.''

''Really?'' he said, pleased. She'd admitted as much before, once they started going together, but he didn't mind hearing it again. He'd had one on her, too, for longer even than he'd been willing to admit to himself as a teenager. What eighteen-year-old boy thought his little sister's fifteen-year-old best friend was hot? He'd been humiliated to catch himself turning down the chance to go out to a party so he could hang out at home just because Nora was spending the night.

Nora punched him lightly in the arm. "You know I did! Molly thought it was hilarious. She kept saying, 'My *brother?* You should see him in his boxers! He's skinny.' Or she'd remind me how you and your friends held those belching contests."

Rob winced.

"I'd get fired up in your defense and remind her that the boys she liked had probably had belching contests, too, and that they were even skinnier. Sam Blumenstein had legs like matchsticks when we'd see him out running in middle school P.E. Molly was madly in love with him."

Deflected, he asked, "Was she really? I was thinking just tonight that Molly wasn't very sentimental. I'd try to egg her about boyfriends, and she'd just laugh. I never thought she even kidded herself that she was really in love with any of them."

Nora made a humming sound in her throat. "I hadn't thought about it, but I guess you're right. Once we were in high school, that is. At twelve and thirteen, when the hormones were raging, she had huge crushes on boys, a new one every month or so. We'd lurk at the library after school, because *he* sometimes went there to study, or we'd oh so casually wander downtown, because he helped out at his father's lumberyard after school, or…'' She stopped and gave a small laugh. ''It added a little drama to our lives.''

He'd stuck on part of her story. ''Lumberyard? You mean, Molly liked that little Peirson punk? The one with the spiked blue hair?''

''Come on, give her a break! She was twelve. She thought he was a rebel.''

Rob snorted.

''Your shaved head wasn't exactly a girl's dream, I've got to tell you,'' his teenage love informed him. ''I was so relieved when you grew your hair again and I could go back to daydreaming about you.''

Involuntarily he ran a hand through his hair.

Nora laughed at him.

''That's the trouble with people who've known you too long,'' he growled.

''Hey, you've stayed in White Horse.'' She had one foot comfortably tucked under her, and he guessed her shoes had been kicked off. ''Most of your clients probably remember your shaved head, too.''

''I like to think *they* have forgotten.''

''Really?'' she teased. ''Have you forgotten their youthful indiscretions?''

Just the other day, Rhonda and Don Hammond had been in his office discussing the house he was designing for them. Rob had looked at her and, like the flick of a projector, seen her drunk at a party, ripping off her shirt and dancing topless on the table. He'd had a hell of a time keeping his eyes on her face after that.

''Uh…''

''I didn't think so,'' Nora said comfortably.

They kept talking about growing up, people they'd

known, laughing as if their friendship had never been interrupted. It seemed easy in the dark car on the freeway, only occasional headlights and tall streetlights illuminating each other's faces briefly. Not having to look at each other, read every expression, be self-conscious, seemed to free them.

They'd left the freeway and were following the long curve of minor highway that led across the river valley to White Horse when Nora said suddenly, "You know, this is the first time since she died that I've been able to talk about Molly without it hurting."

Jolted, he realized this was the first time for him, too. Admitting as much, Rob said, "People don't like to say her name around me. They don't want to remind me of anything sad, I guess. And Mom and Dad and I don't talk about her this way, either. With Mom so wrapped up in grieving still, the subject is too loaded."

After a moment, Nora said, "It felt good, though. As if she came to life for a few minutes. I could almost hear her laughing."

"Yeah." His sister had had a hell of a laugh, one that had scandalized their mother.

"You sound like a donkey," Mom would say sharply, when what she really meant was, *You sound like a whore.* Men would turn their heads when Molly let loose in a theater during a funny movie. That laugh had represented a part of her Rob had really liked: a complete lack of inhibitions, an ability to wholeheartedly enjoy herself without worrying about what other people thought.

"It's sad that it took us so many years to be able to smile about some silly thing Molly said."

Rob shifted down, then reached out and took her hand. "I think about her."

Nora didn't turn her hand to squeeze back, but she didn't pull away, either. "I do things because Molly always told me I should, or I don't do them because Molly would tease me when I did, but...mostly it's subconscious." She seemed sad now. "I haven't let myself think much about growing up, or the fun we had in high school, because she was so much a part of it all that I couldn't avoid thinking about her, too, and that hurt."

Rob had to take his hand back to shift again to slow in preparation for stopping at the red light at the main intersection in town. "Molly would like it if we can let ourselves laugh at things she said, or smile when we remember good times with her."

"Yes." Nora sounded...surprised. "Yes, I think she would."

He didn't want the evening to end, and regretted the silence that developed between them as he drove dark streets to her house. He felt her withdrawal, as she untucked her foot and fumbled on the floor with her high-heeled sandals.

"That was fun," she said brightly, as he turned the last corner.

"I had a good time." Rob pulled into her driveway. "Thank you for asking me."

"And I got such wonderful ideas! It was really worth going."

He hated that artificial tone. It had the effect of distancing him and killing any intimacy between them.

In the driveway, he set the emergency brake and turned off the car engine.

She inched toward the door and reached for the handle. "Gracious, it's late! Thank you for keeping me company, Rob. And letting me bid for you."

"Nora."

She hesitated, then turned with obvious reluctance toward him. "Rob, please..."

"I've thought all night about kissing you. Trying to remember exactly what it was like."

"Can't...can't we just be friends?" she whispered.

"I don't know," he said honestly. "Maybe that's all I deserve—more than I deserve—but...I don't know."

"*You* deserve?" In the light cast from the porch, her eyes seemed to shimmer. "If there's anybody here who should talk about deserving..."

"God damn it!" He reached for her. Silk slid from her shoulders and left her upper arms bare under his hands, her skin warm and satiny. "Maybe we should call it even. Anything to get past this."

"This?" She sounded husky, outraged. "I committed vehicular homicide. I killed your sister. *This* isn't the kind of thing you tuck away in a drawer to be forgotten."

"Forgiveness and forgetting aren't the same thing."

"No." She drew a ragged breath. "Maybe not. I don't know."

"I do know this much." He lifted her chin. "I have never found another woman your equal."

Her pulse leaped under his thumb and she made a small, incredulous sound.

"Don't you ever wonder if it would be the same?" he asked in a low, gravelly voice.

She swallowed. "Sometimes." Her admission was made so quietly, he barely heard her.

"Is one kiss so bad?"

"I...I don't know." Even as she despaired, she lifted her hands to his shoulders. "You shouldn't *want* to kiss me."

Rob didn't bother answering. He bent his head and touched his mouth to hers, a soft brush of lips to lips, breath and sighs mingling. It took every ounce of self-control he had to make the kiss no more than that, to nip her lower lip and suck gently, to coax and taste and never demand. To remind her, to torment himself, but not to take advantage of her, not to scare her.

When he lifted his head, she stayed still for a long moment, face tilted up, eyes closed, skin porcelain but her mouth soft and full, lips parted as if she continued to feel his mouth on hers.

Rob clenched his teeth and let her go. She drew a shaky breath and opened her eyes, gazing at him for a moment before she whirled to open the door and leap out. She slammed it without a word and hurried up the walk so fast she stumbled once.

A minute later, she'd vanished inside.

Not scare her? Rob grabbed the steering wheel so hard, leather creaked. Who the hell was he kidding?

He'd terrified her.

CHAPTER TEN

THE WHITE HORSE CEMETERY had been carved out of the woods not long after the town was founded in 1880 during the logging boom. Widow-makers had insured that bodies had to be laid to rest, and someone chose a peaceful spot on high ground, nestled in a bend of the river. In the old part of the cemetery, granite stones stood solid, moss clinging to incised letters. A few grander graves boasted marble angels with wings or gated walls.

In common with the modern insistence on convenience above all else, only flat stones were permitted in the new part of the cemetery, so the mowers could drive uninterrupted across the velvet green swale. There were rules, too, about when and how visitors could leave flowers and when they had to be taken away.

Colleen rather resented all of that. Every day when she came, she had to drive through the old cemetery, which had atmosphere. Some headstones leaned with age. Scattered old dogwoods and cedars and sycamores cast shade and huge, woody rhododendrons exploded into bloom every spring. It looked like a cemetery ought to look.

The new part was stark, except for the view across the river to the forested foothills and a few white peaks of the Cascades rearing above. The grass was spongy underfoot, the grave plaques perfectly placed to make curving lines across the gently sloping ground. It was quite easy to become disoriented, to follow a line of bronze plaques and realize you'd chosen the wrong one, to have to cast around in search of the grave of your loved one.

Colleen had come so often that she knew just where to pull over. This morning, dew still clung to the grass although the day felt as if it would become hot. At eight-thirty it was too early for workers to be out, for any funerals to be taking place, or even for most visitors to be wandering the grounds. She came in the morning when she couldn't sleep, and because she liked to be alone to listen, in case Molly ever answered.

Tired, she wasn't paying attention to her surroundings and had almost reached her usual parking spot when she realized that another car was already there. A small, battered foreign car. Her foot hit the brake and Colleen turned her head instinctively toward Molly's grave.

Someone was there. A slender woman with hair that glowed with a deep fire in the morning sunlight. Colleen knew immediately who she was, of course, even though her back was to the road.

Paralyzed with outrage and something more complex—anger, perhaps, or panic, Colleen sat unmoving, her car idling in the middle of the narrow asphalt road that wound through the cemetery. She was forty or fifty yards downhill from the other car, and Nora Woods apparently didn't sense that she was no longer alone.

Probably on her way to work, she wore chinos and a sleeveless white shirt with a collar. She stood very still for a long time, head bowed. At last she turned and started back across the grass, her gaze straight ahead and seemingly blind, because she never did notice the Taurus hovering.

Colleen had the horrific thought that she could step on the gas hard, accelerate across the grass and slam into Nora Woods. She pictured the girl's surprised face, her body flying into the air, hitting the ground and bouncing like a floppy rag doll. No one would see.

On some cool level, saner thoughts flickered through her head, memories of newspaper articles. Dented bumpers or broken headlights, body shops reporting unusual damage, tire marks on the soft ground, skin or hair left on her bumper or a paint chip on the body. And what if Nora flew up and hit the windshield, shattering it?

Even as her daughter's friend walked, oblivious, toward her car, Colleen imagined it: Nora staring with shock and too-brief knowledge of her coming death as she hurtled toward the windshield. The spiderweb of cracks and explosion of blood and the mess of that bright auburn head as it squished like a pumpkin against the glass.

Molly had died like that because, foolish teenager that she'd been, she wasn't wearing a seat belt. Nora was. Police told the Sumners later that she didn't even remember putting it on.

''I always wear it,'' she'd said blankly, her shocked eyes staring, her answers slow in coming and dull, as they described it. ''If only Molly...if only Molly...''

She couldn't answer any questions after that, they said, not for a long while.

Nausea swamped Colleen and she pressed a hand to her mouth. She had just imagined committing murder. What had she become, to envision someone else's terror with such relish?

A moan escaped her hand. She panted for breath and fought to keep back the nausea as Nora, still without seeing her, reached the road, circled her car and got in.

Sweating, trembling, bile rising in her throat, Colleen waited for Nora to look into her rearview mirror and see the waiting car, guess who was behind the wheel, perhaps get out and walk back.

But after a moment the Civic—yes, it was a very old, hatchback Civic—shook itself, belched a puff of pollution and started forward.

Colleen lasted until it was out of sight. Then she flung herself out of her car, ran to the edge of the grass, and emptied her stomach in long, wrenching heaves. Tears wet her face even as she vomited.

What have I become? she asked desperately, and was horrified because she knew the answer.

SHE SHOULDN'T HAVE VISITED the cemetery, not this morning. As she reached the exit gates, she realized the road ahead was swimming before her eyes. Black dots swirled as she pulled to the shoulder, put the car into Park and freed herself from her seat belt so that she could fling open the door and bend way over.

As darkness closed in, she thought, *I'll land on my face when I faint.* But with blood rushing to her head, the darkness slowly receded, leaving her shaken.

She hadn't eaten breakfast, had only had a cup of coffee. Big mistake. What if she'd been out on a busier road?

She'd slept poorly, too, both last night and the one before, after she ran away from Rob. That had doubtless contributed to her feeling light-headed.

This was the first time she'd been to the cemetery since one night when she was sixteen and she, Molly and a bunch of their friends had come here to try to scare themselves. They'd dared each other to have a party among the gravestones, play hide-and-seek, taunt the ghosts. Idiotic and disrespectful, but adolescent. They had gathered that dark night in the old cemetery, where ghosts might wear long skirts and corsets and where the trees and taller stones cast deeper shadows that shivered sometimes when the wind blew and gave them goose bumps.

They had never, ever, imagined that one of them would be buried here so soon.

Nora had been thinking about visiting Molly's grave ever since the auction. Talking about her the way they did had made Nora believe that she might be welcome here. Her mother had told her how to find the grave. Monday morning had seemed safest, the most private time to come. She hadn't wanted a witness.

The peculiar thing was, she hadn't felt much of anything. Molly couldn't possibly be here, she'd thought, staring down at the lawn beneath her feet. She tried to picture the raw hole, the casket laid to rest, the clods of dirt thudding down on its shining lid and finally covering it for all eternity, but she still didn't believe in her heart that Molly was in that casket. She had stood there in the morning silence for fifteen minutes or more. The distant sound of cars drifted up the hill. Once she'd heard an angry caw and lifted her head to see a crow chasing a bald eagle above the river. Otherwise, the quiet was peaceful and even empty. Hundreds of graves surrounded her, but this morning the spirits were apparently sleeping in.

She had cleared her throat and said, ''Molly? I'm sorry. So sorry. You know that, though, don't you?''

No hint of an answer came to her ears; forgiveness didn't flow over her. Anger or resentment didn't prickle at her skin like an electric charge. Molly had been far more present in the car with Nora and Rob the other night than she was on this hillside.

Finally Nora gave up. She did say awkwardly, ''I miss you. I wish...'' She couldn't finish, didn't try. Instead she turned her back on the grave and hurried across the grass toward her car, her eyes misting despite herself.

And then the dizziness had struck her.

Cautiously Nora raised her head and finally sat upright in the car seat. The world stayed steady around her.

She needed something to eat, that was all. She'd go by the espresso stand a few blocks from work and get a muffin or bagel. Tilting the rearview mirror, Nora examined herself. Mascara had run, but not badly. She could fix it in the bathroom at the vet hospital. Maybe because of the contrast to the dark smudges around her eyes, she looked washed-out. A white face with haunted eyes stared back at her. The sad thing was, that reflection was more familiar to her than the glowing face she'd seen in her bedroom mirror as she was getting dressed for the auction, and for Rob.

Before he'd kissed her, and reminded her of still more she had lost and could not regain. The depth of her response to him and her longing had scared her even more than coming home had.

Maybe that was why she'd visited the cemetery today. To atone for wanting something—someone—so much when she had no right to be selfish.

Nora had shut her car door and buckled her seat belt when she heard the sound of an approaching vehicle. She readjusted her rearview mirror and glanced in it, expecting to see a truck driven by a cemetery maintenance worker. Instead, the car that came sedately down the curving road was a blue Ford Taurus.

Someone else who had come to the cemetery early. She couldn't make out the driver and didn't really try. But when the car came abreast of hers she turned her head and met the distraught eyes of the woman behind the wheel.

Colleen Sumner.

The moment was fleeting. Almost before she could react, Nora was looking at the flickering brake lights on the Taurus pausing at the stop sign before accelerating onto the road. All she was left with was an impression of a ravaged face, of pain so deep her own seemed pale in comparison.

Nora shuddered. She had done this to a woman she had once casually called Mom.

A horrible thought came to her. Was Mrs. Sumner always so distressed when she visited the cemetery? Or was it that she'd seen Nora at her daughter's grave?

She must have, Nora realized. The Taurus had come along not far behind her. If Molly's mother had come after her, parked, walked across the grass, spent any time at all, she wouldn't be leaving the cemetery right on the heels of Nora's Civic.

Did she believe that Nora's visit had been insulting somehow? Or mocking? Why else would she be so upset?

On automatic, Nora drove to the espresso stand, where she bought a muffin she didn't want and made herself eat it anyway. Once at the clinic, she called hello and slipped into the bathroom before anyone could see her. Quick repair with water, soap and a paper towel left her just as wan. She wished she carried makeup in her purse.

After exchanging more greetings and talking briefly with Dr. Bergstrom about some figures he needed, Nora looked up the phone number of Rob's office and dialed. A secretary answered and forwarded her call.

"Nora!" he said a moment later. "I was going to call today."

Grief and gladness tangled in her chest. Didn't he understand that they had no future? That they *couldn't* have one? Yet, perversely, her heart quickened with pleasure that he had intended to call, that he was stubbornly pursuing her despite everything.

She swallowed. "Rob, I went to the cemetery today."

He was quiet.

"Your mother saw me there. I went…I chose today because I thought I'd be alone. I didn't mean for her to see me. I hope you believe that."

"Of course I believe you!" Rob paused. "Did Mom say something?"

"No. No, we didn't meet. She drove past my car and we looked at each other. That's all." Nora bit her lip. "The thing is... Rob, she looked horribly upset. Like she'd been crying and...I don't know. I feel terrible."

"Don't blame yourself," he said heavily. "Mom's the one with the problem here."

Nora stole a look around to be sure nobody was within earshot or seemed annoyed because she was chatting on the phone.

"Will you check on her? Just to make sure she's okay?"

"Yeah. Of course I will. I'll call you later and let you know."

"Thank you," she said on a rush of relief. "I'd feel better if I knew she's just mad at me and not..." She stopped. Not what? Suicidal? Had she really been afraid that Molly's mom was going to kill herself because Nora had dared to defile her daughter's grave with her presence?

Or, Nora wondered, was it herself she was afraid for? Was she just a little bit scared of Mrs. Sumner?

ROB CANCELED AN APPOINTMENT with Rhonda and Don Hammond, told his secretary he'd be out for a couple of hours, and drove to his parents'—correction, his mother's—house.

If Mom was home, she'd parked her Taurus in the garage. Frowning, Rob pulled into the driveway. No lights showed through the front windows. In fact, the house looked empty, even abandoned.

It took Rob a minute to realize why. The lawn, manicured for as long as he could remember, was shaggy. The window boxes were empty. His mother had not planted them this year with the riot of colorful annuals she tended so religiously most summers. Even the gray clapboard siding and white-and-black trim looked faded, as if the house begged for a fresh coat of paint.

Meant to show Dad how little she needed him, Mom's burst of activity with the lawn mower had apparently passed. And Dad must have taken it to heart. He'd have been up here mowing if he'd seen his beloved lawn going to hell.

Rob rang the doorbell and waited. Silence. No footsteps, no muffled "Just a moment!"

His worry ratcheted up a notch. If Mom hadn't come home, where was she?

The cemetery wouldn't be feeling like a refuge to her right now. He didn't know of any other place where she went to think or brood or find comfort.

A friend's? But as of two weeks ago, she hadn't even told any of them about the separation.

He stepped back and hesitated, about to turn and give up. But Nora wouldn't have called him if Mom hadn't looked really bad. He wasn't sure what she was scared of, but he'd caught her anxiety.

He had a house key on his ring, although he hadn't used it in a long time, not since the last time Dad had persuaded Mom to get away for a weekend and Rob had stopped by to water plants. They'd gone over to the peninsula and stayed in a bed-and-breakfast in historic Port Townsend. Mom had come home looking relaxed, her step lighter, as if the invisible weight she carried had been eased. But the effect hadn't lasted, and that was…heck, two or three years ago. Thinking back, Rob guessed that his father had given up sometime not long after that.

He rapped hard on the door one more time. "Mom?"

When there was still no answer, he put his key in the lock, opened the front door and stepped inside the dim entry.

"Mom?" His voice sounded too loud, as if the house demanded hushed tones despite the sunlight that streamed in the windows.

Rob could see the deserted living room from here. He carefully shut the front door and went through the dining room to the kitchen. The sink shone, the countertops gleamed. He wanted to be reassured, but his gaze went to the sunny windowsill where his mother had always grown herbs. Every plant on the sill was dried and brown. She had quit watering them. Deliberately? Or had she just forgotten they existed?

Disturbed, Rob opened the refrigerator. It was full. Too full. There were—he swore under his breath as he counted—five quarts of milk. Some were unopened and way past their expiration dates. Vegetables rotted toward the back. A plastic container held a garden of mold. His stomach heaved when Rob dumped it in the garbage pail beneath the sink and ran water into the container.

Mom had just been shoving old food to the back and adding more. It was as if she'd been shopping for the same quantity she'd always bought because that's what she did. She didn't seem to have noticed or cared that she hadn't eaten the food already there.

The pantry was well stocked, but he couldn't tell if she was opening cans of soup from time to time or just not eating at all. Remembering the way she'd pushed food around on her plate and the impression of brittleness she'd given the night he'd come for dinner, Rob swore again.

How could he have paid so little attention? He'd called or seen her every day or two, but not for meals, and he'd taken her reassurances at face value. If Nora hadn't called today...

Fear curled in his stomach. He hurried through the house, checking the enclosed back porch and Dad's den before taking the stairs two at a time. Dad had always kept a gun in the closet. Mom wouldn't have...no. Not Mom.

A man who hadn't prayed in a long time, he found himself doing so as he passed his mother's sewing room, the bathroom—in here he pushed aside the shower curtain, wincing at the rattle of the rings, as if he had to be quiet because...because why?—and the closed doors to his old bedroom and Molly's. The master bedroom was at the end of the hall.

It lay empty, too. The bed was made, but sloppily, with the spread hanging farther on one side than the other. That small carelessness bothered Rob as much as the dead herbs on the windowsill. His mother was tidy to the point of compulsion.

"If you're going to do something at all, do it right," she'd always declared firmly.

Rob still made his bed with military precision. Only Molly had defied Mom by not making her bed at all and dropping dirty clothes on the floor and leaving dirty dishes and crumpled wrappers on her bedside table. As she got older, the battles multiplied.

"It's my room, and if I want to be a slob, I will be!" she had yelled just before slamming her door in Mom's face.

Molly. A hand seemed to squeeze his heart, pumping fear through his veins. If Mom ever...did anything, it would be in Molly's room. Close to her daughter.

He was outside the door in a few strides. His hand hovered above the doorknob, and he closed his eyes. He was being an idiot. Mom was probably at the store loading up on more groceries she didn't need. She must have other regular errands, too. The pharmacy, the dry cleaner, the...

She wouldn't be here.

He turned the knob and opened the door.

His mother, dressed as if to go out, lay curled in a fetal position on Molly's twin bed.

"Mom?"

She didn't move.

CHAPTER ELEVEN

"MOM!" Why was someone shaking her shoulder so roughly and shouting into her ear? "Mom!"

It seemed a great distance away. Perhaps she was in that dark hole in the ground and had to scrabble toward the light. Even when she sensed she was there, her lids didn't want to open. Tears had glued them shut.

"Stop," Colleen mumbled irritably, but it came out slurred, like "Shop."

"What?" Her son's voice still had that sharp edge of anxiety. "What did you say?"

"Stop!" she snapped, and pried open her eyelids. Light from the window made her squint.

"God!" He sank heavily onto the bed beside her. "You scared the crap out of me."

She had fallen asleep squeezed into the tiniest ball she could form, as if she were sheltering physical pain—an inflamed gallbladder, or appendix, or pancreas.

Colleen unkinked her fingers, her elbows, her knees, and finally sat up on the edge of the bed like an old, old woman. "I was just asleep." She still sounded...odd, as if the inside of her mouth had been dried with cotton balls that left a coating of fuzz.

Rob frowned at her, looking unnervingly like his father. "Are you all right?"

All right? She examined the question and admitted the truth. She didn't know anymore.

"Yes," she lied. "Of course. Sometimes I nap in here. You knew that."

"No. No, I didn't." Muscles in his jaw flexed and he said harshly, "I thought this was a museum. Nobody lies down for a nap on the bed where Queen Elizabeth I slept."

Colleen stiffened. "This is your sister's room. What should I do? Remodel it? Why? The house is too big already."

His voice gentled. "Maybe you should move."

A shaft of fear pierced her and she hugged herself. "I'm not ready. I can't. I..."

"You were crying."

He was frowning again, his eyes on her cheeks.

She resisted the urge to wipe them. "I might have had a bad dream." Colleen didn't even know why she was lying anymore. Why pretend? she asked herself drearily. Soon enough, he'd wonder why she was napping at nine forty-five in the morning.

A sudden thought struck her. "What are you doing here?" She glanced again at the clock. "It's the middle of the morning!"

His gaze shied away. "I've been worried about you."

So worried he'd let himself into the house and hunted through the rooms until he found her? She studied him, wanting to believe that her distress this morning had mystically communicated itself to him, that he had suddenly thought, *Mom needs me.* But she had never given stock to such nonsense, and she couldn't start now.

In a raw whisper, she said, "Someone saw me, right?" Colleen sucked in a wounded breath. "She saw me. Did she call you?"

He met her eyes squarely. "Yes. Nora called me. She was worried about you."

"Worried about me?" The idea was absurdly, appallingly funny. Despite herself, she laughed, a high, keening sound. Once she started, she couldn't stop. Peal after peal rang out, until tears ran down her face again.

"Mom!"

Her son's face swam before hers.

"Damn it, Mom, I'm going to slap you!"

She clutched at her stomach and rocked, hiccuping in an effort to stop the hysterical laughter. "Oh, dear," she whimpered. "Oh dear, oh dear."

"What is it? What's so funny?"

To her horror, she heard herself say, "I wanted to kill her today. In cold blood. I saw her standing at Molly's grave, and I thought how easy it would be to drive right at her. I imagined it. The surprise on her face, the way her head would smash against the windshield..." She sounded almost dreamy, but she was rocking again, and tears kept splashing down on her hands. "She would have died just the way Molly died."

Her son uttered an obscenity she had never heard him say before. "You hate her that much?"

"Oh, yes." Her voice broke. "Yes, yes, yes!"

His hands were on her shoulders, and he held her still. On his face was a mix of pity and repugnance that nicked at her heart, letting her see yet again what she had become.

''But you didn't do it.''

She sighed so hard she shook. ''No. I actually thought about whether my car would be dented or the windshield smashed. I knew they would check my car, because I do hate her and everyone knows it.''

His fingers bit into her, then released her shoulders so suddenly she almost fell back. ''That's why you didn't do it?'' His voice was devoid of emotion. ''Because you'd have gone to prison?''

Colleen crumpled then, burying her face in her hands. She shouldn't have had any more tears to shed, but they spilled between her fingers. ''No,'' she sobbed. ''No. Because in her death, I saw what I have become.''

His arm closed comfortingly around her, and she turned to cry on her son's shoulder. He patted her back and let her cry until she settled into shuddering breaths and finally struggled free to seek the tissues she kept on the bedside table.

Only after she'd blown her nose and wiped her cheeks did he ask, ''What have you become, Mom?''

She answered indirectly, her voice thick. ''Do you know how little I feel anymore?''

He shook his head.

''Hatred, I feel that. And grief. But nothing else. The two are so strong, they've burned every other emotion to ashes.'' She stared with dry, aching eyes at the poster of a young Keanu Reeves that hung on the wall. ''I've been cauterized. Today I saw a woman I once would have feared and pitied. She is who I am.'' Mother turned to son and gazed without hope at him. ''Molly wouldn't know me.''

''No,'' he said quietly. ''She wouldn't.''

''She loved Nora.'' Colleen went back to staring at the wall.

''Yeah. She did. They were Tweedledum and Tweedledee.'' They had joked once upon a time about the two girls, inseparable from the first day of kindergarten. ''Siamese twins.''

''I felt...left out,'' she said quietly. ''You were, well, like all boys, I suppose. After you started school, you didn't talk to me. I'd say, 'How was your day?' and you'd mumble, 'Fine,' stuff a cookie in your mouth and head for your bedroom. But mothers and daughters, they can stay really close.'' She turned her head, silently begging for understanding. ''Girls come home from school and tell their moms all about their day. Even when they're teenagers. Who is going with whom. Who broke up, what teacher is a jerk, what boy's cute.''

He didn't understand. His bafflement was plain. ''She did talk to you.''

''Sometimes.'' Colleen looked down at her hands. Lately they had become...knobby. She saw in them the beginnings of old age. ''Mostly she talked to Nora. She and I would have a wonderful day shopping, but the minute we got home she'd run to her room, close the door and call Nora. Sometimes, when I'd suggested we do something together, I could feel her impatience. 'Drop me at Nora's,' she'd say, even before we were home. She felt an obligation to me. A fondness that meant she had to indulge me. But she didn't really want to spend time with me, her mother.'' Here, most of all, was the pathetic part. ''I tried to love Nora, too, but I couldn't, because in my heart I believed she'd stolen the closeness with Molly that should have been mine.''

There. It was said. She, a grown woman, had been jealous of a child. A six-year-old with missing teeth, a skinny third-grader, a pimply middle-schooler. Even of the beautiful young woman who had smiled radiantly at her and said, for all the world to hear, ''Thank you to both sets of my parents, shared with my friend Molly.''

Even then, she had felt a pang. A pang of guilt, because she didn't feel what she should, resentment, because Nora had the stage and not Molly.

''Jesus, Mom.'' Rob sounded stunned.

''Don't take the name of the Lord in vain,'' she said automatically.

''I never knew.''

''Even I hardly knew,'' Colleen admitted, eyes downcast. ''I lied to myself sometimes. I didn't like to admit to feeling so petty. I did try. Sometimes, I even succeeded.''

He rose to his feet and paced across the room before turning to face her. ''You wouldn't have wanted me to marry her, would you?''

She struggled to remember how she'd felt before that terrible night. ''I don't know. I thought you two would grow apart.''

''You mean, you hoped.''

''Maybe,'' she whispered, seeing in his face that she had now driven away not just her husband, but her son as well.

Yet another realization darkened his eyes. ''No

wonder you hated Nora so much after the accident. She'd finally managed to take Molly away from you completely."

"She killed her," Colleen said weakly.

"They both got drunk." He stared at her with something very close to dislike. "They got in an accident. Molly was stupid enough, or drunk enough, not to be wearing a seat belt. She would have lived if she had been."

It was true. Colleen knew it was. Molly had been so full of rebellion even as she clung close to home. She wanted her room to be a mess, she wanted to wear jeans to church, she wouldn't put on a seat belt when she could get away with it.

"She didn't wear her seat belt because of me," Colleen said dully. "Because I always told her to, she didn't. If she and I hadn't argued so much, she might not have died."

His face changed. "Mom, she was a teenager. They all fight with their parents! They all do stupid things. It wasn't your fault. She was eighteen years old. She didn't make every decision in defiance of you."

"Then why...why...?" she choked.

"Because that was Molly. She didn't like to admit to any vulnerability."

There had to be a why. "Because that was Molly" wasn't good enough. Her death had to be somebody's fault. It couldn't be just "one of those things," as people had tried to tell her. As if such an idea could possibly be a comfort.

Tragedy wasn't senseless. This one had to be Nora Woods's fault. Because if it wasn't...if it wasn't... Even now, Colleen could barely make herself finish the thought. If it wasn't Nora's fault, then Colleen would have to blame herself.

"I had to hate Nora," she tried to explain.

Rob just shook his head. "You infected me," he said in a voice that didn't sound like his own. "Do you have any idea how cruel I was to her? I loved her, and I looked at her swollen, bruised face and said, 'You killed my sister.' And then I walked away, even though I saw her knees buckling and heard her wail. I can still hear her. Do you know that? I dream about it sometimes. This cry wakes me. Sometimes in the dream I'm turning to run back, but she's always gone. Or I know she's dead, too. I can't go back." He shut his eyes, a spasm crossing his face. "I can never go back," he finished, his voice like bare skin scraped over gravel.

"I'm sorry." She sat on the edge of the bed, lacking the strength even to stand. "So sorry," she whispered.

"Are you?" Rob stared at her with dark, unreadable eyes. Suddenly he rubbed the back of his neck. "I've got to go. I don't know what to say. You've blown me away. I feel like I never knew you. My own mother, and I didn't know you."

"I'm sorry," she said again, inadequately.

"Sorry?" He stared at her, as if astonished. "What good is that now?" And he walked out.

A moment later she heard the *thud, thud* of him descending the stairs. Déjà vu. Then the slam of the front door.

Now she was truly alone, her only company herself—a woman she had discovered she loathed.

Me, myself and I, she thought giddily, insanely.

And not a one was likable.

ROB DIDN'T CALL NORA. How could he? What would he say? "Oh, yeah, Mom's just fine. Peachy keen. Indulging in dreams of smashing your brains on her windshield, but it keeps her entertained." Or, "Yeah, by the way, do you know she's hated you since you were five years old? Of course you killed Molly. You were always out to steal her away from my mother."

Nora had never had a chance of receiving forgiveness from his mother. Now she hated not only Nora but herself as well. The accident that night had been like the explosion of a nuclear bomb, the force expanding and flattening everything in its path, the poisons left in the air and soil working slowly, bitterly.

Mom didn't like who she had become, who she had been all along, perhaps. Well, Rob sure as hell didn't like himself right this minute, either. He'd taken his mother's way today. The way he had treated Nora was Mom's fault; she'd infected him with a vicious virus. He had no responsibility.

Molly, he'd argued, was eighteen years old and capable of making her own choices, foolish and intelligent. Well, he'd been twenty-one, that much more capable. Worse yet, he had let the years crawl by without ever once trying to remedy the wrong he'd done to the girl he loved.

He hadn't had the guts to call her and say, "I'm sorry. I know it's too late, but...I'm sorry." That, at least.

And then he'd blamed Mom.

He didn't accomplish a damn thing all day. His dad

was in the kitchen when Rob got home, banging pans around. "I'm making tacos," he said.

Rob walked in, sank onto a barstool and said, "Mom's falling apart."

His dad turned slowly. "What do you mean?"

Rob told him about Nora's call and how he'd found his mother, curled on Molly's bed, still as death, face crusted with dried tears.

He told him everything she'd said.

His father, eyes sad, only nodded.

"You knew?" Rob said incredulously. "That she was jealous of Nora all those years?"

His father brushed that off. "I knew that for some reason she blamed herself for Molly's death. That's what she really told you today. She's spent twelve years desperately running from what she believes is her own culpability. Wouldn't she have found some peace otherwise?"

"But…that's ridiculous!"

"Grief does odd things to us." Allen circled the counter and sat down heavily on the stool beside Rob's. "Who doesn't think, If only…? If I'd agreed to chaperon the graduation party, Molly couldn't have sneaked away. If we'd talked to both girls, told them it was okay if they got drunk, just to call us for a ride, maybe… If I hadn't let her go at all, if I'd taught her this, if I'd said that, if I'd promised, or forbidden, or…" He stopped abruptly and bent his head, pinching the bridge of his nose as if to stifle tears. "You think those things night after night, without end. You could have done something. You should have. It has to be your fault."

Rob laid an awkward hand on his father's shoulder.

They didn't touch much, never had, but there was a time for everything.

"I didn't know."

"Of course you didn't. You missed her, she was your sister, but she wasn't your responsibility. Parents think they can protect their children. When they can't, it's hard to accept."

"But you've managed."

His father heaved a sigh. "I suppose I have. I know I can't go back. I've come to believe I did everything reasonable. Molly and I had a good relationship. The trouble is, she and your mother were having problems. They butted heads almost from the time Molly was born." He seemed to be looking into the past, his gaze distant. "Your sister was stubborn. If she was told to do it, she wanted to do the opposite. She and I…I guess we compromised. Your mom wasn't as good at that. That last couple of years, Molly was fighting her way free, and your mom was having a hard time letting go."

"And Mom thinks this was part of it. Molly sneaking out to the party, getting drunk, not wearing the seat belt."

His father nodded. "That's my guess. But if Molly's death was really and truly her fault, she couldn't live with herself. So she fixated on someone else. Nora didn't just make a mistake—she killed Molly."

Rob rubbed a hand over his face, understanding what he hadn't this afternoon. "But it wasn't Mom's fault. Teenagers get drunk. They do stupid things."

"But she's afraid," his father said gently.

Rob swiveled on his stool. "If she can't blame Nora anymore, what will Mom do?"

He got a heavy, slow shake of the head in response. "I never thought she'd be suicidal or I wouldn't have left her alone. Now...I just don't know."

"Can you talk to her?" Rob asked...begged.

"I can try." The lines sank deep in his father's face. "There's no saying she'll listen. I've asked her a dozen times to see a counselor. I offered to go, too. She wouldn't hear of it."

"She's...different. Sinking." Rob didn't know how else to describe it. He'd had that feeling today, that she was barely keeping her mouth above water, clinging to the edge of the pool with shaking fingers that would sooner or later cramp and let go.

His father nodded. "Maybe now's the time, then." He looked at the dinner makings he'd spread on the counter. "Do you mind if we order out?"

"No." Rob couldn't remember being so exhausted. "Anything."

Neither of them moved.

"I need to call Nora." He grimaced. "What do I say?"

"Maybe you need to tell her the truth."

The truth didn't sound any more palatable than it had that morning.

"I don't know," he said, rubbing the knotted back of his neck.

His dad's clear blue eyes met his, seeing more than he'd meant to reveal. "Go see her. Face-to-face, you'll know what to say. You can get something to eat later."

"Yeah. Okay." He found himself getting to his

feet because he'd said he would, even though he hadn't consciously decided anything. He didn't know what to say to Nora; he wasn't so sure he'd know when he saw her, either. But otherwise he'd have to call, and that seemed even harder.

On the drive to Nora's, Rob went past his mother's house. He was relieved to see lights on and glimpse her walking in front of the window. If the house had been dark, he'd have had to stop and let himself in again. What if she had been suicidal when he left her this morning? And he'd walked out, dismissing her because she'd confessed to unworthy feelings.

Who didn't sometimes think or feel things they wouldn't want anyone else to know about? Okay, Mom had been jealous of a kid. But she'd hidden it well; she'd made Nora part of the family. Whatever she'd felt, she had done the right thing.

Until the day Nora drove into a tree and killed Molly.

In front of Nora's house, Rob parked on the street and sat for a minute, gathering energy or courage to walk up to her front door and knock. Except for the night he'd picked her up to go to the auction, he hadn't been here in twelve years. Too long.

Lights were on inside and he thought he saw the flicker of blue from a television set. When he rang the doorbell, it must have been a full minute or two before the lock clicked and the door opened a cautious few inches.

"Rob?" Nora swung it open the rest of the way, her eyes anxiously searching his face. "Are you all right?"

"I'm fine." He managed a smile. "I was just hoping to talk to you."

"Come in." She stepped back. "Mom and Dad are in Everett at an Eagles club banquet. They won't be back for a while. I've been worrying since we spoke. Did you talk to your mother?"

He stepped over the threshold. "Yeah. This morning. That's what I wanted to tell you."

"You look like you need a cup of coffee. Why don't you come to the kitchen with me."

It hadn't changed much. New vinyl, he thought, a warm pink and tan tile pattern instead of the fake brick that had been here when he was dating Nora. But the cabinets were the same dark wood, the countertops brown tile. Nora reached for a copper teakettle and said, "Do you mind instant?"

He shook his head. His dad still drank instant, too, and had no interest in trying lattes or mochas or flavored anything from the espresso stands that had sprung up on every corner like weeds in fresh-turned soil.

Leaning one hip against the edge of the counter, he watched Nora bustle, filling the kettle, standing on tiptoe to reach a mug, spooning out coffee and adding powdered creamer without asking him. He liked the fact that she remembered how he drank his coffee. He took pleasure, too, in the mere sight of her in khaki chinos and a thin cotton sweater over a white shirt, her body slender but rounded in the right places. His gaze lingered on her stockinged feet. Her socks added a frivolous note: they had red and turquoise sea horses against a sand-colored background.

"There." She turned to face him, leaning against

the counter on her side of the galley kitchen. "Was your mom fine and I was imagining things?"

"No." His depression settled again like a heavily loaded backpack. "She's falling apart."

Nora made a little sound. "Because I came home."

He shook his head. "Because something had to give eventually. Maybe you were the catalyst. That's all."

She turned her back, as if the teakettle required watching. "I shouldn't have come."

"My dad would have run out of patience anyway." He waited for her to face him. "What's happening would have happened."

"Would it?" She wasn't crying, but her mouth trembled. She caught herself and pinched her lips in a firm line. "I feel like Typhoid Mary."

"In this case, if you triggered Mom's behavior I think it might be a good thing. She couldn't go on like she was. Dad couldn't, I know. I dreaded visiting them. Maybe now she'll deal with how she feels."

"How do you deal with hating someone so much you can taste it?" Nora challenged.

"You think about killing them," he admitted.

"What?" She gaped.

"She saw you at Molly's grave today. She admits she thought about hitting you with the car."

"Oh, my God," Nora whispered.

"Actually thinking something like that is what shook her up so much. She saw what she had become. That's a quote."

Nora made a broken sound. "I stood there at the cemetery thinking how quiet it was, how peaceful. And your mother was watching me."

"I'm afraid so."

She shivered. "I tried to feel the presence of…of ghosts. Maybe they were hiding."

"If Molly had been there, she'd have been at Mom saying, 'What in hell are you thinking?'"

The teakettle rumbled and burped. Nora didn't seem to notice. She gave a funny sort of laugh.

"She would, wouldn't she? I used to admire her for saying things to your parents that I never had the nerve to say to mine. She was always so sure of herself."

"Wrong sometimes," he said, "but sure of herself."

Nora didn't seem to hear him, either. "Your mother. Was she…all right, when you saw her?"

He straightened, unable to stay still. "I thought she'd killed herself."

The kettle whistled and Nora jerked but didn't turn. "Did she try?"

"No." He nodded toward the stove and said over the escalating squeal, "Why don't you pour that?"

While she did, he told her about searching through the silent house and finding his mother curled on his sister's bed. "I don't think she's sleeping much. She must have cried herself to sleep. It was hard to wake her."

Nora handed him the mug. "What did she say?"

"Let's sit down."

In the living room, he settled at one end of the couch and Nora at the other, her feet tucked under her. Rob told her what his mother had said. He hoped he was doing the right thing.

The truth, his father had suggested.

So be it.

"I never knew." Nora's gaze was unfocused, and he guessed she was rerunning childhood films, trying to see now what she hadn't seen then.

"None of us did."

At last her eyes focused on him and she gave a shattered sounding sigh. "What do we do now?"

"I don't know that, either," Rob admitted. "Most of it is up to Mom."

"Would it help if I moved away again? I will, you know."

"No!" He cleared his throat. "No. Don't go."

Her resolve didn't waver. "I can't stay if I'm tormenting your mother. I've hurt her too much already."

"You think it would help to let her sink back into hating you long-distance?" He was making excuses; he knew it. He didn't want to lose Nora again. "She can't heal until she forgives you and herself both."

Nora stared at him, silent for a long moment. At last she squeezed her eyes shut. In a voice so soft he barely heard her, she murmured, "How can you forgive something so terrible?"

Rob set down the mug hard, and coffee slopped onto the table. The crack of stoneware on wood brought Nora's eyes flying open.

"You understand what really happened," he said harshly, "and you say, I can't change it. I am not a bad person. I would if I could. But I can't. All I can do is my damnedest to live with charity and compassion and goodness from here on out."

"You don't have this on your conscience!" she choked.

"No. All I have to live with is having treated you like shit." He made a noise in his throat. "I have to live with the knowledge that I could have killed Molly just as easily."

She gazed at him in bafflement. "What?"

"I drove drunk. Hell, I was a teenager. Once, she made me stop the car, and she walked about a mile home in the middle of the night, with me creeping along beside her begging her to get in, not to tell Mom and Dad." Rob looked away from her. "I condemned you, because I could have hit that tree instead."

"Rob." Nora scooted a cushion closer to him so that she could lay a gentle hand on his arm. "I was blind, falling-down drunk. Just because you'd had a few drinks..."

He moved his shoulders, trying to release tension. "I was blind, falling-down drunk, too." He looked hard at her. "The point is, too many of us played with fate. You lost, that's all."

She flinched. "My best friend died because I did something unbelievably stupid. I can't take that lightly."

"I'm not asking you to. I'm asking you to forgive yourself."

Emotions made shadows in her eyes, shifting as if clouds raced over the moon. Her mouth quivered, firmed, trembled again. "How will that help now?" she whispered.

"There's been enough tragedy." He couldn't help himself. He reached out and cupped her face, let his fingers sink into the heavy satin of her hair, felt her shiver against his palm. "Molly wouldn't want her death to destroy everyone else, too. Live for her, Nora. Don't refuse to live because of her."

"I...I don't know what you're talking about." As if helpless to prevent herself, she leaned her face into his hand, looked at him with huge, dilated eyes. "I've gone on. I just..."

"Won't let yourself love me." He sounded hoarse. "Nora, I need you to love me."

She drew a great, shuddering breath. "Your mother..."

"Don't use her as an excuse." Rob swallowed, made himself say, "If you don't love me, if you can't, if it doesn't have anything to do with Molly, say so. Just know...I've been incomplete with you."

Tears shimmered in her glorious brown eyes, and she turned suddenly and threw herself at him, burying her face in his chest. Sobbing, she said things, of which he heard only, "I have never loved anyone the way I did you. I never can."

His heart clenched with the exquisite relief, then began beating again.

It was only later that he realized Nora had used the past tense: the way I *did* love you. Not, the way I *do*.

CHAPTER TWELVE

HAVING ROB'S ARMS CLOSE around her with bruising strength was like coming home had been. She was just as scared, just as unsure that she was doing the right thing. But, oh, she felt whole for the first time in a decade. She, too, had lived with a hollow place inside where he should have been. She, too, had been incomplete without him.

He held her while she cried. Nora wasn't sure that he didn't cry, too. Her storm was fierce but brief. She quieted, her head against his shoulder, her hand splayed over his heart.

What was it her mother had said? *He turned into just the man I hoped he would.* Something like that.

Mom was right, Nora thought in the still after the storm. Then, he was funny, smart, sexy, kind, and he'd chosen her. She hadn't been able to believe her luck. All those years of daydreaming about Molly's big brother, and he had kissed *her.*

But both of them had been so young. They could have changed in unanticipated ways. How could she know, when she was sixteen or eighteen, that the person she loved might not become money hungry or domineering or impatient? How could she know that he would find wisdom in grief? That his eyes would still be kind, his smile wicked if sadder, his loyalty unshakable? How could she know that he would still want to kiss *her?*

She had never, ever, dreamed that they would meet again as anything but distant strangers, with a painful gulf between them. Even once they had, once they'd become, perhaps, friends again, she had ignored her yearnings. Even his hints that he was interested didn't mean that he would ever again say to her, *Nora, I need you to love me. I've been incomplete without you.*

Now that he had, her heart soared with exultation even as it cramped with grief. He loved her. She was in his arms. Miracles happened.

This one had been born, though reason said it wouldn't. But she knew, with an ache beneath her breastbone, that it couldn't grow and thrive. She couldn't let it. Rob's mother wouldn't let it.

But she could have this much, couldn't she? Just tonight? This knowledge, that he needed her as much as she needed him?

His mother wouldn't have to know. And Nora's own conscience seemed willing. Maybe she didn't deserve eternal happiness, domestic bliss, children and a husband who kissed her every day when he came in the door and the two of them growing old together and holding their grandbabies. But flickers of joy to be remembered, those she could allow, or how could she live at all?

Her tears dried as he rubbed her back in soothing circles and murmured tender words in her ear.

At last she snuffled and gave a watery laugh. "I'm sorry. I don't know why I cried."

"With happiness?" His deep voice had a wry note, as if he knew better.

She lifted her head to smile up at him, her face no doubt blotchy and puffy and squinty eyed, but the expression in his eyes told her he saw only beauty. Or, perhaps, only *her.*

A miracle, someone seemed to whisper in reminder.

He smoothed hair back from her forehead and mopped tears with his thumbs. "Will you run away this time if I kiss you?"

Her heart bumped. Nora bit her lip and shook her head.

"Good," he murmured, and bent his head. But instead of capturing her mouth, he kissed her forehead, so softly, then her swollen eyelids, the tip of her nose, her cheek. She tilted her face up, feeling like a prisoner who had stepped out into the sunshine for the first time in a decade and reveled in the warmth and brilliance. By the time Rob's mouth reached hers, she was melting already. With a sigh, she parted her lips and accepted him.

They kissed slowly, deeply, as if every taste and touch and sigh was infinitely precious. They had forever and no need to hurry. Or they might never have a kiss like this again and so needed to remember every texture, every word.

He groaned at one point and lifted her so that she straddled his lap. Feeling him pressed against her, hard and thick, was incredibly erotic. The here and now played against memories, like double, triple exposed photographs. The two of them, laughing one night when they had first started dating, Rob pulling her onto his lap and tickling her, her sudden awareness of his erection, the way her breath caught and held and they looked at each other, the moment suspended, the mood altering as if a clap of thunder came before the clouds. Later, during the brief month in which they were lovers, she had ridden him once just like this, naked and feeling incredibly wanton, the expression on his face so intense and utterly absorbed in her and only her that she could not break eye contact while they made love, so that they both saw their disintegration in each other's eyes.

He must remember, too. Suddenly he reached under her shirt and filled his hands with her breasts. His tongue plunged into her mouth as if he were possessing instead of savoring. She *wanted* to be possessed. She whimpered and arched and pushed against him.

His hips rose and shoved hard, and he said gutturally, against her mouth, "Nora, I want you."

"Me, too." She blinked. "No, I mean, I want *you.*"

Rob's grin was pure male. "Yeah, I figured.

She loved the scratchy feel of his chin against her palm. "Mmm." Leaning forward, she kissed his jaw, then his throat, tasting his salt with her tongue.

He groaned again, his chest vibrating with the sound. "Damn it, Nora, I want you *now!* And we're sitting on your parents' living room couch."

The raw urgency in his voice made her consider. "They won't be home for a while. They never are."

He unsnapped her bra and gently squeezed. "I'd suggest you come back to my place, but guess what?"

Nora gave a choked laugh. "Your dad is there."

He was playing with her nipples. "Do you feel like a teenager again?"

"No," she gasped. "No."

"Me, either. But where the hell do we go?"

"Upstairs," Nora decided. "They won't be home. And if they do come...I'm twenty-eight years old. If I want to entertain a man, I will!"

"Attagirl," he murmured, a smile in his eyes right along with heat that kept her resolve from dipping. "If you're sure."

She smiled with sexual intent and rocked her hips, loving the way the humor vanished from Rob's face and left pure, blazing arousal.

"In that case—" he gripped her buttocks and stood in one powerful motion "—upstairs it is."

Nora squeaked and wrapped her arms and legs around him. "I can walk!"

His eyes seared her. "But it's more fun this way."

"Oh." Nora kissed his ear and nipped the lobe. "You're right. It *is* fun."

He stopped once on the stairs to kiss her, then carried her straight to her bedroom. Inside it, he kicked the door shut, muttered, "I wish you had a lock," and let her down on her twin bed.

Thank goodness, Nora thought fleetingly, she hadn't had a taste for either pastels and ruffles or rock stars and black lights when she was a teenager, because her room hadn't changed at all. Her mother had always believed she'd come home.

Since she had, all she'd done was set up her computer on her student desk, add a filing box for auction records, and hang her small wardrobe in the closet, pushing aside clothes she'd left behind twelve years ago.

Or perhaps it wouldn't have mattered if the bedspread had been pink and girly, or if Nirvana had stared moodily from the wall above. Rob never once looked away from her.

"You," he said roughly, "are even more beautiful than you were at eighteen."

She knew it wasn't true, and knew he wasn't lying. In his eyes, she had always been more beautiful than she really was. She had felt so drab ever since, because he wasn't there to look at her.

"I missed you," she whispered.

He knelt before her and began unbuttoning her shirt. Tenderly, carefully, he pushed it and her sweater off her shoulders. Nora lifted her arms from the sleeves and looked down as he unbuttoned her pants. The slide of the zipper was exquisite torment, his fingers sliding along the opening over the satin of her panties.

When he nudged, she lifted her hips and he pulled off her chinos, leaving her in bra, panties and—she blushed to notice—socks.

Rob lifted her foot and played with her toes. "You always did like socks."

"I still do." Her toes curled. "They're my...indulgence."

"Are they." His eyes were heavy lidded. Somehow he made the act of peeling her socks off, one by one, an act of foreplay.

Then he kissed the arch of her foot, nuzzled her ankle, nipped her calf, licked the back of her knee. By the time he reached her thigh, Nora found air only one shuddering breath at a time.

He kissed her through her panties, making her

hips buck helplessly. That's when she decided to fight back.

"Not fair," she declared, her voice scratchy. "I want a turn."

With that, she scooted to the edge of the bed and grabbed the hem of his shirt. Still watching her with that same, shattering intent, he lifted his arms and let her tug the shirt off.

She sighed with pleasure and had to pause to touch his chest, bulky with muscles that weren't there twelve years ago, when he was a callow twenty-one-year-old. Muscles rippled as she explored, and strain showed on his face. He made no move, though, as she reached for the button at his waistband.

For both their sakes, Nora took her sweet time inching the zipper down over the powerful bulge beneath. Shudders traveled through him as she trailed her knuckles and the tip of her thumb along his length.

When she reached the base, she kissed him, too, through his boxer shorts, then peeled off his slacks. Rob bent and tugged off shoes and socks, too.

"You should model underwear," Nora said, sitting back to admire the sight of him, lean hipped and broad shouldered, muscles sleek.

The look on his face made her laugh.

"I don't think so," he said.

"Well." She splayed her hands on his chest. "Maybe I should just take a picture for myself."

She couldn't really suggest it, couldn't say, *I won't have you, but I'd like a photo to remember you by.* After all, he thought...what did he think? she wondered. That this was the beginning of the two of them against the world?

Or was he, too, conscious of the poignancy of this night, the impossibility of a future together?

She didn't let herself worry, or brood. Right now, they were together. He was sliding his hands into her hair, lifting her face, smiling at her in a way that squeezed her heart.

Their lovemaking was wonderful: every touch right, every murmured word tender or erotic or funny, every fit—mouth to mouth, fingers entwined, bodies finally joining—perfect. It didn't bother her that he'd brought a condom, as if he had known this moment would come.

They made love with the urgency of their young selves even as they held back here, waited there, teased and took time to savor, because now they had more patience, more awareness—ironically—of the now, because of the aching gulf of years that had separated them.

Pleasure built until it filled Nora, until she could no longer hold it and had to cry out and let it go in a flood of exquisite sensation, joy and sorrow. Her release brought his, and she loved holding him as he groaned and his body jerked inside hers.

He rolled, taking her with him so that he didn't crush her with his weight. With her lying on him, listening to the hard, fast beat of his heart, he said, "I love you, Nora Woods."

The words, *I don't deserve it,* rose to her lips, but she swallowed them. She'd said them before, and what she deserved or didn't had nothing to do with how he felt. *If you love me,* she wanted to ask, *then why didn't you ever call me, ever write, ever come to find me?* But that didn't really matter anymore, either. She did understand the complexity of guilt and regret and pain that complicated every facet of their relationship.

She only lifted her head, smiled, and met his lips in a sweet, lingering kiss.

If he noticed she didn't say, *I love you, too,* he didn't comment.

COLLEEN DECIDED that dinner could be over—she'd sat in front of the bowl of tomato rice soup for half an hour, long enough to qualify as a mealtime, although she'd sipped only a few spoonfuls. Carrying the bowl into the kitchen, she dumped the remainder down the disposal. She washed the pan and bowl—ridiculous to use the dishwasher these days, when it would take her a week to fill it! With her few dishes dried and put away, she hung up the towel and looked around.

Housecleaning would fill her evening, but she had already done everything. Besides, she scarcely seemed to make an imprint on the house. It was nothing like the days when she had two children creating messes and dirty clothes and rings around the tub. If she didn't vacuum or sweep or scrub at all, nobody would notice for weeks or even months. Perhaps a little dust would settle on tabletops or lamp shades or blinds—dust seemed to float freely for no reason she'd ever discerned—but otherwise she not only didn't create dirt or disorder, she wasn't needed to remedy it.

She stood in the middle of the kitchen and realized the truth. She wasn't needed, period. Not by anybody.

The understanding had been creeping up on her. Like most women, she'd begun feeling superfluous when Rob left home and Molly got her driver's license. Still, Molly came home for dinner most days, and Allen expected dinner to be on the table and there was the house to clean and laundry to do. Colleen had been active in the Booster Club at the high school in those days. Even after Molly died, Colleen had still had Allen, at least.

But he'd been slipping away for some time. She had not *had* him for several years, in any meaningful sense, although she had been too absorbed in her unhappiness to notice. But at least he'd eaten here, and she'd done his laundry, and he'd left a scattering of dark bristle in the bathroom sink after he shaved in the morning and the wet towel tossed just anywhere after he showered.

How very sad, she thought, that she'd needed to pick up after someone to give her life validity.

Even sadder yet was seeing that she no longer had any reason whatsoever to get out of bed in the morning. Right this very minute, she couldn't think of a single thing to *do*. She had let friends drift away—no, she'd driven them away with her unrelenting grief, just as she'd driven her husband away and now her son, too. She wondered if any of those friends, women whose children had been the same ages, who had met at PTA meetings and soccer games and dance recitals, would be glad to hear from her if she called.

She looked toward the phone but didn't move. Flipping through the phone book, deciding who to call, dialing, thinking of how to start, seemed to require more commitment or initiative or energy than she possessed right now. Instead, she went to the living room and sat down, looking first as she always did toward the photos of Molly that cluttered the mantel and end table.

Tonight, they were just...photos. Not memories, not reproaches, not anyone or anything that needed her. Except, Colleen thought with a touch of black humor, to be dusted.

She also couldn't help noticing that the photos of Rob—of his graduations from high school and college, induction into the honor society, the first day of kindergarten—were few and lost in the forest of his sister's.

No wonder he had felt slighted! Colleen frowned into space, remembering a time—well, several times—when Allen had tried gently to point out the effect her absorption had on her son.

She, of course, had dismissed him. Even ridiculed him.

Tonight she was too weary even to cry, too... barren inside.

So many mistakes. And it was far, far too late to remedy them.

The doorbell rang, startling her. Who would come calling at this time of night?

Rob, she thought in relief. He regretted speaking so harshly this morning and had come to make amends. Even in her relief, it seemed to take an enormous effort to stand and go to the front door. She had so little energy these days. Perhaps she was coming down with a bug, she thought, as she unlocked the dead bolt and opened the door.

"Rob..." Colleen stopped. It was not Rob on her doorstep, but rather her husband. "Allen."

"May I come in?"

The scene struck her as surreal. He looked the same as always, in a checked flannel shirt, jeans and work boots. His eyes were as blue as ever, his shoulders broad and...and comforting, his large hands dangling at his sides as if he didn't know what to do with them. Yet he had rung the doorbell and was asking permission to step into the house they'd shared for thirty-five years.

"Yes." She stepped back. "Of course. I'm sorry."

Once in, he gently shut the door behind him. His glance around was almost...surreptitious. As if he wanted to be sure she hadn't thrown out his easy chair or repapered the front hall or drawn hex symbols on the walls.

"How are you?" he asked, about the time the silence had stretched into awkwardness.

"I'm fine. And you?"

"Doing all right." He moved his shoulders uneasily. "Looks like the lawn could use mowing."

Colleen wanted to protest that she intended to do it in the morning. The truth was, though, wrestling that huge, heavy machine around the yard had been more daunting than she'd expected. It kept dying, and she didn't know why. Just yanking that cord to start it over and over had been exhausting.

"I could hire a lawn service," she said. "You shouldn't have to do it when you're not living here."

"I don't mind. I can do it this evening. It'll be light for a few more hours."

"Oh. Well." Colleen knotted her hands in front of her. "This once, if you're sure..."

"I'm sure."

With a nod, he went back outside. Colleen closed the door behind him and stood in the living room to one side of the window, the space between the blinds allowing her a filtered view of the front yard. A moment later, Allen emerged from the detached garage pushing the mower.

He bent over it for a moment, which puzzled her. Of course, it started immediately for him, with a throaty roar as if it were eager to tackle the ankle-deep grass.

They went back and forth in front, with the mower falling silent only once when Allen emptied the bag into the compost bin behind the garage. He was nearly done when she wondered if he would leave without coming back in.

Perhaps—it would be only polite, even under the circumstances—yes, she'd offer him some lemonade or a cup of coffee. Colleen hurried into the kitchen and dumped a can of frozen lemonade into a pitcher, adding water and stirring with frantic speed. Pushing the pitcher into the overcrowded refrigerator—goodness, she hadn't noticed how full it was!—she hurried back to the front door.

Her heart bumped. The lawn lay smooth and green, and Allen and the mower were nowhere to be seen. But then she realized that of course his truck was still here, just parked on the street, and there he was, coming out of the garage and shutting the door behind him. She felt oddly light-headed with relief.

He saw her and came across the grass.

"It looks so much better," Colleen said, pretending to survey the yard. "Thank you."

Allen gave one of his laconic nods. "I'll do the backyard tomorrow night, if that's all right."

"Thank you." She nodded toward the front door. "Would you like a glass of lemonade or a cup of coffee?"

"Lemonade sounds good."

Disconcertingly, he followed her into the kitchen, giving it that same surreptitious once-over.

A little tartly, Colleen asked, "Did you think I'd remodel the minute your back was turned?"

He actually flushed. "No. The house just...feels different. Familiar but not, at the same time. I'm sorry. I know it's me."

She concentrated on pouring two glasses full. "It feels odd to me, too. It's so...quiet." Empty, but she didn't say that.

Out of the blue, her husband said, "I'm staying with Rob temporarily."

"I assumed you were." She handed him a glass. "Does it feel peculiar, staying with him instead of the other way around?"

"A little," he admitted. In concert, they headed for the living room. "I've got to be cramping his style. Young bachelor like him."

"Is he even dating?" she asked, afraid she knew the answer. Afraid she knew the woman her son was seeing.

"Dating?" He settled into his chair with a sigh, as

he so often had after a hard day of work. ''Not that I can see. Went to some kind of charity auction last week, but he's pretty busy with that new development out Stone Creek way, plus the addition to the vet clinic and the new law office.''

Colleen relaxed an infinitesimal amount. ''He's successful, isn't he?''

''Very. Good, too.'' Her husband gave an approving nod. ''I've built a few of his houses. Rob uses his head.''

''I wish...'' She stopped. *I wish I'd let him know I loved him as much as I did his sister. I wish it hadn't taken this long for me to wake up and see what a fine man he'd become. And perhaps most of all, I wish I hadn't told him what I did today, to bring that look of contempt into his eyes.*

Her husband was watching her, she realized. Colleen rearranged her expression to hide the bitterness of her reflections.

''He's worried about you,'' Allen said.

She stared at him, outrage filtering through her surprise. ''He *told* you what we talked about today?''

Allen nodded. ''Some of it.''

Along with her anger churned fear that Allen, too, would see how *small* she was. He might not love her anymore, he might have given up on her; but he didn't know—hadn't known—that she had been jealous of a five-year-old girl.

''What did he tell you?'' she demanded.

''That he searched through this house afraid he'd find you dead,'' her husband said bluntly.

''Dead?'' Her voice caught and cracked. ''Why would he think that?''

"Nora called and told him she'd seen you looking distraught. He came over here and hunted through the house. When he saw you curled up on Molly's bed, you scared him."

Allen didn't sound accusing, more matter-of-fact. That was one thing she'd always loved about him, his refusal to be judgmental.

"I was asleep. That's all. I have never said a word to suggest I might be suicidal!" Outrage was winning again. "Why would he think such a thing?"

Relentless as a glacier grinding boulders in its path, Allen continued, "He says you're not eating."

"Of course I'm eating! I had tomato rice soup for dinner."

"Did you?"

She let out a huff of fury. "What do you mean, *did* I?"

"You look like a faint breeze would blow you over." His exasperated gaze swept over her. "Look at you! You're lost inside your clothes."

Colleen stole a look down. The waistband of her slacks was certainly loose, but lost! She was faintly shocked to see that her body made only a tentative outline beneath the shirt and slacks, as if she had no more impact on her own clothes than she did on the house. Her lower arms, exposed by a three-quarter-sleeve shirt, looked like sticks fallen from a tree, waiting to crunch underfoot. Suddenly breathless, she patted her chest and found it sunken, only her collarbone a stark ridge.

"I...I may have lost a little weight..." Even her voice was faint as she battled a sense of disorientation. How could she not have noticed how thin she was getting?

"Rob says the refrigerator is crammed full, with things rotting toward the back." Allen's voice was still steady and even hard, as if he had no sympathy or wouldn't allow himself any. "As if you're buying groceries, never using them and not noticing that you haven't."

She tried to recover her spirit. "He snooped?"

The lines seemed to deepen on Allen's face. "He cares."

Colleen crumpled, then, physically and emotionally. "No," she whispered, as tears ran down her face. "Not anymore. He can't anymore. You should have seen the way he looked at me."

Allen moved, sitting on the couch and pulling her into his arms. "Don't be ridiculous! He loves you."

She shook her head frantically, bumping her nose against his chest. "He can't. Not after what I told him. How can he? I despise myself!"

Her husband made a harrumphing sort of sound. "Colleen, you're human. No more, no less. What have you ever done that was so bad?"

Colleen struggled out of his arms and cried in agony, "I killed Molly. It was my fault she died. And you've always known it, haven't you?"

CHAPTER THIRTEEN

HER HUSBAND JUST KEPT patting her back. "Damn it, woman," he said, sounding only mildly exasperated, "that makes no more sense than hating Nora Woods for twelve long years did!"

"Yes, it does!" she wailed. "If Molly had worn a seat belt…"

"She would have lived." For a moment his voice was grim. "Molly was drunk and therefore stupid, just like Nora was. How was this your fault?"

Colleen lifted a frail, shaking hand to wipe tears from her cheeks. She tried to straighten her spine. "You know how we were fighting all the time. I just couldn't let up. I think I was afraid of the fact that she was growing away from me. So I told myself her life would be ruined if she didn't quit being such a slob, didn't write thank-you letters when she was supposed to, didn't dish up too much food and then throw most of it away…"

Oh, she'd had a litany of complaints, and Molly had known her hot buttons. Other women talked about how difficult their daughters were at thirteen. Molly had stayed difficult. Not with her daddy. That had stung, because Molly got along so much better with Allen than she did with Colleen. But almost from the day she turned thirteen, she had fired the first salvo in a war to stand autonomous from her mother, to be her own person, and she never gave quarter.

Well, Colleen thought wretchedly, her daughter wasn't the only one who wouldn't bend an inch. As the adult, Colleen should have understood Molly's need to forge an identity and given her the freedom to do something so natural. Instead, she'd fought to keep her dependent, or at least to forge an identity of which *she* approved.

"One of the things you tried to drill into her was that seat belts save lives," Allen reminded her. "Why is that bad?"

Grief and guilt swamped her. "Because I knew she deliberately defied me! If I'd just let up, made it common sense instead of a battleground, she would have had it on that night."

"You can't know that," he argued, his forehead furrowed. "She was drunk. Too drunk for common sense."

"Nora wasn't," Colleen whispered. "She wore hers because..." Her throat nearly closed. "Because she didn't have to spit in her mother's face every day."

Although she was trying to hold herself away from Allen, Colleen felt the swell of his breath.

"Damn it, Colleen, those two girls may have been best friends, but they were as unlike as...as a daisy from a delphinium!" He gave her shoulders a shake. "Molly was born screaming. You know that. She'd have spent her life butting heads with anyone who happened to be her mother! Nora always liked to please. You remember what a timid little thing she was, when our Molly was a raucous tomboy? Doing what she was supposed to do was in Nora's nature! Molly..." Grief weighted his voice. "Molly just had to do everything her own way."

"But I could have...I should have..."

"Do you know how many 'could haves' and 'should haves' I've thought since that day?" His fingers bit into her shoulders, then eased as if he didn't like the feel of her bones. But his eyes stayed on her face. "What parent wouldn't think those things? But they don't help." His hands dropped from her, and his shoulders sagged. "They don't help," he repeated softly. "We can't change what happened, Colleen. Maybe we all made mistakes. You, me, Nora, those boys who had a party without their parents' permission, whatever adult bought the booze for the kids. But it's over. She's gone."

Gone. Colleen turned her head and looked at a photo on the end table of a sixteen-year-old Molly being inducted into the Honor Society. She was glowing with pride, and so pretty, her hair up in a French knot and her neck and shoulders slender above a stylish little black dress that made her look—almost—as if she were a sophomore in college instead of high school.

Colleen remembered her pride and pettiness. Molly was smart, but she'd had to work for her 3.8 grade point average, while Nora hadn't, not the same way, and she'd maintained a 4.0 through her four years. But all the same, Molly was up there, too, one of the kids everyone knew would be successful in life.

And she was prettier than Nora. Colleen remembered letting herself savor the knowledge, although she had eventually banished it as unworthy. Nora looked nice that night, too, just more coltish, less naturally stylish, her face a little too pale and earnest. But Colleen had hugged both the girls and taken pictures of them with their arms around each other.

Those photos were in the box in the basement.

"I would do anything..."

"I know you would." Allen gave a sad, twisted smile. "Funny, that's the exact same thing Nora said. But you can't change the past any more than she can. Somehow or other, you have to accept that."

Everything in Colleen recoiled from what he suggested, just as it had all these years. But for the first time, she was able to stand aside from the roiling fear of admitting that Molly truly was gone and see that he was right. Perhaps she never would forgive herself, perhaps she'd spend the next twenty or thirty years secretly saying *But I could have* or *I should have.*

But she could face her most shameful secret, the knowledge that she had always resented her daughter's best friend, and offer forgiveness.

Oh, not to herself. It wouldn't be that easy. But Nora was young enough to make something of her life still. Colleen saw that, if she could help Nora let go, it would be the only remaining gift she could give Molly, who had loved her so.

For you, she silently told her daughter's photo.

Turning back to her husband, Colleen held her head high. "Do you think Nora would be willing to see me?"

NORA SAT ON THE FLOOR next to her bed and knew she should be packing. She'd accomplished whatever it was she'd intended when she came home. She had freed herself, in a sense. Her gaze wouldn't shy away from this area on a map. She could think about home without flinching. She could even visit her parents in the future.

But now…now, she was only causing trouble. She was tearing Rob from his mother if not his father, and her very presence was a torment to Mrs. Sumner.

She was making *herself* unhappy. How had she let things go so far with Rob? Of course she'd missed him all these years, but not like she would miss him now. Then, she had been mourning a youthful love. Now, she would ache for the man who could have been the father of her children.

If only.

Nora let her head fall back against the mattress. "I love you," she whispered.

Damn.

She should at least go to work. At least have the courage to tell Dr. Bergstrom and Dr. Hughes in person why she was abandoning them without notice.

As she started to scramble up, her foot nudged the plastic file box full of copies of the letters she'd sent out and the lists of names and addresses of bed-and-breakfasts and restaurants and river rafters and airlines she had intended to write.

Oh, no! Nora thought in dismay. She had made a commitment! How could she walk away now?

She'd been an idiot to agree in the first place, her stern side chided. She had known from the beginning that White Horse would never be home again, that her stay was temporary. She never should have signed on to a project meant to change the character of a town where she didn't belong.

But I promised! she argued.

You've done plenty. You can hand over your research and let someone else do the rest.

What if they couldn't find someone else? What if she left them in the lurch and the auction was a flop and they didn't raise enough money and the youth center never got built? It could be important. By staying, she could make a difference.

Sure, she thought miserably, she could tear apart any number of lives.

No. She had to leave. Soon.

She had no idea where she would go. Her last job was in Tacoma, but it was nothing she wanted to return to, and the apartment had been crummy and even scary sometimes at night, when she'd had to come and go, or had heard unfamiliar footsteps on the stairs, pausing sometimes on her landing.

The very idea of job hunting made her stomach churn. She wouldn't have a reference from the vets here. They were bound to be angry, with good reason, at her quitting so soon and without notice. She'd saved a little bit living at home, but not as much as she should have.

But none of that was the point. She was the one who had caused everyone else's pain in the first place. If penance was to be paid, she was the one to pay it. She could not selfishly grab for happiness if by doing so she deepened Mrs. Sumner's grief.

Dressing quickly, Nora decided she could take the files and continue writing procurement letters, at least. Darn it, she was enjoying it! She wouldn't be here to attend the auction or see the plans or the foundation poured, but she would visit sometime, once boys in baggy pants were doing flips in the half-pipe and latchkey kids were playing Ping-Pong or basketball in the center.

Just to see what she had helped bring about.

Her parents had both already left for work, and Nora poured a bowl of cereal and ate it standing in the kitchen. She'd be five or ten minutes late, but nobody would mind. Not until she told them she was leaving and wouldn't be back.

Which wouldn't be nearly as hard as telling Rob.

He might understand, she thought hopefully but didn't believe herself. He'd think she was a coward, running away.

She wished she could believe he was right, that if only she summoned a little bit of courage, she could face her dragons and slay them.

But that was a fairy tale. The courageous course was setting out on her own again, letting Rob and his parents heal as they couldn't with her in White Horse, the ever-present thorn.

Nora slipped in the back door at work and thought she'd made it to her desk unnoticed when Joan turned from the counter.

"Oh, Nora, there you are! I took a phone message for you." She nodded toward the desk before making a face when the telephone rang. "It's been nonstop."

"Do you need help?" Nora mouthed, but Joan waved her a thanks-but-no-thanks.

Nora dropped her purse in a drawer before picking up the pink slip. When she saw the name of the caller, her heart did a somersault.

Molly's mother wanted to talk to *her?*

She sank into her chair and stared at the message

slip as if invisible writing might start to appear, offering a clue. When she heard the receptionist end the conversation behind her, Nora said, "Joan? Did Mrs. Sumner say why she was calling?"

"No, don't you know her?"

Nora kept forgetting that not everybody had lived in White Horse forever and knew her history.

"Yes," she said slowly, "she's Rob Sumner's mother. You know, the architect?"

Joan made an assenting noise and went to help someone whose dog apparently had worms that she wanted to describe in graphic detail.

Nora hesitated, then picked up the phone. The number she dialed was as familiar—more familiar—than her home number. How many thousands—millions—of times had she called Molly? They'd talked half-a-dozen times or more a day sometimes.

Her heart was drumming so hard now her chest hurt. One ring. Two. Mrs. Sumner wasn't home. Three rings. Nora was ashamed of her relief. Four. She'd let it ring one more time...

"Hello?"

She grabbed a shuddery breath and didn't know if she could speak.

Miraculously, she could. "Mrs. Sumner? This is Nora. I, um, got a message."

"Yes. I wonder if you would be willing to meet with me." She paused. "I thought perhaps a talk was long overdue."

"You want to see me?" Nora asked in disbelief.

"If..." The other woman's composure cracked. "If you're willing."

"Of course I am! I hoped..." Nora stopped. What

if Molly's mother wanted only to tell her in person how much she hated her?

Or...Nora felt a spark of wariness, remembering what Rob had told her. What if Mrs. Sumner really was crazy and had decided to kill her? Should she insist they meet in a public place?

"What did you have in mind?" she asked.

"Could you stop by after work some day this week?"

Nora hesitated only a minute. She'd leave a message telling her parents where she was going.

"Yes, of course. I can today, if you'll be home."

Hanging up a moment later, she saw with astonishment that her hand was perfectly steady. She felt as if it belonged to someone else.

She worked all morning but couldn't have said afterward what she'd done. She only hoped she hadn't made horrible mistakes.

At lunchtime, she made a rare escape to a fast-food joint, needing to get away. Wanting to be alone, she used the drive-through and ate in her car in the parking lot. If she'd gone in, it would be just her luck to run into Rachel with her kids or one of the women working on the auction. Somebody who'd want to talk, who would notice her distraction.

Another pink slip sat on her desk when she got back.

Rob Sumner, this one said, with a number that Nora knew was his cell phone. She felt a swell of longing that frightened her. Just to hear his voice, to have him tell her that last night had meant...not something. Everything.

He might know why his mother had called.

But what if he didn't? What if Mrs. Sumner wanted only to spill her bitter grief? Nora didn't want to get her in trouble with Rob.

Anyway, she didn't think she could bear hearing him say "I love you" again. No matter what his mother wanted to tell her, welcoming Nora into the family would not be part of it. She'd have to leave White Horse. Not today, but soon.

She put off talking to either of the vets, who were busy all day anyway. She'd wait and see—she didn't know what for, but she felt unsettled now.

It was almost five when Kathy Holmes called.

"Nora, I'm so excited I could hardly wait to let you know! I just checked our post office box, and guess what?" Kathy paused dramatically.

Despite everything, matching excitement stirred in Nora. "We got something?"

So far the box had been empty. She'd begun to wonder if her letters were just ending up wadded in wastebaskets. Auctions were such a popular way to raise money for causes, these places must get a zillion requests for donations.

"Three responses!" Paper shuffled and she said, "Let me put my glasses on. Let's see. A bed-and-breakfast in Port Angeles gave a night's stay for two. The Edgewater Hotel in Seattle is giving a night in a waterfront room valued at $350. Can you believe it? And there's a hot-air balloon ride."

"Really?"

"Yes!" Kathy crowed. "And this is just the beginning! I'd actually started to doubt we could do this. You must have written a fabulous letter."

"I don't know about fabulous..."

"The Port Angeles place is gorgeous," the other woman swept on. "Wait'll you see their brochure. I'm ready to go."

She chattered for bit, her hope contagious. Nora couldn't say *I may not be around to help.*

Hanging up the phone, she realized she'd chickened out all around today. She'd made Joan take a second message from Rob because she didn't have the guts to talk to him. She hadn't quit, and she hadn't told Kathy the truth.

Sitting in her car, Nora wished there was some way she could chicken out of going to see Mrs. Sumner, too. If she couldn't get out of it completely, she wished she'd asked that they meet someplace else.

Part of her had wanted to find Molly again, but another part of her dreaded actually succeeding. What if Molly was there, at home, trapped, knowing she'd never be able to grow up and leave, never accomplish all the grand plans they'd whispered to each other in the small hours of the night?

Frowning, Nora started her car. She was being ridiculous. She didn't believe in ghosts in any literal way. Molly wouldn't be there any more than she'd been at the cemetery. She was...gone. Alive only in the memories of the people who had loved her.

Nora gave her mother a quick call on the way.

"Do you want me to come with you?" Mom offered. "I can meet you there."

She really, really wanted to say yes. But she couldn't. "Wouldn't that make it even harder for her? Or keep her from being honest with me? No. Thanks, Mom. I feel as if this is something I owe to her. You know?"

Her mother was silent for a moment. "I understand. I just can't imagine..." She stopped. "Well, you'll find out soon enough what she wants."

"I'll tell you all about it when I get home," Nora promised, hoping she sounded assured instead of tremulous.

Just turning into the Sumners' driveway brought back memories. She'd come for Molly so many times. Until Molly got her license, Nora picked her up every morning for school. The gravel would crunch, and she would lean on the horn.

Molly was never quite ready. She'd come tearing out with her hair unbrushed or her makeup bag in her hand or gobbling a muffin. She would fling herself into the car with grumbled complaints about people who were early.

More vividly than the present, Nora saw a typical morning.

"On time," she corrected serenely.

"Early," Molly argued.

"On time."

"Early!" Molly glowered, then laughed in an abrupt shift of mood. "Okay. So I'd always be late if it wasn't for you." She casually grabbed the rear-view mirror and swiveled it, leaning forward so that she could peer into it as she applied mascara. "I swear, I'll never take a job that starts before nine in the morning. Ten is even better. Or evening. I am *not* meant to be up at seven."

Nora squeezed her eyes shut as though she could blank out a film running in front of her. The memory banished if only temporarily by her willing it to be gone, she got out of her car and resolutely marched up to the door. After ringing the doorbell, she couldn't help stealing a glance at the exact spot where she had sat on the porch railing the first time Rob kissed her. The lilacs were in bloom again, the deep purple blossoms just beginning to wither. The heavy scent always evoked the memory of her stunned joy and the pain of that last day, mingled so that she couldn't remember one without the other.

She turned back as the door opened, then gaped in shock when she saw the woman who had been her other mother.

Colleen Sumner was skeletal, her careful makeup looking almost grotesque, like too-bright blush on the cheeks of a corpse. She looked like...like people Nora had seen in magazine photos accompanying articles about AIDS or cancer. Was she dying? Why wouldn't Rob have said? The other day, at the cemetery, Nora had seen that she was distraught, but the glimpse was too brief to allow her to notice that she was also emaciated.

''Mrs. Sumner,'' Nora said inadequately. ''I... thank you for calling.''

''Please.'' Without smiling, Molly's mother stepped back. ''Come in.''

Once upon a time, Nora would have said ''Thanks!'' and raced up the stairs, her feet thumping and her hand sliding along the smooth mahogany banister. This time, she only nodded, took a breath and crossed the threshold back twelve years, fifteen years, twenty.

Everything was exactly the same, from the dark wood floor of the entry hall to the Oriental carpet runner on the stairs, muted by years and foot traffic to deep golds and browns and sage-green from what had probably once been brighter colors. The same oil painting in the style of the Italian Renaissance hung on the plaster wall, and the well-worn wing chair still sat beside the telephone stand beneath the staircase.

Nora's helpless gaze turned to the wide doorway into the dining room, where the same mahogany table and chairs kept company with a glass-front buffet that held the same delicate rose-patterned china, taken out only on special occasions. The cream-and-rose striped wallpaper was the same, faded perhaps, but her memories might be more brightly colored than reality.

Nora jerked her attention back to Molly's mom, who gestured for her to go ahead into the living room. With enormous relief, she spotted changes there: a new couch to replace one with a scratchy fabric, a different chair where Mr. Sumner had liked to sit, although this one, too, was massive and homely.

Photos still clustered around an old clock on the mantel. Others hung on the wall above the fireplace. Molly laughed and pouted and gazed solemnly at her, until Nora had to blink. It was like looking into a kaleidoscope, where a hundred fragments of one image made beautiful but dizzying patterns.

"Please, sit down," Mrs. Sumner said.

Nora stumbled on her way to the couch and sank onto the cushion at the end. She was afraid to look at the framed photos on the end table. How could Mrs. Sumner bear to live with Molly everywhere, displaying a hundred moods but never changing, never growing up?

Molly's mother sat stiffly in a wing chair that Nora thought had only been recovered rather than replaced.

After an awkward silence, during which they looked at each other, Mrs. Sumner clasped her hands on her lap and said, "I believe I haven't been fair to you."

"What do you mean?" Nora asked cautiously.

The older woman looked down at her hands. Her knuckles stood out in marble relief. "You were driving that night, but I know that some of the fault was mine. If Molly and I hadn't been having difficulties, she might not have gone to that party at all, or drank so much. She might at least have worn her seat belt." Filled with pain, her eyes met Nora's. "Molly made decisions as much as you did. That's really what I wanted to say. Rob, and my husband, seem to think you've never forgiven yourself. What happened was a tragedy, but it was an accident." With apparent difficulty, she added, "I...seem to have had trouble moving on. But you, Nora, are young. You have your life ahead of you. I'm asking, for Molly's sake, that you not waste it out of regret and grief."

Nora knew with one part of her mind that she was gaping, but she couldn't help herself. Rob had said his mother hated her! That she'd admitted to wanting to kill her daughter's murderer. How could she possibly have gone from feeling such bitter enmity to forgiveness in only a day or two? But why would she invite Nora over to lie?

Nora shook her head. "I don't understand. You must hate me for what happened! I *should* suffer! I should have died instead of her."

Mrs. Sumner's mouth twisted. "I can't deny that I've hurt badly enough to sometimes wish the same. I thank God that choice was never in my hands. I would have made it cruelly, and Molly would never have forgiven me.''

''But she would have been alive,'' Nora said passionately. ''She lit up a room when she came in. She had so much personality, I used to wonder why anybody even noticed me behind her. If I hadn't loved her so much, I would have been jealous.''

Mrs. Sumner's eyes filled with tears. ''But you did love her, didn't you?''

Nora squeezed her eyes shut. Her voice was ragged, husky, just above a whisper. ''When we were little, we pretended we were twins, reincarnated from some former life. We were convinced we could send feelings to each other, that we'd know if the other one was ever in trouble.'' She tasted the salt of tears. ''When she died, I did know. I felt as if...a light had gone out. As if I'd suddenly lost one of my senses. The world had gone dark, or silent, or...'' She shook her head hard. ''I don't know how else to explain. She was part of me, and it's my fault she's gone.''

''But not your fault alone. I've only just let myself understand. Some adult must have bought the alcohol you girls drank that night. Or a salesclerk knowingly sold it to kids way too young to buy it legally. Isn't it that person's fault? And what about the boy who had the party behind his parents' back? And—'' her voice broke ''—I've already admitted it was my fault she wasn't wearing a seat belt.''

This much, Nora could do for her best friend's mother.

Through her own deep emotion, she said, ''I truly don't think Molly didn't buckle up because she was somehow defying you. She never said anything like that to me. I'd make her wear it sometimes, when she was in my car, and she didn't once say, 'You sound like my mother,' or anything like that. She'd always just look surprised, like it hadn't even occurred to her to put it on.'' It was true, every word. Molly *had* resented her mother's nagging about some things, but that wasn't one of them. ''I think...'' Nora groped her way to explaining something she'd always understood. ''I think she felt lucky. Charmed. You know? She was always so sure of herself. You should be proud that you gave her that kind of confidence. I used to envy her, standing up to tell the teacher she'd marked an answer wrong, or marching down to the principal's office to protest some unfairness, or flirting with a new boy, or...'' Nora tried to smile. ''She never felt like she needed anyone—or anything—to protect her.''

Mrs. Sumner was silent for a long time. When she did speak, it was quietly, ''Then that was my fault, too.''

''But...I didn't mean...''

''I know you didn't.'' She wiped her cheeks, straightened her shoulders and got to her feet in a clear signal that Nora should go.

Nora hesitated, then rose, too. Formally she said, ''I'm sorry if I've caused you distress by coming home to stay with my parents. I thought it was time for me to face my own memories. I should have guessed that seeing me would hurt you.''

With dignity and a touch of coolness, Molly's mother said, ''I hoped never to see you again. But some good seems to have come of your return. Perhaps you helped me face my memories, as well.''

Inexplicably, Nora's eyes filled with tears again. "Could I go up to her room? Or…no. I suppose you're using it for…for something else now."

Whatever she'd expected, it wasn't the reaction she got.

Mrs. Sumner's face contorted briefly. Her voice was tremulous. With anger? Or grief?

"I'm going to ask you to go now. For Molly's sake, I can forgive you. That doesn't mean…" She seemed to fight to control herself. "That doesn't mean that seeing you here, in my house, isn't painful."

Nora couldn't speak, wouldn't have known what to say if she could have. She only nodded and hurried past Molly's mother to the front door.

Soft as a sigh, she heard—or felt—Molly grumbling.

Why haven't you come upstairs? I've been waiting forever. Mom isn't that *interesting.*

Blinded with tears, Nora could not, would not, turn to seek the source of the plaintive voice that could only be a remembered replay of some long-ago complaint, when Nora dawdled too long downstairs talking to Molly's mom. Molly wasn't really begging her to come up.

Molly was dead.

The knob turned. She bashed her shoulder on the door frame in her hurry to be outside, running away from this house.

She was forgiven.

And the mere sight of her would forever hurt the woman who had tucked her first lost tooth under her pillow and seen to it that eight quarters were magically in its place come morning, put her height measurements on the wall next to Molly's, as if she was part of the family, sewed the most glorious Halloween costume she'd ever had, because her own mother couldn't manage much but hems and buttons.

Away. She had to get away. Somewhere no one would look at her with grief or loathing, where no one would know she had done such a terrible thing.

Perhaps then she could take what forgiveness and acceptance and even love she had found here and use them to bind her wounds, so that someday she might look in the mirror and like the woman she saw.

CHAPTER FOURTEEN

WHY WOULDN'T SHE return his phone calls?

Rob wrenched off his tie and tossed it in the general direction of his dresser, not looking to see where it landed. His suit jacket went over the back of a chair, and he yanked so hard at the buttons on his white shirt he was lucky none tore off.

Nora was scaring the hell out of him. Wadding his shirt and dropping it in the hamper, he swore under his breath. Face it—he'd been scared since he had kissed her goodbye on her doorstep last night. She'd been so damn vague about when they'd see each other again, about how she felt. If she hadn't made love to him with such passion and commitment, he'd have been wondering if he wasn't just a one-night stand. But he'd *seen* the look on her face when he entered her, when she convulsed with pleasure and—awe, as if she'd found the promised land just as he had.

So why wasn't she calling him back?

There was the question of the day.

Rob grabbed a T-shirt at random from his drawer and pulled it over his head, then changed from slacks to jeans and a pair of worn canvas deck shoes.

Now what? Did he go over and batter on her door until she opened it? Yeah, what would happen is, her father would come to the door, brows lifted, and Rob would feel like a teenager again. If he was lucky, he'd be invited in and he and Nora could perch on the living room couch, side by side, and make conversation with her parents—unless they went into the next room to give the "young people" privacy.

But not enough privacy to rip off Nora's clothes and make passionate love to her.

Rob swore again, but out loud this time.

He was glad his own father wasn't home to see his bad mood. Dad had left a scribbled note on the refrigerator that said he was mowing the lawn. Mom's, Rob presumed. The note also said, "She's coming around. I'll tell you later."

Coming around? To what? Deciding she wouldn't run Nora down the next time she saw her crossing a street?

He should talk to his mother again, too, but first he needed to let everything she'd told him settle. Finding out she'd always resented Nora had made him doubt everything he'd believed about her and his family. It was like taking a photograph in to be restored, and being able to see details you hadn't before. Little things: an expression, the subtle isolation of one family member, the shabbiness of a house in the background, that made you realize you'd been kidding yourself before.

He'd believed his family was loving and complete. Mom and Molly bickered, sure, but there was nothing abnormal about that. As Dad muttered once, they were both bullheaded. Neither Rob nor his sister had ever had cause to doubt their parents' love—or that their parents loved each other.

Now…now he didn't know. What kind of undercurrents had he missed? Had Molly sensed Mom's dislike for Nora? Was that part of their problem? Did Dad and Mom have tensions that he just hadn't noticed?

Did he *want* to know, if it turned out most of what he remembered from his childhood was distorted, or even illusory?

Rob stalked downstairs, to his small kitchen, and stared moodily at the answering machine. No blinking light. He knew she hadn't called his cell phone. Did he try her again, hope he'd catch her unwarily answering the phone, or that she was unwillingly called to it by her mother?

Maybe it would ring any minute, and she'd say, in a tone that was low and intimate and husky, ''Hi. I'm sorry I didn't call. Something happened, but...I missed you.''

Feeling as if his chest was being crushed, Rob flattened his hands on the countertop and bent his head, taking slow, deep breaths.

Sure. That was going to happen.

An e-mail was likelier, one that said something like, *Just thought I'd let you know that I got this great job in L.A. and didn't have time to phone before I left. But...last night was fun.*

Wasn't that about all he deserved, after the way he'd acted twelve years ago?

He ate a solitary dinner consisting of a microwave turkey pot pie and a salad made from bagged lettuce. He could cook; it just wasn't worth the effort most of the time.

He tried to watch television while he ate, but nothing held his attention. He finally left on the Mariners, playing the Oakland A's, but if his father had walked in and asked the score, he couldn't have come up with it.

At eight Rob flipped off the game and decided to call again.

Her mother answered. "Oh, Rob! How are you?"

"Just fine. And you?"

"Oh, fine, fine. I assume you're wanting to talk to Nora. I'll get her. Rob..." She seemed to hesitate, then said, low and hurried, "I'm glad you called."

What the hell? He sat up in his chair and rested his elbows on his knees. Maybe something *had* happened today. But what? This was a quiet town.

Waiting, he ran through wild possibilities. She'd gotten fired. Somebody who came into the vet clinic had realized who she was and told her she didn't deserve to live. She'd fallen and broken a leg. Had a car accident.

God, he hoped she hadn't had a car accident.

"Hello? Rob?" Her voice was subdued.

"Nora." He swallowed the lump in his throat. "Are you okay?"

"Okay?" She sounded vague. "Yes, of course I am."

"You didn't call me back."

"I know I didn't. I'm sorry, Rob. The day has just been...overwhelming."

Trying to decide whether she genuinely felt contrite, he said, "Overwhelming?"

Her voice brightened. "One good thing. I got my first donations for the auction."

He relaxed a little as she told him about some bed-

and-breakfast, a hotel in Seattle and a hot-air balloon ride.

"Hey, seems like a good start."

"Now I have to get a dinner for two in Port Angeles to go with the stay. And maybe some activity? What do you *do* over on the peninsula besides drive up to Hurricane Ridge or go to the beach?"

They talked about it a little longer. Then he probed again. "Things tough at work?"

"Work?" Surprise laced her voice. "No, why?"

"You said your day was overwhelming," he reminded her patiently. Okay, not patiently—through gritted teeth was closer to the truth.

Nora was silent for a long moment. "Your mother called me."

His hand tightened. "What?"

"She asked me to come and see her."

He croaked something.

"I went after work." She was quiet again for a minute. "She told me to forgive myself. That Molly would want me to. She said she knows it was an accident. That it was her fault, too, because she thinks Molly might have worn a seat belt if they hadn't fought about it all the time. And she talked about the kids who put on the party, and the adult who must have bought the booze, and..." Her voice hitched. "It was...weird. After what you'd told me, I didn't know what to think."

She wasn't the only one. Rob was stunned. Baffled.

"Dad left a note." He was thinking out loud. "In it, he said, 'she's coming around.' I didn't know what the hell he was talking about. But maybe this is it."

"The thing is, I could tell she could hardly bear to look at me."

He wanted to kill his mother for hurting her. But he was ashamed of his hot surge of anger, because Mom hurt, too.

Hiding his temper, he asked, "What makes you say that?"

"She finally said so. She asked me to leave."

He swore viciously.

"No. It's…it's okay." A soft sound could have been a shaky breath or a suppressed sob. "I don't blame her."

"Let me talk to her."

"No!" she said with quick panic. "Please don't, Rob! Your mom…tried. She gave me more today than I had any right to hope for. But…" This pause was ominous. "I've been doing lots of thinking."

He felt sick. "About her? Or us?"

"Both. You're tied together. You're Molly's brother."

"I'm the man who loves you."

"Last night shouldn't have happened. I promised myself it wouldn't. I thought we could just be friends. But I think…I think I was lying to myself. Rob, last night we were both lying to ourselves *and* each other."

Fear made his voice harsh. "Maybe you were lying. I wasn't."

"Please…" Tears stopped her.

He hadn't been as terrified as this since the night his father had called and said, "Molly's been in a car accident." The pause had been excruciating; he hadn't wanted to hear what came next. "She's dead, Rob. They say she's dead."

"I want to see you, Nora. Your face, your expressions. I want to be able to touch you. We can't do this over the phone."

She kept talking as though she hadn't heard him. "I don't think I can stay in White Horse. It's not right. You didn't tell me how terrible your mother looks. Did I do that to her, Rob? Is that why you never told me?"

"She and Dad split up. I told you that."

"But it isn't a coincidence that they separated just after I came back to town, is it?" Knowing he couldn't deny it, she continued implacably, "I set lots of things in motion. Maybe some good. I don't know. But some that are bad, too."

On his feet because he couldn't stand to sit anymore, Rob said roughly, "Nora, promise me you won't go before we can see each other."

"Maybe it would be better if we didn't."

"No!" He ran his hand over his face. "No. After last night, you owe me." A lie, but he didn't give a damn. "Tonight. I can come over."

She was quiet for a long time, so long that he began to be afraid she'd hung up.

"Not tonight. I'm confused and upset and..." Only her breathing could be heard for a moment. "Tomorrow. We can talk tomorrow, if you insist."

They agreed on lunchtime. He'd pick her up at the vet clinic.

"I have to go to work. I haven't given notice yet, or quit. I feel like I should just...just *go,* but then I'd be leaving the doctors in the lurch. And I barely got them caught up. Maybe I can stay a week. Or two. If your mother knows I'm going..."

Every word, said more to herself than to him, added to his fear and desperation. Mentally she'd already gone. Would she even listen to him?

"Don't quit until we talk." He made his voice hard. "Promise me, Nora."

She was silent again before saying, "All right. A few hours won't make any difference."

A second later, she'd hung up. Rob disconnected and flung the phone onto the couch. He paced the living room, fighting the urge to kick something, to grab a piece of Inuit soapstone art and hurl it to the ground just to relieve an iota of his raging fear and frustration.

Tomorrow. He had to wait until tomorrow to talk to her, to beg her not to go, to convince her that she loved him. He didn't know if he'd survive until then.

And what if she said no? If she *didn't* love him, not enough?

Then, how would he survive?

COLLEEN HAD ALMOST no appetite—she couldn't remember the last time she'd felt anything but indifference or even distaste when she looked at food—but tonight she made herself eat. Under Allen's keen eye, how could she not?

When he'd arrived to mow, he had casually mentioned that he hadn't had a chance to grab a bite yet.

"If you don't mind something simple, I can put dinner together," she had offered, feeling...well, almost girlish. Excited at the idea of him staying, but not wanting him to guess that she was being anything but polite.

"Sounds good," he'd said, with a laconic nod.

She'd made her carrot and raisin salad that Allen loved and heated some homemade spaghetti sauce that she had frozen the last time she made it. Spaghetti was one of his favorite dinners. She had even found a loaf of sourdough bread in the freezer so that now a basket of garlic bread sat in the middle of the table.

They talked...oh, idly, but in a way they hadn't in a long time. She *wanted* to hear about his day; he seemed to want to hear about hers even though she'd done next to nothing.

"I went to the library," she told him. "Margaret Renfrew was telling me that they have an opening on the board of trustees. Muriel Parker has had to resign. She's had a stroke, you know."

"I heard."

"I thought about putting my name in." She felt timid about the very idea. Perhaps they wouldn't want her, if she'd acquired a reputation as "poor Molly's mother, who has gotten, well, a little odd since the tragedy." But she was also a little excited about it. Colleen thought she'd do a good job. She'd been a member of the Friends of the Library for years, even if she hadn't been active lately. Many of their money-raising events had been her idea in the first place. People might remember that.

Allen nodded approvingly. "I'm surprised they didn't ask you to join the board the last time they had an opening. You'll be great."

"They might not want me."

"Of course they will! They're not idiots."

Colleen flushed with pleasure. She'd forgotten how…bracing he was. Anything seemed possible when Allen believed it was.

"I will put my name in, then," she decided.

"Good for you." He gave her a warm smile, the kind she hadn't seen in a long time. Years, maybe. Sadly, she couldn't remember the last time he had smiled that way for her.

"More salad?" he asked.

She hadn't finished her small helping, which he knew quite well. "Oh, thank you, I'm not done." She took a small bite, chewed and swallowed, actually enjoying the flare of sweetness on her tongue. She followed the bite with another one.

"Have you talked to Nora yet?" Allen asked.

Colleen felt a tightening inside, and she set down her fork. "This afternoon."

Gaze watchful, he asked, "How did it feel to see her?"

Darned if tears weren't stinging the backs of her eyelids. She wished quite fiercely that she could tell him she had hugged Nora and understood how foolish she'd been.

But she couldn't lie.

"It…hurt," she admitted with a sigh. "I did tell her I knew it was an accident, and that she'd loved Molly."

"That's good," her husband said gently.

"I tried." Colleen knew that her attempt at a smile was pitiful and spoiled by the tears that were welling in her eyes. "But… She's changed, but she hasn't. She's still Nora. It hurt, having her sitting there, just like always. Do you remember how she'd pop into the kitchen sometimes, when she came, just to say hi before she raced upstairs?''

He nodded.

''There she was, with that vibrant hair and sad eyes and…so alive! Molly *should* have been upstairs! Getting impatient, calling down. She should be alive, too. Seeing Nora, having her right here in the house, brought back so many memories, I couldn't stand it.''

Creases deepened between his brows. ''Is it so bad, remembering?''

''This was different.'' She struggled to explain. ''I couldn't breathe. I wanted the quiet back! The emptiness. The acceptance.''

There. She'd said it. She didn't want Molly to seem too close. She didn't want to grieve again, not the way she had in the beginning. She had finally crawled out of the tunnel, and she was so afraid that memories awakened by Nora would make her fall in again, that she would have to go back to scrabbling in the darkness, light so far away it never touched her.

Still looking troubled, Allen said, ''You made a beginning. More than a beginning.''

''Yes. I suppose. But I know she could tell how I felt. I may have done more harm than good.''

''You know Rob loves her.''

Colleen flinched. ''I guessed. I was afraid. Are you sure? I thought you said he wasn't dating.''

''I don't know that they are, but I can tell.'' Allen shrugged. ''He's never gotten over her, Colleen. I think, without knowing it, he's been waiting.''

''Would he marry her, even knowing how I feel?''

Her husband met her eyes squarely. ''Wouldn't you be ashamed of him if he didn't?''

All her pleasure in the dinner fled. "So I may lose him, too."

He had that quiet voice that was still stern, the one he'd used when he was disappointed in one of the children. "You don't have to."

"You're asking me to let her take Molly's place. That's too much." Colleen shook her head. "No. I can't. I just can't."

"Would you resent any daughter-in-law?"

"No! This is different!"

He set down his fork and pushed his plate away. "The choices aren't easy, Colleen, but they're yours to make."

She hated the expression he was trying to hide.

"You haven't liked me very much in a long time, have you?"

"You've been a stranger these last years. Not the Colleen I fell in love with."

She sat very still, trying to hide the sting. "Didn't you change?"

"Of course I did." He sounded weary. "But you left me, Colleen. A long time ago."

She bit her lip until she tasted blood, acrid and salty. "I'm sorry. I don't know why I couldn't see my way out."

"Will you see a counselor now?"

"Yes. It would appear I need guidance." She lifted her chin. "There. You heard me say it. I've never liked admitting weakness, you know." She gave a twisted smile. "I suppose Molly and I were alike that way."

"And in plenty of other ways."

"I identified with her, didn't I? Too much, I suppose.'' Colleen looked down at her plate. ''I wish I'd seen...''

Allen laid his hand over hers. '''I could have.' 'I should have.' 'I wish.' You can spend your life saying them.''

''I do,'' she whispered.

His hand tightened on hers, the calluses rough against her skin. ''Tonight, I had dinner with the woman I love for the first time in years.''

This tiny spark of hope was the first she could remember feeling. ''You can't still love me.''

''Why not?'' When she didn't speak quickly enough, his expression went blank. ''Did we lose each other, Colleen? Did you quit loving me somewhere along the way?''

''No.'' She was clinging to his hand. ''Oh, no. I forgot how much I love you, just like I forgot how much I love Rob. I was the one who was lost.''

His eyes were so blue she couldn't look away.

''What if I come to counseling with you?''

''Sometimes, that would be nice.'' Colleen hesitated, then took her hand from his. ''I've realized, with the house so quiet, that I need more purpose. I've done nothing but be a wife and mother, and it's time for me to find out if I can be good at something else. Maybe just find something I care about. I haven't figured out what yet, but I know I want a job, or maybe even to go back to school. If I'm not too old.''

This smile was rakish and swept her back to the days of their courtship. ''We're never too old.''

''You don't mind? Or think I'm silly?''

He firmly took her hand again. ''I never would have minded if you'd wanted a job.''

"Oh." She felt light-headed.

"You have to start eating again."

Her protest was automatic. "Are you giving me orders?"

He gave her a look that she recognized.

"I did eat. You saw me."

"Not enough. But...it's another start." Allen let go of her hand. "I'd best get going. After I help you clean up."

Bereft, she straightened her back. She would not let him guess that even for a second she had believed he might stay. "Don't be ridiculous! You mowed the lawn, the least I can do is load the dishwasher."

"Thank you for dinner," he said gravely. "This has been a nice evening."

"Yes, it has." And yet her heart was breaking.

She walked him to the front door. There, he turned with his hand on the knob. "Maybe we've made a start, too."

Her pulse skipped a beat or two. "Have we?" she whispered.

"Yeah." Her husband bent his head. "I think we have," he said huskily, just before he kissed her.

A moment later, he was gone, and she was left in the silent house, her head spinning.

HER MOTHER WAS READING in bed. Downstairs, Nora had heard the television on. Baseball. Dad was a quiet fanatic. Last year, he'd gotten his hopes up that the Mariners would make the World Series, and then had them crushed in the end.

Nora rapped lightly on the open door. "Mom? Can I talk to you for a minute?"

''Well, of course you can!'' Her mother smiled and set her book down. She took off her reading glasses and patted the bed beside her. ''Come sit.''

Nora loved her parents' bedroom. She had memories of snuggling between them after nightmares or during storms and sometimes just because, feeling so safe. She liked that her mother hadn't remodeled, that the woodwork was still painted the color of clotted cream and the floral wallpaper was the same. The family quilt that used to cover the bed was now folded on the cedar chest at the foot. Mom had gone to a comforter and duvet cover.

''I just fluff in the morning,'' she'd confided when Nora first came home. ''No more bed making.''

Sitting on the bed, one foot tucked under her, Nora said, ''Do you remember when I used to get in bed with you?''

''Mmm,'' Mom murmured tranquilly. ''Molly, too, sometimes. The two of you would giggle and worm under the covers with cold feet and bony knees. Then you'd giggle triumphantly, as if you'd stormed the Bastille.''

Nora smiled, too. ''We never did that at her house. Once, during a really bad storm, I remember her mom coming and sitting with us until we fell asleep.''

''Well, you know, all the parenting books say you shouldn't let your kids in your bed.'' Mom wrinkled her nose to show what *she* thought of the advice. ''I liked having my wriggly worm in here.''

Nora concentrated on the soft, worn denim of her jeans. ''Mom, I think I'm going to have to leave again.''

''Why?''

When she looked up, her mother's eyes were grave.

Nora told her about visiting Mrs. Sumner. "She couldn't stand to look at me. If I stay, we'll see each other sometimes. That's not fair to her. Besides..." She hesitated.

Her mother finished for her. "There's Rob."

"Yeah." She tried to smile. "He says he loves me, Mom."

"And you? Do you love him?"

"Yes." Her eyes filled with tears. "I can't help it! I can't..."

Mom held out her arms and Nora lay in them, as though she were small again. Head pillowed on her mother's shoulder, Nora soaked her aqua satin nightgown with her tears. Pats and murmured "It'll be all right, you know it will," blurred past and present.

He'll never like me! I hate Molly! Mrs. Mitchell was so mean to me!

But this hurt, this problem, was insoluble. Her mother couldn't make it better, she could only comfort.

"I do love him," Nora wept. "I always have. But even if he asks, I can't. You know I can't."

Not until her shoulders quit shaking and she ran out of tears did her mother say firmly, "No, I don't know. Why can't you?"

Nora squeezed swollen eyes shut. "Why can't I what?" she mumbled.

"Love him. Marry him."

"He hasn't asked."

"But you think he will."

Pain swelled in her chest. "I swore I would never be completely happy, because I don't deserve to be."

''What?'' Mom snapped, pulling back to look sternly down at her. ''That's ridiculous!''

Nora sniffed. ''Is it?''

''Of course it is!'' She was angry. ''It was an accident. Besides...do you honestly think Molly would *want* you to be unhappy?''

Drained, Nora lay quiescent. ''No,'' she whispered. ''I forgot, I think, that she loved me as much as I loved her. I felt so guilty!''

''I know you did,'' Mom said softly.

''Being home, it seems as if Molly is all around me, in one way, and yet...not. I guess I understand better that she really is gone, not...oh, just off somewhere, mad and resentful because *she* didn't get to go to college or fall in love and get married or...'' She stopped. ''She's just...gone.''

Her mother kissed the top of her head and smoothed her hair from her face. ''If she heard you say, 'I'll never let myself be completely happy because I don't deserve to be,' can you imagine her expression?''

Despite her misery, Nora's mouth curved. ''She'd be so annoyed with me.''

''With her blond hair and blue eyes, she looked like a china doll, and people always thought she'd be sweet and gentle and saintly.'' Mom gave a comfortable laugh. ''Brisk, brusque Molly, always in a hurry, never one to worry about anyone's feelings.''

Nora lifted her head. ''You think she was insensitive?''

Mom smiled. ''Just unsentimental.''

Nora settled down again, wrapped in her mother's arms. ''I suppose she was.''

"She was so happy that you and Rob were going together. Do you remember the time you were snuggling—well, probably making out—on our front porch, and Molly suddenly popped out of the darkness and snapped a picture of you?"

Nora giggled. "Rob caught up with her halfway home and grabbed the camera. I almost wish now he hadn't taken the film out!"

"I don't think I want to know what it would have showed," her mother murmured.

Nora thought guiltily of last night and everything she and Rob had done right in the next room.

"Nothing that bad."

"Uh-huh."

"Really."

Mom's arms tightened in a quick, fierce hug. "You were good kids. I know you were."

Plaintively Nora asked the unanswerable. "Why couldn't we have stayed good kids, just for one more night?"

"Because you thought you were all grown up, not kids anymore. And how else could you show the world?"

Nora listened to her mother's heartbeat and let drowsiness steal over her. At last, she murmured, "I wanted to help, with this youth center."

"You *are* helping."

"I'll keep trying. I will."

"Of course you will." Mom stroked her hair. "Are you sure you have to go?"

Nora drew a shuddery breath and nodded.

"This time, will you let us help? So you truly make a start, and don't just struggle to pay the rent?"

The pride that had insisted she be independent, that she didn't *deserve* her parents' help, stayed silent. Nora nodded again.

Her mother murmured something that Nora thought was, "Thank God."

A start. For the first time, Nora mulled over ways her start could mean something.

She fell asleep, grieving and planning, in her parents' bed, and scarcely flickered her eyelids when her daddy carried her to her own bed and her mommy tucked her in.

CHAPTER FIFTEEN

COME MORNING, Colleen made mental to-do lists. Putting raisins on her cereal—she had enjoyed them in the salad last night—she mulled over the possibilities.

She would have to research psychologists, not an easy task. She knew a few people who had had their children in counseling for a time, but that had been years ago, and didn't psychologists specialize anyway? Her slight frown cleared. Perhaps she'd ask her doctor.

She wanted to talk to the librarian as well, before too many other people beat her to the post, so to speak. While she was at the library, she intended to pick up a community college schedule for fall quarter. She wasn't at all sure she wanted to go back to school, but she could explore the possibility. Perhaps she could take just one class, for fun. And to see whether she felt out of place among the young people.

But the call to her doctor and the visit to the library could wait. She already knew how she intended to spend her morning.

She'd thought last night about going into the basement to find the boxes of photos she'd put down there twelve years ago. But she wasn't fond of the basement even in daylight, when sunlight peered through the few small windows high on the concrete walls. The bare bulb was garishly bright yet failed to illuminate corners. It felt cold down there, and deathly silent like a catacomb. Spiderwebs multiplied between rough beams overhead and in high corners. Since she'd quit canning, more years ago than she cared to count, Colleen had rarely ventured down the steep wooden steps.

No, she hadn't been quite brave enough to unlock the basement door last night. She seemed so very *weak* lately, the stairs had frightened her. But after her bowl of corn bran cereal with raisins, she was sure she felt stronger already.

She put on heavy kitchen gloves in case there were spiders in the boxes, opened the basement door, flipped on the light and started down.

The furnace filled one corner, a monstrosity that Allen had miraculously kept running into its geriatric years. On the simple wooden shelves he'd built to store canned goods now sat only empty, dusty glass jars. Until Molly died, Colleen had still made jam most years, although she'd become quite fond of the freezer kind that she poured into plastic containers. Other kinds of canning—applesauce, green beans, plum butter—were simply too much trouble. She had let the yearly ordeal, inherited from her mother, go without a qualm.

One end of the basement held the detritus of years: furniture that might be—but never quite was—worth reupholstering or refinishing, years' worth of magazines, childrens' books and toys saved for grandchildren, and of course the miscellaneous unused but perfectly good plastic bowls and kitchen tools and flower vases that really should have gone in a garage sale.

Her interest stirred. Putting one on would give her something to do, and provide some extra money if it got too tight. She would keep the idea in mind.

She found the three boxes that held photographs with no problem. They were labeled in a dark, firm hand. Allen's. He must have done this after she'd carried them down. He had sealed the tops with tape, too. Then, he had still been understanding about her grief and her determination never to see Nora Woods's face again.

Gingerly Colleen dusted the boxes off and carried them one at a time up the steep stairs to the dining room. By the time she set down the third one, she found that she was quite tired. Perhaps she had been expecting too much of one bowl of cereal, even with a handful of raisins on top.

She went to the kitchen for a soda, which she rarely drank. A few swallows energized her enough to fetch scissors and slit the tape on the box that had clanked as she carried it—the one that held framed photos.

"Oh!" she murmured in dismay, separating the flaps and seeing that the glass had fractured on the top photograph. Had she thrown it in with hateful force?

It seemed symbolic: the shattered glass marring the golden innocence of the scene. The two girls, wearing bathing suits, stood at the river some long-ago summer, both skinny and grinning, their arms about each other's waists.

Colleen didn't remember *that* moment, but she remembered all the similar moments. How could she help it? Her family had never gone anywhere that Molly wasn't begging to take Nora.

"It's not fun without her!" she would declare mulishly. "I don't want to go if Nora can't."

Nora had done the same, her mother confessed. "We might as well give up! They're inseparable."

Colleen had shaken her head. "Twins, Molly says."

"Yes, so I hear. Reincarnated." The two mothers had laughed together, gently mocking their daughters and yet...perhaps half believing. How many friendships were so instant and so sturdy? Oh, the girls had fights, but they always made up before twenty-four hours had passed.

Colleen had been rather surprised that they had decided to go to different colleges. Molly probably wouldn't have gotten into Stanford, so maybe the decision had been Nora's alone. Molly never said. As she never told her mother so many things.

Once, she'd felt hurt, sharp and edged, when Molly rushed past her to the phone, or kept a sulky silence. Now, carefully lifting the photograph with the broken glass, Colleen felt only an ache, a kind of melancholy.

Setting that one aside to reframe, she reached for the next, and the next. Silver frames were tarnished, and the glass on others was broken as well. She hadn't been careful, wrapping each in tissue or padding them with old towels. She had looked at each with terrible grief, because she would never see Molly in *that* pose again, but also with corrosive anger, because Nora looked sunnily out at her from each picture.

They were in no particular order. Kindergartners grinned at her, showing big gaps in their teeth. An occasion honoring seniors, when both looked so solemn. Oh, and a dance recital with both in candy-cane-red-and-white tutus, posing in first position, their necks elongated, their hands arranged gracefully.

The two, perhaps fifteen, dressed for a big dance—Homecoming, she seemed to recall—both wearing slinky dresses, their hair up, their eyelids shimmering, looking absurdly young and extraordinarily pretty. Nora, too, Colleen realized, lingering over that one. Her fiery hair was set off by a deep bronze dress, and she was coltish but...classy. That was it. She'd never been as pretty as blond Molly, but she had an air. She could toss a scarf around her neck, tuck a black felt beret over her hair, and look chic.

Colleen remembered delighting in the way Nora's sense of style blossomed. She would never outshine Molly, of course, but Colleen hadn't appreciated the condescending murmurs of other mothers, who said, "How nice that Nora never seems to be jealous of Molly," or, "Oh, dear, she doesn't have much figure yet, does she?" *She* would flare back quite defensively. "Nora is simply a swan instead of a duckling. She'll be beautiful someday." Or, "Perhaps she'll be lucky enough to stay so slender and graceful." She had felt protective and even maternal, a memory she was glad to recover.

Eventually she moved on to the other boxes, to snapshots taken from albums or still in their paper envelopes, ones that were slightly blurry, or where one of the girls squinted or scrunched up her nose or turned her head. But they brought back such a parade of memories, she smiled through tears as she looked at them.

She saw the days, adding up to years, passing so much faster than she knew, too fast. Trips to the water slides, endless softball games, buying soccer uniforms with miniature shin guards. Shivering on sidelines or in bleachers, or roasting on hot summer days. Swim lessons, fifth-grade band, endless chauffeuring with giggling, screechy-voiced girls cramming the back seat. Homework and the dreaded science projects—Nora's always clever and Molly's always desperate and last-minute. Sleepovers, the first whispers about boys, the nights when the girls just had to bake, leaving cookie dough globbed on countertops and heaps of dirty bowls and utensils in the sink.

Days that were mundane, obligations that were sometimes annoying, small triumphs soon forgotten, tedium and laughter and friendships forged for that sport or activity alone.

If only, Colleen thought wistfully, she had known then to treasure every moment. But, no, because that would imply that she always knew tragedy waited around some corner. That would have stolen so much of the joy, the wondering what this small person would become, where her talents lay. Perhaps, Colleen had told herself when she signed the rental agreement for a flute, Molly would turn out to be musically gifted. It turned out that she had been chosen to play the flute because she could coax a sound from it, not because she had any ear whatsoever. But that was all right, because she was pitching for her softball team, and she might be the kind of athlete colleges recruited.

She and Nora both had tried everything—sports, drama, music, dance. Both had been good in all and brilliant in none. But that was okay, too, because they were maturing into loving, smart young women who were beginning to think about careers, with the knowledge that they wanted to be in love, to someday have children, to take their turns in the bleachers.

No, Colleen decided, gently setting aside a snapshot of Nora alone, blurring in an awkward cartwheel, she wouldn't have wanted to know that neither girl would have the future that had begun to seem possible. This way the memories and years were untainted, pure.

Her day passed. Lunchtime came and she made herself eat a sandwich. There were so many pictures, and she was grateful for each one. Oh, yes. *That* day she'd had a dreadful headache and the game had gone on for an eternity, but their eventual win had meant they made the playoffs. Muddy and celebrating, the team clustered around the coach cheering. And that day, right in front of five other girls, Molly had hugged Colleen and declared, "I love you, Mom," just because Colleen had been able and willing to drive them to the mall when no other parent would.

She sniffed, remembering that Nora had hugged her, too. Perhaps first. An odd ache built in her chest. Yes, it was first. "Thank you, Mom," she'd said, with that bright smile. And *then* Molly had hugged her, too.

It was funny—strange, not ha-ha funny. She was having trouble remembering the jealousy, the wish that Molly would suddenly dump Nora and find new friends who wouldn't be quite so close, so she'd have to confide in her mother instead. No, what the photos collectively brought back was her pride in her "second'' daughter, her pleasure because sometimes Nora talked to her or asked her advice as Molly didn't, her gratitude because Molly had such a good friend.

At length she took a handful of pictures upstairs with her and lay down for a nap, looking at them as drowsiness stole over her.

Nora, poking a skinny teenaged Rob with her sharp elbow. Rob in his soccer getup looking patient and resigned to the fact that his two cheerleaders were coming to his game. Molly, mouth sulky, with an anxious Nora at her side.

Molly had always had moods, Colleen remembered, as she slid toward sleep, and Nora had smoothed them as no one else could. Tempestuous Molly and serene Nora.

Twins. Reincarnated.

ROB CAME FOR NORA at noon. She lied and said she'd already eaten, so they walked to the riverfront park two blocks away. Not giving him the chance to start a more serious conversation, she told him on the way about a couple more auction acquisitions: tickets to the Seattle Symphony and a beautiful piece of art glass.

''I wrote the glassblower who made that bowl you bought for your mother. I found him on the Internet. He's agreed to donate a vase. He e-mailed a photo. You ought to see it, Rob! You'd swear the glass is on fire, flames licking up the sides. It's really extraordinary.''

''I might have to buy it, too.'' He was trying to sound humorous, or perhaps just normal, but not quite succeeding. ''Did you write other donors to that auction?''

''Practically all of them,'' Nora confessed. ''That woman was so nice, and then I felt like I was creeping into her garden at night and stealing her ripe tomatoes! But I figured, if they'd given once, at least that told me they were susceptible to appeals.''

Rob glanced at her. ''Don't worry. I'll bet she expected you to do exactly that.''

''Maybe.'' Doubtful, Nora fell silent. Guilt seemed to be her specialty, didn't it? She wished she had a fraction of Molly's blithe confidence.

At the park, a few teenagers hung out in the parking lot and leaned against the walls of the rest room. Mothers pushed young children on swings in the playground, while another gently propelled the merry-go-round in slow circles, delighting a three- or four-year-old boy whose eyes were saucer wide and his laughter nonstop. Watching, Nora couldn't help smiling despite her dark mood.

''Ever thought about having kids?'' Rob asked, killing her smile.

Lying, she shook her head. ''Not really. It didn't seem in the cards for me.''

Beyond the playground, grass stretched to the bluff overlooking the river. Without discussion, they walked toward it, circling a group of kids playing an impromptu soccer game.

''Didn't seem in the cards?'' he asked. ''Or doesn't?''

''Either,'' she said sadly.

Rob was quiet until they paused on the edge of the ten-foot bluff above the quiet, summer-low river.

Sand had been imported to soften the gravel beach. Even on this weekday, the beach was busy, with people sunbathing, older kids swimming, parents yelling at them not to go too far and watching the younger ones splashing in pools, teenagers flirting and preening, and down a ways a fisherman stood out in the current in thigh-high rubber boots, casting.

With a sad but somehow sweet ache, Nora said, "Molly and I and our friends used to come here all the time. It was our summer hangout."

"I remember." He glanced around. "Let's sit, shall we?"

Nora let him guide her to a wooden bench set in gravel. They sat side by side, both looking out over the river to the alder and cedar foresting the other side. Shouts and laughs and the sound of splashing drifted up.

"I love you, Nora," Rob said quietly. "I can't lose you again."

It seemed all she did these days was cry. Nora blinked back the sting of tears. "I shouldn't have come home."

"Yeah." His voice was heavy. "You should. For your sake, and for Mom's. She needed…nudging. And you. You needed to recover your memories."

"Maybe." Nora swiped at her eyes. "But I've made you unhappy."

He looked at her and waited until she turned her head. "No. You've made me very happy. I've found what was missing from my life, and you've given me a chance to redeem myself."

Her chest felt unbearably tight. "What do you mean?" she all but whispered.

He slid off the bench onto one knee and took her hand. His expression was tender, the look in his eyes exactly what every woman dreamed of seeing on the face of the man she loved. "Nora Woods, will you marry me?"

She tried to pull her hand away. "Don't do this, Rob! Please don't do this."

"Why?" he asked intensely. "Why, Nora?"

"You know why!" she cried.

"No." Pain shadowed his face. "Do you not love me enough?"

He deserved honesty, even if a lie might be kinder.

"Yes. Yes, I love you." She studied his face, angular cheekbones, long upper lip, the slash of dark brows and light eyes and wondered if it would ever fade in her memory. "But that's not enough. You do know that, Rob."

"No." His hand tightened on hers. "I don't. I know that it should have been enough twelve years ago. I failed you then, Nora. I won't again." His voice was low, shaking, raw. "I swear I won't."

Her tears spilled over this time. "Your mother..."

"I chose my parents last time. I never came after you because I didn't want to hurt them. But I don't seem able to love anyone else, Nora. Only you. I made a mistake, not finding you."

"No! No, you didn't. I killed Molly..."

He wasn't listening. Wouldn't listen. "Now I choose you, Nora Woods. Please be my wife."

Her tears fell onto their clasped hands. "Rob, I can't. I will always remember that you asked me, that you loved me enough, but...I can't."

His face twisted with anguish. "Why?"

She sounded like a distraught child, trying to explain what was wrong enough to have her sobbing. ''I can't let you make a sacrifice so huge. Your family... No. I took...took so much from you. From your mother. I hurt you all. Think how this would hurt! If she cut you off, if she wouldn't see her grandchildren?'' His face was blurred, but she thought the tears dripping on their hands weren't hers alone. ''What if she does? She can't look at me! Imagine how she'd feel if her granddaughter has my eyes, my mouth, my hair? It would be...torment.''

''We'll move away. Anywhere! Back East. How my parents feel won't matter.''

''It will always matter,'' she whispered. ''Thank you, Rob. Thank you for...for everything. But, I can't.''

''God damn it, Nora!'' He rose to his feet and towered above her. ''Don't do this.''

A sob convulsed her. ''I have to. Can't you see?'' she almost screamed. ''What else can I do?''

''Is this what Molly would want?'' he asked cruelly. ''For us all to live bitter and unhappy, because one night you had a car accident?''

Nora buried her face in her hands and cried.

''You're so determined to punish yourself, you're punishing me, too, aren't you?''

She shook her head wildly.

''Oh, yeah. That's exactly what you're doing. I've seen it coming. You won't let yourself be happy. Well, you know what, Nora?'' he ground out. ''I resent having to be a martyr, too.''

''No.'' She lifted her head to look at him through wet, swollen eyes. ''You don't understand.''

"I understand, all right." He had transmuted pain into fury. "You can live with yourself only so long as you can say, 'See, I'm suffering, too.' Has it ever once struck you how cowardly that is? I thought when you came home it was because you'd found the courage to live. If you did, apparently you lost it."

"Please...leave," she whispered, closing her eyes although she left her face tilted upward. "Just...go."

He swore, and she heard the agony beneath the rage. Then, "I chose you, Nora," and the sound of footsteps in the gravel.

Then she crumpled, drawing her knees to her chest, and sobbed from a heart finally broken.

CHAPTER SIXTEEN

SURPRISED WHEN the doorbell rang the next morning, Colleen hurried to answer. She had already gone out and bought new picture frames and was putting photos in them. She still had the rag in her hand she was using with cream to remove the tarnish on the silver frames.

She opened the door to find Fran Woods on the porch.

"Why, Fran!" she exclaimed, flummoxed. They hadn't spoken a word in twelve years, even when they passed each other with grocery carts at Thrifty.

Hands on her hips, the other woman looked at her with open dislike. "Do you have any idea what you've done to our children?"

"Our children?" Colleen echoed dumbly. "What do you mean?"

Fran's warm brown eyes narrowed to slits. "I'm giving you the credit of assuming you *don't* understand what your grief and hatred has done, even to your own son. So I'm here to tell you."

"I..." Her chest felt tight, as if she couldn't draw a breath. How very bizarre, to have someone from the past arrive on her doorstep to launch a verbal attack on her.

"Shall we talk on the porch?" Nora's mother

asked, her tone sharp. "Or would you prefer privacy?"

"I..." Colleen firmed her mouth. "Come in."

Fran marched past her directly into the living room. She swept the gallery of photos with a comprehensive eye, then faced Colleen with an expression of pity.

"I miss her, too."

Once, Colleen would have broken down. Now she only nodded and said, "Please. Have a seat."

Both chose seats, then eyed each other in wary if not hostile silence.

Fran Woods had aged well, Colleen saw. Gray streaked her elegantly cut russet hair. Faint wrinkles at the corners of her eyes and mouth only lent wisdom and dignity to a face with strong bones. Khaki shorts showed legs that remained lean and strong.

Feeling even more feeble, Colleen said finally, "You know that Nora came by to talk the day before yesterday."

"Yes. She said you forgave her, but could barely stand to look at her."

Deeply ashamed, Colleen bowed her head. "I regret that I let her see how I felt."

"Do you know that she intends to leave town?"

Emotions stirred in Colleen's chest, an uncomfortable mix that included surprise, the expected relief and something that rather startled her: regret, for lack of a better word. "Oh, no!" she heard herself cry.

"Rob asked her to marry him. She turned him down. I heard her crying herself to sleep last night."

"I...didn't know."

"I have let you hate Nora and me both all these

years without protest. But I cannot let you hurt her like this.''

''She turned him down because of me?''

''She says she stole so much from you, she can't take your son, too. He apparently offered to move away, but she felt that wouldn't be fair. She wants you to have grandchildren you can love without—'' Fran hesitated briefly ''—mixed feelings.''

Oh, dear. How *would* she feel, if her grandchildren also looked like Nora, who had killed Molly with her carelessness?

She saw a toddler with Nora's auburn hair and Rob's blue eyes running to her, face alight with glee. Would she ever...*recoil,* because this child of her blood also carried Nora's?

How horrible that would be!

''Rob didn't tell me he was asking her to marry him.'' Colleen closed her eyes for a minute, riding a surge of fierce pain. ''I'm not certain we're speaking at the moment.''

''Because of Nora?''

Not one to bare emotions with casual friends—never mind a woman she hadn't talked to in twelve years!—Colleen found herself saying, ''In a way. Because I told him things he didn't want to hear.'' She took a deep breath. ''I admitted that I sometimes felt jealous of Nora even when she and Molly were children. Molly and I often clashed, you know. I thought, without the closeness between the two girls, she might have turned more to me.''

She braced herself for shock or pity or even repugnance on the face of this woman she once had called a friend.

Instead, Fran only nodded. "I felt that way sometimes, too. Nora and I got along well, but we weren't friends the way I would have liked us to be. She did things with me only if Molly wasn't available."

Dumbfounded, Colleen asked, "You...felt the same?"

Fran examined her hands. "I was ashamed of myself sometimes. Molly was a nice little girl, and I wished she and Nora would have a fight so Nora would tell *me* her troubles. How petty! But perhaps natural. Or so I've convinced myself."

Tears sprang into Colleen's eyes. "Oh, no!" She leaped to her feet. "Here I go again. I've turned into a watering pot. Let me get something to blow my nose." She fled the room, returning only when she'd regained control.

Fran was holding a framed photo of Molly, one from graduation. When she heard Colleen's footstep, she hurriedly set it back on the end table and looked up, her eyes misty.

"I did love her, you know."

Colleen sniffed and nodded. "I know. I loved Nora." *Perhaps,* she thought in wonder, *I* do *love Nora still.*

Was it possible?

Still with tears in her eyes, Fran said softly, "When I look at Nora, I so often see Molly. The way she'll turn her head or tilt it to one side, a certain phrasing, a gesture..." Fran shook her head, as if to shed an inner vision. "I know they're borrowed from Molly, just as Molly sometimes did or said things that were classic Nora. They looked so little alike, and yet sometimes I almost thought they could be..."

When she hesitated, Colleen finished, ‘‘Twins, reincarnated.’’

‘‘Yes. Oh, that sounds silly, but you know what I mean.’’

‘‘They rubbed off on each other.’’

‘‘Yes.’’ Fran was silent for a moment. ‘‘This is what I came to say. The closest you'll ever be to Molly again is Nora. She did something horribly stupid with tragic consequences, but she and Molly were dearer to each other than if they had been sisters. Rob and Nora love each other. Nora has never looked seriously at another boy, or man, in her life.’’

Damn. Tears stung Colleen's eyes again. ‘‘Rob has dated, but…’’

Fran nodded and stood. ‘‘Think, Colleen, about what you'll lose if you hang on to your anger. Think about what Rob and Nora will lose.’’

Colleen rose to her feet as well, but shakily. Fran actually took a step forward as if to grip her arm, but she shook her head. ‘‘I'm fine. Just…wobbly, for a minute. Before you go, I want to show you something.’’

Nora's mother nodded and followed her to the dining room. There, she breathed, ‘‘Ohh,’’ and picked up the photo of the two girls at the beach. ‘‘I've never seen this one,’’ she whispered.

‘‘The glass was broken.’’

Eyes swimming with tears, Fran looked at her in puzzlement. ‘‘I don't understand.’’

‘‘I packed away every single picture that had Nora in it. Yesterday, I went down to the basement and got them.’’ She gestured at the empty frames and brown paper grocery bag full of glass shards. "Some needed repair or new frames. I plan to display them again."

"But you asked her to leave."

Colleen struggled to explain. "Seeing her again was...crushing. I felt so much," she said simply.

"You don't still hate her?"

At random she picked up a photograph, one of the girls dressed in nineteenth-century costumes for the school production of *Hello, Dolly!* Nora's glorious hair was piled atop her hair, and she had padded her brassiere to try to create cleavage. With difficulty, Colleen said, "I'm not sure I ever did. I had to *believe* I hated her, because otherwise I might have to admit Molly's death was my fault, too."

"Your fault?"

They talked, then, the two women, for hours. Fran pressed tissues into Colleen's hand when she cried, and she did the same when Fran wept. Colleen wondered how different all their lives would have been if, twelve years ago when Fran and Bob had rung the doorbell, she had cried and let Fran comfort her. If they had grieved together, instead of separately.

At the very least, she would have had a friend all these years.

But perhaps, perhaps she did again. Just as she might have a second chance at her marriage. If only she could truly, in her heart, forgive.

"NORA," JOAN CALLED. "There's someone here to see you."

Please, please, not Rob, Nora prayed. She couldn't go through that again. *Anyone but Rob,* she begged.

She saved her document on the computer and

stood, forcing a pleasant smile to her lips before she went out to the waiting room.

Colleen Sumner, frail but determined, stood at the counter. "Hello, Nora," she said. "I wonder if I might have a few minutes of your time."

Heart drumming, Nora said, "I suppose I could take a break."

"Can we talk outside?"

"Yes. There's a bench out there, for the people who smoke or..." She stopped, aware she was babbling. "We can sit there."

Mrs. Sumner held her shoulders square and her head high. "Very well."

"Joan, I'm..."

"Taking a break. I heard." Joan smiled at them. "It's slow right now. Don't hurry."

Nora hardly knew what to feel as she walked with Molly's mother out the front door. Befuddled. Perhaps a little angry. Couldn't anybody just let her make her grand sacrifice and vanish from their lives without trying to trip her up?

And, somewhere deep, deep inside, a tiny bit of hope swelled for no good reason.

"Have you given notice here?" Mrs. Sumner asked, once they were outside.

Rob must have talked to her. "Yesterday," Nora said. "They were...understanding."

They had walked halfway along the building before Mrs. Sumner asked, "Have you made plans?"

Why did she want to know? Why did she care?

"Only in a vague way. Has Rob told you about the youth center and the auction to raise money to build it?"

"I didn't know you were involved in the effort."

"Well, I got recruited, and I'm finding that I really love working on it. I feel as if I'm good at it, and I might make a difference." How odd, she thought, that Molly's mother was the first person she was telling about her dreams and plans, so new and delicate she had been afraid to voice them for fear they'd tear into pretty but ineffectual shreds. "I'm looking into classes at the University of Washington and Seattle U. Things like grant-writing and fund-raising. I might aim to be an auction consultant—the person nonprofits hire to put on an auction for them. I could make a living and help, too. I could volunteer my services for causes that seem…important enough. Or I could work for somebody like United Way, or…" She stopped. "Well, there are options, but I thought I'd start with classes. Perhaps even a master's degree. My parents said they'd help."

"I'm considering going back to school myself," Colleen said, surprising her. "I've realized just lately that my life has been too centered around taking care of other people. It's no wonder Molly's death left such a terrible hole in my life. I suspect I would have been depressed when she went away to college, too."

They sat on the small bench, facing the parking lot and street. "Didn't you go to college?" Nora asked cautiously.

"Yes, but so long ago. I was an English major, which isn't much use now. Unlike you, I don't know what I want to do, but I need to find something that *I* believe is important."

Bemused, Nora nodded. What were they really talking about?

Mrs. Sumner seemed to gather herself. She took a deep breath, clasped her hands together and met Nora's eyes. "I believe I owe you yet another apology."

Horrified, Nora said, "No! Oh, no. You were…you were kind the other day. Kinder than I deserve. I shouldn't have asked…" Belatedly, she realized that Molly's mother might not be intending to apologize for asking her to leave the house; she might think she was totally justified. This might be something, oh, trivial, or completely surprising to Nora.

Instead of explaining, Mrs. Sumner said, "Your mother tells me that my son has asked you to marry him."

Nora stiffened. "My *mother* told you? But…"

"You thought we weren't speaking." Rob's mother smiled, if ruefully. "She came to see me. To give me a piece of her mind, actually."

She was undoubtedly gaping. *"Mom?"*

Mrs. Sumner's face briefly contorted. "I'm more grateful than I can say that she did. I think people have tiptoed around me too much all these years. I regret shutting Fran out of my life."

Stunned, Nora didn't know what to say. Her mother had gone to see Colleen Sumner. Nora had never imagined she would do anything like that.

What had Mom *said?*

"I'm sorry. I never dreamed she'd do that. I didn't intend…"

"No, I'm sure you didn't." Mrs. Sumner hesitated. "I want you to understand. The other day, when you were sitting there, you brought back Molly so vividly. You girls were like…two sides of a coin. How could one side be in front of me if I couldn't just flip it over? I felt as if she was so near..." Her hands knotted. "I have finally, I think, begun to accept that she's gone. You endangered that acceptance, you see."

Nora nodded slowly. "I didn't intend that, either."

A thin, cold hand covered hers. "Of course you didn't."

Feeling icy inside, Nora said steadily, "I hope that my leaving town helps you regain that acceptance. It's...been hard for me to find, too."

Mrs. Sumner gazed at the parking lot, her tone musing. "Perhaps, in one way, it might be easier. But I also realized the other day, after you left, that I hadn't felt so close to Molly since the day she died. You girls had such a bond. Having you there brought back the good times, too."

"I'm...glad," Nora whispered. The ice was melting, creaking as the frozen wall prepared to crack and let emotions flood forth.

"I wonder if you would consider staying in White Horse." Voice tremulous, Rob's mother turned her head and tried to smile at Nora. "I hope you'll consider marrying my son. That is, if I'm the reason you refused him, as I suspect."

Tears filled Nora's eyes and ran unheeded down her cheeks. "I don't want to make you any unhappier than I already have. Please don't do this if...if you'll be wretched seeing me. What if we have children? How will you feel then?"

Colleen gripped both her hands. Her cheeks were wet, too. "Just like any other grandmother. More! Life has been so bleak, so empty, these past years.

Having little ones in the house again would be glorious.''

Nora drew a shuddering breath. ''If...if Rob will have me, and we ever have a little girl, would you mind if we named her Molly?''

Crying, her future mother-in-law said, ''I would love it if you named her Molly.''

A huge sob engulfed Nora. ''I would give anything...''

''I know.'' An arm came around her, drew her into a comforting embrace. ''I know.''

AS TIRED AS IF HE HADN'T SLEPT in a week, Rob turned out the lights in his office, grabbed his suit jacket and left, locking up as he went. Everyone else was gone. He hadn't accomplished much by staying late, but pretending to work was better than slumping in his easy chair at home, staring at the wall and considering another beer, and another, and another.

Out in the parking lot, he vaguely noticed that his car wasn't alone. The lot was posted Architectural Firm Parking Only, but right now he didn't give a flying you-know-what. Except, as he got closer, he saw that the car was small and battered.

His heart began to drum.

It couldn't be Nora's. Why would she have left her car in his parking lot? He was seeing things, just as he'd seen her so many times over the years, walking toward him on a crowded sidewalk or bending over to smile at a toddler in the sandbox at the park. Illusions, all.

The driver's side door opened, and Nora got out.

He stopped as if he'd almost stepped into space

from the twenty-fifth floor of a skyscraper he'd designed, because a wall he had expected to be there wasn't.

"Nora."

"I didn't think you'd ever come out."

"You could have come in."

"The front door was locked." She wrapped her arms around herself as if she was cold even though the evening was still warm and light. "And I didn't know who else was still here."

"There was nobody. Only me."

"Oh."

Even breathing hurt. He finally took another step and didn't plummet. "What is it, Nora?"

She looked at him with incredible, aching vulnerability in her brown eyes. "I do love you."

His voice scraped his throat. "I thought love wasn't enough."

"I think...maybe it is." She had the oddest expression. "Not in the way I expected, or meant, or... But who loves us more than our parents?"

He took another step closer, his hands curled into fists at his side to keep them from dragging her into his arms. "What in hell are you talking about?"

Her mouth trembled, and her eyes had a sheen. "My mother talked to your mother."

God. He hadn't known hope could feel like this, pressure squeezing his heart until pain and something incredible blossomed in his chest.

"And?" The one word was raw, released between gritted teeth.

"Your mother asked me not to leave White Horse." Wonder shone on Nora's face, making her skin seem translucent. ‘‘She asked if I would consider marrying you.’’

He didn’t get it. Any of it. He would eventually. Maybe. Right now, all he knew was that a miracle was unfolding.

‘‘Will you?’’

‘‘If…’’ She bit her lip. ‘‘If you still want me.’’ Her voice wavered. ‘‘Maybe I wasn’t brave enough. I don’t know. I thought I was doing the best thing. The hardest, for me. But how could I be selfish, and *take,* when I’m already responsible for so much unhappiness?’’

He took the last step and yanked her against him. He was shaking, Rob realized in astonishment. Or perhaps she was. His cheek pressed against her hair, he said, ‘‘I never learn. I lashed out again, didn’t I? You are the bravest woman I know. You had the guts to make a sacrifice I couldn’t. I love you so much, Nora. So much.’’

They rocked, her arms wrapped around his waist, her face pressed into his chest, her tears wetting his shirt.

His soaking into her hair.

‘‘Come home with me,’’ he murmured thickly. ‘‘I’ll kick Dad out.’’

Nora’s head bobbed against him.

Without letting her go, he found his car key and unlocked the passenger side. Then she let out a sniff and said, ‘‘I’ve got to get my purse.’’

‘‘Okay.’’ But he couldn’t seem to release her.

She looked up at last, laughing through her tears. Need, dark and primal, rose in his throat. Rob bent his head and captured her mouth in a kiss even he dimly knew was meant to claim her, on the most essential level.

Nora responded with need as urgent, if more tender. His brain seemed to haze. When he came up for air, he said in a guttural voice, "I want you."

Her tongue touched her lips. "We can get to your house, can't we?"

He wasn't so sure. "No. I'll let us in here."

Her eyes widened, but she let him hustle her to the front door of his office. Thank God, the keys were already in his hand. Getting them out of his pocket now might have been a challenge.

He locked the door behind them, gripped her arm and all but hauled her through the waiting room to his office, where he released her long enough to let down the blinds. Then he faced her.

"You mean it?" He didn't sound like himself. "You'll marry me?"

Nora nodded, a smile trembling on her mouth even as she looked as if she wanted to cry.

"I love you," he said hoarsely.

She flung herself at him, colliding with the wall of his body as he wrapped his arms around her. "I love you, too. I always have, Rob Sumner. Ever since I realized boys didn't have cooties."

He laughed, although it didn't seem like his, either. "I had a crush on you long before I let myself admit it."

"Molly and I used to say we'd been twins in another life."

"I remember."

"Maybe—" Nora looked up at him, her eyes full of love "—we knew each other in another life, too."

"Maybe," he whispered. "But I'm glad we found each other again in this one."

Her voice was the merest breath of sound. "Me, too."

The next moment, he was kissing her with all the desperation of a man who had come too close to losing his heart's desire.

THE LEATHER COUCH in Rob's office was surprisingly comfortable, although her bare skin was sticking to it. Perhaps she could at least shift so that *he* was on the bottom.

Nora wriggled experimentally. "Um...are we going to stay here all night?"

Rob kissed her neck. "I wouldn't want my staff to find us."

Her gaze fell on the wall clock. "You know, it's only nine-thirty. We could go tell our parents."

"We could." He lifted his head to grin at her. "And then go rent a hotel room."

"Um." Thoughtfully, she said, "Maybe *I* should rent an apartment. Instead of staying at my parents'."

"Hell, no!" Rob exclaimed with surprising force. "Let's just get married. Why wait?"

"Shouldn't we, well, adjust a little?"

"No."

She smiled at him. "Okay."

"You mean it?"

"Yes. Except..." Nora hesitated. "Rob, do you mind if I go back to school?"

"Sweetheart..." He rolled, taking her with him, so that she ended up on top. Smiling up at her, he said,

"You can do anything you want. As long as you include me."

"Deal," she murmured, and kissed him.

It was another hour before they got dressed, turned out the lights and locked up the office again.

In the car, Rob suggested, "My mom first?"

Nora nodded contentedly. She felt as if she were floating in the Mediterranean Sea, the water warm and buoyant, the sun shimmering overhead, the smell of wonderful, exotic food from some taverna promising more delights. She was *happy,* she realized in wonder. She'd forgotten what it felt like.

"Can we go to Europe for our honeymoon?" she asked.

His head turned. "Italy? Sweden?"

"Italy. Or Greece. I want to swim in the Mediterranean."

"I won't ask what inspired that." His hand found hers in the darkness. "We'll go to both countries. We can take a boat across the 'wine dark sea.'"

They were nearing the Sumners' house when Rob said, "Hey, Dad's truck is here."

The porch light was on. As his foot lifted and the car slowed, they both saw two people standing on the front porch, backlit by the open front door.

"I wonder why Dad..."

"Oh! Look." In delight Nora saw the man—Rob's father—suddenly sweep his mother off her feet and carry her across the threshold into the house. A moment later, the front door closed firmly.

Rob swore. "Is she sick? Having a heart attack?" The car leaped forward.

"Rob."

He gave her a distracted, frowning glance. "What?"

"Didn't you see her face?"

His expression changed, slowly. Instead of turning into the driveway, he let the car drift to the curb.

"She was laughing. I think, um, that your parents may be getting back together."

"You mean…"

"Uh-huh."

He stared at the house, understanding dawning on his face. "Right this minute, they're probably…" He shook his head hard. "They're my parents. I don't want to know what they're probably doing."

A giggle broke from Nora's throat, then another. She couldn't seem to stop.

"We'll go see *your* parents," Rob said grimly. "And skip mine until tomorrow."

Swallowing her last giggle, Nora laid a hand on his thigh. "Look at it this way," she said huskily. "Your dad won't be going back to your place tonight."

"True." Rob started the car up again and grinned. "Very true." Half a block later, he said, "You remember when I told you that not everything you set in motion was bad?"

She nodded.

"Convinced?"

She was. She had lost her best friend, and would miss her forever. But it seemed that she had also helped to heal them all.

"I love you, Rob Sumner," she said. "Have I mentioned that, if we have a daughter, I want to name her Molly?"

He put the car in Park in her parents' driveway. "I

assumed as much,'' he murmured, just before he kissed her.

When she surfaced, Nora told him, ''The Northwest Coast Indians believe that ancestors are reincarnated when babies are born. They *know* that a baby is really Grandma, come back. Molly and I were so very sure...'' Her heart seemed to swell. ''Maybe she'll find a way.''

''If anyone can,'' Rob agreed, his hand cupping her face, ''it'll be our Molly. She always was determined.''

''I wish...'' Nora made herself stop, before she became unbearably sad. How could she walk down the aisle to get married without Molly right behind her?

''Don't say it. Don't keep saying it. We go on, and carry Molly with us.''

Nora smiled at this man she loved, and ignored the tears that she would not let fall. Not tonight. ''Shall we go in? I'm ready when you are.''